Blood Royal

BLOOD ROYAL

A novel

MOLLIE HARDWICK

Methuen

First published in Great Britain 1988
by Methuen London, Michelin House,
81 Fulham Road, London SW3 6RB
Copyright © Mollie Hardwick 1988

Printed in Great Britain
by St Edmundsbury Press,
Bury St Edmunds, Suffolk

British Library Cataloguing in Publication Data

Hardwick, Mollie
  Blood royal.
  I. Title
  823'.914[F]

ISBN 0-413-40920-1

To
Michael
who is also
of the
Blood Royal

ONE

ELIZABETH
1498

Cloth of Gold do not despise
Tho' thou art matcht to Cloth of Frize.
Cloth of Frize be not too bold
Tho' thou art matcht to Cloth of Gold.

Who shall this marriage make?

Elizabeth Boleyn, who an hour ago had been Elizabeth Howard, shifted her weight from one knee to the other. The stones of the chapel floor seemed to be getting harder, and the fresh rushes strewn on them contrived to be prickly and lumpy even through the thickness of her bridal dress, a robe of Our Lady's blue shot with silver thread.

Even at sixteen, it was amazing how one's knees could ache. She stole a backward glance at her father. He was fifty and more, poor old man, but the Howard pride would not permit a wince or a frown to cross that patrician face, with its long, flattish nose and humourless mouth. The glory of the Howards might be slightly dimmed at the moment, with the memory of their loyalty to the defeated House of York still in the King's mind, but at least the King was a reasonable and politic man. Barely ten years ago, Elizabeth's father had been a prisoner in the Tower; now the Earldom of Surrey had been restored to him, and much of his property.

A lot of it, however, remained with the Crown. Trust a Tudor king to feather his own nest, particularly the cool, calculating Henry, the seventh of that name and the first Tudor to reign. Nasty-minded people said he should have been a shopkeeper. He would have looked and sounded exactly right bargaining over a counter in Cheapside, weighing out Welsh sausages or pigs' trotters. Instead he weighed out – carefully – the rewards given to the trusty servants he had neatly acquired from the Yorkists left alive.

Elizabeth's father was Chief Justice in Eyre, north of the Trent,

Vice-Warden of the East and Middle Marches, and Lieutenant of Northern England. For which reason he and his family and their horde of servants were living at Sheriff Hutton Castle, near York, one of the great castles of England.

The castle and its inhabitants were expensive to maintain. The Earl could not afford large marriage portions for his daughters, who, good matrimonial catches though they were, would all find themselves married off to fairly undistinguished bridegrooms.

Elizabeth surveyed her own bridegroom critically, out of the corner of her eye. Nobody could have called young Thomas Boleyn handsome. His head was clumsily set on his neck and his features undistinguished, a little too broad in the cheek, with a sharp look to the glance of his eyes, which were the colour of lead and looked as though they might also share its texture, and a tightish mouth half-veiled by a gingery moustache. He and the King might fittingly have shared adjoining Cheapside booths, shouting their rival wares and price-cutting each other by a farthing here and even a penny there.

But of course the Boleyns were traditionally shopkeepers. Thomas's grandfather had sold cloth, so successfully that he had become Master of the Mercers' Guild, then alderman, eventually being made Sir Geoffrey, Lord Mayor of London. In his will he had left a thousand pounds to the poor. His eldest son had also been knighted, by Richard III, and the money earned in trade had come down in the family and purchased fine houses and land in Norfolk and Kent. His son Thomas had inherited a particularly pleasant one, Hever Castle.

But it was not of Hever, or of any material possessions, that Thomas was thinking as he knelt stiffly before the altar, unheeding of the endless drone of the Nuptial Mass. He had an entirely new possession, of which he was prouder than of any mansion of stone and brick in rich green acres.

She was beautiful, his new young wife. Her glittering robe encased her slender body from breast to foot, tight-fitting so that it showed her shape. She was taller than Thomas, even kneeling, delicate-boned, bird-boned, as the Boleyns were not. Her dark straight hair hung to her waist from a maiden circlet of daisies linked with silver; the daisies' petals were of pearl, their centres of gold; and jewels edged her bodice. But it was not at these, or at her form or face, that Thomas was covetously, raptly staring. In his mind's eyes, so clearly that he thought others must see it, he saw written in letters of golden fire about her fair brow a word, a name: HOWARD.

He, whose own name was as often spelt 'Bullen' as 'Boleyn', was marrying a Howard. His immediate forefathers had done well in marriage, for titles, noble blood and inheritance, but he had done best of all. His new brother-in-law, the Earl's heir, own brother to his bride, had married a royal princess in Westminster Abbey. He, Thomas, was now related to the King; no longer would people be able to laugh at him behind their hands or make sly remarks about scissors and yard-measures.

The Eucharist had been administered, and the bridal blessing after *Ite Missa est*.

'*Deus Abraham, Deus Isaac, et Deus Jacob sit vobiscum: et ipse adimpleat benedictionem suam in vobis: ut videatis filios filiorum vestrorum usque ad tertiam et quartam generationem . . .*'

Thomas bowed his head in sincere prayer. He hoped most fervently that he and his bride might see their children's children to the third and fourth generation, and that they might all be blessed with money, lands and, preferably, titles. And, of course, life everlasting.

The silvery voices of the Earl's choristers (he had imported extra children for the occasion) soared exquisitely in the *Nunc Dimittis*. Elizabeth now turned her head and frankly met her bridegroom's gaze. It was ardent, impassioned, adoring, almost transforming his plain face. Almost, but not quite; he was no beauty, but that was hardly a fault in a man, when one was a beauty oneself. He would probably not be very unfaithful – at least, not more so than most husbands – and with worship like that in his look he was virtually guaranteeing her domination in the marriage. She would be able to manage him, that was as certain as the ring on her finger.

Marriage, she reflected, was going to be rather more than childbed groans and ritual submissiveness for her. A wife was expected to be the husband's chattel and shadow, but of course that did not apply to Howards. If anyone was going to be the chattel in their union it would be Sir Thomas Boleyn, under the Lady Elizabeth Boleyn's delicate but firm thumb. Nobody expected to marry for love, naturally; the very idea was preposterous, when great lands and estates were involved. The next best thing was to marry a man who happened to adore one. Some sage had written recently: 'Three ornaments 'long principally to a wife: a ring on her finger, a brooch on her breast; and a garland on her head.' Elizabeth had something else, a husband with a heart already melting for her.

'. . . *et Filii, et Spiritu Sancti.*' Thomas gave his bride the slightest nudge, since she was staring dreamily into space while the Gloria was being pronounced. Hastily, mechanically, she crossed herself, her thoughts not so much on the Holy Ghost as on the marriage feast that was to follow. She had fasted before the ceremony, as the custom was.

It was also, fortunately for everyone's comfort, the custom for the wedding party to retire briefly on their way to the Great Hall and the feasting, which would go on until midnight or later. There were jostling crowds outside every privy, but Elizabeth swept majestically up the stairs towards the apartment prepared for the bridal pair, her maids bearing her silver train.

'Jane, Cecily – take off this girdle and give me the knotted silk one. It's coming unwoven and my lord father will be furious if I lose half the pearls down the floorboards. And fetch my sandals – these shoes are too . . . what are you squealing like pigs for, you silly wenches? Oh.'

The flustered attendants were retreating towards the door, behind the looming figure of the bridegroom. Elizabeth herself became slightly flustered.

'Sir Thomas, you should not be . . . I wish to be tended by my maids. Leave me, please.'

'But I believe,' said Thomas, advancing, 'that this is our bridal bower, my lady.'

'Yes, but you have your own chamber and your own attendants, sir.'

'I happen to wish to enjoy my bride's company for a pleasant moment or two. Be off, ladies.' He pushed them out and slammed the door on them. Elizabeth fumed. She had kicked her shoes off, which made her feel at a disadvantage, though she still stood taller than Thomas, and by now she should have been having a refreshing wash in warm herb-scented water. A Howard should not bawl like a fishwife; she controlled her voice.

'This is most unseemly. Leave at once, sir, and send in my women.'

For answer, Thomas strode towards her, picked her up, carried her to the high broad bed and threw her on it. She shrieked. Nobody heard except Thomas, who took no notice. He was now beside her on the bed, and even more unseemly things were happening. Elizabeth, realistically brought up like every girl of her time, was not surprised by what Thomas was doing (she had several times been an attendant at wedding night ceremonies) but she was deeply outraged at the manner and timing of it. Taking not the slightest heed of her angry protests he proceeded to deflower her, efficiently and painfully, before rolling off and refastening his points as calmly as though nothing had happened.

Elizabeth sat up. 'By the Body of God!' she swore and, reaching out, slapped his face. 'What kind of mannerless lout have I wed? My father shall know of this, by the Sorrows of Mary!'

'There's very little your august father can do to remedy it now, my lady.' His face was flushed, but the red patch on the left cheek burned as though a torch had been put to it. He carefully avoided fingering it. 'I ask your pardon if I offended you, but I was within my husbandly rights. I was impatient only to enjoy my sweetheart as soon as we were one flesh by the laws of God and man.'

13

And to ensure that they were well and truly one flesh before his powers were weakened by the excess of drink that would be expected of him at the wedding feast, and before his bride had time to work herself up to the state of maidenly fantods girls liked to assume on their bridal nights. She was sound, she was virgin – or had been, until a few minutes ago – and with any luck would give him an heir as a result of this, the first throw. If not, then the next time. There would be many throws, many children of his and hers, children who would be half Howards, and he would see to it that they were educated, groomed, polished and fettled to grace the grand inheritances that would be theirs. Thomas was well content with his work, and it had given him a good keen appetite.

Feasts were expensive things, the Earl of Surrey reflected, even in the cause of getting rid of a daughter to a passable candidate. This was the second wedding within a year, even apart from the usual Twelfth Night roisterings. In the previous year his wife Elizabeth had died, and without troubling overmuch about the conventions of mourning he had promptly married again – her kinswoman Agnes Tilney, a pretty, healthy-seeming girl less than half his age, more suited to be sister to his daughters than their stepmother. She was not yet with child, disappointingly. Thank God he hadn't had to pay for the marriage of his son Thomas to Lady Anne Plantagenet, three years before.

He hoped the King would soon notice his stalwart service in the north and restore all the family estates to him. They would pay nicely for the enormous quantities of food on the tables. Three courses to a banquet, some twenty dishes to each course. Lampreys and eels and pikes and bream, quail and larks and wheatears, geese and capons jostled each other with fearful impartiality. From the Earl's pastures had been drawn in countless oxen, sheep and pigs of all ages, from lamb and sucking-pig to full-grown animals. A delicacy particularly liked was wild boar, still hunted in the moors and forests of Yorkshire, and served with a conserve of heavily sweetened fruits.

The swans, of which there were many, were dished up in style, on beds of pastry coloured green. Their feathers were gilded, and around their bodies were draped cloaks of cloth, vermilion-lined, painted on the outside with armorial bearings, as many as possible complimentary to persons of the company, all coloured like the illuminations of a missal. The silver lion of the Mowbrays appeared frequently: the Earl was proud of it.

It stood by itself in a prominent position on the high table, a confection of marchpane silvered, a golden crown round its neck. You could almost hear it roar. The coating was extremely indigestible, and not meant to be eaten (though when it reappeared in the kitchens, all who could get at it fell upon its interior). It was a *soteltie*, subtlety, like the castle of pastry and sugar crowned by a figure of the Earl's name-saint, Thomas the Apostle, and smaller figures of the Earl himself, his lady, the bride and her bridegroom, with yet another tableau of the pair standing (presumably some time later) beside a sugar cradle. Companion piece to the lion was the peacock in his hackle, the bird skinned, stuffed with spices and roasted before being replaced in its skin and displayed with tail spread.

Elizabeth hunched her shoulder haughtily against Thomas and addressed her young brother Edmund, who sat on her other side. 'Any minute now they'll carve the peacock and offer me the first slice. I hate it, it's as tough as a plank and tastes of nothing.'

'Don't eat it, then.' Edmund scooped up a brimming handful of food, administering a routine kick to one of the castle dogs waiting at his feet for spilt morsels. 'I intend to stuff myself – we don't eat like this every day, more's the pity. Shall we go hawking tomorrow? Simon Huntsman says it's going to be a good fresh day.'

'How can I? We have to start our wedding journey after first Mass.'

'If you've got the strength.' Edmund snorted with amusement. 'Boleyn will probably give you a rough night.'

His sister frowned. 'Don't talk of things you know nothing about.'

'Don't I? That's what *you* think. What's the matter, are you angry? I thought you liked him.'

Elizabeth saw her bridegroom's profile, motionless, and knew that he was listening to their conversation, ignoring the general roar of chatter and bursts of laughter. 'Liking is as liking finds,' she said coldly.

'And kissing goes by favour? What a shrew you are today, Bess. Marriage disagrees with you, does it? Pass the salt.'

'Don't be impertinent to your elders – I can't imagine how the Tilneys put up with a page like you. I'm a . . .' She had been going to say that she was a married woman now, but the recollection of this literal truth stopped her lips. Her face flared with furious colour at the memory of the shameless interlude between the Nuptial Mass and the Archbishop of York's grace before meat. A fine piece of work, forsooth. She plunged her hand into her silver-gilt bowl of venison in frumenty and made an effort to eat the food slowly. Hiccups would be undignified in the extreme.

Across the table her eyes met the gaze of a man sitting directly opposite. It was a gaze of intense admiration, something more than she was accustomed to seeing on the faces of men. She looked up and down the row of diners, and gathered many eyes, many frankly admiring smiles. She was, of course, the Lady of the Feast, and it was her special day, but was this something more than the homage due to her?

It was. Reluctantly though she had become a woman, the sudden maturing had set a bloom on her of which she was entirely unconscious. Outrage, excitment, and the hippocras she was drink-ing had brought a lovely wild-rose colour into her face, deepest on the high cheekbones, where it lent brightness and sparkle to her large eyes, Howard eyes, that could appear almost black at times, at others a glowing translucent brown, like dark amber. In the thinness of her young face these eyes now seemed huge, as the eyes of an owl do in its narrow mask. Her mouth, small and thin-lipped in proportion, could smile charmingly, as it was now doing, and

16

her skin was creamy; exposed to sunlight it would have glowed golden-bronze, but a lady's face might not be exposed to sunlight.

A lady might not reach for the steel mirror that hung at her girdle, either, to check her appearance, but Elizabeth sensed that she was in high looks, and made the most of it. As the precious, marketable eldest daughter of an earl, she had never received wooers or had more commerce with men than in the formal dance or the equally formal kiss of greeting, which was no more amorous than the sanctified Kiss of Peace after the *Agnus Dei* in Solemn Mass. Now, all in a moment, she realised that she had power over men, their bodies and affections.

It was almost like having the power of witchcraft: she crossed herself unobtrusively at the thought. Noblemen or stable boys, she could enchant them when she pleased, and would, if Thomas proved an insensitive husband. So, in her girl's innocence, she concluded, not dreaming where that power would lead her and hers.

A chorister, grandson to that Little Richard who had been one of the chief musicians to the Earl's father, was singing a love song in a high voice like a flute. A few polite ladies were listening to him, but the men would have been better pleased with ribaldry. Heads turned when the man who sat next to Countess Agnes got to his feet, none too steadily, and waved his arms for silence.

'Oh, Jesu,' sighed Edmund. 'Jack Skelton. Smother him, somebody.'

John Skelton was Poet Laureate of England, a sort of priest, always on the edge of taking holy orders, and unofficial jester to the Earl's household. (There were two professional jesters, but Skelton considered himself a cut above them and put them down on every possible occasion.) A short, spare, dark fellow with devil's eyebrows, he leered and twinkled at the company from under a crooked wreath of vegetable leaves woven in imitation of a laurel garland. In an astonishingly loud voice he began to shout one of his poetical addresses, pointing to Elizabeth.

O goodly maid,
Sweet Mary aid!
That now art wife,
Faith, by my life,
I rather would thy lippés bas
Than Saint Peter his gates y-pass,
So merrily,
So coningly,
With delice delectable,
With courtesie able,
Her eyen sable wink
Certes, to make man's heart swink,
Her bosom bright of blee
Doth cry *Vide me*!
Her pappes all rose
Sing *Veni ad nos* . . .

To general cries of 'Sit down!' and a push from his neighbour he subsided, catching to him a passing maidservant and embracing her passionately. Nobody took any further notice of him. His words would live for centuries after their voices were still; though not, perhaps, his impromptu address to the Lady Elizabeth Boleyn.

Finger bowls scented with rosewater were brought round before the serving of sweetmeats. Thomas pushed one into a position where it could be shared by him and his bride.

'You're very quiet, my lady. Is the food not agreeable to you?'

'The *food* agrees with me very well,' she replied coldly, cracking a nut so near him that pieces of shell shot into his face. She did not see the tightening of his mouth as he took the nutcrackers from her, his hand enclosing hers.

'Allow me. Your fingers are too fine.'

Elizabeth snatched her hand away, saying, 'I don't wish to eat more,' and turned to Edmund, but he was eating spiced custard, and had neither time nor breath to spare his sister.

When the feeding was all done, the fiddlers in the gallery struck up a tune and the company danced, first a stately *basse danse* in which the Earl led out his wife, before retiring to the dais as the measures grew more and more abandoned. Young Countess Agnes looked on wistfully as the revellers went from a galliard to a passamezzo to the branle and then to a hey, or free-for-all.

Elizabeth escaped from the dancing, pursued by shouts for the bride to come back, laughing as hands pulled at her skirt. The fire in the centre of the floor was giving out a great heat, intensified by that from the bodies swirling and capering around it. Sweating and short of breath, she sat down beside Agnes, across whom her father peered at her reprovingly.

'Your place is with your guests, and with your bridegroom.'

'Spare me a little, my lord, to rest my limbs.'

The Earl frowned, but his mind was not on the present occasion so much as on the State papers he should have been studying. Up here, in the wild north, he felt a very long way from Court and the King's affairs. Besides, there were still affairs to settle with the Scots, though he had given them a drubbing the previous year. After a token five minutes he vanished unobtrusively, followed by his attendant gentlemen.

The two girls relaxed, Agnes sighing at the luxury of being able to lean against her husband's vacated chair, the only one with arms to it. Sitting bolt upright on a bench or joint-stool was very wearing to the spine, however well one might have been trained to it since infancy.

'How I should like to dance,' she said.

'Then dance. My lord has gone, he won't know.'

'He will. He knows everything, sooner or later. And it wouldn't be safe, if I'm breeding.'

'Are you?'

'Not that I know of. But I expect I shall be, before long.' No prescience told her of the years of false hopes, miscarriages and still-births which she would live through before the birth of her son. The first Countess had been fertile; it was her duty to follow suit.

Elizabeth supposed that she too would be fertile. Perhaps all too soon, if that rankling event after Mass were to have results. She imagined growing heavy and cumbrous, waddling like a duck, being unable to see her own shoes. Perhaps her teeth and hair would fall out, and she would grow prematurely old as her mother had done. None of these natural happenings would have troubled her mind at the moment if she were not resentful of her groom for robbing her so violently of the ceremony a bride expects at the losing of her maidenhead.

'A woman,' sighed Agnes, 'is after all nothing but a vessel.'

'Lord, Agnes, how you do talk,' said Elizabeth rudely. Her own mother would have had her beaten for that, but Agnes merely gazed in surprise. 'Has a vessel any choice? The potter throws it, the buyer fills it. Is a woman no better than a piece of fired clay? I have no intention of being a vessel.'

Agnes smiled and shook her head. The Earl had made it clear that she should consider herself greatly honoured to be the vessel for containing future Howard progeny, and she was reconciled to that: if they would only come and get it over.

Elizabeth had somewhat naively imagined that her husband's claims on her person were now fulfilled, and that the usual bedding ceremonial would be short and formal, instead of the boisterous revelry accompanying the bridals of lesser persons. She was disappointed on both counts. True, she was not subjected to the pulling off of her garters by the groom's attendants, but it was tedious to have to be undressed by the combined hands of every unmarried girl in the company, instead of by her own ladies, and to have the pins that held her clothes together pulled out and thrown away.

'Put them aside, all in one place,' she ordered. 'How am I to be dressed tomorrow, without pins?'

'Madam, it is unlucky to leave even one pin about a bride.'

'Then I must be unlucky. Leave them.'

Reluctantly, they left them. There was still the entertainment of taking off her garland and spreading her hair out over the pillows. Two of her younger sisters were particularly boisterous, being both betrothed, one to a Wyatt, the other to a Knyvette – children still, but looking forward eagerly to their own days of glory.

Thomas was led in by his groomsmen, clad in a rich furred robe and nothing else. They had scented his beard, which, exhaling a strong perfume of musk, seemed to enter the room some way ahead of him. Elizabeth noted that he appeared not to be as drunk as most of the other young people. His manner of joining her in bed and sitting beside her to hear their healths pledged and receive marital advice was gravely decorous.

The toasts and joy-wishing seemed interminable. Elizabeth smiled and smiled and wished it all over. A sharp pain stabbed at her temples, and something had disagreed slightly with her. She hoped it was not the dish of lampreys, which were well known to be fatal when consumed rotten. Probably it had been the slightly sour sack.

Surely they would all go now. But the Earl was making a stately entry, side by side with the Archbishop. A slightly bawdy marriage song, led by John Skelton, died away raggedly as their presence registered with the company. Elizabeth let herself stop smiling, and Thomas joined his hands reverently and bowed his head as the Earl pronounced a fatherly blessing. He bestowed a cool kiss on his daughter's brow, and Agnes, meekly behind him, bestowed another. As they retreated, the Archbishop took their place at the bedside. Solemnly, lengthily, in Latin, he intoned a benediction on the young pair and their marriage, while a little boy behind him swung a censer whose incense warred in perfume with Thomas's beard.

At last the final Gloria and Amen had been said, the Archbishop was assisted out of the room by his small acolyte, the bridal company melted away, with many sly backward glances from the girls, and the heavy door was shut.

Elizabeth leapt out of bed and was violently sick into one of the chamber pots thoughtfully provided. She knew that there were ears pressed against the outside of the door; well, she wished them joy of what they heard. When she returned to bed Thomas was still sitting up, impassive.

'If you're quite done, madam,' he said 'we'll proceed.'

'Proceed? With what?'

'With the night's business.'

'I thought that was to sleep soundly,' Elizabeth snapped, 'seeing that we have our wedding journey to begin at early light.'

Thomas smiled, a tight formal smile. 'There are matters more pressing.'

'But . . .' Elizabeth only had time to note that his chest was covered with a thick mat of dark red close-curled hair before he was upon her, assaulting her with the same cold-blooded expertise as before. He was extremely strong, untender in his handling of her. Only an Amazon could have fought him off, and Elizabeth was no Amazon.

Released at last, she sat up. Thomas reclined on the pillows, complacent, not even ruffled by his conquest. Elizabeth spoke deliberately.

'Bullen by name, and bull by nature.'

Lazily he raised his right hand and struck her across the cheek, a cruel blow that set her head ringing again. Tit for tat, a return of the slap she had dealt him earlier. She burst into wild tears.

'You will not say that again, wife,' he told her calmly, though she glimpsed the cold flame of anger behind the leaden eyes. 'This morning you were a Howard, tonight you are a Boleyn – pronounced exactly so. When you have brought me an heir, which I trust this night will ensure, he will also be called Boleyn, an old and honourable name. Will you remember that?'

Elizabeth did not answer, keeping her hand at her cheek, where she felt a bruise rising. She was hurt and afraid, longing to call for her old nurse to come to her with comforting words and healing liniment. But she had made her bed (or rather, others had made it for her) and she must lie in it with this jumped-up young man whose origins were in trade and whose manners matched them. But

22

when out of bed, she would find ways of dealing with Thomas and with the world in which she now found herself.

He let her sleep little that night, but she gave him no more back-answers, detaching her mind from him with thoughts of hawking and hunting.

At first light musicians with pipes and tabors came to serenade the bridal couple, for a reward of silver. By the hour of Matins they had breakfasted, said their farewells, and were on their way southwards to Hever Castle in Kent, their new home.

2

I am the lady of this house

An uneasy beginning, but bride and groom were agreed upon one point – their relief in moving south out of the barbaric north. They travelled with a large train of attendants, guards, men-at-arms and servants from the Earl's household, Elizabeth's ladies, and Thomas's modest squad of personal attendants. A litter was available in case Elizabeth grew tired of riding, and overnight stops were at the best inns and abbeys. Given dull, warmish late summer weather and roads no more atrocious than usual, it was not a bad journey.

Their way to London lay almost directly down the Great North Road, which then had no name, being little more than a general direction and right of way. The greatest town they passed through was York, familiar to Elizabeth; then came Doncaster, Newark and Grantham. After Stamford, before they entered Peterborough, Thomas tried to insist that they turn off to visit his other principal manor, Blickling Hall in Norfolk.

'It will take us too far out of our way,' Elizabeth pointed out. 'Besides Norfolk is damp and disagreeable.'

'Not at all. Who's been telling you such fables?'

'Nobody. The roots of our family are in Norfolk soil. I thought everybody knew that. Blickling is almost at the sea, we shall spoil our clothes with salt air.'

'But it's such a fine house.' Thomas's tone was almost wistful. 'It was my grandfather's, Sir Geoffrey's – he was Lord Mayor of London, you know – and before that it was the great house of the Erpinghams and the Fastolfs.'

Elizabeth yawned, though delicately. 'So you told me. I shall see it in good time. For the present, shall we go on?' She turned away and tinkled a handbell for her attendant Cicely Fleete, who entered with great speed, as though she had been listening at the door of the inn's best parlour – which she had. Her mistress had developed a subtle form of unspoken communication with her handmaidens, from which they understood that her word was always to be obeyed, instantly, unless contradicted by the express orders of her husband.

Thomas knew that he was being manipulated. He was very sharp, quite humourless, and cold as ice in his ambitions. He had acquired a beautiful, high-born, prestigious wife with immaculate public manners, and for those he would put up with a woman's whims and airy notions. He had not made much progress at Court yet, but he would in time.

And he would go to Blickling, when they were settled into their first home. Some of their children should be born there, if it was their father's will. They would be Norfolk born and bred: so much for the damp and disagreeable county. Outwardly meek, he agreed to proceed towards London. Cicely and Jane and Ursula giggled in the maids' quarters.

And so they came southwards and through the High Gate into London. Elizabeth was delighted to see the tall steeple of St Paul's again, the huddled roofs with smoke hanging above them, the fields and gardens that broke up the pattern of narrow streets. She had been a child when her father left London last. As they rode through Aldersgate to within the city boundaries, Thomas beamed.

'The City of London knows no King, only a Lord Mayor, my grandfather used to say,' he told his wife proudly.

She arched delicate dark eyebrows. 'Did he? Well, I think it must be bringing itself to acknowledge a king now, since I hear His Grace lies at the Tower.'

Thomas was startled. 'The Tower? But I expected – Whitehall, or Greenwich are palaces he likes better.'

'Possibly they're being decorated – palaces are always being decorated. However that may be, there he is, for a soldier told one of my men as we came through the Gate.'

Thomas bit his lip, annoyed at himself, the courtier, for not being better informed. The Tower of London's royal associations were not of the happiest. At least two kings had been murdered there, so it was believed: Henry VI, poor old Holy Harry, and the uncrowned boy king, Edward V. The Duke of Clarence had died there too, in a mysterious and unpleasant way connected with a butt of malmsey, it was rumoured. All these violent deaths were the work of King Richard III of unblessed memory. He was not now mentioned in Tudor hearing.

Thomas was astonished that the King chose to lodge in the Tower when two important political prisoners were also lodged there, the Pretender Perkin Warbeck and the young Earl of Warwick, the last hope of the Yorkist cause. But Henry was a cold, cunning, unpredictable man, answerable neither to his subjects nor to their reasoning. He, Thomas, would present his bride at the cheerless Tower as though it were a gorgeous pleasance.

Elizabeth had forgotten how big it was, and how forbidding. She and Thomas and their train entered its walls to a welcome – for her, noble Surrey's daughter – of trumpet blasts, waved caps and shouted blessings. Yet a sudden shudder went through her like the first intimation of a fever, that set her teeth chattering and her hands shaking on the bridle rein. It lasted only a moment, then it was past. Perhaps she was breeding already.

The royal apartments to which they were conducted were in the upper floor of the Norman keep, the White Tower whose four pinnacles dominated the river's sky line. There were one hundred and fifty-two steps to climb, no trouble to the young limbs of the bridal pair. The rooms they led to were splendid but stony-cold, as though the King's character pervaded them like the chill of early winter.

He received them in the Council Chamber, throned on a dais under a purple canopy embroidered with gold lions. On a smaller throne beside him sat the Queen. Their welcome was gracious: the

26

bridal couple knelt and kissed hands, then remained standing, a few steps respectfully distant from the dais.

Elizabeth had seen the King years before, when, to her child's eyes, he had seemed a towering awesome figure. Now he appeared shrunken, wizened, his shoulders slightly bowed, his face much wrinkled. His long nose was as sharp as a pen, his eyes deep-sunk, his mouth a judge's. In his time he had been exiled, poor, hunted and hungry, learning hard lessons in a hard world, fighting with all his Welsh toughness and tenacity to win the throne to which he had only a fragile claim.

Elizabeth felt that those sharp eyes detected everything about her – everything, that was, to his own advantage. There was calm appraisal in his gaze, but no lechery, though she knew herself to be in good looks, flushed from the climb, dressed in her best sapphire velvet. King Henry was known for his strict chastity. No mistress's name was liked with his, no bawds infested his court.

The Queen was fair, though that was not the reason for his austerity. She who had been Lady Bessy, born of outstandingly handsome royal parents, was a pale gold beauty, white-skinned and high-browed, as frailly lovely as a flower that has bloomed too soon. There were faint lines of pain and strain on her face, for she bore babes with difficulty, and had already dutifully brought her husband seven children, two dead, the latest born only months before. A gabled hood framed her face: she would leave her likeness, a white rose between her fingers, on playing cards, the Queen of each suit.

She smiled at Elizabeth and Thomas. 'A pleasure to see you, safe after your long journey. Was the travelling easy?'

They assured her that it had been.

'You left the Earl of Surrey well?' asked the King. Elizabeth said that her father had been in excellent health when last seen. Thomas wondered whether the King might be moved by this happy occasion to mention that he intended to restore the Dukedom of Norfolk to the Earl. But Henry's memory was long, and even if it had not been he would still have recalled vividly that the Howards had backed the wrong side in the Wars of the Roses, and must continue to suffer for it. A good and faithful servant of the Crown Surrey might be; let him continue to demonstrate that a little longer.

The difficult conversation flagged. Thomas was too much a courtier to speak when the King did not, and the King was more interested in summing up people and situations than in chatting. At last the Queen said, 'We had hoped to be at Greenwich by now, in the fresher air. But there's sweating sickness at the Palace.'

'We trust it will soon be overcome, madam, by Jesu's grace,' said Thomas.

'Yes, indeed. Happily our children have their households elsewhere.'

Elizabeth took the opportunity of asking after the health of the children, and learned that Arthur, Prince of Wales, twelve years old, was to be married by proxy to the little Spanish princess, Catherine of Aragon, and nine-year-old Princess Margaret's betrothal to the young King of Scotland was in train. Two-year-old Princess Mary and baby Edmund were as yet unspoken for; and Henry was not spoken for either.

Thomas and Elizabeth expressed gratification at these arrangements.

'We hope,' said the Queen, 'that you will be as blessed in your children, Lady Boleyn, as we have been in ours.'

They thanked her, Thomas adding that on all sides they heard of the beauty, health, and extraordinary sagacity of the royal brood. For the first time the King smiled, tight-lipped because, at forty-one, most of his front teeth had gone.

'It so happens that we have with us the Duke of York,' he said. 'We will present you to him.' A sharp nod at a gentleman-in-waiting caused that official to scurry out and return with two more gentlemen-in-waiting, in different livery colours, escorting a boy richly dressed in white and green, the jerkin lavishly trimmed with jewels, an ermine-trimmed short cloak swinging from his shoulders, a feathered hat rakishly aslant on his springing red hair.

He was certainly a fine child, tall and broad for his seven years, bouncing with health, as though he lived on beef and ale. His complexion was ruddy, his small blue eyes flashed awareness, his limbs fleshed out even the puffed sleeves and wide-cut breeches, his displayed calves were as muscular and shapely as those of a man. It was hard to believe that this was the son of the two frail people to whom he was reverently bowing before greeting the visitors.

They kissed the large, dimpled pink hand extended to them. Elizabeth, raising her hand, met a frankly appraising gaze that was as precocious as the boy's body. There was something between a twinkle and a beam in the eyes cushioned by full red cheeks; Elizabeth, ridiculously, felt herself flushing as though a man had ogled her. Henry, Duke of York, was already a male to be reckoned with.

'We are glad to see you,' he piped crisply. 'How are the troubles in the north going? We hear your lord father dealt soundly with the rebel Scots last year, madam, when Ayton Castle was burnt.'

'Er, yes, Your Highness.' Elizabeth was utterly disconcerted. The Queen was smiling proudly, the King wryly, watching his son discomfit her. 'He – yes, he brought about a truce.'

'You should be grateful to my lord Surrey for that, Harry,' said the King, 'since Scotland's King is to be your brother-in-law.'

'Margaret's husband – I know *that*, my lord,' replied the boy, then, meeting a sharply critical look from his father, added 'by your leave', and bowed. As though he could not bear to remain put down, he addressed the Boleyns in a flood of rapid French. Elizabeth stood dumb, but Thomas, to her surprise, coolly answered in the same language. The King looked on, expressionless. His son was blatantly peacocking, and knew how far he could go. His estimate of Thomas Boleyn went up a point or so.

Having shot his bolt with Thomas, young Henry proceeded to dazzle Elizabeth. 'You know that your Master Skelton is to be my tutor, lady.'

Elizabeth, who had not known, replied that Master Skelton was most honoured.

'Is he a worthy sort of man?' enquired the Duke. 'I only know some of his light pieces, which one can't judge by. "O cat of carlish kind, The fiend was in thy mind When thou my bird untwined!"'

Elizabeth came back smartly with the next lines of *The Lament for Philip Sparrow*: '"I would thou hadst been blind! The leopards savage, The lions in their rage, Might catch thee in their paws, And gnaw thee in their jaws . . ."'

'Exactly.' The boy was afraid of being out-quoted. 'But is the man a scholar?'

His mother gently but firmly interrupted. 'If Master Skelton were not a scholar, Harry, His Grace would hardly be putting you in his charge. Now go back to your apartments, since you have graciously received Sir Thomas and the Lady Elizabeth.'

When he had gone, the visitors, especially Thomas, praised his looks, manners, and royal bearing. Elizabeth sensed that if custom had permitted it the boy would have lingered outside the door to listen. She also sensed that the King had given them enough time and was anxious to get on to whatever business awaited him. So efficient, so strict to the letter of the law, yet his people would never love him, and in years to come nobody would look back with a sigh to the great days of Henry VII.

They went down the long twisting staircase in discreet silence; it would have been unwise to let their escort of four overhear a word that might be carried back to royal ears. Not until they were on horseback again and moving out of the Tower precincts did Elizabeth speak.

'What a forward, bumptious child! My brothers would have been whipped for saying half as much before their father. Do you suppose *he* ever gets the lash on that broad bottom?'

Thomas made a repressive face. 'The Duke has, no doubt, a whipping boy. Anything else would be unseemly. Besides, his manners are quite in keeping with his station in life.'

'But he's not the heir to the throne – Prince Arthur is that, but this one carries himself as though he were. Is Prince Arthur the same?'

'The Prince of Wales is everything he should be. But not as sturdy as his brother, alas. A studious boy, wise and scholarly.'

So that was why Thomas was being so excessively complimentary about Henry of York: if Arthur was not sturdy, Arthur might not survive, and Thomas's allegiance would be to the strutting cocksure redhead. Thomas would always strive to be on the winning side.

Elizabeth had already learned not to put her own opinions forward too much to her husband. His own were fixed, unbendable, pointed towards worldly success, wealth and titles.

If contradicted he grew silent and withdrawn. There was no point in quarrelling with him, so Elizabeth kept to herself her thought that the King had a cruel mouth and a mean cast of countenance; he would have made a good usurer, lending out money at ten per cent and putting the gripes on defaulters. The Queen seemed a sad thing, doomed to facing a childbirth every year, however much it tried her slender body – a vessel, in Agnes's words. It was said that she had had no choice but to marry Henry Tudor. The daughter of a conquered and bankrupt house must take the best offer, and Henry's had certainly been that.

Elizabeth's own father would not have approved the expression of such thoughts, dedicated to duty and the King's service as he was. How mild he seemed to her in retrospect, authoritative yet gentle and courteous, a lofty Howard, so much grander in his origins than these Tewdrs or Tidders who had been brewers or outlaws or messenger boys, depending or which theory you fancied. Cold-eyed, tight-fisted merchants. There had been a hint of that in the boy, strangely, for all his bounce and manly airs.

He had looked at her as a man looks at a woman: she shivered at the memory of that.

They were across the river, across London Bridge where the press of their horses brought other traffic to a halt, while dwellers in the crowded houses on the bridge peered out of their windows and ran down to stand at doors, examining the Howard livery and coat of arms. There was always something and someone to look at for those who lived on the bridge. A few beggars ran alongside the horses of the gentlefolk, but Elizabeth looked through them as if they were not there, and Thomas threw them no money. He had none to spare. These Londoners might think themselves poor, but when he reached Hever he would be poor too, what with the tips he would have to hand out and the feeding and housing of all the attendants from the north.

The little houses of the Borough of Southwark were behind them now, the Tower out of sight. How pleasant it was, Elizabeth thought, to be back in the south, in the green softness of Kent. She hoped she would never have to return to the mountains and barren moors of Yorkshire.

'Do we go to Canterbury?' she asked Thomas. 'I went there once on pilgrimage. There was a window that showed King Edward kneeling with his family. The Queen, our Queen, was there, as a girl, and now I think she's become a marvellous likeness of her mother, the same gold hair and lily complexion. They called her the White Rose of York, didn't they, before she married King Henry?'

Thomas's brow was furrowed with disapproval. 'I too have been to Canterbury – everybody has been to Canterbury. I well remember the window, and it surprises me that King Henry has not had it removed and his own family's portraits put there instead.'

'But that would be ridiculous!'

'Not at all. The Plantagenets have passed, we live in a Tudor age.'

Elizabeth's voice went up a tone. 'The Plantagenets have *not* passed. My own brother is married to one, the Queen's sister. The Duke of Clarence's son is still alive – in prison, by our King's order. His sister Margaret is still alive. There are all sorts of connections . . .'

'I should be careful what you say, madam. One can get into trouble very easily these days by careless talk – such as mentioning the White Rose of York, or the late King Edward.'

'I shall say what I please. King Henry has long ears, has he? A good thing we're travelling farther from him by every mile. I could say, for instance, that he has a very poor title to the throne. My lord father has an illuminated picture showing the House of York as a great tree, and there are no Tudors on it – not even hanging off the end of a branch.' She was deliberately goading Thomas, egging him on to a quarrel which would relieve her pent-up resentment. He, not even a knight except by courtesy, treating her as he had done, speaking to her as though she were a pert page.

'If the Tudors had a family tree you'd be the ivy crawling up it,' she called after him as he touched his horse's sides with the spur and galloped along the line of riders away from her. His attendants were pointedly looking at nothing, or the sky, and Cicely was apparently in the middle of an absorbing discussion with Jane.

It had been decided to press from London to Hever with only one change of horses. The riding was easy, the weather mild. A faint scent of woodsmoke came from garden fires, trees were lightly touched with the first red-gold of autumn. No marauding gangs set on the riders, and few felons swung horribly in cages from the gallows they passed.

Late afternoon was settling into dusk as they turned aside from the road that led south from the town of Sevenoaks. Thomas, who had returned to ride by his bride, said proudly, 'There it is.'

'What?'

He pointed. 'Hever.'

Elizabeth followed the line of his finger. Within a few hundred yards of the building she said, 'But Hever is a castle.'

'It *is* a castle.'

To Howard eyes, used to Sheriff Hutton, Middleham, Alnwick, Lancaster, what lay before them was a cottage – at the very most a small manor house, with battlements. Elizabeth laughed unbelievingly.

'Most amusing. The home of your bailiff, perhaps, or your cowman.'

For answer Thomas rode ahead and gave directions, in obedience to which the leading riders turned and made for the little bridge that crossed the moat. At their approach the portcullis went up, and they passed beneath it.

The handsomely furnished hall was not large, Elizabeth noted critically, and seemed to be full of people. All the best aprons, pinafores, kirtles and collars had come out for the occasion. The servants' faces were washed and their hair combed. They, like the hall, seemed small, round, pink-faced creatures, dolls compared with the northerners who served at Sheriff Hutton.

The women curtseyed, the men bowed, with a general murmur of welcome. An elderly woman rose from her creaky curtsey and came forward to lay a large iron fire-poker and tongs at Elizabeth's feet. Thomas frowned.

'What's this, Dame Joyce? Has Hever turned into an ironmonger's? Do we now keep the smithy in the house?'

'They're for good luck and good housewifery, sir.'

'Lady Elizabeth will not be concerning herself with kitchen matters.' He kicked the objects. 'Take this litter away, one of you.'

Elizabeth put a hand on his arm. 'No. One mustn't turn away good luck. The gift was well-meant. I thank you, Dame Joyce.'

The old woman's disappointed face cracked into a smile. 'Your ladyship's very kind,' she said. A ripple of relief ran through the watching servants. Their new mistress was not going to be one of the Boleyn stable. Blood will tell, good lineage begets good manners. But Thomas still frowned, pushing his way through them with Elizabeth behind him.

'My father waits for us,' he said shortly.

There was a Great Hall, Elizabeth was pleased to see, a fine panelled place, tapestry-hung. In a high throne-like chair with one leg propped on a velvet footstool sat a stoutish man, richly dressed in sober colours, fur-hatted, his doublet ablaze with gold chains, his fat fingers twinkling with rings that caught the candlelight as he extended one hand.

Thomas went forward and kissed it. Elizabeth, obviously expected to do the same, merely bowed over it. Her father-in-law was not royalty; it would be a mistake to start by treating him as though he were.

His face, so like Thomas's, showed displeasure. But this was a

34

haughty Howard girl, and his son was lucky to have caught her. He surveyed her as he would a prize heifer, and from much the same standards. Handsome, if on the thin side. It was difficult to tell in these buckram-stiffened fashions how much of bosom or hips a woman possessed, but one must hope she was a good breeder. His wife, Margaret Butler, daughter of the Irish Earl of Ormond, had brought him three healthy sons and a clutch of wenches. This girl's mother, too, had been fruitful. He managed a smile, though it annoyed him that his wife was not at his side, having affairs to see to at Blickling.

'Welcome, daughter. Your journey was easy?'

'Very comfortable, sir.' Sir William noticed the difference of her voice from the Kentish and London accents he was used to hearing. Perhaps she had caught a few tones from the north, or from her Suffolk-bred father. She was speaking, but he failed to catch all she said. He cupped his ear.

'You must speak up.'

She raised her voice, which was deep and sweet-toned, very pleasant on the ear. He noted that her manners were perfect as she dealt with the wine and refreshments that were swiftly brought, and that she had a long neck and a graceful carriage. Also that Thomas, whose own manners were refined to the point of being niminy-piminy, looked awkward beside her.

Servants conducted them up a twisting staircase to a panelled bedchamber, very small by Sheriff Hutton standards, and only one for the pair of them. So they were expected to live in close marital bliss, huddled together as peasants are. Thomas would like that.

Because there was to be a banquet in the evening, Elizabeth chose a dress of rich burgundy with gilt scroll embroidery. Cicely and Jane carefully attached the sleeves, puffed over under-sleeves of cream satin. Then her long hair was coiled into a pearled net beneath the gabled black velvet hood, since she was now a married woman and could no longer wear it loose and flowing. She sighed and yawned.

'You're tired, madam,' Cicely said. 'I can do this just as well if

35

you sit down.' Jane pulled up a joint-stool, onto which Elizabeth sank gratefully, pulling in her skirts so that the girls could walk round her. She was indeed tired; she would have liked to lie down and sleep for hours, but duty was duty.

'Are your rooms comfortable?' she asked. They exchanged looks.

'Smallish, madam. Just one room. And the fire very low. Dame Joyce hinted that Sir William's mean about firewood, and we mustn't pile it on.'

'But at least it's snug,' said Jane. 'The whole castle is. Chimneys everywhere, instead of smoke all over the rooms. My mother would love it, she likes everything modern, she . . .'

Cicely quelled her with a glance. Jane was young and over-chatty for her station, and needed constant reminders to be swift and neat-handed and quiet. But Elizabeth smiled at her: it was going to matter, having good-tempered, cheerful women about her, if the Boleyns and their cowed staff were anything to judge by.

'I like it, too,' she said. 'One doesn't feel that mildew is actually forming on one, and the draughts are few – so far. Perhaps because the hangings are heavy and good.' She remembered Sheriff Hutton, where the walls seemed to move as old threadbare tapestries billowed out from them like sails, and winds whistled through the edges of the horn fitted into window openings. Here there was glass, good leaded panes, quite a few of them framing coats of arms.

'On the hanging in the Great Hall,' said Cicely carefully, 'there are devices of the Sun in Splendour, and a border of white roses.' Cicely came of a Yorkist family which had lost its estates after the Battle of Bosworth had ended the hopes of the followers of Richard III.

'Yes, Cicely. Sir William was knighted by King Richard. The Boleyns were in high favour then. But – we should not talk about it too much now.'

'No, madam.' But Cicely, who had been named for the Duchess of York, 'Proud Cis', the Rose of Raby, mother to two kings, was happy enough to be in a house where the old discredited emblems were still to be seen.

Jane said, 'I like it that the privies don't stink. At Sheriff Hutton, phoo! But I suppose the moat stinks, in hot weather, since the jakes drain into . . .'

'Jane. Fetch my lady's jewel case.'

Jane recognised Cicely's tone and went, silently. She had felt the weight of a hand on her ear often enough. Meekly she returned to unwrap from their coverings of silk tissue the gold chains, the ruby cross, the little jewelled bird with movable wings, the heavy gold ring that had been found in an old tomb in the grounds of Tendring Hall. Elizabeth's mother had fancied it strongly, her daughter shuddered at its touch, but wore it dutifully since it had been left to her by name.

The banquet was long and sedate. Almost everyone present was old enough to be Elizabeth's parent or grandparent. Country faces, withered-apple faces, plum-cheeks threaded with veins, rheumy eyes, stiff joints. Nobody exalted, merely neighbours – a squire from Edenbridge and his family, old John Sepham from Planers at Shoreham, a Master Polhill from Otford, a very solemn senior priest from the Archbishop's household at Knole, and three or four couples of no note.

All eyes were on Elizabeth, especially the women's, memorising her clothes, her complexion and figure, her dainty table manners. So this was a Howard lady. There would be imitators tomorrow. She observed how frumpish they were, more fussily dressed than the dames of the north, and so very old-fashioned. Here and there was even a hennin, the butterfly headdress, a veil over a great horned frame, quite grotesque. One might as well be back in the days of King Edward and the Wars of the Roses.

Elizabeth kept her gaze away from such monstrosities, smiled politely, talked knowledgeably of general matters, answered questions about her father and stepmother, about the visit to the King. These folk who lived retired were avidly interested in gossip and patently gratified that Thomas Boleyn's noble bride was prepared to entertain them with trifles such as a description of what the Queen wore, and the forwardness of the Duke of York. She responded to toasts and good wishes, and ate and drank, though the wine was not of the finest.

There was to be another banquet, Elizabeth learned, the next night, to present her to her Boleyn relatives, Thomas's elder brother James, young Edward, and their three sisters, with families. Either they all had other engagements tonight or the meal was planned as something altogether more formal. Elizabeth's head began to swim with wine and tiredness, but she bent it gracefully to listen to Sir William's remarks. She hoped his children were livelier conversationalists. The figures in the tapestry began to waver, the horses' heads to move and shake their bridles, the hunters to raise and lower the horns at their lips . . .

'My lady,' Thomas said sharply, from two places away. Elizabeth sat up with a start and an unnaturally bright smile of awareness.

Then, miraculously, Sir William was glancing at the elaborate Italian clock high on the mantel, and the servants were clearing the board. Very soon it would all be over.

In the bedchamber she yawned and yawned as she was being undressed by Cicely and the youngest lady-in-waiting, Ursula, who was all thumbs; Jane had been sent to bed almost unconscious.

When they had gone and she and Thomas were alone she said, 'Your father must be very rich, but the wine was bad.'

Thomas had drunk plenty of it, bad or not. 'He's a miser. A penny-pincher. A skinflint. The clothes I wore when I came to Sheriff Hutton were the first I'd had new for three years. Truth.'

'But the house. The carving is most beautiful – it must have been done by the best craftsmen. The linen, the furniture – look at this bed, finer than my father's. And that tapestry is new, surely. Susannah and the Elders, what a curious subject for a bedchamber. Who chose it, you?'

'I never choose anything.' The wine was distinctly catching up with Thomas, now that he was away from the constrictions of company. 'We're poor, wife, you've married a poor man. Do you know how much we have a year to live on? Fifty pounds. Fif-ty

38

pounds, for clothes and servants' keep and wages, fires and candles and all. Now do you believe we're poor?'

Elizabeth was shocked. 'I had no notion. Then – your father paid for all tonight – the game, the meat? There was plenty, I saw no stinting. That old man next to Mistress Polhill ate like a horse, I thought he would burst before our eyes.'

'Oh, meat, game. The home farm and the woods give us those, and my father owns all. We must live on simple fare, my lady, with no little luxuries. My father married an heiress, you see – not so I.'

'I am also an earl's daughter,' answered Elizabeth sharply, 'and I hope the Earl of Surrey ranks higher than the Earl of Ormonde.'

'Alas, an attainted man keeps a poor thin purse. You came to me with what he could spare – not a fortune. But of course he would not have confided that to you.'

Glad enough to get a daughter off his hands, thought Elizabeth bitterly. And my sisters, when their time comes. But my step-mother, Countess Agnes, dresses like a figure of Our Lady on feast day, no stinting for *her*. I and my sisters may marry poor knights, so long as she has her fineries. It was an unworthy thought, and she pushed it from her. Thomas was perched on the side of their bed, an unimpressive sight in his lawn nightshirt, the melancholy that came of too much sour wine clouding his plain face.

'I meant to make a good show,' he said, 'and I'm to be but a country squire. You were right when you mocked me, my lady – we have no castle but a manor house.'

'With battlements.'

'With battlements.' For the first time in their acquaintance Elizabeth felt a rush of sympathy for her husband: so ambitious, so proud of what he had gained – a Howard wife – yet so poor. He was a sad thing, beneath all the bluster. Impulsively she put her hand on his. He patted it absently.

'We must manage as best we can, then,' she said. 'And there must be some way to build up our fortunes. I know nothing of housewifery, but I can learn, Dame Joyce will teach me the best ways of economy – after all, she did present me with the poker and tongs. I could . . .' She looked round the room, which failed to present her with any inspiration.

'We have two ways to build up our fortunes,' Thomas answered, rolling into bed. 'One: I must carve myself a Court appointment, so as to be in the King's sight wherever he turns, if only to clip the royal nails or empty the royal jordan. Two: we must get our children Court places early, and marry them well.'

Elizabeth, beside him, gasped. 'Our children?'

'You did propose to bear children, madam?'

'Of course. But – they're not begotten yet. It would be years . . .'

'Never too soon to try.'

Thomas was in no state to try, but he did, and would every night, Elizabeth knew, until he saw some result for his efforts. She lay still and straight after he slept, shadows forming out of the darkness. Children: perhaps one conceived tonight, a speck of substance that would be a human creature, with arms and legs and eyes and a voice, and organs of sex – a boy to be drilled into royal servitude, a girl to be sold into marriage?

Poor little ghosts of the future. I will bear you safely if I can, she promised them – but to what fates?

3

Hallowmas

George was a lively baby, with a disinclination to go to sleep at the appointed times, or indeed at all: he seemed afraid of missing something. His wakefulness, trying to his nurses, was an intense relief to his parents, for his elder brothers Henry and Thomas had gone to sleep for ever, very early in their lives, and lay beneath the floors of Hever and Penshurst churches.

But George was going to live. His mother doted on him, and his father was gratified by his son's fine head and clever hands, that grasped precociously at objects, and tore with such persistent impatience at his swaddling bands that they were taken off him long before the usual age.

'The child will grow out of shape and its limbs all awry,' predicted the senior nurse, Mary Pegge. 'You don't supppose Our Lady let Our Lord go unswaddled at such a tender time in His little life?'

'I can't say, as to that,' replied Alison, the wet nurse, as the liberated George made a successful grab at her bosom. 'It may be Our Lord was of a meeker nature. And,' she added triumphantly, 'He don't wear nothing in some of the pictures – naked as an eft, He is, bless the mite.'

'You watch your tongue, my girl, else you might get struck down by a miracle.'

Elizabeth, crossing the lawn, heard and smiled. To her, George seemed something of a miracle himself, after all the waiting and the pain and disappointment. And the sorrow, quite unreasonable, considering how many infants died at birth or soon after, and boys were notably hard to rear.

The children's father had been so disappointed that it had turned him glum and silent: two investments in the future gone, and the awful possibility that his wife might be one of those women who continually miscarry or bear sickly babies. But now George was here, named for the patron saint of England, on whose day he had been born, and christened in great state and at great expense, with Sir Henry Wyatt, their relative and neighbour from Allington Castle, as one of the godfathers. Lady Wyatt had also brought forth a son, to whom in turn Thomas Boleyn stood godfather.

Thomas had not worried as much as usual about the cost of the christening, and the confirmation which, by custom, followed it. (So many children died before they were old enough to make the promises themselves that it was as well to get the ceremony in early.) His father-in-law the Earl of Surrey had given up most of his posts in the barbarous north and was back at Court, in attendance on the King and Queen.

Not only that, but he had been reappointed to the Privy Council and made Lord Treasurer of England, an office which Thomas found strangely appealing, promising well for the Boleyn fortunes.

In July 1503, when George was a sturdy three months old, Thomas accompanied his father-in-law north again, on the cheerful occasion of the Princess Margaret's wedding journey to Scotland. He had not, strictly, been ordered to go, or even asked, but he thought it would look well.

Elizabeth was dubious. 'My father won't give you any important office – he has his own people. And the King won't even notice you. Since the Queen's death he has been in such great grief and mourning that he cares for no company but his councillors.'

The Queen had died, just before George's birth, in childbed of her ninth infant, a daughter who soon followed her. She had never been well since the loss of Prince Arthur, struck down at sixteen.

'I shall join the party at Richmond,' said Thomas firmly. 'It will not go unnoted that I am there. My new purple doublet will do very well for such a show. And I shall take your father the miniature picture of you and George – that will please him. And – there'll be others I should like to see.'

Elizabeth knew very well that the 'others' consisted of one person, the twelve-year-old boy who was now Prince of Wales, Earl of Chester and Flint, and Duke of Cornwall. Once Thomas had jestingly referred to Prince Henry as the young royal turkey-cock, but these days his remarks were respectful, not to say deferential. Henry was a very important person now, with the stature of a grown man, they said, and every sign that he would make a more impressive king than his father.

'Remember me to the Prince of Wales,' Elizabeth said, her eyes on the altar cloth she was embroidering. 'He may even recall me.' In five years of marriage not over-studded with compliments, she had been oddly haunted by that precocious stare of admiration from a young child who ought to have known nothing about such things.

'And,' she added, 'don't forget to tell me exactly what the Princess wore. I hear she has a state gown of cloth of gold, but that will be kept for her bridal, no doubt – and all is new, even her laces and pins and ribands. Cicely had it from her sister in the Princess's service. And her sister said that the royal headdresses were set with jewels. Poor girl, she's fat and plain, but she may grow out of it, at only fourteen. And Thomas – do remember exactly what my stepmother wears, and how she looks, for I hear Countess Agnes is very high and mighty these days, no longer the mouse she used to be.'

Thomas was bored with women's chatter. He was, in any case, much more concerned with his own purple satin doublet, and the elaborate bonnet he was having made, trimmed with feathers dyed gold and crimson. Elizabeth was not sorry to wave him goodbye, a gorgeous figure riding in the middle of as many attendants as he could afford to take.

In any case, she had another preoccupation. She was pregnant again. It was too soon after George's birth, but Thomas didn't

43

believe in letting a field lie fallow. This time she would take great care of herself, not riding to the hunt or in one of those clumsy joggling carriages. Elizabeth knew now that she was capable of bearing a healthy child, but there had been a few frights while she was carrying George.

Thomas was away for a shorter time than he had anticipated. His father-in-law had not made much of him, to his disappointment; the Earl's whole interest was set on getting himself back into royal favour, with a dukedom and lands at the end of it. And the Countess, as Elizabeth had heard rumoured, was now no longer the timid retiring second wife, but an overbearing lady very conscious of her position. It was she who played cards with the Princess Margaret, she who somehow always happened to be there on all important occasions.

'She even outdoes your father in pomp and grandeur,' Thomas told Elizabeth. 'Dancing with the Princess, to show off her own skills – and she only a Tilney, nothing great.'

'My mother was also a Tilney,' his wife reminded him. 'But I'm not unduly surprised about Agnes; she always seemed too meek and mim-mouthed to be true. She didn't, by any chance, push my father aside and give the Princess away in marriage herself?'

'No. But I would not have put it past her. She needs a brood of children to settle her down. And how do you, wife?'

How civil of him to ask, thought Elizabeth. 'I do very well,' she replied, smoothing her gown over her thickened waist. 'I hope to give you another fine son in springtime.'

'Good, good. But I should be pleased even if it were a daughter,' said Thomas magnanimously. There were plenty of eligible male babies about: the infant Thomas Wyatt at Allington, and numerous others he had heard of at Court. He always knew whose lady had recently borne a son. Infant betrothals were such a sound idea.

The new baby was a daughter, and Thomas was duly pleased. So was everybody else, for Mary was pretty almost from her birth, somehow missing the boiled look of most newborn babies. Her eyes were dark, like her mother's, but she was a Boleyn in feature, not a Howard, with Thomas's breadth of cheekbone, a full rosebud mouth and a number of well-placed dimples. Chubby and amiable, she smiled on everybody, particularly if they were male.

'What a flirt-gill have we here!' said Mary Pegge. 'A very mermaid for ogling. She'll need the rod as she grows, to keep her from wantonness and harlotry.'

'Fie!' Alison wound an auburn baby-curl round her finger. 'As if she would, the little love.'

Sir William Boleyn and his lady received their latest grandchild in state at Blickling Hall, chucked her under the rounded chin (which would never be a characterful one), pronounced her a pretty wench, and folded a gold angel into the small pink fingers. As well to let her get the feel of coin early in life.

As Mary grew, it became clear that she rejoiced in her femininity. A new frock or riband would bring a laugh of delight: she drew a sharp scolding from Mistress Pegge for being found lying flat at the edge of a lily pond, watching the reflection of her face in the water and smiling at it. She would never be mistaken for a boy, even at a distance, though boys and girls dressed alike in long skirts and bonnets. As well mistake a doe for a buck or a vixen for a fox as the toddling Mary for her brother, or anyone else's brother. Mall, the household called her affectionately, unless her father was about, to hear and forbid the familiarity.

When she was almost two her grandfather, Sir William, died. From his immense riches he left his son Thomas eight manors. At Hever, things began to improve. New furniture and wall hangings appeared, more servants were taken on, painters and builders improved the house and the family shone in new clothes on feast days. Elizabeth's dark beauty, riper than it had been, glittered with jewels – a carcanet of diamonds and emeralds with a crucifix of Italian work, the Corpus of ivory spangled with ruby blood-drops and set in heavy gold.

George acquired a tutor, Master Nicolas, who had been meant for a priest but was turned out as a novice for frivolity and the singing of secular songs to his fellow novices. George's father was not aware of that, or the fact that his little son's sharp ears were picking up some of the secular songs, and his quick brain learning the way to rhyme. Or that Nicolas was gentler than he had made himself out to be, and between him and George's doting mother George was growing cocksure and spoiled.

Candlemas Day, the Feast of the Purification of Our Lady, was a festival enjoyed by all, a cheerful interlude in the dreary cold of early February. Hever's small old church was full of light, a candle in everyone's hand as they went, one by one, up to the High Altar, where tall candles already burned.

'*Alleluia, alleluia,*' intoned the priest, Father Ashdyne. '*Post partus virgo permansisti: Dei Genetrix, intercede pro nobis.*'

Elizabeth reflected on the miracle that a child should be conceived and yet its mother know no congress with man. She and Thomas were kneeling in the Boleyn Chapel at the north-east of the church. It had been built by Thomas's grandfather Sir Geoffrey, so that he and his family could enjoy the utmost comfort during services, to which end a fireplace had been installed. A cheerful fire burned in it now, and a servant knelt ready to shuffle forward and slip another log on it when necessary.

Unlike the rest of the congregation, Elizabeth and Thomas knelt on cushions. Elizabeth raised her head from her clasped hands and looked along the floor to her right, where a small brass cross let into the stone covered the grave of her small son. *Henry Bullayen the sone of Sir Thomas Bullayen.* Poor little doomed Harry's birth had been a hard one. She wondered what it had been like for the Blessed Virgin, bearing a son lying in straw on the ground. Probably no worse than bearing one in a huge bed with bulbous pillars carved with grotesque beings whose faces came and went on waves of pain. And at least Mary's son had lived.

Elizabeth wished that Thomas, her first-born, lay by his brother. But building works had been under way in their chapel when he died, and Thomas would have him interred nowhere but in the family precinct. So he had asked the Duke of Buckingham's permission to have the small corpse buried in the most prestigious part of Penshurst Church.

Thomas looked around him, congratulating himself on the small size of the church and how much room his family monuments would take up, in due course. There would be space for several in the Boleyn Chapel, counting the wall monuments, which would be painted and of great magnificence. He fancied a table tomb for himself, with a brass effigy showing him in Garter robes, the Howard arms quartered with his own, a chevron between three bulls' heads couped. (It looked very well, already, in stained glass set in a window of the south aisle.) What a pity his father had died at Blickling and been entombed in Norwich Cathedral; and then there were all those Boleyn brasses at Blickling and Salle.

Snow flecked softly against the windows, darkening the rich colours, blue robes and red robes, the Sanctus Spiritus all silver-white, with something gold in his beak and a halo of gold rays round him. It was a gloomy day, but that was all the better for the farmers, they said.

> *Si sol splendescat Maria purificante,*
> *Major erit glacies post festum quam fuit ante.*

Good weather at Candlemas meant a prolonged winter and a bad crop, therefore everyone was pleased to see the snow. Outside among the graves it would be lying gently over the Fair Maids of February, the young snowdrops peering out of the ground to look for spring. Elizabeth smiled, thinking of the months to follow, and especially October.

Father Ashdyne was intoning a very long piece of Latin during which the congregation fidgeted on sore stiff knees. Thomas turned his scarlet-bonneted head as Elizabeth touched his arm.

'I am with child,' she said.

Now that Thomas was comparatively rich he became more restive than ever about the matter of obtaining preferment at Court.

'The King is old, he needs strong young men about him. I shall be seen, I shall be seen.' Bustling to and fro between Hever and London, he made sure he was seen, both by the weary ageing King and the huge tall boy who would be King after him; even by the widowed Spanish princess Catherine, living in poverty, at a loose end since the death of her young husband. One never knew when her circumstances might change, and power come into her hands. It was rumoured that she might be betrothed to the Prince of Wales.

Because the King liked gifts and despised nothing, however humble, Thomas took him gifts by the wagon load, produce from his gardens and land. In spring, ripe stawberries, then the fruits of summer and autumn, presented beautifully in gilded baskets garlanded with flowers. Elizabeth complained that the best fish went from the ponds to Court, and so much game that the household hardly tasted any. Thomas ignored her, for it would all pay off some day.

He came home elated on a warm June day of 1506, with two servants carrying a bale of cloth, rich sapphire-coloured satin.

'For me, for a state robe! His Grace thought my clothing too shabby at the last banquet, and has given me this. How munificent, how gracious! I shall have it trimmed with silver lace – '

'Not ermine?'

Thomas disregarded his wife's sarcastic tone. 'And as His Grace loves jewels so well, for the coronation I shall wear the gold collar my father left me.'

'What coronation? The King is still alive, I understand?'

'Of course,' Thomas snapped. 'Have you gone mad? I mean that on his deathbed my father foresaw that there would soon be another King Henry on the throne, and that the times would be rich and great then. Dying men see such things.'

'Poor King.' Elizabeth heaved a mock sigh. 'Buried before the breath leaves his body. What unseemly haste. Have you suggested that he should prepare his soul in good time?'

Thomas turned on his heel. Elizabeth was getting very tetchy and sharp-tongued these days. He would humour her, however, for he had weightier things on his mind than a woman's fancies.

Elizabeth watched him go with quiet fury. She was glad the King had favoured him, naturally, but her Howard spirit rebelled against the way he lackeyed and crept and crawled for preferment, and she felt a niggle of jealousy that it was Thomas who received all the perquisites while she dragged about at home. The child within her must be a large boy, since she was already swollen so much that she could only wear split robes, becoming neither to her figure nor to her vanity. Since she had quickened at four months the creature had twisted and turned like an eel, kicking so much that she could hardly sleep for an hour on end.

She took her annoyance out on Ursula Fettes, her chief lady in attendance. Cicely and Jane were both married and gone, only Ursula remaining of those she had brought from Sheriff Hutton. Ursula had been clumsy at first, always dropping things and botching her work, and had suffered for it, so much so that she had grown in time to shrug off her mistress's scoldings and grow a protective armour of placidity.

They were embroidering an elaborate headdress for Elizabeth, who had rebelled at sewing any more baby garments. George and Mary had been dressed like tiny adults ever since they could walk – their first robes were as good as new still.

'Besides, how do we know what the thing will be? An estridge, possibly.'

Ursula looked blank. 'Madam?'

'Or whatever they call it. A great outlandish bird that breeds in Africa or the Indies, one of those wild regions.'

'Or perhaps Signor Vespucci's New World?' suggested Ursula helpfully. 'I heard Master Nicolas talking of it . . .'

'The bird has long legs, three yards long like a stilt-walker at a fair. And so has this unnatural child.' Elizabeth jabbed viciously at a silk Tudor rose. 'It kicks me night and day as thought it would bruise me black and blue. What will it be doing when its birth-time comes, if it abuses its mother so at five months, curse the creature?'

49

Ursula crossed herself. 'Oh my lady, never curse a child in the womb!'

Elizabeth looked chastened. 'No. I meant no such thing, God forgive me. If I were not so tired . . .' And I wish I had a dress of that blue satin, she thought, and a waist to tailor it to. If only I could go to Court with Thomas instead of rusting here . . .

'Perhaps,' Ursula mused, 'he will be a handsome gallant, so tall that other men look small beside him, and an accomplished dancer. That would be why his legs are so long and strong. You should be glad of such a son, madam, when many women bear little atomies like dwarfs.'

Elizabeth shrugged impatiently. 'Old wives' tales. My family incline to height, but nothing out of the ordinary – none of my brothers is a giant, nor my father. Why should I have a human estridge inflicted on me?'

Ursula, baffled, suggested that she pray to Saint Monica or Saint Anne. 'The saints are a great comfort, and prayer is very, very powerful, madam. I know it, because when I lost my topaz ring I prayed to Saint Antony of Padua and offered him seven candles, one a day for a week, and there it was, down a crack between the floorboards, where it couldn't have been before or I would certainly have seen it . . .'

Elizabeth let her ramble on, and drifted into a half-dream. Her son would be called William or Geoffrey, if Thomas had his way – she had fought him over George – but she was not sure that she liked either. Thomas and Henry were too common as boys' names, she would not have them. Perhaps she would say she had had a divine revelation that the boy should be called Ambrosius or Romanus or Peregrine or Lucian or Hilarion. Thomas would be terribly annoyed, but there would be nothing he could do about it. The saints were, as Ursula had remarked, such a comfort; one should not offend them. If she said that a vision came out of the panelling in her bedchamber, a beautiful boy with a dove on his wrist, all bathed in light, and commanded her to call her child after him, the priest would believe her and Thomas would have to put up with a fantastic name dangling from his family tree.

In any case, it was all months away, not before October or November.

The storm raged outside, gales of wind and fierce spatters of rain, as though the dead were beating at walls and windows, impatient for All Souls' Night. In the bed where her four children had been born, Elizabeth was struggling to bear the fifth, a battle she was losing.

Old Dame Joyce, who had presided at many births, shook her head and sighed. Martha Pole, the village midwife, was sweating now as much as the patient. She wiped her brow.

'I can't do no more, Joyce, my lady must fight it out. We've said all the charms and the birthing girdle is on, and every knot in the house untied – unless any of you maids has left one fast?'

The girls huddled in the shadows of the hot room (a fire roared in the hearth), murmured that they had unloosed all the cords about them, the lacing of their bodices, the strings of their caps.

'One is tied somewhere, I warrant.' Martha glared accusingly round, then bent to examine the twisting, moaning form under the sheet. 'Nothing else for it, after so long, and not a sign of the head yet.'

Ursula was at the window, peering into the wild darkness, where, against the shine of the wet cobbles, a horse was being halted.

'Dr Philipson is here.'

Martha snorted. 'What can he do that I can't?' Professional jealousy was strong among her kind. 'A man has no place in a birth-chamber.' Yet she was secretly relieved to have help in a case for which neither she nor Joyce had any remedy. She greeted the doctor civilly enough when, his rain-sodden cloak left with a servant, he entered the room.

An hour later they were no further; the patient was exhausted, almost past utterance. 'Her strength is gone,' pronounced the doctor. 'I must bring this to a conclusion, God helping. One of you send for Sir Thomas.'

Thomas, nightgowned, tousled, thoroughly frightened out of his usual hauteur, had been sitting in a parlour, trying to take his mind off what was going on upstairs. There had been suffering for Elizabeth before, of course, but nothing like this. He seemed to be looking at someone who was not his familiar wife, but an ugly stranger, almost a corpse already.

'Her mother bore ten living children,' he said, helpless.

'Your lady is of a different structure, sir.' The physician's sleeves were rolled up and he breathed heavily. 'There's nothing in the pages of Galen to help me with her. I can save her only if I destroy the child. Only you can give that word.'

The women sobbed. Joyce said, 'Sir, we've infused marshmallow and parsley and fennel in Rhenish wine – '

'With oil of sweet almonds,' put in Martha, 'but my lady will not drink, it runs down her chin. Save her, poor bird, I do beg you, sir, for I never saw any woman suffer as she does. I'll christen the child myself before its soul flies.'

Thomas hesitated: his son, another son to make the family name famous and follow in his father's footsteps to Court; or his wife, sometimes maddeningly short-tempered and finicky, yet the grandest lady he could have wedded, her beauty still a pride to him. He imagined what the Earl of Surrey would say to him if his daughter were allowed to die, by Thomas's word.

'Save the mother,' he said.

And as he spoke Elizabeth cried out and the baby's head slid into the doctor's hands.

Elizabeth had been washed and tidied up, given aqua vitae and water and propped up on pillows. She was faintly surprised to find herself alive. Miraculously, the pain had crawled away, leaving her so weak that she felt herself to be made of glass or feathers. She could see clearly, though nothing that was being said by the murmur of voices in the room made any sense to her.

Before the blazing fire one of the maids was kneeling, doing something by the wooden bath that had been placed there when Elizabeth's labour began. Her eyes focused, showing her that she was drying something in a towel, and that the something was wriggling and making noises like a distressed cat. Dame Joyce saw that she was trying to speak, and hurried to her.

'That,' Elizabeth said, carefully, 'what . . .'

'A girl, my lady, a strong healthy wench, blessed be God and Our Lady, after such a mortal travail.' The old woman was weeping with relief. The midwife and the doctor were downstairs, being regaled with food and drink. But Thomas sat by the fire, looking from his wife to his new daughter, and back again.

Joyce had the child in her arms, at its mother's bedside. It was naked, damp, and even to a maternal eye very ugly, thin and long-legged. So that was why Elizabeth had thought a boy was kicking her. A fuzz of black hair crowned the scarlet face, still convulsed by the outrage of birth and the fearful struggle it had made for its life. A strange sister for Mary, who had been like a cherub even so early.

Elizabeth gestured, and Joyce laid the baby against her shoulder.

'Born in the chime hours,' she said, 'this young lady will have the power to see spirits. And she was born under Scorpio, the doctor told us, which will make her strong of will. Aye, she'll have her own way with all of us, and be a good musician and dancer and shine in the world . . .'

Elizabeth found her strength coming back, flowing from the close vital body of her daughter.

'Anne,' she said. 'I shall call her Anne, after Our Blessed Lady's mother who saved us both.'

4

The King's Hunt

'She will have to go into a convent, of course,' Thomas said. His eyes were on his younger daughter, who with her brother and sister was sitting at a table at the far end of the Long Gallery, beneath the window, with Master Nicolas and the young Frenchwoman, Simonette Durand, who had joined him as governess to the three children.

'Anne? Why?' Elizabeth asked sharply. They were strolling in the Long Gallery for exercise, since the heavy rain made hunting or walking impracticable. At the staircase end it was silent, only the faintest sounds coming up to them from the house, and they could talk without being heard by the pupils and their teachers.

'Look at her. Plain as a pikestaff, skin like leather, black eyes, a long neck like a duck's. What kind of husband would she get?'

'Fie on you, Thomas. She's only five, it's not to be seen yet how she will grow. And her skin is exactly like mine, dark-hued, and her eyes are beautiful. As to her neck, swans have long necks as well as ducks. And she has the sharpest wits of the three of them – Mary can sew no better than she, and speaks no French yet, whereas Anne chatters away in it as though it were her native tongue.'

'All the better when she becomes a novice. Only a well-educated girl can aspire to be Abbess. I shall have to pay a dowry, of course, but not so much as to a husband.'

'Money! You think of nothing else, Thomas. Have you ever seen any sign of undue devotion in Anne?'

'Devotion? Not especially. It is not necessary, surely?'

'But desirable. I doubt if Anne has a vocation – her heart would not be in it.' Elizabeth understood her younger daughter better than anyone else. She saw clearly in her the Howard strain, saw glimpses of her own father, sisters and brothers, and of herself. Something bound her closer to Anne than to placid Mary with her milkmaid prettiness or clever-clever George, who could dispense wit and charm like a prince scattering gold to the multitude, and mock his father with such a straight face that only he and Elizabeth knew it.

Perhaps it was the night of Anne's birth that bound them together. They had fought the same battle, the mother and the babe, and it was Anne who had won it for them both by her determination to be born. My nut-brown maid, Elizabeth called her secretly, from a ballad which had been sung at Sheriff Hutton, the tale of a dauntless young woman whom no peril or privation could keep from following her love into outlawry.

Anne would be like that, set on her chosen course, like a falcon.

And like a falcon she must be tamed, said those who had the bringing-up of her. 'She is neither to hold nor to bind,' warned Dame Joyce. 'She'll have her way, as I foretold when she was not an hour in this world. Let them that teach her beat her well, for though it hurts her body it will profit her soul. And work against Those Signs,' she added significantly.

Elizabeth dealt her a sound cuff on the cheek. 'Never let me hear you or any other speak of such things again. Ignorant, superstitious numbskulls, all of you! Keep your tongues off your betters.'

Joyce, with tears in her faded eyes, went without a word, leaving Elizabeth ashamed. It was not courteous to strike an old woman, even a servant, but rage had possessed her at yet another mention of what she would not tolerate to be spoken of in her hearing: the Witch-Signs.

All the old women whispered, and some of the young ones, about the two deformities on Anne's body. One was a great mole or wen at the base of the child's throat, where the hollow lay between the collarbones. Elizabeth had considered having it removed, but Dr Philipson had warned gravely that some evil humour might enter the body through such a cut, and that in any case it would leave an unsightly scar.

The other blemish was on her right hand, a tiny growth at the side of the little finger, like another finger trying to emerge, with a rudimentary nail at the tip of it. 'So the Devil marks his children,' they whispered. 'A teat for his imps to suck of a night, and a hand turning to a beast's claw. The signs are for all to see.'

Anne hated the flaws. If her mother had not strictly forbidden her to attack either with a knife, and made her swear not to in front of a priest, she would have got rid of them herself. Thomas had found her at it once, and beaten her severely.

Not that Thomas was often home to attend to the disciplining of his children. When Anne was still an infant, the King had at last taken notice of Thomas's patient appearances at Court, and appointed him Esquire to the Body: not a resounding title, but an office which would keep him close to the King's person, relied upon, confidential.

Now he spent his nights on a truckle bed (narrow and uncomfortable, but who cared for that?) within earshot of any summons from royalty. When the King rose, it was Thomas who dressed him, garment by garment, the clothing reverently passed to him by a groom outside the door of the royal bedchamber. Thomas loved it all. The King was ill, spitting blood, far from fragrant to be near, but what of it? Queasiness hardly became a privileged courtier.

Then, not unexpectedly, the King died. It would have been treason for any man to say that he was dying, had been dying for a long time, but everyone had known it. A general sigh of relief went up. In his later years he had become more miserly, tightening the financial screws put on his people by his Treasury ministers, Empson and Dudley, and very eccentric, constantly devising unlikely marriages between himself and various young foreign princesses. He was fifty-two, had reigned for twenty-four years, and people were tired of him. It was time for a change.

They got it in the person of his son Henry. Now King Henry

VIII, this large dazzling youth of seventeen had been the stout precocious child who had ogled Elizabeth Boleyn at the Tower in her bridal days. Brought up in the shadow of his father, he craved flamboyance, glitter and personal power.

He indulged all of them, to the delight of his bored subjects. On Midsummer Day, 1509, he gave them a coronation to remember.

Thomas was in Westminster Abbey, close to the new monarch, and wearing his gold collar.

'You see, my father was right,' he had smirked to Elizabeth, 'we were to have a coronation soon, just as he said.'

'Good. I shall enjoy that.'

'You?'

'Of course. I can wear my carnation velvet, and my new hood. My father will expect to see me looking fine, and it would be pleasant to outshine Agnes, who I hear is pregnant – at last.' Elizabeth smoothed her waist. She would never be pregnant again: Anne's birth had torn her, so that all Thomas's efforts to increase his dynastic investments were vain.

'Very well,' he said. 'If you can be spared from your household duties, and the management of the farms.'

'We have good bailiffs. Why keep a dog and bark oneself? The crops will do very well in this good weather, and I shall hardly be expected to supervise the sheep-shearing. No, Thomas, my place is at your side on this happy occasion.' She made eyes at him in pretty mockery, which he ignored. 'Besides, we have a new Queen, who will be pleased to see ladies about her. Poor thing, she will be ready for some festivities after all that miserly living, not knowing whether she was to be married to King Henry or sent back to Spain.'

Queen Catherine was a surprise. Six years older than her bridegroom, she was tiny, dumpy, slightly swamped by her rich gown and load of jewels. Her fair hair was beautiful, her face had a gentle prettiness, though it was not as pretty as it had been (poverty is no beautifier); her best features were a soft mouth and long, languid eyes. Her accent, when she gave her hand to Elizabeth to be kissed, with a shy smile, was heavily Spanish.

'Well,' said Elizabeth to Thomas, at the end of the long day's ceremonies, 'I confess myself disappointed. How does she manage to look such a frump, at her age and with all that money on her back? The late Queen was so lovely, I shall never forget her. They say men who have any choice in the matter always marry women like their mothers. But perhaps young Henry prefers short, fat women.'

'We do not question His Grace's choice,' Thomas answered pompously. 'His Grace seems most enamoured of his bride.'

'Bride – yes, of course. Only two months married. No wonder she still looks on him like a sheep on the biggest ram of the flock. He must be something of a contrast to poor young Arthur, who never bedded her, I warrant – '

'*Madam!*'

'Oh, you may pull faces, Thomas, but I shall say what I like in the seclusion of our bedchamber. If this is your idea of a lodging for me, by the way, I suggest you find something better, for I intend to stay at Court at least until Michaelmas. I expect I shall see very little of you, when you're about your duties. If London should be struck by the sweating sickness I shall have the children taken to Blickling, and join them there while Hever is swept and cleansed.'

Thomas, unconcerned with his wife's amusements, applied himself assiduously to his duties as Esquire, a post he had managed to retain under the new King. Henry was impressed by this highly correct, dapper, ultra-respectful courtier, and in a mood to dispense largesse. Thomas's devotion to the royal person was rewarded. In coronation year he became a Knight of the Bath.

Now he was entitled to wear a new collar of gold. Weighing thirty ounces troy, it was composed of eight devices of Tudor roses, enamelled in their colours proper, linked together with seventeen knots enamelled argent, from which hung the badge of the Order. Doubly a knight now, Thomas Boleyn was a proud man.

Three months later he was created Keeper of the Exchange in England. After two years, his worthy service earned him the appointment of Sheriff of Kent, and a year later he became, in his capacity as a Norfolk landowner, joint constable of Norwich Castle – this office being shared with his neighbour, Sir Henry Wyatt.

His ambitions grew by feeding. He saw an earldom ahead of him, if he played his cards aright (and he would). There seemed no limit to the honours this vital, generous and noisy young monarch would thrust upon him.

And, just possibly, upon his wife.

It began after the heir to the throne had been born, and lost, at less than five months old – from no known cause, certainly not neglect. Conjecture gave many reasons, including infection by contaminated objects, over-feeding, or the constriction of swaddling bands, but nobody knew why Prince Henry, that lusty infant, suddenly died.

He had not been the first progeny. That one, also a boy, was born prematurely. The King was not being over-lucky in his begetting, nor were his pious wife's prayers having much effect. She took to praying even harder and more frequently, joining a religious order and hearing Mass at all hours of the day and night. The King, outwardly as good a son of the Church as she a daughter, admired and conformed, but inwardly was just a trifle bored with it all; particularly as the Queen was visibly stoutening in body, and not only from pregnancy.

The first encounter was in a courtly dance. Elizabeth Boleyn danced most gracefully, had danced almost as soon as she could walk, light of foot, taut and slender. Henry was uncommonly tall as well as broad, but she was tall for a woman, tall enough not to make him feel as though he were dancing opposite a puppet. Flowers, gilt dust and perfumes, spiced food and wines, the music of the rebeck, viol and lute, all combined to make the feast-night intoxicating.

The King was, in fact, just a trifle drunk, the lady drunk only with the knowledge of her own charms and her freedom. She beamed her dark eyes at him and smiled with her slightly thin lips, and Henry found her most seductive. He remembered names well.

'Lady Boleyn, wife of my good servant Thomas.'

'The same, Your Grace.'

'We have met, at our coronation, and since. Yet I seem to know you better than that would warrant.'

Elizabeth modestly cast down her sweeping lashes. 'We first met when Your Grace was only a child.'

'And you were a mere infant, madam.' Henry knew how to flatter.

'Alas.' She shook her head, and the garnet necklace round her throat shook too, drawing his eyes to the charming cleft beneath. 'I am old, Your Grace, old, far older than yourself.' The difference was actually nine years. 'You were too young to remember.'

Henry's remarkable memory rarely failed him. 'But I *do* remember. It was at the Tower. You wore blue. I thought you a most beautiful lady.'

'*Une vrai belle dame*, as Thomas would say.' She mocked Thomas's affected accent. 'Your Grace was fluent in French, even at so early an age, I remember.'

His small light blue eyes dwelt on her face. How very small they were, and his mouth too, a tight rosebud. Was it that their surroundings had grown broader?

'My whipping boy was beaten that day,' the King said, steering her past a slower couple of dancers, 'for my insolence and forwardness to you. I hope you forgave me, since my boldness was a tribute to beauty.'

Elizabeth's complexion was too sallow for easy blushes, but a modest dip of the head managed to suggest a blush. Henry thought it quite charming. His taste lay more in the direction of small plump blondes, but he was at the moment none too particular, since Catherine's extreme piety made her a less than jolly bed companion, and she was always either pregnant or getting over a disappointing pregnancy. He had not been a loose liver, so far. People compared him to his glorious, wanton grandfather, Edward IV but he had not inherited Edward's passion for indiscriminate womanising: it had led to so many disasters, not least of them his premature death, and Henry had no intention of jeopardising either his life or his throne by careless wenching. It was whispered that he had been a male virgin when he married Catherine. That was not true; he had had quite a few adventures into Cupid's country, one or two of them in its less salubrious districts. There had been a few disturbing symptoms, which had mercifully passed. But a married woman of Lady Boleyn's status would be quite safe.

He had the good sense to leave their first encounter with a few more murmured compliments and a lingering kiss on her hand.

The next encounter found them on a wet afternoon which, as wet afternoons will, provided Henry with boredom, leisure, and consequent inclination. He moved purposefully through a crowd of chattering ladies to join Elizabeth on a window seat.

She responded noticeably, though modestly, to his tactful gallantries. She was most honoured, she mumured, His Grace must not speak so within others' hearing. (The others, like a flock of birds on a feeding ground, had moved unobtrusively away to where the Queen sat, and were energetically neither watching nor listening.) No, she would not take a cup of wine just then, she had been eating sweetmeats.

Henry persevered. Since they were in the Palace of Richmond, so sweetly situated by the Thames, she might like to accompany him to a private apartment from which could be seen the new buildings he was adding, in a handsome style designed by a talented Italian architect. He made it sound an enticing prospect, in every sense.

But the lady shook her head, regretfully. Alas, she had strained her right ankle (she exhibited it, for rather longer than necessary) and was trying to avoid undue exercise. Hence her occupation of the window seat.

Henry acknowledged temporary defeat, as one rider in a tourney saluting his opponent.

Within three weeks Elizabeth was graciously offered the coveted post of lady-in-waiting to Queen Catherine.

The young Queen was pleased to add this new attendant to her select retinue. She had only eight chief ladies, all either countesses or the daughters of dukes. They included poor Margaret de la Pole, whose husband had been in the Tower for years for the crime of having a claim to the throne; the Countess of Shrewsbury, the Countess of Derby, Lady Oxford, Lady Essex, and Elizabeth Boleyn's stepmother, Agnes, Countess of Surrey.

Elizabeth herself would rank junior to these, among the Ladies of the Bedchamber, nearly all of whom had husbands who were of the King's household. The Queen had looked Lady Boleyn over, thought her handsome and dignified and knew her to be of high rank. And Henry recommended her particularly, which was enough for the loving, trusting Catherine.

It was not for Elizabeth to refuse such an honour. She knew what it would mean: the persistent attentions of King Henry, and far more opportunities for flirtation, even dalliance, with other gentlemen than she had enjoyed as merely the châtelaine of Hever. Starved of pleasure, hungry for admiration, almost desperate to retain her flying youth and the beauty which would not endure, she made her lowest, most graceful curtsey to her royal mistress.

It was a pleasure to serve Catherine, who was gentle, kind and patient. She was almost abnormally pious, certainly, but not, as Henry's alarming grandmother had been, formidably harsh because of it. She liked to see her ladies constant at their devotions, spoke to them raptly of her joy in Our Lord and His Mother; between them they had the biggest collection of jewelled crucifixes, the Queen's gifts, outside a nunnery.

Elizabeth listened fascinated to Lady Essex's account of an earlier scandal. Two of the Queen's chief ladies had been Lady Fitzwalter, a beauty and a great favourite, and her even more beautiful sister Anne, Lady Hastings.

'Her Grace was with child – that was the first time – and the King was very young, as indeed he is still, and tired of . . . finding himself a bachelor again. So he began to court Lady Hastings, and so did Sir William Compton, a Groom of the Bedchamber, and went to her room, which lay well out of the Queen's sight.'

'Both at the same time?' Elizabeth asked.

'Fie! But who knows? At any rate, Lady Fitzwalter grew afraid that harm would come to them all, and told her brother the Duke of Buckingham, who flew into a passion and burst into their sister's room, where he found Compton with her. Just as well it was not the King, or he might have suffered for it.'

'Did anyone suffer for it?'

'Only the women. That's how life runs, my dear. There was a fearful quarrel, Hastings was sent for and carried Anne off to a convent sixty miles away, and Compton went to the King and complained.

'Of what? Having his mistress removed?'

'Of Buckingham, I suppose, for the King rose from bed in the dark of the morning and had Buckingham fetched to him and called him a meddling prier and poker into other people's concerns – I heard this from a servant who was roused to summon the Duke. And Buckingham stormed out, vowing he would not pass another night in that place. Next day the King ordered the Queen to have Elizabeth Fitzwalter dismissed, and all other women who might be sniffing out mischief about the Court. He threatened to throw every one of them out, neck and crop, but the Queen would not have it, and all Greenwich heard them quarrelling. It was after this that she miscarried, and some blamed it on the Hastings affair. So you'd better be careful, my dear.' Lady Essex laughed heartily, innocently, with no ulterior significance.

Elizabeth brooded on the story. She had better be careful, indeed. She knew the King to be greatly attracted to her, all the more because she kept him at arm's length. Were she to yield, and the Lady Hastings unmasking be repeated, Thomas would be anything but a *mari complaisant*: he would make a scene. Somehow it would get back to the Queen and there would be trouble. For herself, for Thomas, and for the Queen. One could not help but be sorry for that poor young woman, who would obviously have to face a rival with every pregnancy.

Was it worth the risk, to experience royalty in one's bed, and a large lusty young man's ardour instead of Thomas's almost mechanical marital attentions? Elizabeth decided it was not, thanking God for a cool brain to balance a female nature inclined to warmth. Never should the name of Boleyn, much less that of Howard, be coupled with terms so shaming as whore, strumpet, meretrix, harlot, words from the stews.

The day came when Henry caught her as she was passing through a small unfrequented antechamber leading from Fountain Court to the Queen's apartments. The Palace of Greenwich was full of such seldom-used, purposeless little rooms. This one contained only a joint-stool and a pallet, a rough undraped thing which could be dragged into any chamber and used as a bed for a servant.

As soon as she saw him, and the glint in his eyes, she knew that he had been following her. He appeared gigantic in a brightly-chequered doublet of green and gold, like a great tree in foliage above two long sturdy white trunks, his legs.

'Well met, Lady Boleyn,' he said. 'I beheld one fair sun in the heavens – now I see a fairer in my own house.'

She weighed up the distance between herself and the doorway. But he was standing between, rock-like. She smiled in what she hoped was a sickly and pathetic manner.

'I, too, was sitting in the sun, Your Grace, watching the boats on the river, but its heat burnt into my brain and made me faint.' She put her hand on the basquine of boiled leather that encased her stomach. Surely he would not attempt her if he thought she was likely to spew all over him.

But he and his purposeful smile advanced. 'That bold sun kissed your cheeks, too, my lady. And not for the first time, by that gold dust I see on them. Well, I like a brown girl. A country Phyllida.'

He grasped her arms, pulled her against him, and dragging her with him stepped back towards the door and kicked it shut.

Elizabeth prayed. In no more than a moment there flashed through her imagination scenes of horror: Thomas bursting in, Thomas divided between anger with her and deference to his monarch, the words they would say – the Queen making a stately entrance and giving birth on the spot, from sheer outrage – the Queen's confessor, Friar Diego Fernandez, surprising them (he was known to sneak about in lay clothes) and condemning them both to eternal perdition . . .

Just as, struggling, she saw in her mind's eye the Friar's crucifix threateningly brandished against them, the latchet of the door clicked and someone entered. It was none of the personages she had envisioned, but one almost as alarming – her stepmother, Agnes, Countess of Surrey, with a waiting-woman peering over her shoulder.

Elizabeth did not miss the lightning flash of triumph on Agnes's face. They were second cousins as well as step-relations, with only a year or two in age between them, and had known each other since childhood. Agnes had changed much from the meek girl who had sat mum and mim at Elizabeth's wedding, and sighed about women being vessels. She seemed to have grown in height, which was possible, and comported herself with the dignity befitting the wife of the great Earl of Surrey. Her gown was a dark damson-red, suggesting robes of State, with sleeves of cloth-of-silver, none too fresh looking: Elizabeth guessed that they were worn often because Agnes couldn't bear to leave them off and wear something humbler. At least Agnes had not grown in beauty – her face was a map of disappointment from childbearing, the usual story of a woman's life. She had yet to bring the Earl a son.

She swooped to the floor in a huge curtsey.

'Your pardon, Your Grace. I didn't know Your Grace was here.'

Henry pulled himself together, disentangling a hand from Elizabeth's skirts and arranging his flushed face into an expression of airy nonchalance.

'Madam.' His courtly bow gave Elizabeth time to retreat and try to compose herself. 'What a delight, two Howard ladies in a little lowly chamber, two glorious jewels in a poor setting. You must have much to say to each other, since you are just come from Framlingham, I believe, madam?'

'Yes, Your Grace. My lord had much to see to there.' Framlingham Castle, that noble Suffolk stronghold, had come into the Earl's possession at Henry's coronation – Agnes was frequently torn between her Court duties and her passion for living in Framlingham in great state, on her husband's vastly increased income. As Henry bowed again and stalked out, Agnes's eyes met Elizabeth's. This time the triumph was unmistakable.

'I am grieved to see one of my kin behaving like a wanton,' she said in the tone of one who, far from being grieved, was delighted.

'I was not behaving wantonly!' Elizabeth flared. 'It was nothing, a little jest on His Grace's part. You know how he loves to tease.'

'Too well. But was he not being rather more playful than usual – in close retirement, one might say secrecy, and with a lady of your blood? My lord your father would once have had you whipped for that. I marvel that Sir Thomas has not taught you better conduct since you became his wife. As his mother-in-law I think it my duty to warn him to keep a closer watch on you.'

Elizabeth felt rage rising within her, carrying angry blood to her cheeks. 'You'll do nothing of the kind! You are *not* Thomas's mother-in-law, merely my father's second wife, whom he took because you were kin to my mother and he thought you would be like her – poor man, what a sad disappointment to find himself married to a shrew and a scold.'

'And what a sad disappointment for Sir Thomas to find himself married to a light-skirt. Fie, oh fie. Come, Joan.' Agnes saw that Elizabeth's hands were clawed in readiness to rake her cheeks. The girl had always had a temper and might well do her a mischief unless she retreated. 'Calm yourself,' she advised. 'Pray to Our Lady for a holier heart. I shall pray for you myself.' Wheeling round, she gave her maid a push that sent the girl through the doorway.

'Try praying for the King!' Elizabeth shouted after her. 'He needs it, and so do you for your uncharitableness!'

She was ashamed of herself, ashamed of Agnes – fighting like a couple of bawds on Bankside. All spite and malevolence: Agnes must have seen that any exercise in lechery had been entirely on the King's part. She wished she had fought and screamed instead of putting up that feeble defence. But in her heart she knew that she had physically enjoyed it, and would have enjoyed yielding, at another time and in another place, such were the ungovernable lusts of the flesh.

The worst of it was the presence of the attendant. What with her to entertain her friends with the story, and Agnes's spite, the tale would be all over the Court within a few hours.

Which, indeed, it was.

5

Rumour, painted full of Tongues

The whispers went round like snakes' hisses; in corners between two or three, in parlours and bedchambers between many.

'Lady Boleyn is whore to His Grace.'

'No! I'll not hear word of such lewdery. It must be slander.' (Meaning, tell me more.)

'True, as I stand here. Joan Paxton saw it all.'

'In the King's bed?'

'Perhaps that as well. But the place was . . . Joan doesn't know what the chamber is called. There was a bed in it.'

'They were in bed?'

'Joan was too flustered to see. But Lady Boleyn was naked.'

'No, half-naked, Margery.'

'Half-naked, then – her skirts over her head and the King . . .' Whisper, whisper.

A burst of delighted giggles. 'And she so proper and proud. Who'll ever believe it?'

'Lady Surrey, for one. She was there, it was she who surprised them. She will carry it to the Earl and then we shall see what he thinks of his daughter.'

'And Sir Thomas. Oh, Sir Thomas! I can't wait to see how he will look with horns. Will he wear his Bath Order on one, and the Howard arms in little on the other?'

'What's the French for cuckold?'

'*Cocu*?' somebody suggested, making the word sound as unambiguous as possible.

'Bulls have horns,' said Margery. 'Why not Bullens?'

A chorus of cuckooing and bellowing broke out, in the midst of which Elizabeth entered. The chorus stopped as though chopped off with a knife.

The girl Margery spoke. 'We were saying how odd it is to hear the cuckoo so late, Lady Boleyn.'

'Yes,' corroborated Marion Dunne, 'I heard it in the Queen's Pleasance only this morning, and you know the rhyme says "In July away I fly, in August go I must". Yet he is still here.'

Somebody was overcome by giggles and left hastily.

Elizabeth looked round the group, thoughtfully. She was not slow of wit: the cuckoo's cry was synonymous with only one thing, like jests mentioning horns.

'How odd,' she said. 'But perhaps you were mistaken, Marion. Other birds can mimic the cuckoo – the starling, for instance. I think, if you will reflect, you will realise that it was a starling.'

She turned on her heel and walked out, leaving a silent group behind her.

That evening at supper she watched her father very closely. But the Earl smiled graciously upon her when his eyes met hers. Evidently Agnes had not told him. Agnes herself was formal but polite to Elizabeth. Very wise, not to inform on the King: look what had happened in the Fitzwalter-Hastings affair. But Agnes's silence would not shut the mouths of others.

It was as well for her peace of mind that she did not know what gratuitous malice could do. A lady-in-waiting whom Elizabeth had once snubbed severely took it upon herself to remark to the Queen, during the ceremony of disrobing, how well His Grace was looking, and how cheerful he seemed. 'As though he had found a new diversion – the Tennis Court, perhaps.'

Catherine's English was not yet perfect, but she understood perfectly well the language of looks. This lady's expression denoted something besides the Tennis Court Henry had had built recently, its windows facing a pleasant prospect of the river.

'I am glad his Grace has a good sport,' she said carefully.

69

'Oh, it is most good. It gives His Grace such splendid exercise. I believe Lady Boleyn enjoys it, too.'

'Lady Boleyn? I did not know ladies played that game. I should not care to try it.' Her square, stiff farthingales, still of the Spanish fashion she had worn when she first came to England, would, indeed, have made such an activity impossible.

'Perhaps I mistook, Your Grace. It may be that she merely likes to watch.'

'So? I will ask her.'

With intent – for she was not as naive as she had been, and her informant knew it – the Queen did ask Elizabeth. Brown eyes met brown eyes, and the Queen's were sad, suspicious. Elizabeth, pitying, tried to reassure without telling lies or giving anything away.

'I dislike all sports, Your Grace, though in my youth I practised archery sometimes. I feel that they are not good for women – dangerous, even. I do not indulge in tennis – or any game which men commonly play.'

Catherine nodded. 'Good. That is as it should be. *Gracias* – I mean, I thank you.' What she meant was *a Dios gracias*, thanks be to God that my husband is not deceiving me with a lady whom I respect.

Nevertheless, Elizabeth thought it prudent to leave Court for a little while, to give gossip time to die down, and the King's fancy time to cool.

When she left for visits to Hever and Blickling, the rumour spread that she had done so because she was with child by the King. 'She's so thin, it will be hard for her to hide her condition.' When she returned in late September it was clear that no child existed, so the gossips said that it had been born prematurely, that she had miscarried, by good luck, and now was come back to flaunt her figure.

Rumour would live on, long after all of them were dead, and gather embroidery as it lived. The date of her youngest daughter's birth was forgotten, until it passed into oblivion and those who liked to believe scandal could put it about that Anne was King Henry's child. As the Apostle says: 'Behold, how great a matter a little fire kindleth!'

And the King, disappointed of a conquest he would have enjoyed, was self-congratulatory that he had not deceived his wife. Instead, he threw himself into sports, energetic sports which took his mind off such matters, just as he had expressed in his famous song.

> Pastyme with good company
> I love, and shall until I die . . .
> For my pastance,
> Hunt, sing and dance,
> My heart is set;
> All goodly sport
> For my comfort
> Who shall me let?

To vary the sport, he made war on France and Scotland, winning a notable victory on the Field of Flodden – though he did not personally command the winning side. Their leader was the seventy-year-old Earl of Surrey, Elizabeth's father, whom for his valour the King elevated to Duke of Norfolk. He had gained Henry a great victory and a piece of the dead King of Scotland's bloody plaid.

And hardly anyone noticed, except Elizabeth's fellow Lady of the Bedchamber, Lady Margaret de la Pole, that her husband Edmund had been very quietly taken out of the Tower one day and executed on Tower Green, for the treasonable crime of having royal blood in his veins.

Elizabeth was glad the King had abandoned his chase of her, if it was going to cause as much trouble as it had promised. Yet, perversely, she could not resist catching his eye and sending out eloquent messages from her own. She was playing with fire, but something in her nature needed to play with fire.

She needed more and more hungrily to be fed with admiration. Perhaps, even, with a little romantic love, the kind of love that sends a lady passionate verses, comparing her to Venus, Helen, an unattainable star, a glorious flower. *Stella coelis, rosa splendida hortis*. Thomas had never given her such love – she doubted whether he was capable of it – and she was weary of matching him in cool remoteness.

There were gentlemen at Court who found her attractive, some of whom disliked Thomas and had no objection to cuckolding him. So it came about that whispers circulated. Lady Boleyn was light, Lady Boleyn was easy. She thought she could do anything she liked because the Howards were now so high in favour since Flodden. Thus the gossips were most polite to her face, while privily calling her Bess Bullen, the *bona roba*.

Elizabeth cared not at all for them, so long as she could slake the craving within her. It was quite safe, since she was now barren. True, some of her suitors were not young, or very attractive in their persons, but what of it? Beauty was woman's right, not man's.

There came a day of early April, when the sun was nearing the earth and the light harshly bright through the clear glass of the windows. Elizabeth sat at the table in her bedchamber at Hever, turning her hand-mirror this way and that to view her face from all angles. In the cruel light she saw strands of grey in her hair, quite thick over the temples, and lines radiated from the corners of those eyes which the most poetic of her admirers had called dark stars: ugly, deep lines, matched by other, fainter ones from her nose downwards, and a little pucker between the brows.

There were remedies, of course. Cow's milk, lemon water (that would tone down the distressing browning of her cheeks, which the sun had somehow caught in spite of shady hats and thick veils). A concoction of distilled vinegar, new-laid eggs, dock roots, and flowers of brimstone was said to help. Ursula should make it up for her.

But there was something worse. Elizabeth parted her lips and cautiously fingered the tooth which had been causing her unease.

Yes, it was loose, an incisor right at the front, and its neighbour was not over-firm. Nothing would secure them, not aqua fortis nor calcined rosemary nor sugar-and-honey water.

Skelton's rhyme at her marriage feast came back to mock her.

> Faith, by my life,
> I rather would thy lippés bas
> Than Saint Peter his gates y-pass.

No more, Master Skelton. I am almost thirty years old, and my youth is over, my beauty gone.

She tinkled a bell for her waiting-maid.

'Send for my daughters.'

Mary and Anne were very young, but not too young to be taught how to cultivate and care for their looks. A woman's beauty is so short-lived, so soon over, no stronger than a flower.

TWO
MARY AND ANNE
1514

Girls of mild silver and of furious gold.

6

Maiden Mary

The years that took from Elizabeth gave lavishly to her children. The year 1514 saw George, at eleven, tall for his age, as darkly handsome as though the base and noble blood in his veins had blended in a perfect alchemy, and so clever that he had become an embarrassment to Master Nicolas's limited powers of tutelage. It was time he was sent away for stricter supervision and teaching, and he was despatched to the Archbishop's household at Knole, the great house of Sevenoaks. There he succeeded in charming everybody and learning exactly as much as he wished to learn.

Mary, now ten, was such a model of childish beauty that the family chaplain declared her one of the Seraphim, sent to show the face of an angel to mortals. In fact, feature for feature, she was very like her father, with the addition of dark Howard eyes: broad cheeks, straight brows, a largish nose and a small mouth, all transmuted by her sex to great prettiness. The hair which had been first blonde, then auburn, was rapidly darkening to match the eyes, but her complexion was perfect pink and white, greatly admired.

Mary smiled and laughed a great deal, bestowed affection impulsively on everybody from the cook (who gave her more titbits than anybody else) to her austere grandfather the Duke of Norfolk. It was when Simonette found her bestowing affection on Gregory the dog boy, who all but lived in the kennels with his charges, and smelt accordingly, that Mary received one of her rare beatings. But it was a light one, little more than a few smacks. She cried so prettily and so heartrendingly that those who punished her felt like torturers of the most brutal kind.

Thomas, a keen critic of his children, approved his elder daughter's looks, obviously a guarantee that she would make a grand marriage.

Of his younger daughter's appearance he had once not been proud. Frankly ugly as a baby, she had become a thin infant with a sharp unchildlike face and a body lacking Mary's dimpled flesh, and then an equally sharp-faced little girl. Now, quite suddenly, at the age of six, a change had come over her which made her father think again.

Her long skinny limbs had at last gained more flesh. She had a distinct waist, a rare thing in little girls, and her lack of bosom, natural enough at her tender age, suited perfectly the grown-up style of her dresses, just as the long neck he had once thought duck-like had become a slender pillar supporting a well-shaped head.

Her carriage was good, too. Anne never slouched or drooped, but kept her shoulders back and the graceful head held high. She seemed, in fact, a miniature woman rather than a small child: not all that small, since she topped Mary in height.

She had always been bright in intellect, since the days when she had learned her letters from a hornbook, her criss-cross row, the alphabet written on a sheet of horn. Her Latin was now good – as far as a girl's could be expected to be good – and her excellent memory enabled her to rattle off the Psalms, the Gloria, the Credo and the Paternoster so briskly that she clearly gave little thought to their meaning.

And why should she? Nobody did, other than priests and learned men. Thomas gave up the idea of putting her into a convent. With her combination of grace and quickness, Anne was fitted for a very good match indeed, if God spared her to live to womanhood.

Her father was particularly proud of her skill in French, which she spoke fluently and with an almost perfect accent, picked up from the Parisienne Simonette. Thomas had become aware, during his time in France during the French wars of 1513, that his own mastery of that language did not extend to an accent which would deceive anyone. It would be a great asset to a girl to be able to chatter away to visiting diplomats. Or even royalty.

To his delight, he had been sent by the King as ambassador to Marguerite of Savoy, the ruler of the Low Countries. His residence at the Archduchess's court had given him ambitious ideas for his daughters.

The two girls were at Allington Castle, near Maidstone, in the Lady's Bower, when their friends the Wyatt children heard the news. Tom was eleven, just George Boleyn's age, and his sister the gentle Margaret was born in the same year as Anne. Sir Henry Wyatt, a widower since Margaret's birth, sometimes sent for the Boleyn children to come over and keep his own brood company. (His second son, also a George, seldom stayed, preferring the society of the village children, huntsmen and grooms.)

None of the children, nor any children of their time, knew a proper and acknowledged childhood. For them there was no Age of Innocence and smiled-on play. Their extreme youth was an inconvenience to their elders, something to be got over as soon as possible. They were far older in thought and speech than their years, because they were being taught to be adults. If they were poor, they must be fitted to work and bring in wages; if rich, to marry well, serve in high places, beget heirs. That was the whole purpose of education.

The Boleyn and Wyatt children would not have dreamed of disputing these hard but inescapable facts, whether they liked them or not.

Margaret ran to Mary, who was weeping over her embroidery.

'What ails you, Mall darling? Is it a pain? Has someone hurt you?'

Mary shook her head violently, sobbing even louder.

Anne, with a patient sigh, raised her head from the book she was riffling through.

'She's being sent away. Father's packing her off to the Archduchess in Brussels, and she doesn't wish to go. Ninny.'

'Oh, poor Mall!' Margaret knelt, her arms round her heaving friend. 'So young, to go to a foreign land. Must she go, Anne?'

'If Father says so. And why not? What is there to do here? I wish I were going. George is a spoilt pet at Knole, and Mall going to Brussels, and I am stuck in Kent like a clod.' She banged down the book and went to stare out of the window, at the river and the gardens of the castle, a pretty house larger than Hever, but much like it.

Tom Wyatt's heart felt as though it had plummeted into his shoes. He would not be a man in body for years, or even, strictly, a youth, but he was going through early pains of romantic love. He read avidly when not at his lessons, his head stuffed full of courtly tales and poetry. His favourite book was Ovid's *Amores*. He understood very little of it but felt it all.

Anne was his Corinna, the adored mistress of his heart, his ideal. That she was so young was no matter, in four years or less he would be considered old enough to marry her, in name only, of course. But if Mary was to be sent abroad, Anne would be, and soon.

Mary sniffed, wiping her streaming nose and eyes. 'Father *might* send you instead, Nan, if you asked him.'

Anne laughed, a sharp mirthless laugh. 'Can you see it? No, as the elder you must go. I am the baby, made to stay behind.'

'But I c-can't speak French as you can, Simonette is always pinching me for it. Nobody will understand what I say.'

'Then you'll have to mime it, like the clowns in the mummer's plays.' She rattled off a hailstone shower of French, at which Mary cried the harder. Her tearful outburst was to be her last effort at rebellion against her all-powerful father. Henceforth she would obediently do as men told her: after all, they must know best.

After dinner, which they all took together in the Great Hall (it passed for great at Allington, but was modest enough to Anne's eyes, for she longed for the size and splendours of Sheriff Hutton, as described by her mother), Anne and Tom walked by the river, Anne still restless and impatient.

'I'm writing a poem to you,' said Tom.

'Another? You're always writing poems,'

'Oh, this is the best one yet. Shall I tell it to you?'

Anne shrugged thin shoulders. He began, in nervous self-conscious tones, knowing that she would laugh at him.

> With lilies white
> And roses bright
> Doth strive thy colour fair;
> Nature did lend
> Each finger's end
> A pearl for to repair.

Yes, she was laughing at his poor verse, and spreading out her small hands.

'Lilies and roses, Tom? Do you see any in my face? I think you mean cowslips. I shall be as yellow as my mother when I'm her age.'

'No. She . . . you . . .'

'And as to pearls, my nails aren't very like pearls, are they.' She hid the deformity on the right hand under the other fingers – not even her poor slave Tom must look at it. 'Now if you were to give me real pearls, that would be different.' She picked up a stone and threw it into the river. 'I love pearls, more than diamonds or rubies or any such thing, and when I marry my husband shall give me boxes full of them, to wear all over.' She was thinking especially of carcanets, necklaces, strings of pearls to hide that hated hideous wen at the base of her throat. The white linen partlet whose top was framed by the square neckline of her gown did not come up high enough to cover the thing, and her mother let her wear a double row of simple coloured stone beads to fill it in.

'I would give you pearls. When you're Lady Wyatt, you shall have a dress covered with pearls.'

Anne could not have said how she knew that she would never be Lady Wyatt, but she did know it. She sighed, thinking of the dress covered with pearls. They would shimmer and shift colour, like bubbles, making her dark skin look rich, as her mother's complexion sometimes did when she wore pearls. She would look like a water nymph in one of the fantastical Court plays her mother recounted, in which the Queen's ladies were sprites or fairies or damsels from the old times, and the King's men hunters or knights or champions of fairy tales, or heroes from the stories travellers brought back from foreign places too far and strange to imagine.

Tom sighed too, because his small lady seemed unhappy. He took her hand and bent down to kiss her cheek. But she pulled away, because the last time she had fancied playing at courtship Tom had been too shy to touch her.

'"He that will not when he may, When he would he shall have nay." There's a poem for you!' With a laugh she began to run, faster and faster along the river bank until trees hid her from his sight.

Sir Henry, watching from a quiet bower where he liked to sit with official papers, was saddened. He had known the pains of adolescent love, though not so precociously young as Tom: a feeling all made of uncomprehended urges and airy fancies born of other men's thoughts, something all young animals felt but had the sense to know was not yet for them. How fortunate were the beasts of the field. If his Tom and Boleyn's dark daughter had been a couple of young otters there would have been no heartache, none of the bad verses which Tom's tutor was accustomed to finding among the lad's papers. Henry Wyatt knew Boleyn, the man's ambition, money, and growing authority at Court. Certainly there was a Howard–Wyatt connection, but not a strong one – they could just be called cousins, which would not be good enough for Boleyn.

Sir Henry was already on the look-out for a husband for Margaret. She was a tender creature, and should be married early enough to spare her this sort of pain, for maids might suffer as well as men. He hoped the dark child would not suffer.

Mary was despatched to Brussels without undue ceremony or sentiment. Her wardrobe was lavish, designed to make the most of her childish charms and advertise her father's wealth. Having voiced her distress at Allington, she made no further resistance, but endured all the preparations, then all the well-wishing adieux, stoically.

It was hardest to part from Anne, for they had been close, though so unalike.

'They may send you out to join me,' Mary said.

Anne shook her head. 'That would be unlike our father, sending two arrows after the same beast.'

'Beast? What beast?'

'Oh, Mall, how stupid you are. I mean that he intends to rule one court through you, so he must mean me for another. Why should I care? I may go to London, to be one of the Queen's ladies. That will be much grander than Brussels. Who ever heard of Brussels?'

But Anne's eyes glistened with tears and Mary's soft lips trembled when the groom helped her up on to the horse that would carry her on her way to Dover. Her father rode beside her, suitably escorted, the armorial bull of Bullen displayed everywhere room could be found for it, on the uniform of the attendants, on the horses' saddle cloths.

Elizabeth waved and waved until the small figure on the brown horse was out of sight. Her straight square shoulders drooped as she turned away and went back into the courtyard. It was the best thing for the girl, of course; Thomas had done well to use his influence for her. But she would be glad to get away, to Blickling, or back to Court, anywhere away from the sight of Mary's empty gowns and the place where Mary had sat at table. She would never see that child again. A young woman resembling her, perhaps, if they both lived. But never the Mary who had ridden away, and had not looked back.

Mary would like to have held the hand of the equerry presenting her, but only people of the common sort did such things. He stood beside her in the Audience Chamber of the Grand Palais, the royal palace of the Netherlands on the Coudenberg, looking down on Brussels. They were alone between ranks of courtiers, who maintained a grave mien out of respect for their august mistress, and took no serious note of the young girl.

She wore her best farthingale and the blue hood with a veil which she had longed to wear since it was made, but now had no pleasure in. She knew that her face was pale and her eyes heavy with weariness. The sea crossing had been rough and the land journey from Antwerp so tiring that she had not been able to enjoy the foreignness of her surroundings.

Bouton took her hand and led her forward to where the Archduchess sat in state. Mary made the very low curtsey she had been practising, raising her eyes just high enough to take in the long elegant feet in jewelled shoes and the embroidered hem of a rich flowing gown. Then a hand was thrust forward abruptly for her to kiss, and as abruptly withdrawn.

Marguerite of Austria, daughter of an emperor, twice widowed, had at the age of twenty-six faced a life of emptiness, unless she were to have a third try at marriage. Then, suddenly, her brother the Archduke had died: Philippe le Bel, the handsome young man everyone expected to reign as long as his father had done.

Marguerite was strong-minded and capable, if a trifle hard-featured, with a little too much of the family nose. Her father was sensible enough to appoint her Regent of the Netherlands, and guardian of her young nephew Charles, who would be Emperor of Germany when he came of age. Marguerite had taken to power like a duck to water, and was now, after seven years, as deeply respected as any male ruler could have been.

'Look at me, demoiselle,' she commanded. Mary raised her eyes, carefully keeping all expression out of them.

'Charming,' said Marguerite, and the attendants around her murmured agreement. 'They grow pretty faces in England, I see. Ladies, you must look to your beauty – such as it is.' They smiled demurely, and Mary allowed a dimple to appear in one cheek. She could control its appearance and disappearance, and knew that it usually had a disarming effect. The great lady was speaking. '. . . delighted to receive another Boleyn' (she pronounced it Boullen) 'at our court, since your father's most valued service as ambassador to our own father, and to ourself.' So Marguerite used the royal 'we': Mary was duly impressed. 'We are sure you will do honour to the name, demoiselle. Your father's letter gives a good account of you, and we shall hope to prove it. You may retire.'

Both were pleased, mistress and servant. Mary because she had found a royal lady who might be stern but could also be kind, and Marguerite because, like other plain rulers, she liked to have fair attendants around her. Childless herself, she had a fondness for children, and although Mary was ten, well on the way to womanhood, she seemed very young, vulnerable and winsome.

The Archduchess proceeded to take this promising chick under her wing. Mary's father was informed that Marguerite 'hoped to treat your daughter in such a fashion that you will have reason to be content with it . . . I find her of such good manners, and so pleasing in her youthfulness, that I am more obliged to you for having sent her to me than you are to me for receiving her.'

So everyone was happy, Thomas in an exceedingly good temper that his elder daughter had proved as good an ambassador as himself, Elizabeth reconciled to Mary's absence and taking a fostermotherly interest in Margaret Wyatt, while Anne bided her time.

It would come, she knew. Hever and Blickling were familiar, dull, Tom Wyatt's devotion something she took for granted. She tried not to read Mary's letters with envy. They told how Mary had forgotten all her French at first so that she hadn't understood a word anyone had said to her, but then it had all come back by being forced to speak it. Now she could chatter on like a millstream, making her noble lady smile at her so-English accent and give her a jewelled brooch shaped like a parrot as a reward. Also how one of the courtiers, whom she would only coyly refer to as Jehan, had refused to believe she was so young, and had got her into corners and made the most outrageously passionate proposals

85

to her. The Flemish food was richer than they got at home, so much cake and so many sauces made with cream that she was growing twice as fast as she had done.

'I am growing too,' Anne told Margaret. 'I shall be taller than Mall when she comes home, because she will have grown fat and wide. You know they talk of Flanders mares? Well, she'll be one, a Flanders Mary.'

'Don't talk so sharply, Anne. You know you miss her. I do, we all do. You should be glad of her good fortune.'

Anne, who did indeed miss her sister, flung away, suddenly swamped by one of the dark moods which came over her for no reason, moods which Simonette called *les chiens noirs du diable*. She was not close or dear to anybody now, it seemed. George was always at Knole or gadding about, her father only wanted her for her educational possibilities, and her mother seemed absent-minded these days. She should have been bearing more babies to occupy her time and energies, but that was not possible; it was as though she had lost her way in a maze, where nobody could reach her through the high yew hedges.

Tom Wyatt was not allowed to see Anne often. His father had been spoken to by Thomas Boleyn. 'My daughter is not for your son, Sir Henry. The choice is not mine but Our Lord's, who destined her for high places. I would have been pleased with such an alliance, it goes without saying, but I am powerless in the matter.'

Sir Henry wondered whom Our Lord had in mind for Anne: he would put nothing past his country neighbour, in the way of ambitious matches. He also wondered when his son Tom would get over this youthful fancy, which was becoming slightly unnatural. Obviously, as a good Christian he did not believe that the child Anne was a witch, but it did seem as though she had put some kind of enchantment on his melancholy, verse-scribbling boy. He trusted that it would fade with the years, as surely it must when she was betrothed – and Tom as well. Lord Cobham had a little daughter.

He would ride over to Cobham Hall with Tom, and see how the two young things got on together.

Mary prospered at the Archduchess's court. Everyone took to the child, particularly the gentlemen, since she was well grown for her age and promised beauty. Besides, she already had a come-hither eye, and knew how to get her own way so prettily that people failed to notice how she managed it.

On a morning when she was not officially in attendance, she was sent for. The Archduchess was sitting surrounded by ladies-in-waiting, who were putting the finishing touches to her elaborately curled hair. She had more colour than usual in her cheeks, and looked almost handsome.

'Ah, *mignonne*. A countryman of yours is awaiting an audience with us, and we thought it might cheer you to see him.'

Mary dipped to the ground, as she now did without even thinking about keeping her spine straight and raising her eyes to exactly the right level. 'Not my father, Madame?'

'Not your father. The Duke of Suffolk. He visited us last year, with King Henry, after the French wars.'

Mary's sharp eyes detected a grin, hastily wiped off, on the face of the lady who was busily adjusting the back of the Archduchess's coif. What was so amusing about the Duke of Suffolk? Her father had been on that royal visit, and spoken very highly of the Duke, she remembered. He was in favour with the King because his father had fought on the right side at Bosworth and been killed, and the boy had been brought up with the royal children . . .

The Duke was announced. Mary swooped down into another curtsey. When she rose she saw a large man, tall, broad and powerful, with a ruddy face, bright red hair and a square spade-beard to match. (It would have made a good yard broom, so thick and coarse it was.) He strode confidently forward and implanted a smacking kiss on the royal hand.

Mary noticed that this rather unpolished salute – the merest brush of the lips was customary – was amiably received.

'*Enchanté de vous revoir, ma chère et très belle Madame.*'

Heavens, how terrible was the man's French! He spoke it like a coster. No wonder the ladies smiled. Yet Mary's strong female instinct told her that they found him attractive, that Marguerite herself found him attractive, even though he was so ignorant as to address royalty as Madame on an initial meeting. He was chatting away now in his execrable accent, getting his grammar wrong and making ludicrous slips, and yet the Archduchess smiled on him. Mary listened hard – one had to, to make out what was being said.

'The ring, Madame. Once more I offer it to you.' There was a flash of great diamonds in his huge hand. Marguerite shook her head, but she was not displeased.

'I told you before, sir, that we do not accept stolen goods.'

'But I got it fairly! I swear to you, Madame, I did.' (*J'ai le fait honnêtement*, dear me: the ladies silently giggled.)

'We called you a thief then, and we call you one now.' But she was laughing, teasing him. After that Mary got lost in the dialogue, so clumsy on the man's part, so sparkling on the lady's. When wine and cakes had been brought in, and the Archduchess and her guest had retired to another part of the room, Mary questioned Madame Louise, her particular friend among the junior waiting-women.

'Why does he speak so badly? I thought he was a friend of the King's. Does our King speak like that?'

'*Dieu*, I hope not. No, the Duke's father was only a country squire; he is nothing, he only got the title because your King beheaded the last Duke for being related to him. This man is a great peasant, a boor, yet he came here last year set on marrying Madame.'

'Oh. I should have thought he was married already – he's quite old.'

'About thirty, and he *has* married already – three times.'

Mary looked shocked. 'You mean they all died?'

'Only one, the first – and he married her twice, because the first *noces* were annulled. In between he married a rich widow and got rid of her, and then an heiress – but she is out of the way now, and he's free again. Oh, we know all about the gallant Duke, we maids. He'd get his way with any woman if he wanted. Best keep out of his way on dark staircases, *ma fleurette*. But I shouldn't be prating to children on such things, or such men.'

Mary knew quite well, as everyone did, what could happen to her if she were to meet the dangerous Duke on a dark staircase, and was rather more thrilled than alarmed at the prospect.

'Then will he marry our mistress?'

'I think not. Oh, I think not.' Louise shook her head rapidly, many times. 'She's too wise to give herself over to an English place-seeker, with a courtesy title. No, I think he came here for another reason. As a test, perhaps. I saw the look on his face when she teased him, and he was in a way satisfied, like a great cat that has had all the mice. Now he knows, and he can go courting elsewhere.'

'Where?'

'How should I know, child?' She swept away, seeing a senior attendant beckon. Mary was left thoughtful. As long as Charles Brandon, Duke of Suffolk, remained at Marguerite's court – and it was not long – she watched and noted him. He noted her, once, as the smallest of all who waited on Marguerite, and came to loom over her, like a cliff over a flower on the seashore.

'*Quel âge avez-vous, ma petite?*' he asked, tilting up her round chin, staring down with hot bold eyes.

'I am ten years old, my lord,' she answered in English to disconcert him. But he was only amused.

'Oho! A little countrywoman of mine. And who might you be?'

She told him, very primly, then flirted with him, also primly, turning her head aside in mock modesty when he said that she was like a pink rose in bud. 'I warrant you've felt no thorns yet?'

Mary perfectly understood the naughty *double entendre* and, looking him straight in the eye, replied, '*Je ne connais pas les épines.*' How extraordinary that with such fiery hair he should have eyes that were almost black, under marvellously straight brows like a beautiful woman's. He was not handsome, and yet . . . With her new courtier's diplomacy she turned the conversation to interesting features of Brussels, asking him if he did not think the great copper figure of St Michael on the tower of the Hôtel de Ville resembled the golden angel high above Christchurch, Canterbury.

Suffolk, who never noticed such details, agreed that it did. He would take a particular note of the Canterbury figure when he passed through on his way to London in the next few days, and think of Mistress Bullen.

'Boleyn,' corrected Mary politely. She was sorry when he left Brussels, and the maids whispered that the Archduchess was sorry too, for he amused her, though never, never would she have married him. He would not come back, this great bull-frog who would a-wooing ride.

But Mary was to meet him again, and sooner than she thought.

7

Princess Paradise

The next time Mary was called to the royal presence the summons came by way of a page, Guillaume, a young man with scented hair and languishing eyes who had a strong fancy for her.

'*She* wants you, *chérie*. A letter from England.'

'About me? What does it say?'

'Alas, I wasn't told. Her Highness's confidence in me must be waning, so sad. Have no fear, she's not angry with you, but with somebody else. Shall we go the back way, round the Painted Corridor?' With an arm round Mary, which was strictly against court etiquette, he strolled slowly with her, stealing a few kisses, to the chamber where Marguerite received ordinary folk, as against ambassadors and people of state. The twittering of little birds in golden cages filled the air; a tiny monkey, dressed in miniature soldier's uniform and shivering with cold, perched on a day-bed cushion. The Archduchess was fuming. She held a letter.

'Ah, Marie. Your good father has written to me. This he says: "My very dear and renowned lady, I recommend myself as humbly as possible to your good graces. I venture to beg of you a great favour." What a stately style he has, Sir Thomas. "It will be known to Your Highness that the sister of King Henry, the most noble and fair Princess Mary, is shortly to journey to France to become the bride of His Grace, King Louis of France."'

She laid the letter on a side table and banged her fist on it. 'No, it was *not* known to me. Last time I heard of the matter the Princess was betrothed to my nephew Charles, had been since they were children. It was all settled and ratified last year – your King sent me a company of archers to strengthen my army, and told me how highly he esteemed Charles. And so I should hope!'

Mary murmured, 'Of course, Madame.'

Another bang on the document. 'Yet now, in spite of the truce he and Spain and I made against France, I hear that Charles is out and old Louis is in. Am I to know these things from lackeys?'

Mary was not rash enough to protest against her father being called a lackey. She listened patiently while Marguerite raved about the indignity she had suffered, promised the English King a flea in his ear when he eventually condescended to write to her, and treated her ladies to an unflattering description of King Louis. 'A doddering old man of fifty-two, three times that girl's age, and feeble and pocky besides. What kind of bridegroom is that? King Henry wants to put his sister to bed with a dotard, is that it? They say Louis has lost his teeth and dribbles like a baby. Besides, he's had two wives and is worn out. What kind of heirs will he beget for France?'

Mary listened attentively, eyes downcast, to this diatribe, wondering what it all had to do with her. Eventually, the worst of her wrath spent, Marguerite informed her that her father begged to state that the Princess had requested the company of his daughter on her bridal journey to France.

'He asks me, most humbly, to release you. Well, child? Are you willing to leave me for this – this burletta? Do you wish to accompany this sacrificial maiden, this Andromeda, to her drooling dragon?'

Put like that it sounded a most unappealing prospect. Mary was very comfortable where she was, but orders were orders; she recognised the steel behind the velvet of her father's letter. She had never met the Princess, never even seen her, so why would her attendance be so particularly requested? This was Thomas Boleyn's doing, and his daughter feared him.

She was sorry, she told her mistress, she wept to leave the Palais, and Brussels, and the beloved royal presence. It was only that she was commanded, that she was in the habit of obedience, that she felt it her duty . . .

'Good child. That is very well understood. You shall go, then – and I wish you joy of it. You shall have one of my birds to take with you.'

Mary managed to evade the bird in its gilded (but not jewelled) cage; it would have been an embarrassment, and there were plenty of birds in the trees. She left, however, with a number of charming presents, some of them valuable, and the good wishes of everybody. Guillaume wept. He had decided to marry her when she reached the age of twelve.

Her royal mistress still could not believe in the reality of the English-French match. Even after she heard that the marriage had officially taken place at Greenwich on 13 August, and that the bride had been symbolically bedded with the Duc de Longueville acting as Louis's representative (one bare leg in chaste proximity to a feminine foot peering from beneath an embroidered nightgown), she scoffed at the news, and sent an envoy to England to protest.

'And tell King Henry he need send no more jumped-up dukes here with diamond rings. I shall marry a man young enough to bed me himself, if I marry at all. One foot in the bed, forsooth! One foot in the grave, more like. Or both.' Almost to herself, not caring who heard, she added, 'I would never have married that red-haired upstart. I told Henry I would not, and that he must stop playing tricks with me. They think women are fishes, to be caught in nets, but they shan't catch an emperor's daughter so.'

For the rest of the day, her ladies remarked, she was noticeably out of temper.

Mary, with her escort, rode up to the gate of Hever on a fine summer's evening. A watcher on a tower saw her train approaching and sent word to the house, so that her family were awaiting her in the courtyard. Even her father was there, seeming pleased with himself.

Elizabeth saw that her daughter was indeed changed, even in just a few months. A polish had been added to her manners, looks, even her appearance, though a few minutes of her chatter showed that behind the foreign gloss she was the same affectionate, simple child.

They heard all she had to tell, interrupting and questioning, Thomas often nodding approval, Anne very quiet. Mary had presents for them all, including the head servants, chosen from the gifts made to her. For her mother there was a pomander enclosed in an orange of gilt metal studded with brilliants, for her father a small ornamental dagger. Dame Joyce, nursing a finely embroidered handkerchief, tut-tutted at Mary.

'You should never give a knife, Mall child – knives cut love.'

'But this will not – I hope I know my love and duty to my father. Nan, this is for you.' It was a pendant, a charming tiny figure of Our Lady and Child in an embossed setting studded with turquoises.

'Blue for the Blessed Virgin, you see. Do you like it?'

'The chain is very short, no longer than would fit a dog,' Thomas said.

'Yes, sir. I – that is how it was given to me.' But Mary lied: she had changed the original chain for a shorter one, so that Anne could wear the pendant resting at the base of her throat, hiding the wen. Anne knew it, and thanked her sister with a hand clasp.

Elizabeth, swinging her gilt orange which was her gift, told Joyce to go and lay out the clothes which Mary was to take as her French wardrobe. Mary rose eagerly, then remembered the question that had puzzled her, that her father could answer.

'How did it come that the Princess asked for me to go with her, sir? She never saw me, nor I her, and it was not Her Grace the Archduchess who mentioned me . . .'

'I recommended Her Highness to take a small number of carefully chosen girls. There will be Lord Grey's sister, the two sisters of the Marquis of Dorset, and Lord Dacre's daughter, besides you and Anne.'

'*Anne!* Anne is going, too?'

'Why not, pray?' Thomas's tone was chilly.

'But I thought . . . I thought I'd been chosen because I was experienced in waiting . . .'

'Then you thought wrongly. Go and inspect your wardrobe.' Mary went, curiously deflated, her pride a little dented; yet when she considered it she was happy that she was to have Anne's company among so many strangers, it would make the journey easier than the one to Brussels. Always there was to be ambivalence in the sisters' feelings towards each other.

Thomas was pleased with the coup he had brought off – two daughters in one select company, close to the young lady who would be Queen of France and wield immense influence. He knew, for such were the ways of kings, that when the Princess was married in fact as well as by proxy, King Louis would dismiss her English attendants, for fear of the undue influence they might have on her. Children would be allowed to remain, however, since they could not influence anyone. He would have two sets of eyes and ears constantly on the new young Queen, Boleyn spies in the French camp.

Mary was puzzled that Anne seemed so little excited at the thought of the adventure before them.

'You always wanted to go abroad. You were a little jealous – now weren't you? – when I went away. And now you have a chance to get away from England, which you find so boring.'

'I do find it boring. There's nothing to do but lessons, and Simonette is getting so old and so crabbed. But . . .'

She found it hard to put into words that now her great chance had come she was afraid of it. Suddenly Hever, and beautiful Blickling, seemed safe, places where no harm could touch her. She had had so many bad dreams, and last time she had ridden over to Allington she had seen a ghost on the staircase of the Solomon Tower. She had known it was a ghost because it was so evil-looking, a brown shape, very squat, with a sly human face of which she had just caught a glimpse before she fled screaming down the stairs into the modern part of the building.

95

To Mary she said, 'I am so ugly. Who would want me as an attendant? Look at me, like a toad.'

'Toads have fine brown eyes, and so have you.'

'Thank you. *Tu te moques de moi, je crois.* They say the Princess Mary is so beautiful, *belle comme un ange* – she will only want pretty girls about her, like you.'

'Father knows best, and he thinks well of you. We must always do as he says, without question.'

'Yes.' Anne heaved a long deep sigh. She valued her father's esteem and trusted him. If he thought her worth sending to a princess, then he must be right.

It was only at the final parting, when they were to leave Hever to join Princess Mary (or Queen Mary of France, as she must be called in future) that Anne's brittle nerves betrayed her, and she wept. Not in her mother's arms but on the painful sharp shoulder of Simonette. The governess, almost forty years old, was now wizened and shrunken, like a little old woman, and her graceful movements were stiffer because of the rheumatism life in England had brought to her bones. She peered now out of eyes grown weak with reading and writing. Soon she would be turned away, she feared, unless Lady Boleyn showed great charity towards her. Perhaps they would pay for her to return to France to what remained of her family, her dead husband's old grandmother.

'I shall be *réduite à la mendicité* – a blind beggar. I thought they would leave me you for a few years yet, but no, they are sending you away, you, my Nanette, little and tender as you are.' Simonette sobbed, and Anne, who stood taller than the governess, embraced her and kissed her wrinkled cheek.

'My mother would never send you away. She's kind-hearted, only rather taken up with Court affairs. I shall speak to her, to find you another place.'

Simonette continued to sob. Anne's tears were dry now that she had someone to fight for – it was useless to fight for herself.

'I shall speak to my mother as soon as I see her. You taught me so well, there must be some family who would be glad to have you.'

'Did I? Did I teach well?' Simonette sniffed damply.

'Of course. I speak French perfectly, don't I? You and I never speak anything else. And I keep my back straight and eat daintily, and know how to wait on my elders at table, and I can dance – a little – '

'As well as possible for your poor partner's crooked back!' interrupted Simonette hysterically.

'That is nothing. And I play the lute – I can play "Mopsy's Tune" and "Lady Lettice's Dump" – and handle a hawk and send an arrow straight, and I manage the hounds better than Gregory does. So you see. My mother *must* recommend you.'

Elizabeth Boleyn agreed that Simonette must not be turned away. She later told Thomas that it was the worst of manners to dismiss a good servant; no Howard would dream of it. Thomas made a poor mouth at the prospect of parting with a pension to one whose usefulness to him was now over.

'Send her to Wyatt's,' he suggested.

'To do what? Tom is at Cambridge and George gone as a page to Penshurst. Sir Henry hardly needs a governess for himself.'

'He should have married again and got more children,' Thomas growled.

'That fails to answer my question. What are we to do with Simonette? She could have helped Tysoe with your papers and correspondence, if her eyes were not so bad.'

Thomas brightened. He loved to dictate letters and have useful documents copied for his library – and extra help would be free.

'Get her a pair of spectacles.'

'What an excellent idea! Of course, the perfect answer. We'll take her up to London with us and she shall have the best to be had.'

So it was that Simonette kept her board and lodging and the roof of Hever over her head, and became the possessor of a clumsy pair of lenses cut from a thick block of glass, which were indeed the best to be had, but that was not saying much. At least they magnified so that she could easily read, and once she had mastered the art of keeping them on by cords tied round her ears, she was as content as she could expect to be in her situation.

Anne and Mary were awed into silence by their presentation to their new mistress, in the Great Hall of Greenwich Palace.

Princess Mary Tudor was eighteen, and as dazzlingly beautiful as they had been told – or more so. Tall, slender, delicate-boned, she had the fairest of complexions, exquisite features, and bright golden hair flowing to her waist. Beside the beauty of the wearer, her rich clothing was hardly noticeable, though Anne's eyes dwelt on the thick embroidery of pearls which covered her sleeves and bordered the square neckline of her dress; the pearls were no creamier than her skin. A great sweetness of expression and the intelligence which beamed from her large blue eyes helped to explain why even flatterers were lost for words to describe her. One Venetian had named her simply 'Paradise', and it seemed difficult for anyone to write about her without mentioning angels.

Elizabeth, who was in attendance to present her daughters, saw in the Princess her mother, the long-dead Queen, the fragile lady, lily-fair, who had received her and Thomas at the Tower on their bridal journey; and behind this likeness the bright reflection of the Princess's grandmother, her beauty caught for all time in the stained glass at Christchurch in Canterbury. Two dead White Rose queens, and a girl alive, in bloom, more lovely than either.

'Is she happy?' Elizabeth wondered. But no, it was impossible, with a bridegroom as repulsive as report said. But the angelic face smiled at the little girls who were to wait on her, and the voice was gentle and tranquil. The pink lips were generously sculpted, full, tender: the lips of a woman capable of passion, perhaps. In which case, God help her in France.

Mary Boleyn, who had been so pleased with her own improvement at the Archduchess's court, felt fat and clumsy in contrast to the Princess. Anne deliberately looked at her deformed hand, then touched the wen under her collar of silver filigree; it seemed to throb. She was dark and ugly, she would never be anything else.

Yet none of them who viewed the glorious Princess could be jealously resentful of that heavenly beauty, any more than they would of the beauty of Our Lady when they eventually reached Her throne.

Thomas, ever the opportunist, lost no time in arranging to present his girls to the King. 'He must be like a god,' Mary said to her mother, on the way to the royal antechamber. 'He must be the handsomest man in the world.' Elizabeth made a noncommittal sound.

When they saw King Henry, seated in a carved chair at a table covered with State papers, both sisters made a deep curtsey and used every second of their arising to take in the royal appearance. He was very tall, indeed large, broad-shouldered and thick-necked, his face very round, pink and white, the complexion of a baby. He was, indeed, not unlike an enormous baby boy, a giant's child. His hair was bright golden-auburn, cut short to just below his ears and fringed high on his brow. A faint sheen of hair was on his massive chin and upper lip.

Anne wondered why, since the royal sister's eyes were so large, the brother's should be so small, hardly more than pale blue gleams between heavy lids, and why his mouth did not match the Princess's, being a small tight purse of a mouth, out of proportion to the large face.

Mary thought him a very fine man indeed.

He looked up from his letter-signing, nodded courteously to the family group.

'Ah, Thomas.' His voice, too, was unexpected, high-pitched, slightly squeaky.

'May I present my daughters, Your Grace – Mary and Anne?'

The King gave a mere flick of a glance over the childish figures. The only children of interest to him would be his own, and as yet he had none. The elder was reasonably pretty, the younger frankly plain, a swarthy, skinny wench. At a quick glance one would think someone had given her two black eyes, but a second inspection showed that Nature was responsible.

'Mistress Boleyn, Mistress Anne. We greet you. We understand you are to accompany the Queen of France on her coming journey.'

They chorused that they were, that it was a great honour. Henry returned to his papers and the children and their father left, stepping backwards. Neither of the girls said much to their mother about the King, except that he had received them graciously. They had been well drilled in the art of uttering little or nothing about royalty while at Court, and not too much away from it.

On a late September morning a procession left Greenwich for the Dover road. It was the most gorgeous procession ever to have been seen by the gawping, respectful crowds who watched it pass. Nobles, lords and ladies, their attendants, their guards, pages, maids, trumpeters and musicians, household servants, all dressed in their best. Silks and satins, velvets and furs (particularly furs, for it was cold and would be colder at sea), jewels and gold and silver thread: even for a royal train it was resplendent. Henry intended to show King Louis what England could do in the way of magnificence.

The crowd cheered for him and for Queen Catherine, bravely riding beside him, though an impending child swelled her purple gown, for she was six months' gone. She was not very beautiful, people murmured. Some of them could remember her first arrival in London, such a pretty creature. Now her short stature and breadth were noticeable, and her paleness and double chin; and her smiles seemed forced. But she was so much older than the King, and had lost two babies already, or was it three?

They cheered much louder for the heroine of the hour. The one who had been their Princess, and was now by title Queen of France, looked as matchless on horseback as at all other times. She wore a gown of cloth-of-gold laid on crimson, a cloak of brown furs without and white furs within, and a great hat of looped crimson silk aslant on the sunshine hair, now braided up as befitted a wife. Round her neck, dancing on her breast with the movements of the horse, hung her bridegroom's gift, the huge, pear-shaped diamond that was called *Le Miroir de Naples*. Innocently it gleamed there, the beautiful gem which was to cause such a tempest of royal squabbling before it mysteriously took itself off, its final destiny unknown to recorded history.

The journey to Dover was long and tedious. Mary and Anne heard that the bride was little pleased by the long stay the procession made in Canterbury and annoyed that it delayed her arrival in France. 'She's impatient to get the whole thing over. They say the King had terrible trouble getting her consent to marry Louis, and now she regrets it bitterly, but he's promised her something as a reward – nobody knows what.'

But stay at Canterbury she must, for the King in his piety ordered it. The royal party lodged at St Augustine's Abbey, where the King worshipped at St Augustine's shrine and at the Rood of Grace. Then (for rivalry between St Augustine's and Christchurch was hot) he progressed to Christchurch to prostrate himself at the High Altar, the shrine of St Thomas à Becket and the shrine of Our Lady Undercroft, giving at each sacred place an offering of one mark, which was good money and pleased the monks.

The Boleyn sisters were lodged, with the other small girls, in cottages near the Abbey which were not so much humble as sordid. They had never been so lowly housed before and were critical of the poor conditions, hard narrow beds, rushes on the floor which had not been changed recently, and a general stink.

Mary boasted slightly, as a travelled person. 'I saw worse in the Low Countries. And the Archduchess's palace was not all that clean.' Anne wrinkled her nose in disgust at the lice; she was the first to use the communal washing bowl. At Hever she had a little marble bath of her own – she would have given her soul for it now. But too much protest would have been childish and undignified. Apart from set lips and whispered comments to Mary, she put up with it all.

The lesser members of the royal train were exempted from attendance at the various shrines, but Mary and Anne spent most of their time marvelling at St Thomas's shrine, where countless miracles had been wrought. They stared and stared, not from precocious piety, but from wonder and awe at the unbelievable splendour of the begemmed thing.

On a marble base stood a huge gilded ark, glittering sarcophagus to the coffins inside it, one within another, the last of all holding the bones of the saint. There were arched openings into which pilgrims might put their hands, to touch the outer coffin. Those humble hands ventured into a blaze of colour, an encrustation of jewels given in tribute by the rich and noble: ruby vying with emerald, sapphire, diamond, pearl, turquoise, beryl, opal, chryso-phrase, amber, topaz, coral, flung on as though by the prodigal hand of a giant. Between them shone artefacts of enamel, gold and silver. A gilded angel figure pointed to a shape like a celestial egg made of rosy light.

'The Regale,' said Anne. 'The Regale of France, the great ruby. They say that at night it glows like a fire.'

'The Regale,' Mary murmured, half hypnotised by all that glittering, shining beauty.

'They say the King Louis that was King in Holy Thomas's time would not give it, but as he knelt it jumped from his finger to where it is now.' Anne was pleased with her gleanings of history. She had a strange desire to pull off handfuls of the jewels and cover herself in them, until she too was all sparkle and light. The guide, a watchful monk, pointed his silver wand at them and suggested that they move on. He distrusted boys anywhere near his precious charge, and he was not too trustful of girls, especially those with huge dark eyes and an eager look to them.

Outside, in the crisp cold air, Mary looked up to the tremendous gold angel poised on the gable of the south transept, and thought, not for the first time since her meeting with him, of the Duke of Suffolk.

The procession reached Dover, where they stayed several nights in its frowning castle, waiting for the weather to improve. In the dark of an early morning they rose by torchlight to embark for France. King Henry leaned his horse towards his sister's, and kissed her heartily on both cheeks. It was observed that she caught at his cloak and held him earnestly in conversation for several moments, her eyes searching his face, and that he nodded repeatedly and patted her hand.

'He is promising her something. I told you.'

'What? A fortune if she bears a boy for France?'

'That's impossible. They say . . .'

Mary eyed the Strait of Dover and shivered. It swirled and boiled with leaping waves, ominously grey like the lowering skies, tipped with white foam. The sailors were having trouble with the ships, which seemed not to agree with them that the waters were now calm enough to set sail.

'Holy Christ,' Mary said. 'We shall be very sick. It's like the sea when I went to Flanders. I thought I would die.'

Anne, too, thought she might die, tossing on those waves, she who had never been to sea before. She was cold, her head was beginning to fill up with a rheum, her bones ached from a bad night on a hard pallet. Therefore she sat up even straighter than usual on her small horse, and gave her hand with a gracious smile to the man-at-arms who was helping her out of the saddle.

'*Soyez brave . . . courage, ma mignonne,*' Simonette had said. There was no danger that she would forget to be brave.

8

Children of Honour

Lady Margaret Guildford, Mistress of the Robes, chaperone and titular Mother of the Maids, went from one pallet to another in the stuffy stinking cabin of the Princess's ship.

'Ladies. Get up. We have landed at Boulogne.'

One of the older girls sat up and found her voice. 'In the harbour, madame?'

'In fact, on a sandbank.' Lady Guildford's smile was forced. She too had suffered during the awful four days at sea, but she was of tougher stuff than these delicate girls, who looked more dead than alive, white and drained from vomiting. They had been in danger of their lives from the storm that thrashed the Channel, and had known it. Lady Guildford had never heard so many prayers in her life: she had given up asking the Princess's chaplain to step down and administer spiritual comfort, since he was as ill as any of them. Her beloved charge, the Princess, was in no better case. But at least it was over, and somehow they would get off the sandbank and onto French soil.

The youngest of the attendants had been very ill indeed. Anne looked like a ghost, her skin a dull saffron and her body as thin as though she were the last survivor of a siege. Hell, she had thought: Hell is like this, not fiery as they say. At one point she had wished not to live. Only having Mary to comfort had kept her conscious. Mary had wept a great deal in her sister's arms. Lady Guildford shook her head over the little girls. She had never thought it a good idea to bring them.

Even now, with the galleon motionless, the ordeal was not over.

A stretch of water separated it from the harbour, to which the passengers must somehow be conveyed. After much contriving, a large rowing boat was brought alongside, a rope ladder lowered, and the Queen-Princess carried down it with great difficulty and placed in the boat. She was a Tudor and uncrowned Queen of France: she summoned up every ounce of courage and gave her rescuers all the help she could. The waves between sandbank and shore increased in ferocity, making it impossible for the boat to land. At last, afraid of losing her to the sea so near to safety, tall powerful Sir Christopher Gervase carried her in his arms through the billows to the beach, the wild water sometimes mounting over their heads and swamping them. On the shore, the Queen fainted at last; she was carried up towards a waiting litter in a state of utter collapse.

At least the royal bride was safe. The intrepid Sir Christopher fought his way back to the galleon, from which he and the strongest of the sailors eventually rescued the other wretched voyagers. First to disembark were the Duke of Norfolk and Duchess Agnes. The Duke, a tough, hardened campaigner, had preserved the dignity of the Howards throughout the dreadful voyage. About to descend the swaying ladder after his wife had been helped down it, he said to Sir Christopher, 'My granddaughters. Are they safe?'

'Safe, my lord.'

'I thank God. See first to them and the other young ones, will you?'

So it was that Mary and Anne arrived in France. They would never recall much of being transported by litter up to the Haute Ville and through the gates of its sturdy walls to a lodging where they were stripped, bathed, dried and put to bed.

'My Book of Hours is gone,' Mary said. 'Father will be so angry.'

'Father will be too glad *we* are not gone to worry about your Book of Hours.'

'Do you think so, Nan? I wonder where he is.'

'Safe. Somewhere.' Sir Thomas had sailed in another ship of the scattered fleet, but it did not occur to Anne to doubt that Death would not have dared to sink it. He would certainly not seek his daughters out for their own sakes, even if the ship had got into Boulogne: his one aim would be to rejoin the Queen and her company, and be seen near her when she first met her husband.

It was two days before the bedraggled little company was sufficiently restored to set off for Abbeville, where King Louis was to meet them. It was only twelve miles, but in their weakened state they had to pause several times on the way. Sewing women had been hastily gathered in Boulogne to replace garments ruined by the sea. The Princess, pale and thinner as she was after her voyage, was splendid in cloth-of-silver, a jewelled coif glittering beneath a hat of red velvet. Her white horse was caparisoned with gold, those of her thirty-six ladies adorned with embroidered crimson velvet. At least the palfreys were well dressed. Anne addressed hers in French, to which it seemed to respond amiably enough.

After the riders followed three chariots, all glorious – the first covered in silver tissue, the second in cloth-of-gold, the third in crimson velvet wrought with the heraldic devices of Louis and his English bride. The last was filled with roses, grown and kept fresh by a small army of Boulognois gardeners, who had sat up with them all night.

The procession was brought up by companies of archers and carts full of treasure – including wall hangings. The English organisers had thought of everything.

They were still some miles from Abbeville when a forerunner came galloping back to report that a party of riders was approaching.

'The King!' Word went round and excitement was high. But the noble personage who led the train was François, Duc de Valois, Comte d'Angoulême, senior Prince of the Blood Royal: a very important personage indeed.

The impressive six feet of him was decked in a coat of gold and silver cloth, from which the fitful sun sent out sparkles. Beneath his plumed hat streamed long chestnut hair, framing a pale clean-

shaven face with a long drooping nose and a thick-lipped mouth –
not a combination that made for handsomeness. Yet the large tawny
eyes and the curious smile on those full lips carried a royal, wicked
charm all François's own. He was twenty years old, with the
sophistication of a man ten years older. He was also heir presump-
tive to the French throne.

His greeting to the Princess was one of utter gallantry, and his
words, unheard by her attendants, brought a faint touch of colour
to her pale cheeks. Mary Boleyn's mouth fell open in awed surprise.
In her time at the Archduchess's court she had seen no man to
touch him, either for grandeur or what in a woman would be called
allure. The image of the Duke of Suffolk began to fade from her
mind. She was moving under the spell of the second of those
infatuations which would rule her life.

Gracefully François guided his procession to fall in behind the
bride's, so that she would be the first to meet King Louis.

He was approaching, riding on a modest hack and dressed as for
hawking – just a country gentleman out for a morning's exercise:
very English and casual. When bride and bridegroom caught sight
of each other for the first time, her ladies with one accord stopped
breathing for a second or two. The tawny eyes of François watched
her face closely, and the lips curled in a gleeful leer.

As she prepared to dismount, the sun went in and it began to
rain, a fitting omen. The ladies drew in their breath again. Not a
face changed, but the same thought ran through all minds.

He was as bad as rumour had said – worse.

Louis was fifty-two, but might have been seventy-two. He
stooped over his bridle reins because his spine was failing him. His
face was scrofulous, the eyes bleary, the grey lips turned down. His
body was bloated, shapeless. Some remarked that his nose resembled the snout of a wild pig.

The rain grew heavier, soaking the light canopy which had been
held over the Princess and her horse, but by etiquette she must
dismount and kneel. Fortunately the silver brocade of her gown

was almost stiff enough to stand by itself, so that when she knelt it kept its shape, flowing round her in shining folds.

King Louis raised her (it was noticed that she gave him a lot of help) and kissed her pale cheek, then, when she rose, flung his arm round her shoulders. The tableau was that of a young nurse supporting an elderly patient. Her splendid hat was knocked askew, but she was too good-mannered to straighten it.

The English contingent lodged at Abbeville that night, the ladies in a dormitory kindly lent to them by the monks of St Vulfran's church. Lady Guildford did not approve of the small ones, the Children of Honour, being together with the older maids, for fear of what they might overhear. She had a good idea what it would be. Plentiful wine, after the fatigues of the journey, was having its effect.

Kathryn Paget, who was generally considered the wit of the older party, lived up to her reputation.

'He is not poxy, as they said, girls.'

'No? Are you sure?'

'Very sure. You see, nobody would come close enough to give it to him.'

Everybody laughed, but a shrill voice pointed out, 'He must be poxy, you can tell by the children. His daughter Madame Claude limps like a beggar and has a terrible squint, they say.'

'A leper's squint? Possibly she got it looking both ways for her husband François, who runs after every woman he sees.'

'*Can* he see them or does his nose get in between? What noses they have, these French! The King's is more like an elephant's than a boar's, even.'

'Oliphant,' whispered Mary Boleyn to Anne. 'The word is truly oliphant. It says so in my bestiary.'

'*Tais-toi,*' hissed Anne, who was listening to the conversation.

'The royal nose certainly droops,' someone ventured.

'Everything droops,' pronounced Kate Paget. 'That's obvious. But on the wedding night all will go well – with the help of two strong equerries.'

Lady Guildford, entering on the gale of giggles that followed the remark, clapped her hands sharply.

'Enough, ladies! Mistress Paget, you go too far. Children, you are to sleep at that end of the room, by yourselves. Pick up your mattresses and sheets and follow me. You will be watched tonight by servants from the King's household, while I attend on Her Highness. Anne, you are small but you speak French well – I count on you to interpret and keep good order.'

'Yes, madame.'

When the dormitory had settled down, Anne lay looking out of the high window at the red glow in the sky. A fire had broken out in the town: it was said that a dozen or so houses had been burned to the ground, and some lives lost. It was not a good omen for the royal marriage. Anne was too exhausted to wonder what sort of omens boded for herself in the service of the Princess. She still had a bad cold, her head ached, the insides of her knees were chafed from riding in a sodden skirt. But it was all interesting, not at all *ennuyeux*. She was beginning to think in French all the time. What a pity her father had not reached Boulogne in time to see her in her crimson velvet saddle, and hear her speaking to her horse in its own language. He would have been proud of her, might even have said so.

Beside her, Mary slept curled up, puffing out gentle puppy-like snores.

The wedding in the cathedral church was the most magnificent in memory, the bride the most magnificent figure, dressed in cloth-of-gold trimmed with ermine, strewn with diamond clasps like raindrops. Her unbound hair fell to her waist in a shower of gold, from a coronet of sapphires and rubies. Round her neck hung a ruby and diamond carcanet given to her as a wedding token by her bridegroom, and below it, between her breasts, flashed the Miroir de Naples. Her beauty blazed with a supernatural radiance, though the face between the jewels was candle-pale.

The bridegroom was also in cloth-of-gold, but it failed to give him the appearance of a matching figure in an illuminated missal. He was suffering acutely from gout, brought on by his ride in the rain, and fidgeted noticeably throughout the ceremony, his face creased with pain. He dribbled somewhat, a courtier ready at hand with a kerchief to wipe his mouth.

After the wedding came the banquet and the ball (though the King had not danced for years), lasting until midnight. The Children of Honour were not required to attend this, but the Boleyn sisters watched until Lady Guildford discovered and removed them. Tight-lipped, she then repaired to the Queen's bedchamber to assist at the disrobing and bedding ceremony. She wished she could sit by the royal bed all night, tapping her foot, so that the dotard would not dare touch her darling.

The next day the maids and children were kept strictly under her control, so that they should not hear the scandalous rumours that were going about concerning the royal wedding night. The King was '*très joyeux et très gai*', was he? And he had '*traversé la fleuve trois fois*', had he? So he had told the Venetian ambassador, but François d'Angoulême knew better, having had a spy posted behind some curtains. He was happy today, all cat-smiles; now he was quite certain that the King was not capable of fathering children. Before long the old man would die without issue from the English marriage, and it would be *le roi François* instead of *le roi Louis*.

That day the King should have set off for Paris, to prepare for the coronation, but unfortunately he felt unable to undertake the journey. Abbeville rang with happy laughter – behind closed doors. Everyone was to remain in the town until the King felt fit to travel.

Three days after the wedding the maids, in morning attendance upon the Queen, were cheerfully sewing on jewels and laying out delicate garments when Lady Guildford burst in upon them. Behind her, surprisingly, was the Duke of Norfolk.

'She looks like the wrath of God,' whispered Kate Paget. 'And why the old man?'

They soon found out. Lady Guildford ostentatiously stood aside, leaving the Duke facing a startled audience. It seemed to discompose him slightly.

'You have something to say, my lord.' Lady Guildford's voice was trembling with temper.

'Yes. Yes. Ladies, His Grace King Louis has commanded me to dismiss you all.'

The shocked silence disconcerted him even further. He was not reassured to see, framed in the doorway of the antechamber, the young Queen, an angel in floating white this morning, unbejewelled and heavy-eyed from sleep.

'I thought I heard you say, my lord Duke, that the King had ordered the dismissal of my maids.' Her voice was bell-clear with Tudor imperiousness.

'It is true, Madame. He has so ordered. Also the whole of your suite, but for half a dozen or so gentlemen, a chaplain, a physician, and a secretary. Whichever of your retinue Your Grace may choose, of course.'

'May I ask why?'

It was not in order for a duke to shrug in the French manner, but a shrug was implied in Norfolk's answer.

'I can only suggest that you speak to His Grace yourself, Madame.'

The blue eyes blazed with fury. 'I shall indeed speak to him! Am I to be humiliated, treated like a criminal? What have my followers done, to be dismissed? Are they not good enough for him, do they not come up to French standards? Does he complain of my bad behaviour, caused by bad servants? Answer me!'

Norfolk, mighty in war but not much use in women's matters, turned to Lady Guildford, who ignored him, addressing her mistress.

'Even I am to go, Madame. I who have been your faithful and loving governess since Your Grace was very young.'

The Queen looked very young now, her lovely mouth tremulous, her eyes filling with tears. 'You have always been a mother to me, my lady, and I need you at my side in this foreign country. They shall not send you away, and that is my final word.'

'It is also the King's final word that my lady shall go, Your Grace,' said Norfolk.

Used to controlling herself, she choked back the tears. 'You didn't approve of this marriage, did you, my lord? And you never liked Cardinal Wolsey, who personally chose my retinue. Is this your revenge on the Cardinal? Yes, I see it now. This is all a game of chess, and my servants are the pawns – that's so, isn't it? My poor ladies and the rest are to be banished because you, *you* have whispered in the King's ear.'

'I have said nothing to the King, Madame,' replied Norfolk, so shiftily that he might as well have agreed.

'Nonsense, I can see your hand in this. Well, I shall write to my brother, at once – while I still have someone to find me pen and paper.'

'There, er, there is just one small exception.' Norfolk was retreating towards the door. 'The King consents that you shall keep four of your maids, selected from the Children of Honour.'

He bowed himself out, away from the chorus of questions, protests and sobs, devastation in the dovecote. So shaken was he that he ventured to present himself again before Louis to report that the grief, distress and general disturbance caused to the Queen seemed so great that he humbly begged the King to think again whether it was necessary.

Louis was even more unwell than usual, his sickly constitution violently upset by the recent abuses inflicted on it. He was tired of putting a good front on things, grinning and telling everyone that he and his bride were in perfect love and accord, that he was as much of a man as the next one. It was his inclination to tell Norfolk to go and jump into the River Somme, but he summoned sufficient patience to give this stiff-necked Englishman an explanation.

'If you have finished, milor . . . From the moment of our Queen's arrival in France, Milady Guildford has taken upon herself to rule her in all things. She will not leave us alone – as though a married woman required a chaperon. Now, *la reine Marie* is young – if there is ruling to be done, her husband must do it.'

'*D'accord, mais . . .*'

'If we are never left alone, how can we – be merry together? You understand me, I think. If Milady Guildford remains, then the whole future of France is doomed. As for the maids, she rules them formidably, they will follow where she leads. No, they must all go, except for a few of the little ones, not old enough to matter. We have spoken.'

Crushed, Norfolk left the King to face the fury of his Duchess, who was included in the sentence of banishment. It was true, he told her, he had never cared for the French alliance, he detested the jumped-up Cardinal Wolsey, but he had only been a spokesman in the matter, not a prime mover. Agnes loosed on him a tirade of tears and temper. He reflected that he had been much happier amid the carnage of Flodden Field.

The Queen wrote to her brother immediately. No reply came: she had made her bed and must lie on it, thought Henry. By the same messenger she wrote to Wolsey, who obeyed her and wrote to Louis in diplomatic terms, asking for the recall of Lady Guildford and a reprieve for Mary's courtiers. His polite pleadings were refused.

The departure of her ladies, weeping and complaining loudly, distressed the Queen so much that she went to her husband and berated him in round English as well as in French. He immediately succumbed to a violent attack of gout which put him to bed – alone. So much for the liberating absence of Lady Guildford.

For the small attendants who were allowed to remain, the Queen picked the Boleyn girls and the sisters Elizabeth and Anne Grey. The girls who had not been chosen fell on the Boleyns like furies.

'You! Norfolk picked you because you're his granddaughters! He planned it all, the old fox, so that sweet Mall and precious Nan should stay and get all the favours and we should go back and starve, for all anybody cares.' Scratching and hair-pulling ensued, and Lady Guidlford was not there to separate them, having already left the court.

Mary wept and struggled, Anne fought back, to such effect that her attackers retreated with a black eye and a cut cheek apiece.

Thomas Boleyn, who had stayed in the background of all the dismissals, rejoiced greatly. His wisdom had been justified. Of all the banished maids, his two daughters remained, to pave their way to power and influence.

And also their father's. He found himself dismissed from France, as was Norfolk, but it mattered not at all – he had left worthy representatives behind him.

It was noted by the King's courtiers that Queen Marie brightened considerably in manner soon after Lady Guildford's going. She was said to have told somebody that now she could do what she liked. How extraordinary the English were, especially their women. She began to show nothing but kindness towards her invalid husband, sitting by his bed, giving him medicine and reading to him, like a veritable *soeur de charité*.

Soon he was well enough to be prepared for the coronation journey, managing to set out on it without suffering a relapse. About half way, at Beauvais, the procession halted for a few days to give the King a rest. The day after their arrival they were joined by a troop of English nobles, sent to convey greetings from King Henry.

Mary and Anne, riding alongside their mistress, obediently halted their mounts when she did. Mary was startled to hear a curious sound from her royal lady – an unmistakable cry of joy which seemed excessive merely for the greeting of an embassage. She looked up, inquisitive. The lovely face beneath the jewelled chaplet was glowing with colour, the lovely mouth smiling. *La reine Marie*, always angelic, had become the Angel of the Transfiguration.

The gentleman at the head of the English party swept off his hat, revealing a blaze of carroty hair which matched the jutting beard.

'*Mes félicitations à Votre Grâce*,' he said in his execrable accent, and approached so near that their horses' noses almost touched.

Only Mary Boleyn, riding close, heard the Queen of France greet the Duke of Suffolk as 'dearest love'.

On the first of January 1515, in the midst of the worst storm Paris had ever known, King Louis XII died at the Palais de Tournelles. His marriage had lasted eighty-two days.

Six weeks later, in the chapel of the Palais de Cluny, Mary, Queen of France, became the Duchess of Suffolk in a small private ceremony. Her brother had promised her on the beach at Dover that she should wed the love of her choice when the King died, and she had forced Suffolk to overcome his qualms and agree. On 13 May they were married again at Greenwich Palace. Suffolk had their portrait painted, and beneath it his own attempt at poetry. Somebody had corrected his spelling.

> Cloth of Gold do not despise
> Tho' thou art matcht to Cloth of Frize.
> Cloth of Frize be not too bold
> Tho' thou art matcht to Cloth of Gold.

And the Boleyn sisters were also back at home, without employment. Mary, yawning over embroidery, sought out Anne, who was reading French with Simonette. The governess's reunion with her favourite pupil had been ecstatic. The hideous spectacles improved her sight so much that she could positively enjoy the work that had been so trying before.

'I shall die of ennui here, Nan,' Mary announced, throwing herself down on a window seat to illustrate her physical weakness.

'Do something useful, then.'

'*Et parles toujours en français, Marie,*' Simonette reminded her.

'Why should I?' Mary answered rudely in English. 'Since we're no longer in France and never likely to go back there.'

'I shall go back.' Anne's eyes were on her book.

'How do you know? How much do you bet – a groat, a mark? I

think I shall forget France and beg our mother to let me go to Court with her. Queen Catherine must need a few fresh faces about her.'

Simonette shook her head. '*La reine est malade.*' Catherine had lost yet another premature baby son a few weeks before Christmas.

'Oh, how *triste*. Long faces and prayers all day, I suppose.' Mary kicked discontentedly at the hearthstone. 'The peacock is dead, the old one. I went to see, and one of the gardeners was burying it.'

'You killed it,' Anne said. 'You chased it and made it run.'

Mary's eyes brimmed, and she ran to the window and pressed her face against it. Simonette sighed. She wished very much that Lady Boleyn were at home to control her daughters, who had seen a bigger world than Hever. One could not keep a child like Anne for ever at her books and lute practice, and Mary was already too much a woman for her years.

But Lady Boleyn spent little time at home, or at far-off lonely Blickling. There was a certain widower with a handsome manor house at Eltham who had no scruples about courting her when her husband was away on diplomatic business. Nor had she any about accepting his courtship, while the remains of her beauty lasted, and that indefinable elegance which had come down to her younger daughter and was more fascinating than mere beauty. To the elder she had passed on an insatiable hunger for love – the love she herself had never enjoyed. Simonette intended to pray for them all, the three Boleyn ladies, with extra fervour, when the feast of her patron saint Agatha, virgin and martyr, came round.

But before that day there arrived letters from Sir Thomas: his untiring efforts had found places for both his daughters. Mary was to join the court of François, the new King of France, and Anne to become a maid-in-waiting to his Queen Claude, who kept a separate household. They were both sternly ordered to study hard, particularly the French language, on pain of losing their father's goodwill towards them.

Mary begged Simonette to write on her behalf, saying all the correct things. Shrugging, the governess agreed, for the child had no gift for composition. But she made Anne write her own letter. It was a good one, in pretty, delicate script and passable French, with no crossings-out or blots; her father put it into his pouch, to read over again, then kept it among his papers.

Almost five hundred years later it was still clear and legible, a child's voice speaking, promising her father duty, diligence, and a love based on such great firmness that it would never grow less.

Which of these virtues, duty, diligence or love, was to rule her life and her sister's? The answer lay over the sea, in France.

THREE
MARY AT COURT
1515

Live in delight even as thy lust would,
And thou shalt find when lust doth most thee
please
It irketh straight and by itself doth fade.

Sir Thomas Wyatt

9

Mignonnelette

'You will do well for youself,' Thomas Boleyn told Mary, newly
arrived in Paris. It was not a prophecy but a command. 'You will
strive to please, to gain royal favour. You will work hard at your
accomplishments and perfect yourself in them.'

Mary bowed her head. 'Yes, sir.'

'These nobles are of a higher sort than you knew in Brussels. If
you apply yourself you will gain honours, preferments, riches. You
will advance our name and our family fortunes. Otherwise,' he
took her hand, not to caress it but to grip it hard, twisting it as he
did so, with his nails biting into her flesh. She bit her lip, knowing
better than to cry out. 'Otherwise I shall be very sorely offended.
Do you understand?'

'Yes, sir.'

'Simonette has told me you are slow at your lessons and too fond
of sport. That will change. You will be obedient and dutiful to the
King, to Madame Louise the Queen Mother, to the most virtuous
Madame Marguerite, his sister, to Her Grace Queen Claude. I had
good reports of you from the Archduchess and I expect to hear
even better ones.'

'You shall, sir.' Thomas's grip on her wrist was now acutely
painful and his eyes were hard and cold, blind to all but ambition.
This elder daughter was a considerable investment for him. Properly managed, she might marry a French noble and become a
duchess. France was a fair and rich land, where titles and estates
were worth having. He was doing very well in England, and in his

diplomatic career, and he fancied advancing his prestige abroad by good matches for his daughters.

His parting words to the younger one were less harsh. 'Anne, you show much promise. Do as well as you did in the former French Queen's service, and I shall be proud of you. Curb your temper, watch your French grammar, and attend your music lessons every day. And Anne, you are too thin and puny – eat well, put flesh on your bones.' Affectionately, for him, he chucked her under the pointed chin. It was a pity she was not likely to become the beauty her mother had been, but grace and accomplishment would make up for a lot.

And so Anne took her place as the youngest among Queen Claude's maids, in what was virtually a finishing school. The Queen was plain, gentle, excessively pious, insistent – though without harshness – that her ladies should be so busy with virtuous pursuits that they would have no time to spare for the other kind. Anne was too young to be interested in the other kind. She listened, and watched with her great eyes, and in her learning was as hard on herself as her tutors, or harder. People liked her for her quietness and were amused by the occasional lapses in decorum which showed her still a child.

Mary's appearance at the Maison du Roy caused a sensation. She, too, was of tender years for that court, but then it was well known that her father regarded his children as junior ambassadors. If Mary had been a babe in arms he would have found some employment for her at court, they said.

As it was, *la petite Boullen* charmed everyone. So English! Such a fair complexion! Such a terrible accent! Even a touch of Flemish in it, picked up at Brussels. Yet so pretty, so plump a little pigeon. If you looked carefully at her face, then at her father's, it was amazing to see the likeness between them, mercifully tempered by the cunning hand of Nature. And then she was so amiable, ready to run errands for senior ladies, or do menial tasks which others despised. As she was already trained in the ways of a court, she was neither clumsy nor so ignorant that she had to be told what to do.

Not ignorant, but innocent. It was a popular sport to tease her with *doubles entendres*, make her repeat highly indecorous words and phrases, then translate them and watch her blush.

'What society has she kept in England – monks and nuns?'

'Well, Sir Thomas is not exactly a *gaillard*. He must have kept her under lock and key.'

'But she learns quickly, *la mignonnelette*. The other day I heard her say . . .'

'*No!* Pink as a rose, was she?'

'Not a blush. She's learning, I tell you.'

Mary was indeed learning. Her father's high-flown description of the personages at court had been polite but both inaccurate and incomplete. At the head of the pyramid was what might have been termed an unholy trinity: François, his mother and his sister. One heart in three bosoms, people said.

François was twenty-one, bursting with youth and confidence. 'There was never a King in France in whom the nobility took such joy', was said of him by an admiring squire. A military leader in the most showy way, he had just beaten the Swiss, recaptured Milan for France, and distinguished himself at the battle of Marignano, wearing a splendid new suit of German infantry armour. They made up a song about him:

> *Victoire au noble roi François!*
> *Victoire au gentil de Valois!*

He was not exactly handsome, having an over-long nose – *le roi grand-nez* was an affectionate term for him – but he could make people believe that he was, simply by his fine bearing and cheerful expression. Somebody had rather shrewdly mentioned the 'lying merriment' of his looks. There was something of the devil in his face, something of the satyr, something of the tom cat (as Mary had noticed on the road to Abbeville), and something of the fox. He was magnificent, jolly, and boundlessly lewd.

123

His sister Marguerite d'Alençon was also lewd, though at the same time mystical, religious in an airy, unrealistic way. Unlike François, she was truly beautiful, a golden-haired, blue-eyed nymph whom people called *La Perle des Valois*. Marguerite meant pearl, and they said she had been born not of her father's seed but of a pearl her mother had accidentally swallowed. She was a brilliant scholar, a mistress of languages and a gifted author, with a sense of humour that was by turns spiritual and crude.

Louise of Savoy was young enough to have been elder sister to her two children. Marguerite had been born when she was sixteen. She was pretty, almost as striking as Marguerite, but dark and slight. She was amused by her son's amorous adventures, and doted on him. They said that she ruled France from behind his back, which may or may not have been true.

They also said that François and Marguerite were rather more than brother and sister to each other. That, too, might have been true, or a shocking slander, but after a few months at the French court Mary would not have been shocked by anything.

Others were very close to the King. Guillaume Gouffier, Sieur de Bonnivet and Grand Admiral of France, who, Mary thought, resembled the Duke of Suffolk, and who had tried to imitate that Englishman with an attempt to seduce Madame Marguerite by getting into her bedroom through a trapdoor.

Then there was de Montmorency, climbing his way up to being Constable of France and married to the daughter of the King's bastard uncle. And Boisy, another bastard, half-brother of the Queen Mother, and the charmingly named Fleurange, Captain of the Swiss Guard, and several more, all of whom grew beards when the King grew his.

Mary was soon aware that the mild Queen Claude had formidable rivals. François's appetite ran to large, startling ladies – *la petite bande*, as they were incongruously known, since there was nothing *petite* about them and they were not united in any way. Marie de Langeac was as round-faced as a wooden doll, and so was Marie de Macy, Dame de Montchenu; while Marie d'Assigny,

Dame de Canaples, had brilliant dark eyes and the figure of a well-nourished hen pheasant. François enjoyed his own very public *affaires* and loved to hear about those of his courtiers.

Unless ladies absolutely thrust themselves upon him he felt it below his dignity to go looking for them. Admirably fitted to be his procurer was the great, expansive Cardinal of Lorraine. He had been a bishop since he was ten and Church matters bored him. He held his own court at the Hôtel de Cluny in Paris, where he could do exactly as he liked, and did.

It was at a ball held there that Mary's ripening beauty was first noted by the trawling Cardinal. Nearly a woman now, almost fourteen, she had an air that was fashionable, very much of the court, altogether *de rigeur*, yet quite plainly not French. Flemish, Dutch? No, English, decided the Cardinal. He did not fail to notice the likeness between this female cherub in blue and the King of England's assiduous ambassador.

Mary found her hand taken from her dance partner's. A tall, gorgeously-robed man was smiling down at her.

'Mademoiselle Boullen. You are sad. May I cheer you with a little wine – or comforts? blancmange? herbolace?'

It was flattering to be addressed by the great Cardinal himself, who usually sent his minions to summon those he wished to converse with. Mary made a deep obeisance to him and answered most politely that she was not sad, and that at the moment she wished for no refreshment, although she was deeply sensible of His Eminence's graciousness. Her partner had retreated hastily, leaving her isolated with her host.

'That young gentleman is your *bel ami*, your lover?'

'No, Your Eminence.'

'But you have a lover – many lovers, surely? Let me know them, so that I may tell the King, who takes such pleasure in the happiness of his court.'

'I have none as yet, Your Eminence. I am very young.' And, she might have added, thoroughly frightened of her father finding her out in some scandal which would spoil her matrimonial chances.

He was always popping up when least expected, checking on his girls, and particularly on the prettier one.

'Not too young, surely? Does the Lady Venus ask the ages of her nymphs?'

Mary smiled, giving no answer. The Cardinal was disappointed.

'So. A nymph of Diana, not of Venus. Well, well, we must see . . .' He drifted loftily away. Mary sighed with relief.

That was in the first year of her time at court. In the second year, when she had become fully a woman, no longer a child, and knew her market value to be thereby increased, something happened to change her cautious way of life and open her eyes to the meaning of what went on around her, and why.

François and his court were at the Château of Blois, in the Valley of the Loire. It was the ancient palace of the royal family of Orleans, so ancient that the King determined to improve its dilapidated condition and make it fit for a Renaissance prince to live in. Using the finest builders, he added a north-west wing, high-arched on the cliff looking down on the town of Blois, a wing of great elegance with just a hint of the glorious new Vatican buildings about it. Within its courtyard was a marvellous staircase of white stone, wonderfully carved with the forms of small noble creatures, the fiery salamander, François's personal emblem, and the royal ermine, and embellished with the initials of François and Claude. It was open-fronted, so that the King's guard might muster on the platforms to salute him when he rode into the courtyard. At night they carried torches that glinted on their silver halberds and flashed from the diamond buttons and gold clasps of the King's garments.

Within, the Château was of matchless beauty. Its low ceilings were covered with ornate designs of plasterwork, its panelling elaborately carved and gilded, its walls glorious with the Italian paintings François bought so lavishly, the highest treasures of art. Some were by an ancient painter whom François almost worshipped, and had brought over the Alps to live in France, at his expense. Leonardo da Vinci was feeble, very near his death. He was not a painter like other Italians, nor were his holy personages like their handsome but commonplace madonnas and children. His women wore a strange, enigmatic smile, with a touch of what was perhaps heavenly humour. His Virgin, a woman grown, sat on the knees of her mother Saint Anne, seeming amused at the sporting of her baby son with a lamb. His John the Baptist pointed to Heaven with a look that indicated a divine secret known to nobody else. St John did not appear wholly masculine, and that applied to Messer da Vinci too.

Mary understood nothing of art, but was deeply awed by its splendours: artists must have eyes specially created to pierce the clouds, she thought, and see beyond to Paradise. She was impressed in a very different way by the paintings that adorned walls and ceilings in apartments used only by the King and his intimates. They were certainly not of Paradise. Their gods and goddesses were naked, given to very earthy behaviour, and their courtiers were not cherubs but cupids who likewise dispensed with clothes in that balmy pagan climate. They also dispensed with conventional conduct. Mary was curiously stirred, as she had never been before, by their uninhibited gambols.

The first time she was troubled by these stirrings she hastily took herself to Père Jérome, the confessor of the maids, and shyly confessed them, not knowing how to find the words.

The reverend father had never heard such a naive confession. These English, how long do they keep their children in the nursery?

'My daughter, the good God in His mighty wisdom sends such feelings to prepare virgins for that estate to which He has destined them.'

'Marriage, motherhood?' Mary suggested. She could think of no other destiny beyond the obvious one of being promoted to an estate and a title.

'As you rightly say, daughter.'

'Then what should I do when they come upon me?'

'Cherish them as holy gifts, signs of grace. But,' he felt bound to add, 'remember also the things of the spirit, and yield to no evil promptings from the Devil's emissaries.' What a pious hope, in that court, he reflected, imposing on her ten Aves and half a dozen Paternosters.

Horses were in the courtyard, young voices ringing in the clear air. Excellent, said the King's ladies, fresh company, news from Paris, perhaps a few songs we haven't heard before. There was laughter and excitement in the King's salon. Mary did not join in, being engaged in reading aloud to one of the Queen's senior ladies, who was ill. She found the pious book difficult and dull, only caring for the gorgeous illuminated capitals.

Having been excused from her duties, she left and made her way down a corridor, winding among the maze of turrets, bays and pinnacles, the roof of the more ancient part of the Château. She paused, wondering which way to turn, just as a young man appeared from the further end of the corridor. Both stopped. Both spoke at once.

'Can you tell me, mademoiselle . . .'

'M'sieur, do you know whether . . .'

He smiled and shrugged. 'Pardon, mademoiselle – I am lost. I am a stranger to Blois.' He stared at her. 'Marie!'

'M'sieur?'

'It is Marie de Boullen, surely? I couldn't forget such a face.'

Suddenly she remembered. He was older, taller, more manly, and an overpowering perfume of musk no longer wafted from his hair, but without question he was the boy who had wooed her so ardently at the court of Archduchess Marguerite, and had wept when she left.

'Guillaume! Oh, I'm so glad to see you!' In the frank impetuous fashion of English ladies, which Guillaume found so daring but so charming, she offered her lips for a kiss of greeting. Enthusiastically he gave it, and took another, then held her at arm's length.

'But how you've grown, and how beautiful you've become – you always were, of course, but in Brussels you were a bud, and now I see a rose. What are you doing here? I thought you were sent for to London . . .'

'I was, but everything changed.' They began to walk, her arm lightly linked with his, as was the fashion of courtesy, not caring now where the corridor led, or whether they would ever find their way down to the rooms below. He told her how his father wished him to gain a wider experience than he was getting as a page at the Archduchess's court, and therefore strings had been pulled to remove him to the French King's. He was betrothed to a demoiselle of Anjou, a good match, of better family than his own, but as she was still a child the marriage would not take place for two years. 'And you, Marie?'

'Neither betrothed nor spoken for – that I know of.'

'You astonish me. I thought milor your father had great ambitions for you.' (The self-seeking, pompous ass, how could he have begotten a rose like this one?)

'I am to finish my education first,' Mary said demurely. 'I am not clever like my young sister.'

'With such a face, who needs to be clever, lady? Ah, you can still blush – I remember your blush. And your perfume is delicious.'

'Unlike yours, as I remember. It overpowered the incense in Madame's chapel.'

'Ah. I was a silly boy then, a *poseur*. I am a grown man now.'

'I like you better,' she said shyly, and blushed again. 'Shall I show you the palace, or do you want to go back to your friends?'

'I want to be wherever you are.'

'You're very bold.' She was charmed by this new, manly Guillaume, a match for any gallant at Blois, and he was even more infatuated with the ripe young woman than he had been with the pretty child.

She showed him, with pride, the wonderful rooms of the Château. She sat, Guillaume reclining adoringly at her feet, while someone read to the King after he had dined, often from one of the romances of chivalry, the history of Troy and the rape of Helen, *Le Romaunt de la Rose*; sometimes from one of the naughty stories from Giovanni Boccaccio's *Decameron*, which Madame Marguerite's secretary had translated for her from the Italian. At moments, the eyes of the two young people would meet, and her hand stray down to his.

They hunted together in the forests of Blois, hunts that were like pageants performed to the music of sonorous brass and silver trumpets. At supper after the hunt they managed to find each other in the throng, and dance together the pavane or the galliard, or listen to love songs sung to a lute.

Or they would wander off together through great rooms lit by scented candles and torches, into moonlit galleries sweet with the air of the gardens where twinkling fountains played; and so on up until they reached a little turret room which belonged to nobody except, it seemed, themselves.

There it was that Mary, on the improvised couch of Guillaume's velvet cloak, found out at last the cause of the strange stirrings which had troubled her, and passed through brief pain to unimagined pleasure. And, through Guillaume's young, gentle teaching, to the discovery of herself. For this I was born a woman, was her thought; to this most beautiful hour, all my life has been directed.

10

The King's Favourite

The delights of the flesh were greater than Mary had ever dreamed of, a pleasure which mere acquaintance with the facts had not prepared her for in the least. Her delight in turn delighted Guillaume. Experienced youth though he was, he had never encountered a maid so naturally ardent, so frankly sensual. Perhaps it was the nature of the English, though he had not noticed it in the few of Mary's countrywomen at the court of Brussels.

He adored her. But he also adored roast quail and sucking-pig dressed with apricots, yet had no wish to live on those delicacies. Mary's very innocence began, ever so slightly, to bore him. She could teach him nothing that he had not taught her, which was frustrating in itself. After a few weeks of enjoying her at every possible moment, and some almost impossible ones (they were caught twice, but in that court this was no matter for comment), his fancy began to stray.

There was attached to the King's court a band of highly superior prostitutes, *les filles de joie*, who followed everywhere, shepherded by an alarmingly correct Madame. These girls were all lovely, well trained in the arts of love, clever enough to converse with sophisticated gentlemen or lower themselves gracefully to simpler ones. Very few of them were over the age of twenty, some not yet twelve. Every May Day, Madame took the King a most splendid bouquet of flowers, the leaves powdered with silver and gold dust.

Among this select company was a girl slightly younger than Mary, a contrast to her in every way. Valentine (it was not her christened name, but she had chosen it as a suitably amorous one) was whip-slender, with a three-cornered smile, eyes as round and shining as black cherries, and two thick dark plaits which resembled tarred ropes or well-fed snakes. She was reputed to be the most accomplished young whore ever to have been recruited to *les filles*. It was said that François himself resorted to her when his appetite was jaded and he wanted to learn something new.

Guillaume, a young man desirous to complete his education in every way, had his eye on Valentine. She would cost good gold, but his father was generous and would provide the extra cash if Guillaume could give a valid reason for doing so. He would think of a reason. Valentine and he had exchanged long, slow, appreciative glances; he knew that for the price of a new doublet she could be his for an hour. More than an hour would rate as much as a new horse with all its equipment.

The obstacle was Mary. He was a kind-hearted lad, and the girl wept so easily, even for joy. If he were not careful she would be bewailing his betrothal, or making some ridiculous vow to follow him wherever he might go, even after his marriage. He began to look about for ways of escape.

Among the Gentlemen of the Bedchamber was a young nobleman called Gaston Daubigny, who had been at court only a little longer than Guillaume. A handsome, craggy personage, noted for his powerful wrestling and skill with the foil, he was known not to have a mistress. Indeed, the King, who liked people to enjoy themselves, had reproached him publicly for it, and Gaston had smiled with tight lips. He came from Normandy, where they were less free in their ways than men of the south.

Guillaume insinuated himself into Daubigny's company after a game of tennis. A good player himself, he had deliberately let the other man win. They drank a cup of cold wine together.

'You are silent, friend,' said Guillaume, who had been chattering merrily for the last ten minutes. 'A man of deeds, not words.'

Gaston nodded.

'Yet you seem not to engage in the pleasantest sport of all.'

'Which is – ?'

'The joys of Venus.'

'Oh, that.' Gaston shrugged. 'My days are well filled with other things.'

'And your nights?'

'Well. Since you ask. I've found no special lady to my taste.'

'Not tried to find one, perhaps?'

'Not particularly. I dislike rebuffs.'

Guillaume tried to look as though a brilliant idea had just come into his head. 'I know – and this is a very marvellous thing – of a warm and lovely girl who would not rebuff you, her heart is so kind. If you were to win her favour, you'd be a happy man indeed.'

'And how would I do that?'

'Why, in the usual way – woo her.'

'I'm not much skilled at wooing.'

Guillaume suppressed impatience. 'I know her well, I can prepare the way for you. When the time's ripe, I'll tell you, and you need only take her aside, walk with her, pay her a compliment or two. All women love compliments. Tell her of her beauty, say you're not given to idle praises, but your heart has been slain by her eyes – that sort of thing, you know. Very easy.'

The Norman surveyed, suspiciously, this youth who was so anxious to wish what sounded like an ideal paramour onto someone else. 'And you, what benefit would you get?'

'Freedom. Variety,' Guillaume said frankly. 'I admit it. I need a change, and so will she, when she comprehends how much better a bargain you are than I.'

'You're not by any chance trying to father a bastard on me?'

Guillaume crossed himself. 'Holy Saints forbid! So, shall I sound her out?'

'If you commit me to nothing.' Daubigny was still suspicious and not at all confident of this glib youth's good faith. But he longed for a mistress, and the King's taunts had struck home.

Guillaume's first ploy was to pretend languor. On a perfect evening, with summer just merging into autumn, stars coming out in an azure sky and nightingales still singing, his love-making was so lacking in enthusiasm that Mary sat up, alarmed.

'You're unwell, my loved one. What is it?'

'Alas, *ma belle*, I don't know, but I'm not at all myself tonight. Forgive me – not your fault, mine. My head . . .' He put his hand to a brow which he hoped looked fevered. 'My eyes burn, and I have an inclination to shiver. Oh, it's nothing, perhaps just the early autumn chill.'

'Not – the plague? Oh, not that!'

Guillaume patted her. 'Calm yourself, Marie, there's not a hint of it about – not even in Paris this year. No, this is just a stupid infirmity. It will pass.'

The next time he pronounced himself better, but still lacking in his usual vigour. Mary was not suspicious, even then. Not for a week did she tell him reproachfully, that he had changed towards her. 'I'm ugly, is that it? I'm growing fat, I'm not pleasing you any more. Tell me, only tell me, and I'll try to make myself prettier, thinner . . .'

'Marie, oh Marie! What a delicious *crétine* you are. Of course you're not fat. And who ever wanted to shoot down a thin partridge?'

Mary reflected that he seemed not to wish to shoot her down, fat partridge or thin, very often. She was hard to put off without actual unkindness on his part, yet somehow he contrived it; all female that she was, she took the hint at last. His passion had cooled, she was not the ideal lady in his life, as he was the ideal gallant in hers.

Or had been. She was not without pride, and managed a wan smile at what she guessed rightly would be their last encounter.

So ended her first love affair, and so it came that one evening, instead of joining in the dancing, she sat aside, watching wistfully, her childish mouth turned down. At that moment Gaston Daubigny dared to seize his chance. Darting to her side, he asked her to dance, and awkwardly started a conversation as they paced in the slow pavane measure. He could think of nothing better to discuss than the weather, which suited Mary's English taste perfectly. She found his accent almost incomprehensible, and he hardly took in a word she said, so unused were his ears to her version of courtly French.

Yet it made no difference: their glances and their bodies said all. Gaston was more virile than the volatile Guillaume, a fighting and hunting man of impressive strength and vigour, with a sort of determination about his love-making which pleased her very much.

On its nourishment she bloomed. Her father, visiting Blois, was delighted by her new beauty and maturity. He was still not sure where to make the best match for her, but she was becoming a greater prize all the time. He gave her a new dress, marigold-yellow satin strewn with silver leaves and brilliants, and a great topaz to wear about her neck.

The court was on the move, back towards Paris, while Blois was being swept and sweetened. Behind the King swarmed a procession numbering thousands, on horse and foot. Nobles, merchants, soldiers, courtiers great and lowly, jesters and priests, bears, monkeys and caged birds, the poor pregnant Queen in a litter, François riding in glory and splendour – they all streamed through the countryside, halting at night to sleep in luxurious tents.

Mary was too young to mind the inconvenience of travelling so far, and so nomadically, and she never felt the cold. Travelling, she was separated from Gaston, but that could be borne cheerfully enough, after their vigorous nights at Blois. She enjoyed the fresh country air, the tables spread at night with the best of food and wine, quite as though they still had a château's roof over their heads, the roaring camp-fires, and the savoury smell of roasting meat. She liked bedding down in a pavilion of a tent, on a pallet of wool covered with furs, more furs above her, candlelight and laughter. It was excitement, adventure – anything could happen.

Cardinal Jean de Lorraine was travelling with the cortège. Ever watchful for his monarch's pleasures, he regretted that the beautiful Françoise de Foix had not yet come within the King's net, for with the Queen pregnant again a new royal diversion was needed.

He had watched Mary Boleyn's progress with interest. He was perfectly aware of her broken liaison with the young Flamand and of her present one with Gaston Daubigny – a common, unworthy fellow, in the Cardinal's opinion. She was a pretty creature, growing increasingly more luscious. He disliked Thomas Boleyn, after a clash of wills with the English ambassador. It might be doing Boleyn a favour to bring his daughter to the King's notice, but on the whole the Cardinal thought it would have just the opposite effect, since all these jumped-up tradesmen looked for great family marriages, and too much promiscuity tended to spoil the market. It was a wonder Boleyn had not thought of that before sending such a ripe piece to a court from which no woman – maid, wife or widow – departed chaste.

Since he had not thought of it, and the moment seemed right, the Cardinal had a word in the royal ear on a certain chilly, starry night a few miles south of Paris.

In the tent Mary shared with many other ladies, the chattering and giggles drowned the voice of the page who insinuated himself through the throng of girls, dressed, undressed, abed or gracefully disposed on furs and cushions in conversation with their lovers.

'Demoiselle Boullen, His Grace desires your company.'

Mary, brushing her hair, which she had just washed in scented water, was startled enough to drop the brush.

'*My* company? Why? Are you sure?'

The page was sure. He would lead the way, if the demoiselle would dress herself sufficiently to face the night air.

Conflicting thoughts whirled through her head as they went. Why should the King send for her, a humble lady-in-waiting? Was he about to tell her some terrible news – that her father was dead, or her mother? Had some misdemeanour of hers been reported to him, and if so, what? It could only be to do with Gaston. They had been incautious at times, as she and Guillaume had been, but surely the King was liberal enough to excuse peccadilloes . . . unless the Queen had heard and insisted that she be dismissed. Or . . .

They were at the blue and golden royal tent, the lilies of France fluttering above it in the night breeze. She was being murmuringly announced.

François lounged on a couch of skins beside a glowing brazier from which came an incense-like perfume. He was all white and silver: white velvet, white satin, gleams of silver and diamonds, a white cloak lined with ermine. His head was bare, the firelight reflecting gold in his hair and the elegant pointed beard he now wore. He looked like a white heraldic leopard reclining along a forest bough.

'Mademoiselle Boullen.' He stretched out one white hand, covered with rings. Mary was too nervous to take in his exact words of greeting, but they were something to the effect that it was gratifying at last to have leisure to talk to her, the fair daughter of King Henry's distinguished ambassador. She bowed her head, still half-curtseying, half-kneeling. The jewelled hand gestured.

'Pray do get up. I have an excellent view of the top of your head, mademoiselle, but none at all of your face, which is a pity. Come and sit beside me.'

The hovering gentleman glided forward with a carved stool which he placed a foot or so away from the couch. Mary perched on it in her best In Attendance attitude, back poker-straight, feet together beneath the spreading skirts, hands meekly clasped in her lap. François, glancing behind him, clicked his fingers, at which somebody out of sight in a far corner of the tent began to touch the strings of a lute. The gentle languishing music was like a curtain of sweet sound behind them. Mary knew that she must not speak until the King did.

'You speak our language like a Frenchwoman, mademoiselle,' said the King charmingly if untruthfully. 'Did you learn it in our country?'

'No, Your Grace. As a child. My sister and brother and I had a French governess. But they both speak French better than I do – especially my sister . . .' She stopped abruptly, remembering that chatter about one's family could not possibly interest the King of France.

But to her astonishment, he began to ask questions about that family, about her Howard relatives, the old Duke – 'seventy-five years old, a noble age, would we all could look forward to matching it,' and he added something in Latin which Mary failed to understand. Now her father's houses, were they châteaux, in the style of Blois and Amboise, and what was the hunting like?

Mary began to stammer descriptions of Hever and Blickling, noticing miserably as she heard herself talk that she made them sound like peasants' mud hovels. She babbled of Penshurst and Allintgton Castle, and the royal residences she had seen (which were few indeed); described, in answer to keen questioning, her one encounter with King Henry in London and her glimpses of him at Dover.

Yes, the whole kingdom had rejoiced at the birth of a daughter to Queen Catherine – so she had been told by her father – and no, there was not yet any sign of another royal heir. As to the Queen . . .

At some point in her chatter she realised that the exalted personage on the couch was not going to eat her, or order her immediate execution, or send her out into the night to walk back to the coast. He was simply a charming gentleman whom she knew perfectly well by sight; he had even bestowed on her the kiss of courteous greeting when she first arrived in Paris. It was not at all difficult talking to him, and she no longer stammered or stumbled into the occasional word of English.

François listened with half an ear, studying her with the eye of Europe's greatest connoisseur of women. He knew all about her amours with one of his pages and a Gentleman of the Bedchamber. He had been delighted to hear of the latter, since he considered any courtier lacking a mistress to be a paltry *petit-maître*, a *damoiseau*, little better than effeminate. Now he knew that Daubigny did not deserve such a label.

He chatted with that young man one night, when Daubigny was for once fairly drunk, and had persuaded him to talk of his sweetheart. As the good wine flowed, so did the probing questions and increasingly bawdy answers. How did she look when she . . .? Was she talkative or silent at such times? Was she fertile in invention, in the *ars amoris*, or pliant and submissive? It amused him enormously to hear such details – he would laugh and laugh as they were recited. But, in accord with the ideals of chivalry, they must not be publicly told. The Queen would be most shocked if they reached her ears; gentlemen talked only in private about such things.

From what he had heard of Mary, she was most promising material: warm and willing, inexperienced enough to be taught, quick to learn, even, charmingly, occasionally proffering naive little suggestions of her own. She was very pretty and faultlessly young and perfect in body: he liked to know that, his own wife having a bad limp, a squint, and being of such dumpy stature as to seem almost dwarfish, poor thing. To François a beautiful woman was like one of the works of art he collected with such knowledge and assiduity.

And she was English, which lent her just that touch of intriguing strangeness and piquancy. Daubigny had not mentioned that, but then in some ways he was a clod, a peasant. François would soon find out for himself, now that the conversational conventions had been observed.

'I see your hair is damp, mademoiselle. Is it raining, or are you a disguised mermaid?'

'I washed it, Your Grace. Tonight. The dust of the road had got into it.'

'Of course. Then you should dry it, for fear of catching cold.' Casually he twitched off the crimson shawl she had hastily draped over her head and shoulders before leaving her tent. Damp, dark, curiously sensual, the long hair hung over the loose white *peignoir* she wore. It was not as long as Anne's hair, or of the same quality, but Mary was proud of it.

François left his couch to stand beside her, and lifted the damp strands, lock by lock, spreading them out like fans, letting them fall again. '*Une sirène, une vraie sirène,*' he murmured. Mary did not know what a siren was, but hoped it was something pleasant. Then, in one practised movement, he pulled her to her feet and drew the loose garment down from her shoulders to her waist. Obediently she pulled it down to her feet and stepped out of it, extremely thankful that her smock was of fine linen and richly embroidered. She knew very well what François would do next; and indeed he did, stripping the heavy bearskin from the couch and laying it on the floor in front of the brazier.

The tent was very quiet in the many-candled golden light. The lutenist was still playing, so softly that the notes hardly reached the two now lying on the bearskin. Mary sensed that there were other persons present, perhaps one or two, invisible and inaudible, attendants to a recognised ceremony.

She was unprepared for the impact of François's possession of her. It was neither conquest nor seduction, but something of each. His artistry in love-making not merely surpassed what Gaston and Guillaume had practised; it seemed not a simple physical accomplishment but a skill allied to those which produced the other features of his court, great paintings, architecture, gardens, poetry. Gaston's simple embraces had made her a woman: in François's, she knew the joys of a nymph of the Elysian Fields.

François found her everything he had hoped for, and more. She was amazingly teachable. To every town on his progresses through France he was accustomed to make a *joyeuse entrée*: none more so than this one. It was he who tired first, leaving Mary still eager. She was disappointed, but one did not argue with a king.

Mysteriously, the same gentleman who had ushered her into the pavilion was suddenly there, silent, ready to escort her through the encampment. There was no sign of the lutenist or anyone else. François kissed her hand with the utmost graciousness, saying, '*À demain.*' If not tomorrow, then the next day, or night. She was a priceless discovery.

The King's mistress. It was unbelievable rapture to think of herself in those terms. She was transported with pride, walking on air. As she walked she broke into little trills of song; at Mass she could not keep her mind on the prayers. Her cheeks dimpled into smiles at the least thing.

'She's drunk,' suggested Lysette.

'No, mad.' This was Èleanore.

'Or perhaps merely *exaltée*. She's seen a vision.'

'Of what?'

'With Marie, it could only be one thing.' They laughed heartily. Mary knew well what they were saying, but she only smiled and smiled, and hugged her secret, which would soon be no secret.

She gave Gaston Daubigny not another thought and he, oddly, never came near her again. Of Guillaume she had long ago lost sight. Within a week it was known that she went to the King's bed, and when the court reached Paris, settling at the Hôtel des Tournelles, Mary was given the key of the little door which was hidden behind a loose tapestry and led to a staircase and another secret door into the King's bedchamber. She wore the key on a gold chain between her breasts, beneath the topaz her father had given her. François disliked Tournelles, but its dark ancient rooms were undoubtedly convenient for intrigue.

It was not the first time he had condescended to a lady-in-waiting, but unusual enough to cause a little jealousy among those who thought themselves more beautiful and desirable than the English girl. Her very Englishness was a cause of rancour. Nobody dared speak openly against her, or mock, for it was well known that François would not tolerate ribaldry concerning ladies, even from other ladies. But they whispered.

When she appeared in a new and splendid dress of mulberry red, the kirtle embroidered in a lattice pattern of small emeralds and brilliants, barbed remarks were made.

'She has joined *les filles*. Every New Year the King gives each of them a dress. New Year is a little late, that's all.'

'What a vulgar dress. Most suitable to a tradesman's daughter.'

'Not daughter, surely. Milor Boullen isn't a tradesman, even though he looks like one. It was his grandfather.'

'That makes no difference. The blood is still bourgeois.'

On the night she first wore the mulberry dress Mary found dead toad in her bed.

She was not cast down by the whispers. Her heart was filled with immense pride – pride in her capture of the King. It was as though she had ridden ahead of all the hunt and slain the finest stag in the forest. Her pride was not only for herself, but for her father. He had commanded her to gain royal favour, to work hard at her accomplishments (and so she had, though her principal accomplishment was perhaps not one that had occurred to him) to gain great honours and advance the family name. She had done all these things, and he would be delighted when he returned from his present duties at the English court and found her so exalted.

He was a very important man indeed, now: Sheriff of Kent, a power in the country as well as the city. When the heir to the throne, little Princess Mary, had been christened, Sir Thomas had held the canopy. Yes, he would be proud of the daughter who had fulfilled his wishes.

Mary was not only proud but happy. She found François not only a superb lover, but a kindly, considerate and free-handed man. His air of *diablerie* was something apart, a faun's mask he wore. It was easy to see why his mother and sister worshipped him. She knew (though not from his lips) that it was largely due to his diplomatic handling of the situation that the young Queen of France, Mary Tudor, and Suffolk had got away unscathed with their rash marriage. King Henry, his promises to Mary forgotten, would have had Suffolk's head for it, but François's returning of the Queen's rich dowry had placated him, greedy as he was.

From François, at intimate moments, Mary heard something of his feelings for King Henry. They had not met, but sensed each other's personalities from afar. Now they had both been beaten in the race for the title of Holy Roman Emperor, following the death of the Emperor Maximilian. François, Henry, and Charles of Spain had been in the running for it, and Charles had won.

'I was not, frankly, pleased,' he told Mary. 'I offered handsomely for my stake in the prize, three millions of gold and the Princess

Renée. But I lost to Spain. Ah, well, it suits me not to have to carry the cares of an empire on my shoulders. Or at least that's what I say.' He laughed. 'And better Spain than England.'

'Don't you think King Henry would have made a good Emperor, sir?'

He pulled at his beard. 'Only God could answer that. For me, I hear and I mistrust. Henry seems a great handsome bold giant, a giant stalking through a country fair, so magnificent that all the people cry "Ah!" and fall back as he passes. But within the giant of plaster and stuffing I think there is a child – a greedy, shifty, cowardly child. A cruel child too, I think.'

'Why, sir? What has he done that was especially cruel?'

François glanced sideways at her, with a lift of his diabolical eyebrows. 'Did you not hear of the *malheureux Jour de Mai* two years ago? Your Londoners don't like foreigners, did you know that? Not only us French, but Germans, Spaniards, anyone. They put their heads together and rebelled against these strangers who were eating their food and taking their trade. There were riots – on May Day, of all joyous days to choose. The Duke of Norfolk – your grandfather, *chérie* – put down the riots with soldiers and cannon. Then the ringleaders ran away, so that only apprentice boys were left. They were tried for high treason and found guilty.'

'Boys, sir?'

'Boys. Many were not yet thirteen. Your King had some of them hanged, drawn and quartered. Indeed the city gates were decorated with their quarters as with triumphal garlands.'

Mary was shocked. 'King Henry did that?'

'Ah, but he pardoned many after Queen Catherine and Cardinal Wolsey begged for their lives, because they were so young and small. Then the people shouted "God save our merciful King".' François shrugged. 'It was a necessary measure, to execute the children, I suppose. But it tells me something about King Henry. The boys had done nothing but run about and make a noise. I think I would not have killed them. I might have done, but I hope not.'

Mary remembered the big, rosily handsome young monarch she had seen in London and Dover. Surely he would not execute children. There must be some good reason. Knowing what she now knew of men, she wished she could see King Henry again.

She did not have long to wait.

The English Mare

François, who was fond of scribbling verses, had scribbled one on a window pane:

> *Souvent femme varie*
> *Bien fol est qui sy fie.*

The man who trusts too-often fickle woman is crazy. Yet it was amusing when women surprised one by being suddenly capricious. His favourite mistress, the lovely young Jeanne le Coq, liked to tease him. Another, a new one, the massive Françoise de Foix, was always fighting and making up again, being jealous and giving cause for jealousy.

It was a little tedious to have a mistress who, however wanton and charmingly lascivious, could always be relied upon: almost like having a second wife. He liked Mary Boleyn, was not in the least in love with her, and his mischievous sense of humour went to work to try whether she was as wanton as she seemed.

One night Mary was summoned, in a note brought by a page, to a tryst in *La Chambre Jaune*, a room high up in the refurbished part of the Hôtel des Tournelles which François sometimes favoured as a meeting place with his *belles amourettes*. There were many twisting stairs to climb to the quaint little room where everything was gold or buttercup-yellow, from the cherubs playing on the plaster ceiling to the rare, elegant carpet.

She arrived breathless, panting, aware of the extra weight she had put on with good food and plenty of it. The bed, its gold canopy held up by buxom gilt nymphs, already had an occupant.

So he had nodded off, even before . . . With a smile of maternal understanding, Mary approached the bed and gently touched the humped shoulder of the recumbent figure.

It started up, making her shriek with surprise. The man who sat up in the bed, grinning, was not the King at all. He was bigger, older, heavier and coarse-featured, with bold light blue eyes, peasant cheekbones and a bristling brown beard.

Even more breathless than when she had entered the room she gasped, 'Monsieur de Bonnivet!'

The Grand Admiral of France, the King's closest friend, was a dashing character almost equal to his royal friend in womanising, soldiering, and hunting.

'*La p'tite Boullen. Venez, venez, fleurette.*' He held out bare arms to her, throwing back the bedcovers.

'There has been a mistake . . .' she faltered.

'None, I assure you, none. I was lonely, my good friend the King promised to find me company – and what do I see but a bonny rose of England? Come and keep me company, demoiselle. Unless – you mislike me? But no, it's impossible.' Before she could answer he was out of the bed, a huge naked figure, embracing her, pulling her with him.

There was no possibility of polite or shocked refusal. Much to her surprise, Mary found herself enjoying the experience. It was an entirely new one, full of a rough gusto she had not known before. This was the man who had tried to seduce, or rape, La Perle herself, the Duchess Marguerite, by climbing into her bedroom through a trapdoor. Mary could believe it. When it was all good-humouredly concluded she felt that Marguerite had missed something.

She could not have explained how it was that not many days after that encounter she came to be sharing the awesome bed of Bonnivet's brother, the Cardinal de Boisy. He was quite old, over forty, and rather feeble, much gentler than Bonnivet, but highly instructive, in his way. (Alas, he was not long for this world and she was never to repeat the experience.)

After that her partner was another great friend of the King, Anne de Montmorency, whose feminine name belied his harsh character. He taught her a few painful lessons she would rather not have learned, and she was glad to be suddenly recalled to the royal bed.

François seemed to know about her encounters, teasing her lightly about them. From her replies he knew that he held in his arms a natural courtesan, a girl formed by some trick of Nature for man's pleasure and her own. She was addicted to sex, *s'adonée*, as another might be to wine. He was known to his huntsmen as the Father of Venery, and might be called so in another sense. He fully understood Mary and her kind, even, perhaps, why she had become what she was, given her cold-eyed, cold-hearted father. François was a devoted father to his own daughter, the little Princess Charlotte, and had wept bitterly when her sister Louise had died at three years old. Women needed all kinds of love, paternal love included.

Yet, such is the nature of men, that from the day, or night, when she began to circulate among his courtiers he valued his pretty Englishwoman less. He began to think of her in loose terms, not usually in his vocabulary of courtesy. In years to come he would remember her as *una grandissima ribalda*, a great prostitute.

Mary was well brought up enough to be discreet, not to chatter about her lovers or give away intimate secrets. But her behaviour did not go unnoticed.

In a room of the magnificent new wing at Blois, two women were talking. The noise of hammers was a background to their conversation, for the wing was still unfinished: it was to have the finest apartments in the world, François declared.

Louise de Savoie was pacing up and down, her skirts of peacock-blue satin trailing on the marble floor, her hands playing restlessly with a fan. At forty-three she was still beautiful, if the beholder did not compare her too closely with her daughter. Marguerite wore white, emphasising her angelic fairness (and as a kind of mourning for her love, Gaston de Foix, the great soldier, dead so young in battle). The table at which she sat was covered with books: missals, breviaries, histories, romances, books of poems, each a work of art, bound in velvet of white or green, crimson, russet and blue, clasped and studded with silver. She was always reading, but her large blue eyes were still bright and clear, alight with intelligence, with, irony.

Her mother paused by the table.

'I dislike it,' she said. 'It is extremely distasteful. My son, my Caesar, King of France, associating with a vulgar little harlot, not even a lady.'

'He has associated with many others, not always of irreproachable virtue.' Marguerite turned a page.

'I know that. It is not for you or me to act as guardian of the King's morals. I was forced to speak to him about his night wanderings in the streets of Paris, playing silly jokes. Amusing, but so very dangerous. He could have been abducted, murdered, anything. Well, he seemed to listen to me, and I think he will take more care in future. But this girl. She sleeps with half the court – did you know?'

Marguerite put down her book. 'I find it as distasteful as you do. The child is ignorant, not properly sensible of our ways and conventions. Sooner or later she will do harm to François's reputation, damage his honour. She should go, I think.'

'I'm glad you agree, *chère fille*. François will not miss her, and most emphatically neither shall we. But how, do you think? Boullen will be offended if we simply order her to leave the court.'

'He'll be offended in any case, pompous little man.' Marguerite meditated, looking down her rather long nose at the bright book open before her. A smile curved her mouth.

'I think I see a way,' she said. 'At the end of the month King Henry and Queen Catherine come to France for this great ceremony which is to join the two countries in amity. A pious hope, in my opinion, but never mind, it will serve. Mary Boullen will simply be sent back in Queen Catherine's train of attendants. I will speak to Claude, who will speak to Catherine. Claude dislikes the Boullen girl, I know.'

'But she is devoted to the other one, the younger sister. Perhaps she won't agree.'

'She will if I suggest strongly that she should. I can be very convincing, *ma mère*, and I understand Claude. She's quite saintly in her tolerance of François's little diversions, but there is a limit, and it has been reached. I shall have a personal word with the girl's father. I think he should know what kind of daughter he has bred. Don't you agree?'

'Utterly.' They exchanged mutually congratulatory smiles, these two who might have been sisters instead of mother and daughter.

The open-air pageant which would be known in history as the Field of the Cloth of Gold would never be surpassed for magnificence. François was determined to show Henry what French splendour could be, and Henry was determined to do the same for the renown of England. François devised a setting which he hoped would baffle description, and it did.

The field itself was a valley called the Val Doré, a few miles from Calais, where the royal ship *Catherine Pleasaunce* had landed more than five thousand English, headed by Henry and his Queen. The place was near the little walled town of Ardres, whose inhabitants shrank back behind their crumbling walls in awe at the sights spread before them.

François, too, had some five thousand people in his train. He had always enjoyed his own very grand form of camping, and now he established himself happily in a great pavilion of cloth-of-gold striped with blue, sewn with fleurs-de-lys. Above it, a life-size statue of the Archangel Michael stamped down a realistically painted dragon.

Queen Claude's pavilions were of gold, silver and violet. Hundreds of banners floated above them, brilliantly coloured and of the richest materials, and everywhere that the arms of France and its nobility could appear, they did appear. It was a loud, clear statement of supremacy, the supremacy of the Valois dynasty.

Henry's quarters had a solid English look. A castle that seemed to be real was in fact a fabrication of wood and canvas, cleverly painted: it had real glass windows, frowning battlements and a gatehouse all beflowered with the crimson rose of Tudor and a profusion of statues of persons sacred and profane. Fountains gushed wine, supplied in cups of silver to the multitudes who rolled up to avail themselves of it and proceeded to get spectacularly drunk.

As well as the English King and Queen, the King's sister Mary was of the company, Duchess of Suffolk and Dowager Queen of France, and the mock castle also held Cardinal Wolsey. He slept in cloth-of-gold sheets. The hall of the castle was a small palace in itself, all gold and green with a silk ceiling and a floor covered with taffeta, Tudor roses blooming everywhere, a chapel behind it in which life-sized gold statues of the Twelve Apostles dumbly challenged St Michael to descend from the French King's pavilion and outshine them – if he could.

The honours were about even.

When the two Kings met on the Feast of Corpus Christi, 7 June, in yet another gold pavilion, they were equally resplendent, François in cloth-of-silver and gold, crusted with jewels all over, Henry scarlet and gold, on a white horse. Two men like great living jewels. Two men jealous, uncertain, nervous of one another, fencing, as it were, with bright smiles on their faces, each expecting the other to draw blood first: a rivalry as much personal as national. Not the least concern of each was that they were pledged to become united through their children, for Henry's three-year-old Mary was betrothed to François's one-year-old Dauphin.

In the jousting that followed, the two Kings did not challenge each other, but they tried a wrestling match, and the Valois threw the Tudor heavily in a *tour de Bretagne*. A point to France. Both their wives were plain and dumpy, but Claude had borne three children, including a lively heir, and Catherine had only a daughter. Another point to France.

Mary Boleyn was delighted to be able to view both Kings at once from a vantage point so near them. The lesser ladies-in-waiting had abominably primitive accommodation, which Mary thought hardly suitable to her but, being anxious not to cause trouble, said nothing about it. What was a pallet of straw and a few fleas, after all, when one would soon enjoy so much grander lying?

She was overawed by King Henry. He looked so much more splendid than he had in the murk of Dover beach, so young and ruddy and strong. She compared him with the Duke of Suffolk, who had accompanied his wife. Yes, they were very much alike. Now that she knew so much more about men, she reflected that her knowledge came late. If she had only realised in Brussels the marvellous attractiveness of Suffolk, how different her life might have been. He had openly flirted with her, young as she was; why had she not had the wit to lay the foundations for something more?

But it would still not have been as grand as her present position. Her gaze went back to the magnificent figure of the English King. He was, she thought, the handsomer of the two, certainly very virile, though it was strange that so many of the Queen's babies had died; perhaps she had a fault in her womb, a worm, a blight. How sad for the King: Mary sighed. The butchered apprentice boys were quite forgotten as she gazed at him.

On the third day of the festivities she was summoned to the presence of her father. He awaited her in a sumptuous tent, over which flew a painted banner of a lion rampant, much resembling King Henry in the face.

None of Sir Thomas's retinue was present. Just he himself, in a black velvet doublet slashed with crimson satin, and a white-plumed hat. He stood, feet apart, one hand on the pommel of the dagger at his belt.

Mary ran forward eagerly, made her curtsey and rose to offer the kiss of greeting. The hand left the dagger and cracked across one side of her head, then the other side, knocking her in a heap on the floor.

Gasping with pain and shock, she stared up at the grim face glowering down at her. Before she could gather her wits to speak, he had moved away and was regarding her as though she were some poisonous reptile he had just killed.

'You have been whoring, mistress, I hear.' His tone was like a blast of January wind. Mary struggled to sit up, not daring to stand in case he struck again.

'Sir, what do you mean?'

'I mean what I have just said. You have turned common whore and strewn your favours about the court of King François.'

'Sir, father . . . no. You heard lies. I am the King's mistress.'

'*You!* Are you mad? King François's *maîtresse en titre* is Madame Françoise de Foix, Dame du Chateaubriand. You had perhaps not noticed the lady?'

It would have been impossible not to notice Madame de Foix. She was tall, imposing, darkly handsome and of a fiery temper. Mary knew that she had an *amour* with François, but so she had with Bonnivet. Surely it was impossible that François cared more for that loud-mouthed virago than for her, Mary. Still kneeling, she tried to defend herself.

'The King sent for me months ago. Since then I've been his favourite. I thought you would be pleased, Father.'

'You – thought – I – would – be – pleased. When I have heard from the King himself that he favoured you because he knew of your reputation as an easy harlot, one already well handled by men? I was told this by Madame la Duchesse d'Alençon, who thought I should know it for my own good. I then ventured to enquire of the King myself. It is not his habit to defame a woman, but he had to confess to the truth in your case. He also reported to me that he had passed you on to various of his friends, thinking you might amuse them as much as you did him. A strumpet, a meretrix, a bawd – those are your titles, *vos titres, maîtresse.*' He then added some remarks in Latin, for decency, more to relieve his feelings than to upbraid his daughter, who had no idea what they meant. Reverting to English, he informed her that she had brought the name of Boleyn to shame and ruined her marriage chances, that her mother's heart would break when the dreadful news was told to her, and that Queen Claude desired so little to look upon her face again that she was to be banished from the court and sent back to England when the ceremonies were over.

'The mere sight of your whey face makes me sick.' With the flat of his hand he hit her hard about the head several times, rocking her off balance so that she fell again.

At that he rang a handbell to summon a servant.

'Take this – young woman – away. I have finished with her.'

Imapassive of face, the man waited for the sobbing Mary to get to her feet, then silently escorted her out of the tent.

So this was her reward for pleasing the King of France. Mary crawled off to her bed of straw and lay on it, weeping, for hours. Her pride was in ruins. She knew, as far as she could reason clearly in her distress, that she had truly thought herself to be fulfilling her father's ambition. She had not known what she did, in bedding with the other men. The King had wished it, she was his to dispose of as he liked.

He had indeed disposed of her, for good.

She told no one how her face came to be so bruised, only shook her head. Silently, she crept about her duties, which fortunately kept her away from Queen Claude. When she could escape she walked, wandering away by herself. Near the edge of the valley was a farm, its lands sprawling down many acres of young crops, grazing beasts, barns, slaughterhouses and sheds of all kinds. In one of these, used as a winter store, there were iron hooks in the ceiling, strong hooks from which flitches of whole carcasses could hang. She measured the distance between the floor and the hooks. With a stool or a chest, she might be able to reach up to them. But she had no rope, and her own stockings would not be strong enough.

In the woodland there was a large natural pond. Animals drank there, and sometimes swam. Mary could not swim. She stood on the edge, looking down into its muddy depths, where water beetles darted and tadpoles clustered, already half frogs. Then she turned away. She had not even the courage left to drown herself.

*

On the high dais above the tilting ground the two Kings were watching the jousting and chatting idly in French, since François's English was poor.

Henry laughed, the genial laugh which shook him all over and set others laughing too. 'Impossible! The daughter of our highly correct ambassador? I remember him when I was a child, and he wore a hanging face even then, when he was not smiling diplomatic smiles.'

'I assure you, brother, it's true. As loose a young fish as I ever knew – and my experience has not been small, I flatter myself. God forbid I should speak so of a lady, but *la p'tite Boullen* is an accomplished harlot. I think she does it merely *par joyeuseté*, mind you – some women are like that. I have a name for her, you know – my *jument de louage anglaise*.'

'Your English mare. Because you've ridden her so many times?'

'Exactly.' Both monarchs laughed uproariously.

'But this,' said François, 'you may find out for yourself when she joins your court. I believe the chief gentlewoman of your fair consort has been instructed to add Mistress Boleyn to the number of the royal attendants – in a humble capacity, by her father's request. Emptying *vases de nuit*, perhaps? Sir Thomas would like that, being so incensed against her.'

Henry was thoughtful. His consort was anything but fair these days, poor lady, worn out with fruitless pregnancies, stout and frumpish, no longer the pretty girl he had married, still virgin though she was his brother's widow. His mistress Elizabeth Blount was unfortunately pregnant, near her time; he would have to send her away from Court and marry her off, to avoid embarrassment to himself. He was still young, only twenty-eight, the Plantagenet blood that mingled with the Tudor hot in his veins.

'Your English mare,' he said. 'What a good phrase. It reminds me so much of a scurrilous rhyme of ours about a wench in a bawdry-shop: "Ride, an you will, ten times a day, I warrant you she will never say you nay."' He translated for François' benefit.

'This young mare. She has no sign of the *morbus indecens*, the *nephandam infirmitatem*, has she?'

François was shocked. 'Holy St Denis, of course not. I would have no diseased persons about my court. Her only fault is a lack in her French vocabulary: the word *non*.'

The populace, watching them more than the tourney, thought how pleasant it was to see the great Kings of England and France so happy together.

'Good,' said Henry briskly. 'I shall take it most kindly if you will have her sent to me tonight, brother.'

Such was the story behind Mary Boleyn's return to England as the mistress of King Henry VIII.

12

Desire, your man, Madame

Anne was coming home.

Two years had passed since Mary had seen her, before she was packed off to England, her known disgrace mitigated by the quickly spread rumour that King Henry had taken a fancy to her. Two years as discreet concubine to Henry, ostensibly in the service of Queen Catherine, but with her own apartments, her own servants, so that all might be done without public offence to the Queen.

Until the evening when Mary had told the King that she was pregnant.

After his many disappointments over still-born or moribund infants she had thought that news of any coming child would be good news. She was shocked to see his face alter, the expression of genial lust wiped out as though by a visor slammed down. The small eyes contracted and the small mouth tightened: bad signs.

'A child?' (A hippogriff, a chimaera, a circus freak? implied his tone.)

'Yes. I am two months gone.'

He surveyed her figure critically. She was plumper than she had been, but still attractive. At two months the unborn thing might be shaken out of her by violent exercise – hunting over rough ground, for instance. But it was a remote chance. He strolled away from her, picking up objects here and there, a scent bottle, a pair of gloves, thinking, planning.

'I had thought you were more ... accomplished than to get trapped.'

Mary blushed. She knew all the devices of contraception, very necessary to know at the court of François. They were, unfortunately, not infallible. She murmured that she was sorry.

He smiled a pursy smile. 'Well, well. It seems that I am too much a man for such frail defence. Manhood will have its way, no gainsaying that.'

'If it is a boy, sir . . .' Mary was thinking of Henry's bastard by Bessie Blount, Henry Fitzroy, openly acknowledged by the King, and destined for great honours, though his mother had disappeared from the Court before his birth and had not been seen since. It was said that she was soon to be married.

Henry, too, was thinking of his former mistress. 'High time you were married, Mary. How old are you – seventeen, eighteen? Yes, high time. We will have to find a suitable gentleman for you. Meanwhile I think it better if you leave the Court before your happy state becomes visible. Let me see, your parents are now with us here at Baynard's Castle, I think. No doubt Lady Boleyn can be spared to accompany you back to Hever. You'll be pleased, no doubt. I remember how pleasantly snug that little place was, last time I hunted down there. Yes, I will have it arranged.' He turned to go, quite comfortable in his mind. He liked Mary, had even been quite in love with her once. She was the placid, docile, wifely type of woman, like Catherine in temperament, no arguments or silly floutings of his authority; not particularly stimulating, but sensual enough to keep him satisfied, trained as she had been by François and his attendant satyrs.

Mary dared to run after him, catching his arm. 'Please, no, sir!'

'No?'

'I mean – could I not stay a little longer, or . . . or go to one of the other palaces?' Seeing his expression blank, she burst out, 'I am not welcome at Hever.'

Henry was bored with the discussion. He was pleased to have secured himself another possible male heir, though a bastard one, to serve as a second string to Henry Fitzroy, since infants were fragile, as he knew only too well. When the girl was safely married and the child born, he would probably take her back, little Boleyn with the curves and the dimples, much like his wife had been when he married her, before she grew fat and painfully pious.

'Go where you will, but away from here,' he said, and left her.

She subsided onto a couch, trembling at the knees. Home was not home any more, neither Hever nor Blickling. Her father's wrath towards her had never abated, only cooled into a blank ignoring of her presence. It was clear to him that she had no effective power over the King, any more than if she had been one of the many wives of an eastern Sultan. She was just an accommodating whore whom the King had been gracious enough to elevate, always careful not to offend by her presence the godly wife whom he honoured so much, even though he now stayed away from her bed.

Sir Thomas was now Controller of the Royal Household, a very great man indeed, just slightly below the Lord High Treasurer in status. The Lord High Treasurer had, until retirement, been his father-in-law the Duke of Norfolk, and his brother Edward was a member of the King's household. Thomas was exceedingly rich. His wealth now included half the English lands of the Earldom of Ormonde, which numbered among them thirty-six manors. He knew that there were other riches and perquisites in store for him. He was not pleased to be known as the father of a whore.

Mary's mother followed where he led. Elizabeth Boleyn had grown hardened and somewhat embittered in her life at Court. Her beauty had faded, surviving now only in her slender body and the fine bones of her face, illuminated by her still handsome eyes, a paler brown than once they had been. She no longer thought of Mary as her pretty little daughter, once so precious, so missed; only as a fool who had let down the family reputation. The Norfolks treated Mary no more kindly: they were all only civil to her because to be otherwise would have been to insult the King.

Family hostility or not, there was no alternative for Mary but to
home. George, who was sympathetic and made no moral
was furthering his career at the court of the German
As she was unmarried, it would not be proper
herself.

So she went back to Hever, with her mother, who scarcely spoke to her, and there she waited miserably, growing ever larger, until she was summoned to London to marry Sir William Carey, Esquire to the Body, a knight from a modest Devonshire family. He was a personable, gentle young man, popular with the King because his behaviour was highly correct and he gave no trouble. He admired Mary, thought himself lucky to be getting a lovely well-connected young wife with the King's especial approval, and a ready-made child whose origins he did not question.

The child proved to be a girl. The King immediately lost all interest in it. Mary named it Catherine, after the Queen, who had never been anything but kind to her. Carey was fond of the carrot-haired baby who bore not the slightest resemblance to him or to Mary. He was neither censorious nor ambitious, and made Mary reasonably happy.

So they were at Hever, this February of 1522, Mary and baby Catherine and the infant's wet nurse and nursemaid, among other servants, waiting to greet her sister. Thomas was not there: he had not been at Mary's marriage either, but that was to show his disapproval, and now it was because he was detained in Greenwich on the King's business. He had escorted Anne back from France, and then proceeded from Dover to London.

A coach was rattling over the drawbridge, a dark beetle lumbering across the winter greys and whites of the landscape. The company assembled in the Great Hall stirred, exchanging glances and murmurs. Lady Margaret Boleyn, the girls' widowed grandmother, was there, massive and elderly, adoring her son while disapproving of almost everybody else on principle. She wore mourning black, heavy with marten fur. Elizabeth Boleyn was resplendent in a kirtle of dark crimson velvet over an underskirt of green brocade, many chains and jewelled bands encircling her neck to hide its folds and wrinkles, a touch of artificial colour in her now sallow cheeks. She had to compete with a daughter of fifteen. Mary wore her favourite blue beneath a heavy over-robe of lynx fur, rather shabby. Her husband was not rich, the King had given her no presents since she had left Court. She was a little ashamed of her figure, still very plump since the baby's birth. She sat very quietly, not drawing attention to herself.

The steward of the castle appeared at the door. 'Mistress Anne, if you please, my lady,' he announced to the company in general.

In the doorway stood a vision. Not a heavenly one, for it was clad in the height of fashion and superb style. Mary had a swift impression of velvets, darkest mulberry and black, embroidered work glittering with points of jewelled light: but all muted, almost sombre, so that one saw the wearer, not the clothes. Mary did not know that she gasped aloud, or that her mother did the same.

The thin child she remembered had turned into a tall young woman, slender, graceful in her least movement. It was said of her that she walked as others danced. Her complexion was like ivory, with little colour in it, yet glowing with youth and health; her mouth a rose.

But all else was eclipsed by her eyes. Such eyes, dark as the eyes of the Howards, huge and lustrous, slightly slanting, the eyes of a lovely doe in a woman's face. They drove men wild with love – had already inspired numberless songs and sonnets. A poet of François's court had tried to describe them but found his vocabulary inadequate: 'Those alluring eyes . . . she knew the right time to keep them still. At other times they would send out a message of secret meaning from her very heart; such was their potency that all must obey their commands. The power, the force of those eyes . . .' He gave up, he was only a poor scribbler, mad about her like all the men, even his King.

Elizabeth's heart felt a strange sharp pang, part simple jealousy, part love and pride. 'My mother.' Anne went to her side, and was taken into an embrace Elizabeth did not often bestow nowadays. Lady Margaret smiled benignly on this granddaughter who bid fair to fulfil all the Boleyn hopes. Mary jumped up to enfold Anne tightly and give her the triple kiss of greeting customary in France, one on the mouth, one on each cheek. Anne's cheeks were cold from the February air, like winter roses.

When she spoke it was not in the voice they remembered. For almost eight years she had spoken nothing but French, so that the rhythms of her speech and her intonations were purely French, lending an exotic charm to everything she said.

'Oh, I'm glad to be home! But how small everything is – *une petite cabane* . . . no, I must speak English, my father says.'

'It must seem so to you, after those châteaux.' Elizabeth could not keep a tinge of tartness out of her voice. 'But Hever can still provide comforts. You must be cold, child, and hungry.'

Anne was at the fire, warming her hands. 'Both, madam, though we took some hot cordial last time we changed horses. How well you all look! *Madame grandmère*, you are younger than when I saw you – ah, how many years ago.'

Lady Margaret shook her head, but preened herself. 'You've brought a flattering tongue back from France, I hear.'

'And my mother, not changed at all – what magnificent *colliers* . . . I mean chains for the neck – you'll have to correct me. Mary, you're quite a matron, but it becomes you. How is your little boy? *Excusez-moi*. I mean girl.'

The day, the evening, raced past in conversation, laughter, admiration of Anne's clothes and rapt attention to her stories. She selected them carefully, giving her family a heavily edited version of the cheerful amorality of François's court and the scandalous conduct of almost everybody in it. They heard a lot about Queen Claude, her extreme piety and sobriety of life, and the strict régime she imposed on the young ladies in her care; all tinged with not unkind mockery.

'It was really most like being a novice nun, always at Mass or at the weaving loom. You would not believe the intricacy of my *broderie* now – I must have embroidered the image of every saint in the calendar and enough altar cloths to cover all the plains of France, not to mention an archbishop's cope. As for prayers, we said them at all hours of the day and night, we said them in our sleep.'

'This man Luther.' Lady Margaret spoke up sharply. 'I hope no taint of his vile heresies reached the court.'

'Martin Luther the monk?' Anne's tone was limpid with innocence. 'There was talk of him. The King said that he and all who listened to him should be burned.' She omitted to add that the King's sister Marguerite, with her passionate interest in dogma and mysticism, had listened very closely to stories of the monk who had questioned the doctrines of the Catholic Church, and had thrown open the dangerous subject to those about her. It was possible, Marguerite said, according to Luther's belief, that indulgences bought with money could not save souls from Purgatory, possible that God did not save or damn the sinner according to his merits, possible that the soul did not leave the body at the moment of death and fly out of the window.

Anne also omitted to add that she, sharply intelligent and an expert at listening to what others were saying, was interested in Luther's strange, shocking theories. She chattered and laughed, gestured with her lovely hands (why was her 'extra nail' not noticeable any more? But of course, because of the long, billowing inner sleeves she wore, which hid the little fingers of each hand) and in general made her listeners see her exactly as she wished.

And they, three worldly-wise females, hung on her words and took her in with their eyes, and were dazzled and charmed.

When bedtime came Anne dismissed the two maids she had brought with her, after they had unpinned her. She stood in her smock, like a tall white candle, her hair now freed from the gabled French hood edged with pearls. It was coiled in plaits all round the back of her head, secured with pins of ivory. Sitting on a stool before a mirror, she gestured to Mary, who moved behind her like a trained servant and began to take out the pins and untwine the braids.

The hair lay all about her, covering her like a black waterfall, rippling below her waist. It had always been long in her childhood, but now it had acquired a lustre, a shining, from fine brushes, costly oils and good nourishment. Mary brushed it now, watching Anne's eyes close and her head go back on the long graceful neck, as a cat relaxes when stroked under the chin.

As Mary touched her, lifting the hair away from white shoulders, moving it away from the high forehead, the conviction came to her that her sister was still a virgin. On impulse, she blurted out a question. The eyes opened, pools of dark light reflecting points of candle flame.

'Yes.' The word was almost a sigh. 'Many men loved me *à la frénésie*. Some offered to die for me, and one tried it. But his hand was too unsure, or the knife was too blunt.' She drew a finger across her throat. 'I was not impressed. I was promised treasures, but there is one treasure a woman has already and must not lose – except to a husband. So our father taught us. Yet you gave yours away.'

'Yes.'

'I remember, though I was only a child and they kept the gossip quiet in my hearing. Then, later, I heard it all. Were you not a little foolish, Mary?'

'I was a complete fool,' Mary said bitterly. 'I know it now, but what use is that? At least it got me back to England, and I was never happy in France.'

'Were you not? I was. In a fashion. It taught me so much. . . . So. What is King Henry like as a lover?'

'He . . . what can I say?' What dare I say, more like, for any words critical of the King had a way of getting back to him and provoking one of those rages which lasted a short time but were terrible. It would not be safe to tell anyone, even her sister, that for all his impressive size and ruddy good looks he was not as virile as the Frenchmen she had known, nor as sensual nor skilled in performance. He was an ardent wooer but, the prey once caught, a prosaic enough lover who might as well have been a mere husband.

'He's most kind,' she said. 'Full of thought for me. It wasn't my wish to bear a child and lose my place at Court, and he understood that and permitted me to, er . . .'

'What a mealy-mouthed little *mijaurée* you are. I know perfectly well what you mean. Yes, I should think he is kind. I remember how well he behaved to his sister when she married Suffolk so rashly. Another king might have had Suffolk's head for it. He is too chivalrous to injure a woman. And now you're safely married – do you like that?'

'William is very kind, as well.'

Anne laughed, her own ringing laugh. 'How fortunate, to be surrounded by kind men. And you're still in the King's favour?'

'As far as I know. In the spring I'm to return to Court. I'm glad. I hate Hever now. Our mother has taken against me, our grand-mother says the Howard blood in my veins has turned to sour ale, and our father hates me. How glad I am to have you back, Nan! You seem so much older and wiser than I am, for all the three years between us.'

Anne patted her hand lightly, turning to view her own reflection in the mirror. She was not perhaps strictly beautiful: her nose was a shade large, with an unfashionable slight tilt to the tip, and of course there was still that hideous mole. She had been given a pearl collar by the kindly Queen Claude, four rows of pearls linked with gold which quite hid the deformity. In any case it seemed smaller than it had been.

And her eyes would make up for all. What a wise virgin she had been: and was.

On a fine crisp morning a few days later Thomas Wyatt and his sister Margaret rode the twenty-odd miles from Allington to Hever. Tom was eighteen, the oldest of the young people, married two years, the father of a one-year-old son. Margaret was fifteen, the same age as Anne, a pretty, gentle-natured creature, very much her brother's sister. The children who had played together before the departure of Mary and Anne for France were met, all grown and changed.

The susceptible Mary thought Tom very much improved. He was a budding courtier now, Cambridge-educated, tall, slender, brown-eyed and with the beginnings of what would be a fine brown beard. His voice was soft, deep and pleasant, his manner modest. Like Margaret, he seemed more of the country than of the town.

Mary thought, with a half-jealous dart of pain, that watching Tom's reunion with Anne was like watching a man take a bullet in the heart and fall, mortally wounded. His face flushed, then paled, as he confronted the beauty who had once been the child Anne. Margaret, after one startled look, clasped her friend in a warm embrace. But Tom dropped to one knee and kissed Anne's fingers. She took the kiss like a queen.

Anne would remember that day, the day when she first knew that she had power in England. How they talked, the four of them. Mary had been to Hever so seldom of recent years. Baby Catherine was admired, no comment made about her red hair and fiery blue eyes. 'She has the temper I used to have, you remember,' Anne said. 'I am *si calme maintenant, si douce*. And I *will* remember not to speak French.' She took very little interest in the baby.

But Margaret adored it, laughed fondly when it roared with anger and bunched up its tiny fists against her. 'I should like to be a nursemaid. Why was I not born to it?'

Yes, she was betrothed, to young Anthony Lee of Cheshire, and she might before too long have babies of her own. She tried not to sigh, for she had an old fancy for George Boleyn. But George was to marry Jane Parker, daughter of Lord Morley, King Henry's Gentleman-Usher – if Lord Morley could raise the enormous dowry Thomas Boleyn was demanding. Margaret could see a bright shadow of George in Anne, and had conceived a marvellously girlish hero-heroine worship for her, at the instant of meeting.

Anne would always remember Tom Wyatt's love-struck face that day. She was used enough to infatuated young Frenchmen, but here was an infatuated young Englishman who would take love seriously: if he said he was going to kill himself for her sake he would probably do it.

She asked him, lightly, about his family. Elizabeth was very well, he thanked her, and the baby, another Thomas. His father was very well too, acting as Treasurer of the Chamber, and high in the King's favour. His father thought him, Tom, too extravagant, positively wasteful. And yes, of course Elizabeth would ride over to Hever herself one day, while Mistress Anne was still there. He had no idea whether Solomon's Tower was still haunted, but on the whole thought it was a foolish story some nurse had put about. Yes, the black pigeons were still at Allington.

'*Black* pigeons?' Margaret interrupted. 'You mean brown, Tom. Whoever saw a black pigeon?'

Tom corrected himself. The word black filled his mind. Throughout dinner, throughout the conversation, he had been gazing at Anne's eyes, wondering how it could be that their pupils sometimes appeared to fill the whole of the iris, yet by another trick of light the black-seeming surround turned to a lovely velvet-brown, the colour of a humble-bee's furry body. And her hair – a long plaited loop escaped the gabled hood – that sometimes appeared to have a raven's wing blue-black sheen, at others to glow like dark copper. She was a palette for God's own use in His painting.

At some time, when dusk was falling and candles were lighted, the lutes were brought and they sang, as everyone did when company gathered. Old songs, songs they had always known.

> My Robin is to the greenwood gone,
> My Robin has left me all alone . . .
> Bonnie sweet Robin is all my joy.

And 'Lamkin' and other country stuff, which Anne at first affected not to remember. Tom sang to the lute some verses of his own, very melancholy and full of repetitions, at which Anne most elegantly pretended to yawn. She took the lute from him and picked out a tune, no less melancholy than his. Her voice was trained and strong, a pure soprano.

> *Gentilz gallans de France,*
> *Qui en la guerre allez,*
> *Je vous prie qu'il vous plaise,*
> *Mon amy saluer.*
>
> *Comment le saluroye*
> *Quant point ne le congrois?*
> *Il est bon a congnoistre,*
> *Il est de blanc armé . . .*

'No, no,' said Margaret. 'Those are foreign words, you should sing the right ones. Thus:

> As you came from the holy land
>   of Walsingham,
> Saw you not my true love,
>   On your way as you came?
>
> How should I your true love know
>   From another one?
> By his cockle hat and staff,
>   And his sandal shoon.

Anne bent her head to her lute, rippling her fingers across the strings. Tom gazed and gazed at the picture she made, the long white neck that seemed too slender to support the weight of the small hooded head, the glimpse of her young breasts where the lacy line of her partlet crossed them, the lowered eyelids and long dark lashes on pale cheeks.

'I remember now,' she said. Without lifting her head she sang almost under her breath:

> He is dead and gone, lady,
>   He is dead and gone,
> At his head a grass-green turf,
>   At his heels – a stone.

Then she looked up. Tom met the full force of her eyes, and saw in their dark starry depths knowledge of her own power over him, pity for his captive state, response to him as a comely man.

A long shudder went through him. For as long as he lived, twenty more years, that tune, and the name of Walsingham, would always have the power for a second's space to still the beating of his heart.

FOUR

TOM WYATT'S NARRATIVE

This book abroad is sent
To tell men how in youth I did assay
What love did mean . . .

1522

Brunet, that did set our country in a
roar . . .

Sir Thomas Wyatt

Venus estoit blonde, l'on m'a dit:
L'on voist ben qu'elle est brunette.

Venus is blonde, they tell me: yet
It's plain to see that she's brunette.

Le Roi François I

13

Beauty

'I will not marry him,' said Anne.

My heart gave a great leap. Perhaps there was a chance for me, after all my despair. I had been struck with love for her at Hever. When she appeared at Court that February day, it had been to me as though high summer from some foreign land had suddenly transformed our grey cold climate with glowing sun and the warm perfume of spices, intoxicating my senses, making me faint and languid with love. My eyes were dazzled by her bright beauty, my ears enchanted with her speech which was like quick music. I could have fallen at her little feet and kissed them, like any slave.

Then it was told to me that by the King's decree and Wolsey's she had been destined to marry her cousin, James Butler, heir to the Earldom of Ormonde and its much-disputed riches. He was a cousin of the Boleyns. I knew him slightly and had thought him an inoffensive fellow, but now I hated him bitterly.

'How could you go against the King's wishes – and your father's?' I asked her.

She shrugged. 'Nobody can make me marry him if I don't wish to. Even if they dragged me on a hurdle to the altar I should shut my lips tight and refuse to make the vows. So!' She made a thin line of her lovely mouth, and I turned weak with love.

'What ails this Butler?' I asked. 'He is not old or deformed, is he?'

'Older than you – twenty-four perhaps, how should I know? And straight enough. But his hair is foxy and I like a dark man.'

I stroked my beard, which was becoming satisfactorily thick.

'And his voice! So barbarous, like the whine of a bagpipe. How can he still talk so, when he grew up in England and knows perfectly well how to speak properly? Besides, I should have to go and live in Ireland, where the savages fight like wild cats and go about half-naked. Our Lady only knows if they're even Christians!' She gave a pretty, affected shudder. 'I should die, die utterly. So you see, Tom, the marriage is impossible. Besides . . .'

'Besides?'

'Nothing. I forgot what I was going to say.' It was not a blush that came over Anne's cheeks, for she never blushed, but a faint tinge of rose in their creamy hue. My heart leapt again. Could it be that she felt a kindness, or more than a kindness, for me? If so, my future was a paradise of unimaginable happiness. I truly believe that in that moment of hope I forgot the existence of my wife Elizabeth.

There was a banquet at the Palace of Greenwich that night, in honour of the ambassadors of England's ally, the Emperor Charles V, visiting the King on their way to Spain. Up the river they came, in splendid painted royal barges, dark suave men who had mastered enough English to mingle at Court without embarrassment. Queen Catherine was delighted to greet her countrymen and speak a little Spanish to them. Wrapped up warmly against the chill air, she watched with pleasure the jousting in the new tiltyard, a fine spacious arena with a viewing tower, many-windowed, where ladies could sit in comfort. In summer there would be a pavilion built for them. I saw Anne, now appointed one of the Queen's ladies, demurely inconspicuous, as far as she could ever be inconspicuous. She wore a hood deeply edged with fur, and I, mad, besotted boy that I was, envied the dead animal whose skin touched hers.

The King took part in the jousting, an immense figure in silver armour on a silver-draped horse, carrying a shield whose blazon was a bleeding heart and the motto *Elle mon coeur a navera*, 'she has wounded my heart'. It must be in compliment to his Queen, whom he always honoured at tournaments in the old style, wearing a favour of hers in his helm and dipping his lance in salutation before her.

Odd, though, that love-wounded motto, at their stage of marriage. He was thirty-one and she thirty-seven, looking ten years older than her age, no longer a knight's ideal Queen of Love and Beauty, poor lady. Could someone else have wounded his heart? (Though it would have been highly unchivalrous to advertise the fact.) Bessie Blount's day was over, except as the mother of the King's bastard son, and Mary Carey, though known still to be his mistress, was hardly a new enslaver. It did not occur to me for one moment that Anne might have charmed him, and indeed I am sure that it was not so, at that time. Perhaps he had a secret light o' love. He always saw himself as a boy looking for romantic adventures.

Two days later the Master of the Revels surpassed himself with a second banquet given at York Place, close to Westminster, the magnificent palace of Cardinal Wolsey, Lord Chancellor, Archbishop of York, the most powerful man in England after the King.

The banquet was held in the Cardinal's presence chamber, where he sat apart under a canopy of purple and gold, the Cloth of Estate. Many tables, put together end to end to form one long table, ranged along one side of the chamber, the King seated at a separate one beside the Queen, and at the long table a lady next to a gentleman, then another lady, and so on, making conversation easy and pleasant. I gazed at Anne so long and intently that the food went cold on the gold plate before me. James Butler sat next to her, chatting away in his garrulous Irish fashion, but she seemed to answer little, giving her smiles to a man on her other side, nobody I knew. At a point quite early in the banquet she rose and flitted away, as did many more ladies.

I was composing a poem in my head, so that I hardly noticed when a herald with a silver trumpet summoned the whole assembly to remove to another place. But I did notice, as I followed the others, that the King left first, with his gentlemen, briskly, as though he was concerned in the entertainment which we all knew would follow.

We were used to magnificence; but the sight of the Cardinal's Great Hall brought from us gasps of wonder. It was ablaze with light from countless wax candles, which brought to life the figures in the great wall tapestries. Half the huge room was taken up by a mock castle, brilliant green as though made of emeralds, with battlemented towers.

On the battlements were grouped what looked like angels: ladies in gowns of white satin spangled with gold, each with a headdress of Venice gold set with jewels, and round it her name written – the Virtues, Mercy, Pity, Honour, Kindness and so on. The Countess of Suffolk, still known as the French Queen, was Honour, Mary Carey was Kindness, and Jane Parker, George Boleyn's affianced, was Pity, which attribute fitted her sharpness very ill. Anne was Beauty. On the ground at the castle's foot were other ladies, dressed in bright barbaric colours and crowned with black velvet, their complexions darkened to seem like Indians: they were the Vices, Unkindness, Scorn, Jealousy, Disdain, Danger, Strangeness, and Malebouche (which I suppose meant Gossip or Slander). My sister Margaret was one of these far from evil-looking Indians.

Music floated from the castle, the Cardinal's boys of the chapel singing, and instruments playing. Then, out of sight, a trumpet and drum sounded, and the shouting of men; and there entered a great cloaked figure all in crimson, rivalling the scarlet figure of the watching Cardinal, with eight blue-clad knights behind him. Round his masked head was written 'Ardent Desire'.

Well, so there was a mock siege, the knights flinging dates and oranges at the castle, the Indians hurling back sugar plums and rosewater, and everybody laughing, until the Indians were vanquished and the angels plucked from the battlements to be carried off by the knights. Beauty was the prize of Ardent Desire, the King, of course, but it seemed to me that several struggled with him for her possession. Then there was unmasking and dancing, the rest joining in until the floor was full of leaping figures.

I stayed out of it, having no great hopes of getting Anne to myself. James Butler was not dancing either – I saw him talking animatedly to a group of young men, all drinking ale. How could he not be at her side constantly, wooing her?

Somebody was at her side: the King, jumping and twirling like a monstrous flame, sometimes taking her hand, holding it as she leapt too, holding her waist with his own huge hand, which almost spanned it. I saw him glancing down from his great height, summing her up, almost weighing and measuring her, wearing his small smile which somehow was not merry. But why should he not? She was new to Court, he had hardly seen her as yet.

There was a little stir, a rustle as the ladies curtseyed to the Queen, who was leaving. I had noticed her, not watching the dancing but leaning back in her high carved chair, her eyes half shut and her lips moving slightly, as though she were silently praying. She was pale, puffy, and frog-like in her gown of unbecoming tawny yellow. Everyone knew that she wore underneath it the harsh shift of the Third Order of St Francis. She would have been happier as a nun, surely. Yet they said that she loved the King, had borne all those dead infants most willingly for his sake . . .

Anne had coquetted with him. It meant nothing, but I asked her next day how she liked him, afraid to hear that she found his size and air of power alluring.

'*Liked* him? As a good subject should, I imagine. I hope you're not a troublemaker, Tom. One should never criticise the monarch.'

'I meant as a man.'

'Oh, as a man. Come aside.' She drew me close to the wall, laying a finger on her lips and making exaggerated signs of caution. 'Since you ask,' she whispered, 'I think he has the neck of a bull and the eyes of a boar. His dewlaps hang like a bull's, too, and he sweats like one, though the scent of rosewater struggles to disguise it. His cheeks always seem full of something, as though he chewed the cud, and his belly would hang if it were not held in. And he squeaks like a piglet. The man's a walking bestiary.'

'Anne!'

'You asked. Besides, he's so old, twice my age, think of that. How he manages to leap so high in the Lavolta I wonder at, truly.

But there, he spoke to me courteously enough, and I think he is kind. After all, bulls can be gentle with ladies – think of Europa.' She broke into a chime of giggles and ran off.

I thought of Europa. In legend she was a princess of Phoenicia whom Zeus, disguised as a bull, had carried off to Crete and there sired three sons on her. It was an unpleasant comparison, because so close. Anne had been indiscreetly right about the King's appearance, and his obsessive desire was to sire bull-calves, so to speak. I was as loyal a King's man as my father, ready to die in his defence, yet I could not trust him with my jewel.

It was in the late spring when Anne was summoned to Framlingham Castle, where her grandfather the Duke of Norfolk lived in retirement. His other grandchildren were there. He was seventy-eight years old, in good health for his great age, but he had suffered a sudden illness which frightened him enough to want all his family around him.

Anne was serious, for her, when she returned.

'He'll recover soon, I think. It pleased him to see us, and he made much of me. Agnes was kind, too, though she was once always sneaping and sniping at me. She gave me a gold lace partlet – see. But Tom, do you know why he left Court and went to Framlingham, last year?'

'Not I. I was at Allington.'

'Of course. I forgot you were so young a courtier. Well, it seems that when the King came back from the Field of the Cloth of Gold he ordered the Duke of Buckingham's arrest on a charge of high treason.'

I had heard of that in my country exile, and been shocked, as everybody was. The High Constable of England, with royal blood in his veins, the noble Edward Stafford, condemned on trivial charges: he had listened to astrologers who prophesied that he would be King one day; he had said what a pity it was that he had not had Wolsey's head chopped off, when he had the chance, in the late King's reign. And he had boasted that if he were sent to the

Tower, his friends would raise ten thousand men at once to free him.

He had gone to the Tower, and not one man had risen to free him.

'He was Wolsey's enemy,' Anne said, 'and it was put about that the Cardinal wanted him out of the way. But my grandfather told us it was a secret design on the King's part, because Buckingham had so much wealth and his manors would be forfeit.'

'I know. He was Lord of Penshurst, by Allington. I remember him entertaining the King there.'

'It seems the King's memory was short, then, because it was he who conducted the Duke's trial, and got out of the witnesses all these silly stories. My grandfather was presiding as Lord High Steward, so it was he who had to give the sentence of attainder and death, and he Buckingham's best friend, for thirty years. He wept, Tom, so much that he could hardly get the words out. It was after the Duke's head was off (did you know it took three strokes of the axe? Horrible!) that my grandfather resigned all his Court appointments and went home to Framlingham. "It broke my heart and spirit," he told us.'

'Your grandfather is a very old man, easily upset.'

'You would not say that if you knew him as well as I do. Your face tells me you think I'm being indiscreet. Am I?'

I kissed her hand. 'A little. The thing's over and done with. Since you find the King kind, speak of him kindly. Diplomacy should be in your blood, with your father climbing so high.' Sir Thomas had just been raised from Comptroller of the Royal Household to Treasurer.

Anne was thoughtful. I liked to see her so, quiet, her dark fires banked. 'Yes,' she said. 'It must be in Mary's blood, too, since the King has taken her back into favour. She has her own apartments and servants again, while we poor lesser ladies dine at mess on mutton and ale.'

'Then mutton and ale must be Beauty's own food. How goes . . . Sir James's suit?'

She made a *moue* of disgust. 'That barbarian! He thinks his suit so secure that he takes no trouble to woo. Do you know, I believe he cares for nothing but horses. He talks horses, he spends his days with horses, and his nights for all I know. He smells of horses. He even looks like one, with his long face, *un alezan*.'

'Have you told your father yet that you don't wish to marry a chestnut horse?'

Anne looked sideways. 'Not precisely told him, no. He listens to my mother, and my mother listens to my grandmother, who was herself a Butler. So I say little and keep out of this *alezan*'s way. I would hardly even call him a stallion, more a *cheval hongre*.'

A gelding: the man who was incredibly fortunate enough to be betrothed to Anne allowed her to think of him as a gelding. He must be demented.

If Butler spent his nights in the stable, I spent mine in my chamber, writing verses and more verses, all of Anne and my passionate love for her. When I pressed her to walk alone with me and kissed her, she reminded me gently that I was married, the father of two children. I knew it but too well.

What did I expect of her? She was a maid, warned by her sister's example to guard her virtue. I could never marry her, even though Elizabeth and I were ill matched; my wife and I had never cared much for each other. I rued the day I had ridden to Cobham Hall with my father and been to pay my addresses to Lord Cobham's daughter. I hated the richly carved bed we lay in when I was at home, and the round tower bedchamber that held us, as cold as our feelings for each other. In my mooning infatuation, I would sometimes sit in the Long Gallery at Allington, trying to see a figure from the past who had been there, a thin dark child who had wished for a dress all covered with pearls. I had adored her then: I adored her now, fool that I was. It was hopeless. Yet I hoped.

I hoped until the day, late in that beautiful May of 1522, when Wolsey and his train of attendants came to dine at Greenwich with the King. Anne was there, waiting upon the Queen. I watched her avidly, as always. When the meal was done she did not come to talk with me, as she often did. She was in conversation with a young man I had not seen before.

He was tall, so tall that he stooped slightly, not handsome, long-nosed, pale, with a soft gingery beard, not so luxuriant as my own. She had said she disliked men of a foxy colour. Yet she was looking up at him as though she liked him a great deal, her face alive with excitement and pleasure. She seemed to be the one who talked, while he listened with a smile, occasionally nodding his head. He was nothing to look at, seemed to have no wit: yet Anne's face . . .

I asked someone who he was.

'Young Harry Percy, Northumberland's son. New in the Cardinal's household.'

Ah, God. That encounter boded no good for me. I had been to Mass that morning, St Dunstan's Day. I had prayed to the saint for myself. If I had known what his day would bring me, in years to come, I would have run to the Chapel Royal and crawled like a worm before the altar.

14

Thanked be God it hath been otherwise

I should have laughed, if I had been of a laughing disposition, to think that in the years to come they would accuse Anne of being a witch. If any spell had been woven, it was by young Percy upon her, and a more unlikely-looking warlock was never seen. When I came to know him I was bewildered that she could even waste a minute on him. He seemed more a boy than a man, stammered slightly, with a strange accent of the North, his *r*s sounding like *w*s, his vowels twisted and tortured, and he had neither wit nor light conversation.

The only advantage that I could see in him was that he was heir to the powerful Earl of Northumberland. If Anne married him she would be the lady of vast estates, lands in both the north and the south over which the lion of the Percys roared. Anne would be a countess without peer.

I sought out her sister Mary Carey. She was, as ever, cautious. Women did not please the King by being loud-mouthed.

'I doubt if Nan has even thought about the title,' she told me.

'But your father must have done – many times.'

Mary looked down, twisting her rings. 'Our father knows nothing of it. He sees young men around her, admiring her – not any particular young men.'

'But he would surely approve?'

'He wants the Ormonde title – and the Ormonde money.'

'Why not the Percy title, and the Percy money?'

'Father is curiously obstinate. He thinks of a thing, and that thing he must have.'

'But the Percy lands – Alnwick, Wressel, Leconfield – and how many others? He'll be a Croesus when his father dies.'

'His father was very well when I last heard of him, and of a violent temper. This Harry is quite otherwise, a gentle, sweet young man. Nan likes that. She needs velvet to set off her own diamond nature – Lord, how poetic I grow. Harry Percy is poetic, too, and loves books and learning. So does Nan, because she moulds herself on La Marguerite; and she longs to have a castle in the north. Our mother used to tell us tales of Sheriff Hutton, where she grew up when Grandfather Norfolk was Lieutenant. It sounded so grand to us, living simply at Hever. So you see, those two are perfectly matched.'

'Does anyone who matters know of this perfect match, Mary? The King, or the Cardinal?'

'They know what they can see with their own eyes.'

That was all I could get out of Lady Carey. She was concerned to keep herself, her husband and her infant daughter out of trouble, now that she could no longer depend on her father to defend her, and she would say nothing compromising to anyone dear to her.

I understood that Anne and Harry Percy might well escape notice in that Court, where wooing and mock-wooing was as popular a game as card playing, a Court of Cupid as the French one was the Court of Priapus. I had joined in the game once, and was jokingly called Anne's Knight of the Bleeding Heart, but now I stayed outside the circle. Gloomily I watched as those two sat close, touched hands and knees, gazed into each other's eyes, and generally behaved like fools. My brilliant, sophisticated Anne, so young yet so polished in manners and accomplishments, behaving like a milkmaid with a farm-hand – which Percy could well have been.

I came upon her once alone, and was goaded by my jealousy to speak.

'Your rustic swain is otherwise occupied? How remiss of him.'

'Satire doesn't become you, Tom. I know how you dislike Harry.

181

You may as well save your pains, since we're heart in heart, and ever will be.'

'Heartfast but not handfast. I hope you know he's pre-contracted to Shrewsbury's daughter, Lady Mary Talbot?'

'What kind of ninny do you take me for? Of course I know. It was done six years ago, to ally Harry to the Dacre family who rule half the north and guard the Border – but never mind that. Harry detests the girl. He has renounced her and pledged himself to me, just as I have renounced Butler. All is settled. I shall be Lady Percy. We will live at Wressell Castle, where Harry grew up; it looks onto a river, as Greenwich does, and there's a fine chamber in it called Paradise, with shelves along every wall to hold nothing but books. Imagine that! And verses painted in scrolls. I shall have one painted saying *Amor vincit Omnia*.'

She was sewing industriously at a sampler, working the golden wings of a bee in her exquisitely tiny stitches, calm and composed as though she were already a matron, Percy's wife. I felt as though the needle were piercing my heart at every stitch. With a sudden cruel impulse I wished that it might pierce her as well; and at that moment it did, the sharp point bringing a drop of blood that fell on her sampler. She cried out, putting her finger to her mouth.

'Now the Queen will scold me! Blood is so hard to wash out. Fetch me some water, Tom, and a cloth, quickly.'

I called a passing servant and told her to do Anne's bidding. Now I was bitterly remorseful, sure that my ill-wish had caused the accident, feeling her pain. I began to apologise, but she shook her head impatiently and went on sewing at a blossom inches away from the blood-spoiled bee.

'Anne,' I blurted out, 'have pity on me! If he is gentle and book-learned, so am I, surely, and I loved you so long ago, and you showed me kindness until he came. I'm dying for you – do you know that? I have no pleasure in my life any more. Yet for a silly fancy –'

'It is not a fancy.'

'Call it what you like. Your father will be against the match, and

182

so will the King and Wolsey. I know their minds better than you do, raw though I am at Court. Listen to me, Anne!'

She laid down her needle and looked at me, unsmiling.

'Who are you to talk about pre-contracts – you, a married man and a father? You would have dishonoured me, if I had let you. Harry means honestly, Mary Talbot or no Mary Talbot. The Devil may take her for all we care, we are vowed to each other.'

'Before a justice or a priest?'

'Before witnesses. Friends, who know our intent. As for the King, he is kind and sympathetic to lovers. I was there, in France, when his sister married Suffolk, and he forgave them. So he'll forgive us. As for Wolsey, surely a king has more power than a cardinal? I will tell the King myself how greatly Harry and I love each other, how he is the only husband for me, and if my father chooses to cast me off as he cast Mary, why then it's a pity, but we shall live. Whereas if they forbid me to marry my love, then we shall both die of grief, and no one will have any joy of the matter.'

I began to argue, but she flashed out, 'Oh, go away from me. You talk, and all to no purpose.'

Now I believed her. I went away, into a secluded arbour by the river, where my tears would not be seen. For I confess I was not ashamed to weep. I was only nineteen. Then, as always, I began to scribble, as though writing down my grief were like letting blood from a diseased body.

> She sat and sewed, that hath done me the wrong
> Whereof I plain and have done many a day . . .
> And as she thought 'This is his heart indeed',
> She prickèd hard, and made herself to bleed.

Fool.

What followed next I was not witness to. Those who were, lost no time in spreading it abroad. I heard various versions, but this seems to be what happened.

Anne and Percy had met together in one of their accustomed

places, a parlour off the Queen's anteroom. There, by mischance, Anne's father had come to find his daughter, and found her indeed, locked in Percy's arms.

He heard Anne's explanation, made, charmingly, on her knees, Percy pulled down to kneel beside her, hand in hand, like a bridal couple before the priest. Sir Thomas said not a word in answer, but strode away to demand an immediate audience of the King.

'The King was much offended.' Those mild words are a pale shadow of the red wrath which was King Henry's rage. It flooded over Sir Thomas like a fiery torrent. How could he have allowed his daughter to commit such a folly, to have gone against his express wishes and betrothed herself to Percy, when he himself had designed another match for her? (Curiously enough, he did not name James Butler.)

Thomas Boleyn protested that it was none of his doing, he knew nothing of it, he would reprove the girl soundly. The King silenced him with a bellow and ordered him to summon Cardinal Wolsey, if he was still about the palace. Sir Thomas ran like a hare before the hounds.

Among the Cardinal's train there was a young man called George Cavendish, his Gentleman-Usher, devoted to his master, anxious to lose no word Wolsey spoke: people said that as soon as he had bowed himself out of the Presence he hurried to write down all that the Cardinal had said. He repeated it, too, unless any particular secrecy was demanded of him, and in this case there was none.

The King deputed the Cardinal to handle the matter. The wretched boy belonged to his household, and it was below royal dignity to deal with such things. What else he said to Wolsey, Cavendish failed to report: perhaps he did not know it – then. Perhaps he was dismissed before it was spoken.

At York Place Wolsey summoned Percy, and harangued him, not in private as might have been expected, but before a room full of attendants: the better to humiliate the boy. So far as I heard, the lecture went something like this (picture Wolsey in his scarlet robes, seated in state, on a throne raised three steps from the ground, his heavy jowls nestling in the folds of his cassock, his fat face like an angry sun):

'You – boy. I am amazed, utterly amazed, to hear of this peevish folly of yours, to tangle yourself up with that silly girl at Court. I mean Anne Boleyn, as you well know. Have you not considered the estate to which God has called you in this world? After the death of your noble father, you will be the inheritor of one of the greatest earldoms in this realm.

'I would have expected you, therefore, at least to have asked your father's consent, and to have informed the King, begging for his favour and advancement in the matter. But by your wilfulness, see what you have done. Not only have you offended your father, but also your most gracious sovereign lord, by allying yourself with a girl of whom neither can be expected to approve.'

Percy began to stammer, but Wolsey cut in. 'I tell you now, beyond question, that I shall send for your father, who will either break this rash contract or disinherit you. His Grace will demand this of your father – for he had purposed to match Mistress Boleyn with another person, and had almost reached the point of doing so. Had this gone forward it would have pleased her greatly, I have no doubt.'

Percy burst into tears. Fighting with his stutter, he got out that he was very sorry, that he thought he was old enough to choose a wife for himself, that he had expected his father to make no objection. That though Anne was only a simple maid, a knight's daughter, yet she came of noble stock, of the Norfolk blood on one side and the Earl of Ormonde's line on the other. She was equal in descent to himself, in fact. That being so, he most humbly pleaded for the Cardinal's kind intercession with the King.

Wolsey had been tapping his foot. Now he answered, and not kindly. 'You think the King and I know nothing of our business, boy? Yes, I see you do. Very well. I will send for your father from the north, and we shall act as His Grace the King thinks best. Meanwhile, I charge you in the King's name to avoid Mistress Boleyn's company, or put yourself in peril of his great wrath.'

Percy was in no better position than a fox with the hounds baying round him. My heart bled for the lad when I heard the Earl had promptly come down from the north and descended upon his son like Jupiter from a cloud. He roared, he bellowed, he tore young Percy's pride to tatters, he threatened disinheritance – 'for I have more choice of boys than such a proud, presumptuous, disdainful, unthrifty waster as you, a prodigal, who would cast away all the riches and honours your progenitors have gathered.'

And so on, until the boy's resistance was utterly quelled and he could fight no longer. He gave in. He would marry Lady Mary Talbot: his promise to Anne was cancelled. He would be in all things as his father, Wolsey and the King desired. He would go home to the north.

In that hour, a man was broken as once men were broken on the wheel. I will tell his fate very shortly, since it only touched Anne's twice more.

He married Lady Mary in the following year. They were bitterly unhappy – it was said that they hated one another from the start, and that the marriage was never consummated. She left him and returned to her father, while he sank into the illness which in the end killed him. I believe myself that it was a malady born of grief and disappointment. He was not a weakling, poor Harry Percy, only young and nervous, and these were forces he could not combat.

I sought out Anne. Only to comfort her, God knows, and not with any thought that she might turn to me now that her sweetheart was gone. But she looked at me as though I were yet another enemy. Her face was like ivory, her eyes like burning coals. I have never thought to see a Fury, one of the terrible Eumenides, but I saw one now.

'I am banished,' she said. 'My father is to take me home to Hever. I must stay there until it is the King's pleasure to send for me again.'

Grieved (alas, for myself!) I touched her hand, but she shook me off.

'May God curse him! May he burn in Hell, frying in his own fat, *cette grossièreté de cardinal*. I could watch him burn, and laugh! Tom, I swear to you now' (and she fell on her knees, as though she prayed) 'that if it ever lies in my power, I will do as much to him as he has done to me. I – will – do – as – much – to – him. *Je le jure. Hic voveo per Dominum.*'

With that dreadful vow on her lips she turned and ran from me. I heard her wild sobbing until a door shut it off.

The summer dragged past. We went to war with France, after the Emperor Charles had paid a state visit, attended one of Wolsey's sumptuous banquets, and somewhat unenthusiastically watched a masque which I had devised. The Emperor was an unsmiling young man with a long ugly face. Queen Catherine rejoiced in his presence, and no doubt in the fact that he had ostensibly come to betroth himself to little Princess Mary.

Wolsey, throughout the six months' visit, behaved as though he were co-ruler of England with King Henry. He smiled fatly at the Emperor, though he hated him, having heard one of Charles's few English jokes against him, to do with 'the butcher's dog' (Wolsey) having pulled down the fairest buck in Christendom, the late Duke of Buckingham. The King made as though he were vastly amused by this, but we about him knew that he was not and that he would remember it against the Emperor.

The King enjoyed preparing for the French war. He sent Anne's uncle, the Earl of Surrey, to Calais to make trouble for François, by what the French called very foul methods, burning houses, farms, even a church. (But the French blamed Wolsey, not the King – that was the measure of Wolsey's power.)

The King was bored, I was bored. I had no war to make, and wished to make none. I read Petrarch, scribbled endless poems about frustrated love and my own imminent death from it. I wrote mad lovesick things in the margins of books, such as 'I am yours, Anne.' George Boleyn had come to Court in the Emperor's train, and I used to gaze at him moonishly, seeking for resemblances to

Anne. I saw them now and then in a glance, a turn of the head. Sometimes he caught me staring at him, and I knew that he knew why. We had been friends all our lives.

Autumn set in early after that dry summer. As the leaves fluttered down I became intolerably melancholy, asked for leave of absence, and rode to Hever.

At first I thought the castle was deserted. There were no lights in the gatehouse. I rode over the bridge, my manservant John behind me, but no one came out of the hallway to take our horses. John pulled the bell. It was answered at last by a startled man wearing a leather apron, who seemed to have been busy with something to do with cobwebs, since he was covered in them. I had never seen him before, nor he me: it was my first visit to Hever since February.

He told me that Mistress Anne was at home, and that the Dowager Lady Boleyn lay ill upstairs. I sent him to find Mistress Anne and ask whether she would receive me. He went, hardly seeming to know the direction of the stairs. I wondered what had happened to Sir Thomas's staff of servants, until it occurred to me that the chief ones would be with him at Court, in the splendid lodging he and Lady Boleyn occupied.

The Great Hall was cold, the fire low. I kept on my cloak and paced about, rubbing my hands. John had gone to see to the horses and (I suspected) find himself a quart or so of ale.

When Anne came into the room I hardly knew her at first glance. She was thinner, her cheekbones sharp, the line of her collarbone visible. There were umber shadows round her eyes, as though she had been weeping or had not slept. She looked older, and plain, as I had never seen her look since childhood.

But her face lit up when she saw me. 'Tom! It *is* you! James is such a numbskull that one can hardly tell what he means.' She came to me and gave me hearty kisses of greeting, two on the cheeks and one, very lightly, on the lips. At her invitation I sat in the best chair by the hearth, while she rang for servants to make up the fire and fetch wine. Then, to my pleasure, she sat herself down on a joint-stool by my chair. She was wearing a gown of dull red which made her skin look sallow. She had lost so much weight that her figure was almost flat, like a boy's. I noticed that on one thin hand a heavy gold ring slipped about loosely; I recognised it as having belonged to her mother, a thing dug up long ago at Tendring Hall out of a Roman or Saxon grave. Anne disliked it, I knew, and I wondered why she wore it.

'I'm so very happy to see you, Tom. This place is like a tomb.'

I had not been sure of my welcome, and even now I guessed that she would have been as pleased to see any face from Court that would lighten her exile. Nobody else had visited her, she told me, except George.

'My parents are here very seldom, and Mary – well, Mary is not anxious to be seen associating with one out of the royal favour.' She laughed bitterly. 'If it had not been for George I should have turned into a piece of furniture by now. Mercifully he never brings that lemon-faced betrothed of his, Jane Parker – she wouldn't come within a mile of a leper like me, and I thank God for it. George can't abide her, but she's one of the heirs to Lord Morley's fortune, and our father would never let a match like that slip through his fingers.'

'You've had no word from the King – no hint that you might be invited back?'

'Nothing. And I should refuse to go, while that sanctified toad sits at York Place. If the King wants me, let him come and fetch me! But tell me everything – all the news, who and who? How is your sister Meg, and does she like her new husband, and why has she not been to visit me?'

'Meg is happy, and has not forgotten you. She will come when they are settled in their marriage. We talk of you often.' (How often, indeed. Kind, patient Margaret would listen for as long as I would talk. Her bridegroom Antony Lee was fortunately also of a patient nature.)

The wine came, and food, which we ate in a small parlour with a fire that warmed it, and us. The wine and the talk brought colour to Anne's face, and with thankfulness I saw the black pall of bitterness slip from her, the sparkle come back into those wonderful eyes. I kept the conversation away from anything that might touch on Harry Percy or the events that had led to her banishment. After we had eaten she brought her lute, and played and sang: French ditties and other songs which she knew I would like, among them a setting of one of my lyrics. She knew so well the art of pleasing: I was flattered and charmed, and it was for me alone that night.

I told her that I was riding on to Allington, and must leave soon, for darkness had fallen, and there was no moon.

'Stay,' she said. 'There are enough bedchambers to house an army. No, not true, but there is a pleasant one where you could be snug, George's room that was. I'll have a fire lit and linen warmed.' She rang the little silver handbell, which brought a maid hastening to take orders.

'Will your lady be anxious?' Anne asked. 'I will send a messenger to tell her where you are.'

'No. A kind thought, but don't trouble. She knows nothing of my leaving Court, so I am not expected.' I kept silent about the coldness between Elizabeth and me, the estrangement since the birth of our infant daughter, the hints my tactful father had tried to drop about Elizabeth's light behaviour. On that night I cared not a straw what my wife was doing, whom she was entertaining.

The cobweb-festooned James had, on Anne's orders, brought us a flask of choice muscadel, a wine she loved, and between us we had contrived to drink most of it. Suddenly, to my surprise, she set down her cup, rose and stretched her graceful length.

'It's late, Tom. You must be fresh to ride tomorrow. And I must go and read to my grandmother. She likes to hear the Scriptures, and the priest is too fat and lazy to come out to her, except to bring her the Sacrament on Sundays, so she must make do with my poor Latin.'

Candles were brought, and we were lighted upstairs. At the door of old Lady Boleyn's chamber, Anne said a matter-of-fact good-night to me, and coolly offered me her cheek to kiss.

I was alone in the handsome room now glowing with firelight and candleshine, George's own damask-covered bed waiting for me, covers turned back to show downy pillows, a fur-lined night-robe laid out for my use.

Better than a cold ride through the night to Allington. Yet I felt a curious flatness of spirit, a kind of heart-sinking. I reproached myself for the sin of *ingratia*. We had spent a pleasant evening, I had had Anne to myself – a rare thing – I had found her sad and left her almost merry. Best of all, I had seen and talked with her again, after a summer's starvation.

Yet I lay sleepless, and restless, staring at the wall carvings, scenes from the Scriptures, Boleyn and Ormonde armorial devices. Snatches of words and tunes from Anne's songs chased through my mind. I should have been at peace, yet was not.

The click of the latch startled me. The door opened and she was there. She wore something of filmy white which floated round her like mist. If I had not seen her eyes gleam in the firelight, and the black wealth of her hair unbound, falling to her waist, I would have thought her an angelic visitation.

She came to my bedside, padding softly on bare feet, and stood, looking gravely down at me. Hardly believing, I put out a hand to her. She took it and held it against her breast, then stooped and kissed me on the mouth: not the formal brush of the lips I had had from her in greeting and goodnight, but the sort of kiss we had taken and given only in my dreams.

'Dear heart,' she said, 'how like you this?'

I may have answered, or not, for I was almost beyond speech. At her gesture I pulled back the bedcovers and she mounted the three steps up to the high bed and climbed in beside me.

I was in her arms, she in mine, for the first time; and all my dreams had been poor fantasies compared with this reality. She had not yet turned her sixteenth birthday, but she knew the hunger of a woman's flesh for a man, had been starved as I had. I think I never knew such delight as with Anne, so hot in passion, so delicately skilled in French ways of wooing. Other women I had known seemed like stone images beside her; and I had loved her so long, and despaired of her until this hour.

Only she would not let me break the knot of her virginity. I think her father's threats of what might become of a maid who threw away that jewel, and the warning she had taken from Mary's misspent life, were stronger than my pleading. It can have been nothing else – then.

I was glad, in my heart, to know that Percy had not taken her. He came into my mind, but I pushed away the thought of him, even though I wondered later if it were not the thwarting of her longing for him that had now driven her to my bed.

But it mattered not at all, now that she was there.

She was happy that night, and I almost out of my senses with joy; and I know that she loved me, Tom Wyatt, then.

I rode to Allington next morning in the state of a man who has seen a vision. The world looked unbelievably beautiful to me. My man seemed to think that I was drunk, for he kept reminding me of the way we were going – as though I had not known it as well as the back of my hand.

We reached Allington to be met at the gate by my steward, wearing a long face. One of our farm boys had met John and me a mile or so from home, and run back to the castle to tell him we were approaching.

'Oh, Sir Thomas – that you should come home today! Oh, sir, my lady!'

I thought that Elizabeth must have died in the night, he and the other servants sent up such a clamour – even the infant was shrieking in its nurse's arms. But it was not so: only that she had run away, bag and baggage, with a neighbour of ours whom I had thought a friend.

Later I would be angry and bitter, riding over to tell Lord Cobham that he and my father between them had married me to a whore. But that morning, to the shocked surprise of my household, I was calm, almost placid, able to write a letter to my father at

Court without a tremor of the hand. My heart was too full of Anne, my body alive with memories of her kissings and her sweet words and embraces, to care for any other thing in the mortal world.

This much of my story very few knew then, or shall ever know. Anne's story is known to all England, and beyond the seas. I shall tell it in brief, partly for the grief it still causes me, partly because they allow me only scant paper for writing here in the Tower.

To end the tale of my heaven of happiness at Hever, I will write only this: Anne had said that night, in her defiance, 'If the King wants me, let him come and fetch me!'

He did want her, and he came to fetch her.

15

This gorgeous lady

I should have known better than to take things at their face value when Anne was banished from the Court. Was I not a poet, a thinker, one who should see into men's hearts? But who, except God, could ever see into the King's heart? He was a secret man, more enamoured of secrets than any Frenchman or Italian, devious as they are famed to be: an expert in duplicity, smiling one minute, raging the next, twisting people and circumstances to his advantage.

Perhaps the secret quality came from his Welshness. For all his Plantagenet blood, he was a Welshman like his father, who had kept St David's Day and flown the crimson dragon of Cadwallader on Bosworth Field, where he plucked the crown from a thorn-bush and had the slain King Richard carried naked and disgraced on the back of a horse for men to see and mock at.

But these are disloyal thoughts. A Wyatt cannot afford to be disloyal. My being here, in the Tower, is proof enough of that. I have fits of shaking, which disorder my thoughts a little at times.

I should have known that Wolsey had no axe to grind in parting Anne from Harry Percy. He was merely told to do it, by the King. Why, being parted from her sweetheart, was she not then forcibly married to James Butler? Why did Butler melt away into the shadows of the Court? Why did the banished Percy not put away his hated wife, when his father died, only five years after all the trouble?

There was one clear answer to all these questions: the King wanted Anne for himself. The Queen was past child-bearing and he was out of love with her, and with Mary. Mary would have been his *maîtresse en titre* had there been such a position at the English Court, but there was not; and with maternity and marriage to Will Carey she had become noticeably staider and more matronly, less eager to show off her French accomplishments. He was looking round for a successor when Anne came back to England in that momentous year, 1522.

She was so different from pink-and-white Court beauties, with her light French voice and her dancing feet and deer's eyes. King Henry loved youth, and wit, and accomplishments, especially musical skill, which she had in abundance. He loved to see himself as a *preux chevalier*, a squire of dames, flirting and sighing mock sighs. He would leap into ladies' company disguised as a Moor or Ethiop, then tear off his mask and reveal himself. Not that anyone was deceived for a moment, with his bulk and the way he had of throwing his presence about, like the inescapable heat of a fire.

So this new and rare young arrival, Anne, was indeed meant for 'another person' than Northumberland's heir, a royal person, used to getting his own way in all things. He had been known to tell a Venetian ambassador, 'I will not allow anyone to have it in his power to govern me, nor will I ever suffer it.'

He left her alone at Hever, by design, for as long as he guessed it would take to cool her anger and grief. We had that late autumn, all the winter, and early spring of the next year to ourselves. Little did the King guess that Anne was far from unhappy in her exile. I visited Hever as often as I could, hoping that my absence from Court would not be noticed unduly.

We had that enchanted castle and all the countryside for our pleasure. The River Eden was well named indeed, for us, as we rode along its banks, two lovers innocent of the retribution to come. We dressed plainly, like country folk, so that nobody remarked on us but those who knew us, and they thought nothing of it. The servants at Hever were discreet, having learned service under Sir Thomas's rule.

And the servants at Allington thought nothing amiss, or pretended they did not, when I took Anne there, at a time when my father was absent at Court (he was now Master of the King's Jewels). Anne had her maid Dorcas with her, and a bedchamber removed from mine. But at night that round tower where I had been cold and wretched so many nights was warm with her presence, transformed by her magic. It would never seem forbidding to me again.

I still had not enjoyed her fully, but I let it be as she wished. A misbegotten child would bring her father's wrath down on her, and she seemed to despise the French tricks which would have prevented conception. I was content with what I had of her, even though I longed to have her all mine, as Our Lord ordained for marriage: *erunt duo in carne una*. That was how I loved Anne.

It was in May, that ominous month for me, that Sir Thomas and Lady Boleyn descended on Hever. I knew something was afoot, so portentous was Sir Thomas's air, and it was significant that the King's Treasurer should spare the time for his Kentish house.

He was closeted for a long time with Anne. I was not there, but I had word from her by a messenger: 'My father wishes me to return to Court. It is the will of His Majesty. But I have told him I choose not to go. I will not be a ball, to be tossed to and fro.'

Sir Thomas was angry, but it was below his dignity to drag his daughter back to London by force. Lady Boleyn was troubled. Out of her husband's hearing she said, 'Be careful, Anne.'

'Of what, madam? Disobeying the King?'

'No. Of obeying him.'

Anne laughed. To His Majesty (we had to call him that now, no longer merely His Grace) she thought she was the foolish girl Wolsey had called her, a chit who had had the temerity to choose the wrong man. He could hardly punish her further for that. Let him leave her to work out the pleasant punishment he had devised for her.

The next time the summons came it was in the person of the King himself. A train of attendants and huntsmen behind him, he came galloping down the rough road that led from Greenwich. The sound of hunting horns alerted the household. Panic followed, as the foreriders approached to announce the royal visitor.

Anne received him; her manner was cool but gracious and correct. He expressed surprise that her father was not in residence, just as though he had not seen him at Greenwich only the day before.

All the castle's resources were summoned to provide a meal for the King and his retainers, stocks raided, the wine cellar half emptied. Anne played hostess, the King at her right hand. In his conversation he made it quite clear that it was his personal wish that she return to the Queen's service – there was no question of punishment, only of compensating her for her banishment. Some reward – gifts – just a hint of ennoblement. Anne bent her slender neck like a swan and murmured gratitude. She would give the matter much thought.

That was all she gave it. At Hever she remained, but now I saw her less often, and she was chary of granting me her favours. I sensed her father's influence in this.

Time went by, another year, and the King's occasional visits became more frequent. Sometimes she consented to see him (it was now the subject, not the monarch, who was bestowing the favours); at other times she kept to her chamber, on pretence of being ill. I cannot tell how she behaved to him, but I believe it was not in her nature to resist the chance of tormenting an abject suitor: and what a suitor! I believe she played him like a fish, led him on, then laughed at him, and charmed him all the more. It was all a game to her – she told me so – and to him at first, a game whose rules he understood. But a dangerous one. I would not tell her that thoughts of a divorce from the Queen had begun to creep into King Henry's mind.

I now spent more time at Court, and had become close to the King, a favoured companion, sometimes his confidant. He had a way of walking beside me, an arm about the shoulders, almost leaning his weight on me, talking, musing, telling what seemed to be secrets – yet he only told them because he no longer intended them to be secrets.

'My beloved wife is past her time of child-bearing, Tom. Yet I must get an heir for England. How shall such a thing be done?'

I shook my head, being able to think of no sensible answer.

'I can beget sons very easily,' he boasted. (Alas, not true.) 'There's my son Henry Fitzroy, a fine, sturdy little fellow. I intend to create him Duke of Richmond soon.'

'Your late father's title, sir.'

'Yes. A proud one. I might even marry him to my daughter Mary, now that she is no longer betrothed to the Emperor Charles (a treacherous business, that.) What do you think of the idea, Tom?'

I thought it was improper and shocking in the highest degree, as the children were half-brother and half-sister, and would therefore be committing incest. If the King realised this, he blithely dismissed it because it was counter to his wishes and plans.

'Yes, I could make young Henry my heir,' he mused. 'Do you think the people would accept him happily?'

'I have no idea, sir. But he's a comely boy.' No one could deny that: all the Tudors, bastards or not, were of striking red-headed looks. Nothing was said of the King's latest son, Mary Carey's new-born baby. He too was a fine child, another redhead with hot brown eyes, lusty and big-built, quite unlike his supposed father Will Carey, but for some hidden reason the King was not prepared to acknowledge him and seemed to ignore his existence. I knew from Anne that poor Mary was now out of favour, relegated to the status of a mere lady-in-waiting, though Will remained a Gentleman of the Bedchamber. Her father would have nothing to do with her after the birth of this, her second Tudor child.

'She has thrown away all her chances by being too soft and pliant, she has not forced the King to acknowledge her boy,' Anne said. 'She had not fulfilled my father's plans for her.'

'What of his plans for you, Anne? Why does he not make a good match for you?'

'Who knows? But I must stay chaste until he does.' She slanted her eyes at me. 'Comparatively chaste. I would be happy if he would match me with you, Tom. But that can't be. Why did you marry that Cobham *putain*? Now it is impossible for us.'

There would certainly be no divorce for me. Though she had left me, Elizabeth would always be my wife in the eyes of the church. But the King had better hopes. In a certain text in the Book of Leviticus he had found a weighty argument for his marriage to Queen Catherine being invalid. She had been wife to his brother Arthur, and according to Leviticus a man might not marry his brother's wife, or widow. 'It is an unclean thing . . . they shall be childless.'

All the world knows the King's longed-for divorce was the scandal of Europe. He truly wished above all things for a legitimate heir, and to get one he was prepared to bastardise his young daughter Mary. For the Queen's injured love and pride he came to care not at all. She would neither acknowledge that she had never been his legal wife nor retire into a nunnery, as he suggested. Now he hated her.

But this was not all to get an heir. He was besotted, infatuated with Anne. She refused steadfastly to become his mistress, a course in which she was encouraged by Sir Thomas, who saw a far higher prize for her: a crown.

She knew it in time, from the King's own lips. She had shown me his letters, laughed over them. He called her his *'petite mignonne'*, his sweetheart and well-beloved, sighed about the pain of separation, signed with a device of a heart containing her initials, A.B., and *Autre ne cherche*, 'I seek no other'.

'"Darling"', she read out to me, mocking the King's squeaking voice and bluff manner, '"I trust within a while to enjoy that which I have so longed for to God's pleasure and our both comforts. No more to you at this present, mine own darling, for lack of time, but I would you were in mine arms, or I in yours, for I think it long since I kissed you."'

She saw my jealous look. 'Tom, it was a most chaste, respectful kiss. His Majesty is strangely backward in wooing, more like a schoolboy than a man.'

'*Do* you let him embrace you?'

'Not I. Not beyond a touch. I tell you, I'd as soon embrace a boar.'

I believed her. I knew her to be delicate and fastidious, one whom I could have trusted as a wife even though I had been a thousand leagues from her.

She came back to Court, not like a person creeping home after banishment, but like a queen, as she now knew it was possible for her to be. She was dressed more richly than any lady there, far more so than she had been before; her father had laid out a fortune on her. Instead of cabuchons and garnets, diamonds and rubies blazed about her, and the pearls she loved, pearls edging her French headdress, pearls against the pearl skin of her breast. She took to wearing a pearl collar, the initial B wrought in diamonds hanging from it, hiding the mole.

I wrote her one of my sonnets, telling her what I saw in that glittering initial letter:

> Who list her hunt, I put him out of doubt,
> As well as I may spend his time in vain,
> And graven with diamonds in letters plain,
> There is written her fair neck round about:
> '*Noli me tangere*, for Caesar's I am,
> And wild for to hold, though I seem tame.'

She read it in my presence, and said nothing, but kissed me sweetly. What had been between us was over. I was now only part of the company that surrounded her, as stars the moon; poets, wits, song-makers, musicians, young courtiers, gentlemen of the King's Privy Chamber like William Brereton, Sir Henry Norris, Sir Francis Weston, her own brother George.

George had been given a handsome share in the family ennoblement, and would be given more, as Viscount Rochford and lord of the King's fine manor Beaulieu in Essex. Perhaps his new wealth and honours helped to compensate him for his unhappy marriage. Jane was a sour, unpleasant young woman given to hysterical jealousy; indeed she was all made up of envy and malice, hating Anne for her splendour and the favour she enjoyed, and for the fact that George loved his sister as he did not love her. I thought she was possibly a little mad at times.

I see us all now, as we were at the end of that decade, the 1520s, young men with lutes and scrolls of verse, young women who were possibly more formally pretty than Anne, but like shadows beside her proud radiance.

And I see Anne, looking back, not only as the 'gorgeous lady' as one observer called her, but as a figure in a tapestry landscape, with dogs about her, leaning against her knees and across her feet, long lean hunting dogs, rough dogs like animated mats, spaniels and lap-dogs. They were not encouraged in the chambers of state but Anne loved them and was kind to them, as all were not. It was odd that she, who in looks was more like a beautiful eastern cat, should be so attracted to these rougher creatures.

But it had always been so, since her childhood at Hever when she had shocked her nurses by making a friend of the dog boy. Here at Greenwich she had made a friend of Robin, the royal spaniel keeper. Her favourite among the big dogs was the wolfhound Urian, a huge beast who would hardly leave her side even for the hunt; and of the small ones, the one she called Little Purkoy, because his big enquiring eyes always seemed to be asking, '*Pourquoi?*' He had been her pet since she came back to Court, where each lady-in-waiting was allowed a spaniel of her own. The dogs adored her for herself, not for the favours she could bestow. Perhaps they too felt her extraordinary powerful charm, as most people did.

The Spanish ambassador, Chapuis, did not feel it. He watched her slyly, twisted all her actions maliciously when writing to his sovereign. Cardinal Wolsey did not feel it. Anne had never made a secret of her bitter resentment towards him for banishing Harry Percy. Yet Wolsey was stupid, for all his worldly wisdom. He let the King deceive him – he who knew what a skilful deceiver his master was. The King was angry with him, and his anger was fuelled by Anne, for not having eased the way to the royal divorce. Wolsey failed to smell the smoke of that dangerous fire. He knew that he was hated at Court by some, but he did not perceive that the 'foolish girl' Mistress Boleyn headed them.

Therefore, not perceiving her as a danger to him, he continued to work hard for a divorce for Henry; and went on embassy to Rome to persuade the Pope to issue a Papal Bull to allow the King's re-marriage even before the annulment of his union with Queen Catherine. He of course failed, and this was the beginning of the Cardinal's slow but certain destruction, the dreadful spiral of a man falling from a great height. It is all there, in the documents, on the lips of those concerned in it: I will not tell it again.

What touched me most at this time was the hopelessness of my love for Anne. I wrote many poems lamenting it, pleading with her. But I did not send them to her, for by then I knew the ambitious side of her had won: she meant to be Queen, and nothing would turn her aside.

It is very cold here in the Tower, even in May. I wish they would allow me a fire.

FIVE
MARY CAREY'S NARRATIVE

16

Farewell ye little fishes, that in the river swim, O,
I'm going to be a dancer, a dancer in yellow.
O beware! O beware!

It was summer, and the year 1528. I was twenty-four years old, and June roses clustered in the gardens of Greenwich Palace, and beautiful Hampton in Surrey, the dream house Cardinal Wolsey had given to his royal master (but much good it did him.)

Anne intended to be Queen of England. I knew it, and George knew it. George lounged on the day-bed in the lodgings Will and I had at Court in Greenwich, admiring his long elegant hands.

'I suppose Anne and I get our hands from the Howards,' he said. 'Yours, Mary, are pure Bullen. Well, I suppose all this ennobling means something. Our father has an earldom to come. Earl of what, I wonder? Kent? No, there is one already, and Suffolk and Norfolk are claimed. Ah, well, we shall see. And I have the manor of Beaulieu. How curious of His Majesty, to take possession of so many fine houses and hardly live in them. He paid a thousand pounds for Beaulieu, did you know?'

'I wonder you're not there instead of here.' I looked round the slightly shabby room, with its view of a narrow alley and a stable yard. My dear Will was too easy-going to complain about our lodgings, and I dared not, now that I had no hold over the King.

'Oh, I find myself very comfortable at Court,' replied George, 'so long as I keep my distance from Jane. In any case she prefers our aunt's company. Rather she than I.'

'Or I.' Our uncle, Edward Boleyn, was a member of the King's household, his wife was a member of the Queen's. They were stiff, cold-hearted people who despised me and paid only lip-service to Anne. I knew that George's own choice of companion was another relation of ours, Sir Francis Bryan, a raffish man who amused the King very much and wrote extremely bawdy verse. Our grandfather Norfolk was dead, four years since, buried in a magnificent tomb at Thetford; but his widow Agnes, no older than our mother, still took a lively interest in Court affairs, though she was supposed to be living in retirement at Lambeth. In those days we were still a strong force, we Boleyn-Howards.

My four-year-old son Harry rode noisily into the room on a wooden horse he propelled with his feet, lashing it with a toy whip and encouraging it with shouts. 'Gee up, I'm your dompter, your dompter. Hurry or I'll beat you . . .' George studied him as he clattered noisily out again.

'That child is very large for his years.'

'Yes.'

'His hair is turning darker, I see – almost brown. Matching his eyes.'

'Yes.'

George's shapely eyebrows rose. 'That doesn't sadden you, Mall – that he looks less like the Tudor he is?'

'Why should it? His royal blood has done no good to Will or me. He might as well have been another girl. A second daughter would have pleased me, if she had a milder temper than Catherine.'

'Catherine is a little termagant, certainly. You know, she has a look of the Princess Mary . . . poor child. The King's darling once, but not now – too fond of her mother for his liking. Mall, do your servants spy, listen at doors?'

'What servants? We have but three, barring the children's nurse-maid, all as stupid as owls.'

'Are owls stupid? I'd hazard they look uncommonly wise – to a wood-mouse. I was about to say, if no ears were listening, I shall be vastly surprised if the King ever gets a healthy son, for to my mind he has the burning sickness in his blood.'

I started, crossing myself. 'Jesu! Is this one of your jests, George?'

'I wish it were.' George's handsome, good-humoured face, with its full-lipped mouth, was for once grave. 'They have a new name for it in Italy, Syphilis, after a man in a poem by Girolamo Frasastore.'

'George, stop prating and tell me why you say this terrible thing!'

'I had it from a man who was at the Field of the Cloth-of-Gold, and knew one of the French whores produced by François for His Majesty's pleasure. She was infected, he said, though the signs only came later.'

'But the Queen conceived before that and bore children who failed to survive.'

George shrugged. 'So, he may have caught the thing before. Who knows? Not even the physicians. There were plenty ready to spoil his virginity, they tell me. How witty of Fate to have made him the one to have whores branded on the face with hot irons for meddling with his soldiers. Did you notice ...?' He described horrible symptoms: I did not recall any on the King.

'But my children,' I said. 'If what you say is true, Harry and Catherine might carry it, if it can be carried. Do the doctors know if it can?'

'Never ask me, sister, I'm no physician. But I shall take care in future. I would not risk having a son born diseased. Or sons.' He had a child by one of his mistresses, and his wife Jane was pregnant. 'So far I have only a chance-come daughter. She brought her mother no luck, since she lost her place at Court and was sent home to the country. But the child was healthy enough, and the image of me, a Boleyn to its fingernails – no infection there. King or no King, I'd wager your progeny are as healthy as mine.'

'Where is she now, your little girl?' I asked.

George shrugged. 'With good enough people, well paid for keeping her.'

'Who?'

'I shall not tell you, or you'll make a drama of it and go visiting your niece. They live in Bishopsgate and are known to be honest, that's all I'll say. I even had her christened, Margaret, with Meg Lee standing godmother. There, that's enough.'

'George,' I said, 'don't tell Anne about the King.' His eyes were deep and dark and beautiful, with a sadness sometimes that contradicted the laughter in his face. I knew he would not tell Anne, for he loved her too much.

Will looked in briefly, wearing that air he had of a bird with its feathers slightly ruffled. I was always straightening his bonnet or shaking out a fold in his cloak, or picking a button off his doublet before it fell off by itself. He had the quaint speech of Devon which made everything he said sound faintly comic. He had always been infinitely kind to me, seeming to take no heed that my children were neither his nor at all like him, being both headstrong and unamiable. He cherished me like the faithful wife I had not been to him. The King had a good servant in Will Carey, and I a good husband. The best.

The girl who passed for a lady-in-waiting to me then came running in to say that Mistress Orchard waited to see me, and seemed impatient. Hannah Orchard had been an upper servant of my mother's, now passed on to Anne, who had her own household; I knew that she had been grateful to receive into it a woman who had known her long and was not a time-server. Mistress Orchard was some ten years younger than our mother, comely and plump, a widow who would still have worn mourning clothes if they had not been considered too sombre for Anne's retinue.

She was indeed impatient, flustered.

'Madam, my lady says you are to leave at once, to go with her to Hever. His Majesty is concerned that the sickness is spreading.'

There was no need to tell me what sickness. It was the Sweat, the deadly fever that swept England in summer. Next to the plague, it was the most dreaded curse, an affliction of Job visited upon us: it could kill within hours.

'But,' I said, 'the Court was to leave for Waltham this morning. Surely that's far enough from London?'

'Not far enough, madam. One of my lady's maids is ill. The rest of us are to leave at once, and you too.'

'Are those the King's orders?'

Her glance slid past mine. 'They're my lady's orders, madam.'

Of course, they would be. My sister cared for me, the King cared not a fig whether I lived or died, now that I was no longer his bedfellow. But I dared not go to Hever, even to please Anne. My parents were in residence there, and my father would not have me within his doors. There would be a scene, a scandal which would be reported.

I said, 'I think it better not to go to Hever. But tell my sister I will make other arrangements to go into the country.'

'My lady will not be pleased with that.'

'She will understand.' Mistress Orchard was not pleased, either, to have her mistress's command disobeyed. She adored Anne, almost as though she had taken on our mother's anxious devotion to her.

I sought out Tom Wyatt and told him the news. Willingly, eagerly, he offered the hospitality of Allington to me and my family, though I knew he would ten thousand times rather it had been Anne who needed it. He had been appointed Marshal of Calais, and would be there more often than in England. I think he was glad and wretched at the same time to be going away from Anne; and the King had been cool towards him lately. He offered to send an escort for the children and their nurse, as soon as they could be got ready. Will and I would follow later.

But Will said, 'I see no necessity for us to go. If God wills us to catch the Sweat, we shall catch it. If not, He will protect us wherever we are. Here at Greenwich we have good air, and with so many away we shall be mercifully quiet. I would enjoy,' he added wistfully, 'your company alone for a while, my dear.' Will loved the children as though they were his own, but their high temper, and the constant noise they made in our small rooms, sometimes tried him.

We decided to improve on those familiar, stuffy rooms. We would go up the hill to Duke Humphrey's Tower, high above the royal park and palace, looking up the river towards London. Beside it was a small pavilion, built in the late King's reign. It was fitted out well enough to live in, once some of our possessions had been carted up to it.

There, in that beautiful early June, we were like country folk, alone and quiet and free from cares; it was as though the Sweat had come as a blessing to us. When we heard, as we shortly did, that Anne had been taken with the sickness almost before she reached Hever, and that our father had it too, we were thankful that we had not gone there. George had it too, and many other gentlemen about the King – who had run as though the Devil were after him, and was now at Wolsey's house of Tittenhanger, shut up in a tower with one of his doctors, making numerous prayers and confessions. He had sent another physician, Doctor Butts, in haste to Hever.

I remembered too well how Henry had always flinched from me if I had so much as sneezed, shooing me away as though I were a wasp. He thought he was *in extremis* if he had a pain in his little finger.

A week after we had been at our rustic home, Will came in from walking and sat down heavily, seeming exhausted. His face was pale, in spite of the heat outside, and he said that his head ached.

I gave him a drink of cool wine, but he put it down after a few sips. The ache spread to his back, then to his stomach and further, until he was in too much discomfort to sit, but lay on the floor, writhing.

'I'm on the rack,' he gasped out. 'They're torturing me, Mall. Stop them, tell them . . .'

I knew then what was the matter. I ran down the hill to get help. But no one would come, and there were no medicines to be had. I searched wildly in the gardens for herbs, – feverfew, scabious, marigold, betony, all plague remedies, as were sweet marjoram and dandelion – but though I found some I had no notion what to do with them. I soaked them in hot water and wine and aqua vitae but Will could not take the mixture. He was raving, his skin burning with fever, his hands like lumps of ice. I covered him with blankets, on the floor where he lay, and knelt beside him, talking to him and praying.

Just on the turn of the night he died.

I wished I had gone with him, wherever he was.

It was months before the pace of life steadied, like a clock that has stopped and is re-started. The Sweat had killed so many of the Court that it was harder to recall the names of those who had not died than those who had. Yet all of us Boleyns were spared: why? I wonder that now.

Anne had been very ill, almost on the point of death. When the terrible infection was gone, she came back to Court, thin as a reed, her skin transparent, more like a spirit walking than a woman. Her great eyes burned as though there were a light behind them, and when she held up her hand one could see the bones of it. I let myself hope, at first, that the shadow of death had changed her, showing her the emptiness of mortal titles. If only God would call her to a nunnery, she might die one of His saints, not Henry's Queen.

In the third month of my widowhood the King sent for me. This I knew to be unusual, as he generally avoided those he had finished with. He had me summoned to his presence chamber, where he loomed over his attendant gentleman on a raised throne. Anne was already there, seated, by special royal privilege.

I was not invited to sit after I had made my curtsey. I stood before the King on the precious strip of blue carpet which here took the place of rushes. After a quick raking glance, which took in my black robes and widow's hood, he looked away quickly. He disliked anything savouring of death.

After some formal, hasty condolences, regretting the loss of so good a man as the late Sir William, he said, 'We understand you are not well provided for, madam.' (He used the royal We to *me*! I could almost have laughed.)

'No, Your Majesty. My husband had almost nothing to leave.'

'Ah. He was a second son, of course. No inheritance.'

'No, sir.'

He had not taken his eyes off Anne since glancing away from me. Now he spoke to her, in quite different tones, languorous, caressing.

'You have had word from your father about this, Lady Anne?'

'Yes, sir. Walter Welsh wrote to him, as you so graciously asked. But he will not offer my sister a place under his roof.'

Anne's cool voice made no comment on the truth behind this. News of my husband's death seemed to have sharpened our father's dislike of me, and his illness did nothing to mellow it. He had flatly refused to give me money or shelter, even adding some coarse suggestions as to how I could earn a living, having proved myself no better than a harlot.

So Anne had written to the King from Hever, begging his intercession. He had not written personally, but had told a secretary to write for him. It had done no good, not surprisingly, for my mother had turned against me too, in her strange nervous state: I hoped her age was to blame, and the stress of living with my father for so many years. They both rejected me out of hand. Even Anne could not fight them.

The King muttered something, appearing to confer with the secretary who stood beside him, the man Welsh who had written for me. But I believed there was nothing to confer about – it was already decided. Welsh stepped forward, armed with papers, and began to recite to me Will's assets: almost no money, very little land, and some Crown offices. He had been Steward of the Duchy of Lancaster, Constable of the Castle of Plashy, and keeper of two royal parks.

These had all been disposed of, Welsh informed me, to 'worthy gentlemen'. I waited for the King to intervene and reassure me that

I should have something from them to keep me and the children, but he stayed silent, twitching the fingers of one hand in a way he had when impatient.

'As to your son and daughter, madam,' said Welsh, 'they are to be in the care of your noble sister, who is to provide for them and protect your son during his minority. A suitable match will shortly be arranged for him.'

I heard myself gasp. Harry was four years old, no more. The King was sweeping us all out of the way with extreme thoroughness.

'You must be gratified to know of this provision for your family, madam,' said the King. 'What better hands to care for them than those of their most godly aunt?' This extraordinary description of Anne reminded him of something else. 'As to that matter of your late husband's sister, Dame Eleanor Carey, we have made a strong recommendation to my Lord Wolsey for her appointment as Abbess of Wilton Priory. This was Sir William's last wish, we believe.'

Was it? His last wish, if he had been conscious enough to make one, would have been for me and the children, not for Eleanor, a ragtail not fit to be a nun who had had two children by two different fathers, both priests. Will had said something to me in his last hours of health about hoping that Eleanor would be appointed Abbess, because then she would be forced to reform her ways. I had mentioned this to Anne, who had passed it on to the King, to give me some comfort, as she thought. As though I cared what became of Nell Carey, that lewd woman! I was being treated as no better than a lewd woman myself. No word was said about my future: the audience was at an end.

I know now what I did not then: that behind the King's callousness towards me there was a reason, typical of that devious man. The strongest ground for his divorce from Queen Catherine was his claim that she had been the true wife of his brother Arthur, and so within the forbidden degree of consanguinity. Anne and I were sisters, and I had been his mistress, his concubine – so in blood we too were within that forbidden degree. If the King publicly ignored his past connection with me, nobody would dare to bring it forward. He wished it blotted out.

'Squire Henry means to be God and do as he pleases,' the heretic Luther had said of him. Master Luther was right.

In Anne's apartments, alone with her, I wept bitterly. I had been too proud to weep before Henry.

She put her thin arms round me and rocked me, as though she were the elder sister, and I no older than my Catherine. 'Hush, hush,' she said, over and over.

'What will become of me?' I sobbed. 'Where can I go? How shall I keep the children?'

'You shall stay with me, here at Court, as one of my ladies.'

'The King won't like that.'

'He will like it if I say so. Have no fear. But not the children, Mall. Even I could find no place for them. And our mother would not take them. No, they must be reared in religious houses.'

I wept more, then, at the thought of my two little ones among strangers, obeying harsh rules, Catherine among women who had never been mothers and Harry among men sworn to chastity. They were both wilful, they would be beaten, perhaps starved. Anne assured me that it would not be so; both monks and nuns were perfectly capable of taking care of noble orphans, and she would provide ample funds for their food and clothing. All would be well with them, she would see to that.

And so it was. Both were placed near London, so that I could see them when I liked, and Harry's headstrong nature improved visibly under the firm discipline of the Father Abbot. But Catherine resented from the first the change from her nursery to the sisters' care, and I shall always believe that this helped to make her the Puritan she later became.

Anne made only one condition about my joining her attendants: that I should leave off my mourning. 'It would cast a gloom on my other ladies. And you would not wish to look like a crow among finches, would you?'

'But Will . . . I owe it to Will.' I would have worn black for ever, in memory of that beloved man, the only man who had ever been wholly kind to me. But Anne told me, very prettily and persuasively, that white had been the colour of mourning in Spain until only twenty years or so ago, and that in parts of France they wore yellow.

'It would suit you. I would wear it myself if I had your cause. Wear yellow for my sake, Mall!'

And so I did, though I got some cold looks from ladies who thought me callous, or worse. Anne found me some damask of dark gold, the colour of a fading leaf, from the shop of her linen draper at the Sign of the Dove, so that I should not seem too gaudy. I knew that Will would understand, wherever he was. Surely they would have released him from Purgatory even so soon, and taken him into Paradise, the good soul.

From that time there was splendour upon splendour, as Anne moved into the full sunlight. She had made her return to Court from Hever only after our father had begged her on his knees, even wept in entreaty. Then it was for the King to find a way of having her close every day, yet not living under the same roof.

First he bestowed on her (through Wolsey) all the revenues of the See of Durham, and the Bishop of Durham's official house, on the banks of the Thames, near Wolsey's York House. Our father promptly moved in with her, delighted to have his own painted barge moored by his own watergate.

Then, because Durham House was not modern enough, Anne was given Suffolk House, which was next to York House. So close, that the King would not resist borrowing York House from the Cardinal. There was a stairway on the Suffolk House side, and a little courtyard, not much frequented. Soon it became known that it was to remain completely unfrequented, for the King's use only.

At Suffolk House Anne lived in royal state, with daily levees. For these occasions she wore a cloak with an ermine-trimmed train, carried by a page. The King continued to live at York House, and it became clear that he was never going to give it back to Wolsey.

The Cardinal took it all with a smile, though a false one. Did he hope that Anne, so available now to the King, would let herself be seduced? If so, he was over-hopeful. I knew that, though I saw little of my sister in private now that she lived in such state. It was only to be expected.

When she went to Hever, as she often did, I stayed at Suffolk House. She went there partly to visit our mother, who was never well, and partly to tantalise the King by her absence. But at Christmas she came back to Court and stayed all through the festive season at Greenwich, where the Queen also was.

Two Queens in one palace, presiding over different Courts. A fat dumpy Queen in old-fashioned Spanish clothes, wearing all her jewels at once, like an overloaded statue of Our Lady, yet managing to look dull and ordinary. A wand-slender Queen who wore few jewels, being as bright as any of them herself, who flashed and sparkled from one great occasion to another, singing and playing the lute for the King, acting in masques, a figure of fairy glamour. The King desired her more and more: by this time he was like a boy under the spell of first love.

'What will become of her?' I asked George. 'You see more than I do. How can the King's passion last, with so much against it?'

'Passion is a slow fire and burns long. Besides, he's under challenge. The people know that he means to put Anne in Catherine's place: they love Catherine and call Anne names – the Goggle-Eyed Whore is one.'

'But she is chaste.'

'Tell that to those who listened to him making a public speech about how joyful he would be if only his marriage turned out to be legal. Did they believe him? No. Not a man of them but supposed Anne already in the royal bed. And Wolsey hates her very much. For her he has lost houses and lands and favour. And there is the small threat of the Bible.'

It was known in Court circles that Anne had been much influenced in France by Madame Marguerite, who was almost a heretic, they whispered, favouring the shocking idea that the Bible

216

should be read by all, not merely priests. It had already been translated into English.

'There,' reflected George, 'my lord Cardinal's authority would be undermined. A great Prince of the Church no longer in control of the Holy Scriptures! Imagine the scene – our sister at the King's knee, reading to him – *iter ergo ad exitus viarum, et quosconque inveneritis, vocate ad nuptias.*'

'What does that mean?'

'"Go out into the streets, and invite all you meet there to the wedding."'

I found it impossible not to laugh at George's choice of texts, and the vision it raised of Wolsey's outraged face.

'Well, that will never be,' I said. 'If Nan ever gives in, there'll be no wedding. Queen Catherine would have to be dethroned first, and the Pope defied.'

I was wrong. I had underestimated my sister's strong will, and the single-mindedness of her and the King.

I saw Wolsey routed when he tried to discredit Anne by taking a Lutheran book of hers to the King. But it was she who discredited him, coaxing the King to read it himself and come round to her opinion.

I saw Wolsey fail to persuade the Pope's Legate to grant the King a divorce. And, by Anne's contrivance, brought down, stripped of all his worldly goods, and banished: and at last arrested on a false charge of high treason, by none other than Anne's old love, Harry Percy. So she had her revenge at last, and rejoiced when Wolsey died of a disease, escaping the axe which waited for him in London.

I saw Queen Catherine banished to one damp wretched manor after another, separated from her beloved daughter Mary, and left to waste away in loneliness until she died. But that was not yet.

I saw the King turn to Thomas Cranmer, my father's friend and chaplain, in Wolsey's place, and Cranmer take the side of Anne and the King in the matter of the divorce. (He was a sweet, gentle man, anxious to please, wholly sincere, which was rare in a churchman

217

or anybody else at that Court.) When he was appointed Archbishop of Canterbury, Anne's cause was almost won.

I saw the Duke of Suffolk banished from Court because he had spitefully told the King that Anne had been Tom Wyatt's mistress. The King turned a deaf ear and sent his favourite away – for a time. I was glad, for I had found out that the man who had so impressed me at the court of Marguerite of Austria was no more than a great vulgar bombast, faithful to nobody, not even to the King's lovely sister.

Strangest and most unbelievable of all, I and a bewildered country saw the King turn away from Rome and proclaim himself Protector and Only Supreme Head of the Church in England.

I saw our father invested with the title Earl of Wiltshire.

I saw Anne created Marquis of Pembroke – not Marchioness, but Marquis, a man's title ranking only below a duke, making her a peer in her own right. She wore crimson velvet for the ceremony, ermine-bordered, with a coronet of jewels on her flowing hair.

I did not see the strange wedding which I had told George would never happen. Anne had told me nothing beforehand, and told me very little afterwards. It was not the ceremony she had dreamed of.

At the end of January 1533, a few people met together, shivering in the dark of the dawn in a small room in a turret of the new Palace of Whitehall, which had been York Place and was now being re-built – to please Anne.

Our father and mother were there, and George, and Anne's attendant, a Mistress Savage. For the groom there was Henry Norris and Thomas Heneage, of the Bedchamber. Nobody else, besides the priest, a royal chaplain who was not sure why he had been summoned or what he had to do.

When the King told him, he hesitated, but the King reassured him – the Pope had pronounced for the divorce, he said, and he held a dispensation for re-marriage. The King looked him in the eye, and lied.

The Nuptial Mass had never been said more quickly. When it was over, the last, binding words spoken – *Quod ergo Deus conjunxit, homo non separet* – the company rose from their knees and fled like ghosts at the coming of day.

This I heard from George, after he came back from a mission to France, to tell the French King confidentially of the marriage. It was Anne herself who betrayed her secret – to Tom Wyatt, of all people, meeting him in an anteroom, crowded with people. She was all glowing with excitement, like a flame, a rose tree.

'Three days since I had an uncommon fierce desire to eat apples,' she told him, loudly enough to be heard by all. 'I never liked them before. The King says it's a sign that I must be with child. But I tell him no, it cannot be!'

Laughing wildly, she ran from the room.

Those left behind stared, a whole room full of people shocked into silence.

17

'Come on shore, come on shore,' said the crow to the frog, and then, O,
'No, you'll bite me, no, you'll bite me,' said the frog to the crow again, O.
'Madame, you're welcome.'

In the joyful pageantry that followed this wedding I was only a small, unremarkable figure in black velvet, one of Anne's sixty maids of honour – thirty more than Queen Catherine had ever had. Some were in cloth of gold, some in crimson, but I chose the black, though not from lack of rejoicing for my sister.

I was more glad for her triumph than anyone except Anne herself. Yet I was made uneasy by a small thing which I doubt that any other observer saw, unless it was our mother, who watched Anne with constant devotion, but would not speak to me beyond the civilities of every day.

It was that the King's eyes, in watching all the festivities, were not on her face, as they had been at all times, but on her rapidly swelling belly. It was now May, and she was about four months gone; the child showed more than in another woman, so slender was her frame.

She and I had only spoken intimately once since that clandestine wedding. She was suffering from a sickness of early pregnancy, in which she wanted nobody but me to be with her: how strange. Mistress Orchard, resentful, fetched me.

I sat by Anne, sponging her brow with rosewater. Her face was greenish-pale, and she looked forty, though she was only twenty-six, lying on her bed like a lady of marble.

'The King is good to you?' I asked. We both knew what I meant.

'Yes. Everything I could wish . . .' Her eyes opened. 'He's colder than I expected, Mall. The first time – he was so eager that it all went amiss. He was maladroit and I was gauche . . . Or that was how it seemed.' She added something in French that I did not catch. 'The next time it was better. And since he has known about the child he has treated me like gossamer.' She laughed, her sweet high laugh, but I did not join in.

Stroking her brow, damping the cloth, I pictured her fragility under that massive weight, which I well remembered. It was far more now that it had been, by stones. He had never been a subtle lover, even in his younger days. And she had been virgin.

We had never spoken of her and Tom Wyatt, but I knew, without her telling, how it had been between them. And between her and Henry. With the latter it had always been the chase, not the quarry, which is soon killed and eaten, as a woman is soon taken and cast aside. I had been lucky to be kept so long, but then I was very different from Anne – I was a wifely sort with a whore's tricks, a depraved child like one of the half-grown harlots of Bankside, grown to womanhood.

She had been frightened and hurt, and Henry – Henry had simply been disappointed. After six years and more of sighing and panting for her, the elusive tantalising nymph had proved to be a maid cold at heart towards him. God knows what strange delightful arts he had expected from her.

I asked, as if casually, 'Does he – take your fancy at all?'

She turned her head sharply away from me, giving me my answer.

Pressing, I said, 'Do you still love Harry Percy?'

'No,' she snapped. 'How you question. Leave it. I don't wish to be examined like a prisoner in court. You may go now.'

We were mistress and servant again, and the thing was no more spoken of. I prayed every day for her to all the helpful saints I could think of, and most particularly to Our Blessed Lady, who by my reckoning would have the most divine knowledge of women's problems, though she had of course been spared anything like Anne's.

That had been in the winter. By the spring the sickness had passed and all was joyfulness, except for the sour faces of Anne's baffled enemies – Chapuys, the Spanish ambassador, Suffolk, and Uncle Thomas Howard of Norfolk, who hated her. Archbishop Cranmer had given his formal judgment that the marriage between King Henry and Queen Catherine was invalid, and his re-marriage with Anne lawful. Now she was to be crowned Queen, on Whit Sunday, the Holy Day of Pentecost, in this year of 1533.

First came the Progresses, to show Anne to her new subjects. She sailed up the Thames from Greenwich to the Tower in a barge which had been Queen Catherine's. Her armorial bearings had been removed and Anne's substituted. Whether this touched the King's conscience with guilt I cannot say: but he made a fuss about it, saying that any other of the royal barges would have done.

He was waiting at the Tower to receive her, having had the old building modernised and made more luxurious for her comfort. Down a river thick with boats and loud with music she came in that barge bearing her own colours of purple and blue, other barges and little boats full of dignitaries clustering round it. One bore a mummer in a dragon skin, capering and spitting fire, ringed with attendant monsters and wild men.

Anne's personal badge, the White Falcon, had a barge to himself, a large effigy wearing real feathers, gold-crowned, sitting on a golden stem branched with red and white roses, and maidens singing to it – the words were impossible to hear in all that noise, but I suppose they were about Anne representing the tree which should bring forth roses, the blended red and white of Plantagenet and Tudor. Falcon's eggs. On every barge flags waved, hung with bells that tinkled in the fresh wind.

She stepped from her barge at the watergate of the Tower, as the guns boomed out their salute. A shining figure in cloth-of-gold, she moved with stately tread towards the King, who bent to kiss her reverently, then placed his hands on her sides, showing off to spectators the curve of her belly. Smiling, proud, triumphant, she stood between those huge hams of hands. Then he led her through the postern gate, and we, her Ladies of Honour, followed them to her splendid new apartments.

All night the trumpets and hautboys and citterns played and revellers sang, increasingly drunken as the hours wore on (there were a few bodies floating in the river next morning) while the dragon and his hideous friends continued to leap about and breathe flames until the artificial fire gave out. I and some of the others retired and fell into an uneasy sleep, but I intermittently heard Anne laughing and chattering far into the night, and the King's falsetto laugh joining in.

That was on 29 May. On Saturday, two days later, she made her Progress by land, from the Tower through the City. The weather was so hot that the procession could not start until five o'clock of the afternoon.

The splendour of that Progress was bewildering: what queen can ever have seen anything like it? The streets were hung with tapestries and cloths of crimson, scarlet, silver and gold and velvet. And the people of the procession were one great rainbow of colour – the French ambassador's party, in blue and yellow, Knights of Bath, scarlet-clad. And us ladies, on palfreys, older ones in chariots – our mother, haggardly beautiful, Agnes of Norfolk, her sharp glance taking in everything at once.

Fountains ran with Rhenish wine, children made painfully learned speeches, girls and boys dressed as Roman gods and Muses offered blessings, and choirs sang ballads and hymns in the new Queen's praise. Nobody ever saw such a show. And the Queen the brightest of all, in her surcoat of silver tissue and ermine-lined mantle, 'sitting in her hair', as they said, her tresses a dark mass falling round her like a heavy cloak, topped with a coif circled with rubies.

I glanced often at her face, smiling excited smiles, turning from side to side, enjoying triumph. Nobody would have guessed she was in her fourth month of pregnancy, in that flowing robe of silver. Even when she saw the triumphal arch of the Steelyard, a lovely structure over which some resentful German merchants had placed a great imperial eagle, the badge of enemy Spain, her bright gaze did not swerve. Or when at Leadenhall a child stepped forward from its place beside the image of St Anne, Our Lady's mother, and uttered a long speech ending: 'From her sprang a fruitful tree, the like shall spring from thee.'

St Anne's offspring had been one daughter, Our Blessed Lady, and from her Our Lord Christ. Glorious indeed, but hardly fruitful. Was that the malicious intention of the author, directed at a queen who above all things desired a Tudor son? Who was to know?

There were many caps on citizen's heads, but few doffed in respect, few cries of 'God save Your Grace'. Anne smiled and smiled, and would not be daunted. The people might want Good Queen Catherine and her carroty-headed daughter, but they must do without her. This Anne had said to me, not mincing her words.

'The Devil take them all, they shall have *me*.'

Oh Anne, my sister.

The next day, Coronation Day, excelled all. About nine of the morning Anne came into Westminster Abbey, her train held up by Agnes of Norfolk. The bright June sun beamed through the stained glass of the Abbey windows on her surcoat and mantle of purple velvet, the net of pearls and gems covering the crown of her head, and the circlet of rubies she had worn the day before. Even she had only one such coronet. Before her walked Suffolk, newly back in London, bearing the crown, hiding his sneer behind his spade-beard, and by him walked our father, so puffed up with pride that his face seemed about to crack. I saw our mother weeping. There seemed to be Howards everywhere, a good few of them among the female nobility of England, ranked stately in their scarlet velvet, ermine bars across their stomachers.

At the most awesome moment of the ceremony, the crowning,

Archbishop Cranmer, his look tender and fatherly, placed the great Crown of St Edward on her head, and delivered to her the sceptre and the ivory rod bearing the dove.

But her long slender neck was not able to support the weight of that great crown: when the choir had sung the *Te Deum* he anointed her with the sacred oil upon the brow and breast, and removing that crown substituted another, lighter one, specially made for her.

In that moment I had an unworthy thought. It might have been me. If I had been different, had played my cards wisely, held off and coquetted – if I had not been so free with my favours in France – if I had not given myself to young Guillaume in the turret room at Blois – if I had played on the young King Henry's susceptibility, when I first came back to England . . . then he might have made *me* his Queen, not my sister.

And Anne could have married Percy – or Tom Wyatt. And everything would have been quite different.

It must have been my better angel who tapped me on the shoulder, shaking its head and saying, 'Mary, Mary, consider well.' I considered, and was my humble self again.

When Queen Anne returned in procession from St Edward's shrine at the end of the ceremony, the hand that bore the golden sceptre was supported by our father, the other by Lord Talbot, brother-in-law of Harry Percy. It was an irony which I suspect nobody else noticed – except Anne herself.

At the coronation feast the King watched from a distance, in a specially built cabinet, for he meant the day to be all the Queen's. At the high table, twelve steps up, Anne sat in state, Cranmer on her right, throughout endless courses served up to the sound of trumpets. When she washed her hands in a gold finger-bowl it was Tom Wyatt who poured the water from the ewer. His face was completely expressionless.

Triumphantly crowned, Anne was not yet out of the wood. Catherine still considered herself Queen and would not call herself anything else, although by royal proclamation it was death for anyone to call her so. For two days the King's agents argued with her to acknowledge herself as Princess Dowager. She would not, and they left, defeated.

In revenge, the King moved her to the Bishop of Lincoln's house, Buckden in Huntingdonshire. It was remote and undesirable. On her way there the people cheered her and called down blessings on her.

Anne heard, and was furious. Unfortunately her fury spilled out over the King, as though it were his fault. He soothed her and tried to excuse her – a woman so far gone with child was bound to be unreasonable.

She tried to think of ways to get back at Catherine. In the richly appointed royal nursery, she looked round at the furnishings, which included a gorgeous cradle upholstered in crimson satin fringed with gold.

'I have it!' She turned to me exultantly. 'The Spanish baptismal robe she brought from Spain when she came to marry Arthur. She was always flaunting it, saying how many children it had wrapped. It shall wrap mine.'

I thought this was unkind, and said so. But she turned her back to me, and a letter was sent to Buckden, Catherine returned a hotter answer than usual. The robe should not be used in a case 'so horrible and abominable'. Anne was very angry, throwing things about, even in the nursery itself, which some of the maids thought bad luck. It was finally decided that the coming child should have a christening robe of imperial purple velvet, wrought with gilt lions.

It was not good news that the Pope had declared the marriage of Henry and Anne to be null and void, her child illegitimate, and Henry excommunicate – unless he put her away before the end of September and took back Catherine. The King might have renounced Pope Clement, but it was all ominous. People heard of it, and growled and grumbled, saying that the Whore had called down the wrath of Heaven on herself, at which Anne cursed them and ordered the King to punish them.

He reasoned, then argued, then walked away.

226

I said, 'Nan, be careful,' but I might as well not have spoken.

It was only a month or so before the expected birth that I heard something else. Anne had gone to Windsor, by the King's orders, to be in more peaceful surroundings, while he remained at Greenwich. I was about to follow her, when George arrived there from Rome, where he had been on embassy. I cornered him, though I could see that he was worried and did not seek my company.

'George, is it true? Is the King courting Lady Carew?'

He looked dartingly around him. 'Hush. What do you mean?'

'Well, rumour says he is. She's very beautiful, I should not be surprised if he is. But does Anne know?'

'Why ask me? Have I been here, to take notes of the King's smiles? I've barely combed my hair or had a drink since I set foot in England, and now I must go posting off back to Rome to persuade His Holiness not to grant King François an interview. Must you mutter at me about Lady Carew, or Lady Anyone? Uncle Norfolk is going half-mad about the Pope's matter, and so shall I unless I get some peace soon. Not at Rochford Hall – God forbid, Jane's there.'

Jane Rochford, in one of her madder moods, had objected publicly to Anne's coronation. Nobody was really sorry when the King, at Anne's suggestion, had had her committed to the Tower, to cool her heels and be a warning to others. Especially to our Aunt Norfolk, that bitter woman. I hoped George's infant son would not inherit his mother's half insanity.

I went to Windsor to attend on Anne, with the two other Annes, Gainsford and Savage, and Meg Lee, Tom Wyatt's sister.

The old castle was as chill and forbidding as ever, more like a fortress than a palace, even though the King had spared no expense on furnishings and tapestries.

As we entered the Queen's antechamber, screams and sobs could be heard coming from the room beyond. We glanced at each other. Mistress Orchard, hearing us, came out.

'The Queen is not well,' she told us flatly.

Meg started forward. 'Not the child, yet?'

'No. She has heard something she ought not to have heard, something that has disturbed her very sorely.'

I knew what it was, and my heart sank. And from their faces I saw that the others knew.

'Who told her?' asked Meg.

Mistress Orchard's face was grim. 'Lady Rochford. She posted here from Essex on hearing that the King was – diverting himself, and burst in here without my permission. No thanks to her that Her Grace didn't miscarry on the spot. She should be sent packing back to the Tower, to one of the dungeons. I'd see her whipped for the crazy bitch she is.' Mistress Orchard was working herself up to a temper that matched what we could hear of Anne's.

'May we go in?' Anne Savage pleaded. 'She should have company surely.'

'If you must, but be gentle, ladies, she has had a severe shock.'

The hysterical weeping had quieted when we entered Anne's bedchamber. She was lying huddled on the bed, a magnificent piece of furniture all carved with monsters and allegorical figures, and hung with damask, dazzlingly embroidered. The King had given it to her a month or so earlier, boasting that it was among the spoils of the ransom of the Duc d'Alençon.

She wore black, as though in mourning for her illusion that she still ruled her husband's heart. It was not funeral black, but a beautiful gown of flowing black satin, lined with taffeta of the same and trimmed with velvet. Its skirts stiffened with buckram, it spread all about her like a pool of ink. Black, to flatter her creamy skin and shining hair: the skin that was now blotched with weeping, the great eyes diminished by puffy pink lids, and the hair uncombed, wild about her swollen body.

In her arms she clasped Little Purkoy, now and then kissing his head, which was damp with tears. Urian the hound lay on the bed beside her, muzzle on paws. At our approach he growled: none of us dared go too near him. Recently he had killed a cow, for which the owner had been handsomely compensated.

Anne looked from one to another of us, fixing her tragic gaze on Meg.

'You own a wise head, Margaret. What do they call a female cuckold?'

'Madam?'

'Well? Do you not understand a plain question?' She had control of her voice now, husky though it was with weeping. 'Whatever the word is, the King has made one of me. Me! His lawful wife and the mother of his heir! No thanks to him if the boy is not born crippled. So faithless, so foully unkind . . .' As she began to sob again, the cry of hunting horns sounded from the courtyard below. Mistress Orchard hurried to the window.

'Jesu, the King. To come now, at such a time! Madam, you must not see him. Let me send word that you are sleeping – or that you have a fever – that will keep him away.'

'I will see him.'

'Better not,' I said.

'I will see him,' she repeated, louder. She looked like one of the Furies. Mistress Orchard bustled us out, herding us into the antechamber like sheep.

The King strode in, flushed from riding, jovial and brisk, a huge ruddy-visaged figure in forest green. As he passed the four of us he slapped Nan Gainsford on the rump. Me he did not acknowledge, which was usual.

At the bedchamber door he shouted, 'How's my boy today? Kicking lustily? In practice to be a great wrestler like his father?' Then, as he caught sight of Anne's face, 'What's amiss?'

We heard her answer on a high note. 'Your boy! Have you given *her* a boy as well, another bastard like Fitzroy? Is he to grow up a brother to our son? How do you write to her, if you're ever long enough away from her to write – are you *son seul H.R., qui ne cherche autre*? Well, answer me!'

We heard her using words that might have come from the bawd she sounded like, a trollop from the stews, words I had never heard

229

Anne use before. She was not herself. She had been so unwell throughout the last months of her pregnancy, had lost so much sleep – and there was the stress of waiting for the birth. The news of the King's amour with Lady Carew had dealt a blow all the harder for the many protestations of undying fidelity.

> As the holly groweth green, and the ivy too,
> So am I, ever have been, unto my lady true . . .

He had written that song for her. I could understand her well, a goddess whose shrine had been abandoned and desecrated.

But as she shouted and sobbed, and he tried to answer, I wanted to go in and shake her soundly, and shout myself: Fool, fool, be quiet! That's the way to lose him.

For I knew, nobody better – even Queen Catherine – that to please the King his woman must never argue with him, nor blame him for anything, nor cry – he could not stand tears. His pride must never be pricked, as Anne was doing now, at the top of her voice, within our hearing. This was the only way to keep, in the simplest sense, the King's Peace.

Without those rules I should have been out of his bed and his favour long before I was. But it had come easy to me, after life with my dominating, critical father, who had been proud of Anne but not of me. Under him I had learned to behave to the King like an obedient dog, affectionate and gentle, with only the very faintest show of pretty petulance when I thought it would amuse him: much the way Little Purkoy behaved to Anne. I had kept my own character – alas, such as it was! – so well out of his view that he had seldom called me by name, Mary, but more often Malkin (as we call cats), Mouse, Mignonne, or, if I were ever melancholy, Mumpsimus. That was how I had kept him so long.

Anne had broken these rules so often since becoming Queen. There had been the fuss she'd made about some people who had shouted against her. The King had done nothing about them, in spite of her nagging. And when she had heard of the Pope's decree she had created a noisy scene, much like the one we were listening to now.

I was angry with her and wretched for her. Poor displaced goddess, she had the fickle, dangerous King for a husband, and I had had Will. (With curious pain I found that I could hardly remember his face now. Five years dead, he was not even a ghost any more.)

The King's voice topped Anne's. I had just thought of him as dangerous. Now he sounded it.

'Have you finished, madam? Then listen to me for a moment, by your leave. I say nothing of what displeases you. If you mislike it you must shut your eyes and endure it, as your betters have done before you. I think you understand me.'

Indeed she did, we all did. Queen Catherine had been likened to Patient Griselda in her endurance of her husband's infatuation with her lady-in-waiting; not a wrong word.

'Therefore, madam, you must know that as much as I have raised you up, it is in my power to cast you down again – and lower than you were. Take heed of that!'

He came out of the bedchamber, slamming the door behind him. His face had turned the livid blackish-red colour few of us had been unlucky enough to see. He stood, legs astride, thumbs hooked in his belt of wrought silver, while we huddled like birds, saying nothing. Then we saw the furious flush die out of his face, as though by the effort of his will, and the tiny mouth actually smiled. He was again the image of the genial monarch, the people's Good King Harry. Provided you did not look in his eyes.

'Well, mistresses! The Queen is fretful today. Frampold, I think the old wives call it, eh? You, Mistress Orchard, I hear you have a special skill in brewing soothing draughts, but nothing over-strong, mind, that might disagree with my son. But the auguries are splendid, you know that, of course?'

We murmured something.

'Yes, the astrologers assure me that my son will be born in my very image, a Tudor king in little, even in his cradle.' (I reflected

231

that so had my son been, and much good had it done him.) 'They all say it, to a man – and woman, for a very notable sorceress of Norwich has offered to stake her life on it. Hardly needful, ha ha!'

We laughed dutifully, except Mistress Orchard.

'What shall we call him, eh? Henry, or Edward, for his noble great-grandfather, and the other great Edwards? What do you say?'

We said nothing, having been so shaken by the Queen's outburst. He muttered irritably, 'Well, well, well,' and strode out of the room. Downstairs we heard him roaring at someone. I hoped it might be Jane Rochford.

'Go in to her, you two,' Mistress Orchard said to Savage and Gainsford. 'Say nothing untoward, be calm and usual, make her bed comfortable. Ask her to be good enough to persuade that monstrous dog off it.'

To Meg and me, with a grave face, she said, 'I have a terrible fear. The fortune-tellers may say what they like, or what the King wants to hear. But I've seen more women nearing their time than he has, or many about this Court, and I know how a child lies in the womb. That one is no boy, by my reckoning.'

We must have looked as appalled as we felt. Meg fell on her knees then and there, crossing herself and muttering prayers. She herself was pregnant, and should by rights have been at home, but her love for Anne had kept her in attendance. Rising, she whispered, 'What shall I bear?'

'A boy.' (This was true, as we knew by the end of the year.) 'Any child must be,' Mistress Orchard went on, 'either boy or girl, by the laws of Nature. Does Nature favour either gender, to put more men into the world than women, or endow an unborn child with male members because its father is a king?'

'God,' I murmured. 'The will of God.' Mistress Orchard threw me a contemptuous glance and swept into the bedchamber.

Anne was to lie in at Greenwich, by the King's choice. In the Chamber of Presence the Great Bed of State awaited, and in the bedchamber were two more beds, the Duc d'Alençon's ransom and a pallet bed, for Anne to receive company after the birth. It was our duty to see that everything was ready for the event, the sheets of finest lawn prepared, the special birth-pillows plumped up invitingly, the canopied cradle of estate with its ermine-edged covering turned back, waiting for the baby.

Gainsford said to me, 'The King told someone that Her Grace was lucky to get the French bed when she did, for after the business of Lady Carew he would not have given it to her.'

'Who was this someone?'

'I don't know. Nobody who matters.'

'Then don't repeat what nobody-who-matters says. Why is the pallet bed only used for receiving? It would be better for the mother to be delivered on it, then those who needed to help her could be at close grips.'

Gainsford stared. 'It's the custom! Any servant or fishwife can lie on a pallet.'

In early September the time came for chamber-taking, the day when Anne was to be shut up in the room where her delivery was to take place. It had all been formally arranged by the King's father, Henry VII, and kept up rigidly by his fearsome grandmother, Lady Margaret Beaufort (who herself had been brought to bed at fourteen and doubtless took a grim delight in the sufferings of other royal ladies).

First, though not yet in labour, Anne was taken to the Chapel Royal to hear Mass. Then, under a Cloth of Estate, she was served with the traditional cup of spiced wine. Her Chamberlain prayed that God might send her a good hour, after which she was escorted by George and our Uncle Norfolk into the Privy Chamber, accompanied only by us, her women.

Not all, of course, only a chosen number. Anne had beckoned me close to her and, smiling for the public view, said, 'Stay with me.'

She had chosen for one of her mottoes *La Plus Heureuse*, The Most Happy. But I saw no happiness in her eyes, only wild fear of the thing she could not escape. Yet she smiled and smiled, as they took her into the chamber from which (by order of the long-dead

Lady Margaret) all light except candlelight had been excluded, the windows shrouded, like the walls, in rich tapestries. Here and there a fugitive ray of sunshine glittered. It was increasingly hot, even under that high ceiling, increasingly stuffy and sweaty. I thanked God that I had been lucky enough to bear my royal children on the wrong side of the blanket, and in the humble condition of Will Carey's wife.

Our mother was there, and Agnes of Norfolk. As elder ladies they were allowed to come and go as they pleased, though with due ceremony. Agnes, used to such scenes, had brought her tapestry frame and sat working at it and chatting as Anne's pains began.

'I wonder if Suffolk and his new bride are married yet?' she said to our mother. 'I shall always think he killed the poor Princess Mary with his infidelities. Always at Court when she lay in the country so ill, and taking one inamorata after another – no wonder she pined away. I knew that man was of common stuff the first time I set eyes on him.'

'"Cloth of Frize"', said our mother, who was not embroidering, but had her eyes fixed on the bed where her daughter lay, invisible for the cluster of people about her.

'What? Oh, yes, that rhyme round their portrait. Truly she was cloth of gold, poor thing – the best of the Tudors. Princess Margaret, Queen Margaret I should say, was too silly, and young Mary is all too clearly her mother's child, as Spanish-obstinate as Catherine . . .'

I had heard it all before, and so had our mother. She beckoned me.

'Go and see how she is.'

It was the first time she had spoken to me voluntarily for all of two years. It took this fateful occasion to allow her to forget her disapproval of me.

Anne had not reached the worst yet. She sweltered under the weight of bedclothes, a counterpane of hot-looking scarlet on top of them all. Her arms were outside, and I saw her fists clench as the pains took her.

She had a terrible labour, far worse than either of mine. She was so narrow-hipped and slender, not made for child-bearing. It was a woman's lot, of course, the Curse ordained by God on Eve, but if there was one among her attendants who did not pity her then, I would have been ashamed in the name of womanhood. She laboured all that day and night, and the day that followed, until between three and four of the clock in the afternoon of Sunday, 7 September, with our mother gripping her hand, she gave birth.

To a red-haired daughter. A fine well-formed child, with a lusty cry, but a daughter, not the Prince of Wales for whom the King had confidently arranged.

A girl could not carry on the Tudor line. Whoever heard of a Queen Absolute? It would all be to go through again. My heart bled for Anne, who herself had bled quite enough already, poor creature. The fine lawn sheets were not what they had been.

Our mother told her, trying to smile about it, and Agnes, the appointed chief godmother, brought the yelling scrap to the bedside on a gold-edged pillow no more scarlet than itself.

Anne's eyes were glazed with pain, and she hardly seemed to know what she saw, but she turned them towards our mother and whispered, 'Elizabeth.'

And Elizabeth, the bitterly disappointed King agreed, was a good enough name, the name of his Plantagenet mother. It mattered very little, after all, since she was only a girl.

It was three months after this, when the Palace of Whitehall was ablaze with Christmas candles, and the baby Elizabeth, now firmly in the King's favour as Princess of Wales, was holding court very graciously, that I met and fell in love with William Stafford.

18

When he came to the merry mill-pin,
'Lady Mouse, are you within?'
Then out came the dusty mouse:
'I am the lady of this house.'
'Hast thou any mind of me?'
'I have e'en great mind of thee.'

There was masque after masque, of course. Some were rather on the pagan side for that season, but the King, in his new capacity as Head of the Church, had no objection. Yule had been a pagan festival before it became a Christian one.

Anne's Chamberlain, a man of pious nature, thought a more holy masque might temper the general spirit of levity. (These Puritans were creeping in everywhere.) So Tom Wyatt somewhat wearily devised a Masque of Angels and Devils – hardly a new idea, but it gave everyone a chance. Francis Bryan observed that we might as well all be on the side of Hell, since that was our natural habitat.

Anne danced in it, but only at the beginning, and formally. The older ladies had been recruited as masquers, some reluctantly, like our mother, some enthusiastically, like Agnes of Norfolk who was proud of her still neat ankles and agile limbs. Our mother was St Elizabeth of the Roses, a pretty compliment to her name and her granddaughter's, and Agnes also kept her baptismal name, carrying a toy lamb.

Anne represented St Barbara, I have no idea why. She was the patroness of storms, which was appropriate enough, and of artil-lery-men, which was not. She wore a low-cut gown of white, trimmed with ermine, rose-coloured satin knots catching up the full sleeves, a crown – unofficial but of real gold. Her hair was plaited in great loops round her head, and she looked truly queenly, carrying a chalice holding a symbolical musket ball as though it were the Orb itself.

But her face, when she was not dutifully smiling, fell into sad lines. Not much more than a week earlier they had taken the baby Elizabeth away to live in her own household, at Hatfield House in Hertfordshire. The baby in her nurse's arms had been carried through the streets in an open litter, so that the people could get a good view of her.

Anne missed her baby sorely. Since that terrible birth she had kept Elizabeth with her day and night: I never saw a mother so devoted to her child (I certainly had not been to my little shrew Catherine) and the child seemed to be more at ease in her arms than in its wet nurse's, though the nurse was the one sho supplied the food which is all that is supposed to matter to an infant.

Elizabeth. Not only Anne's stake in the Tudor dynasty, but the only person who had ever been truly hers. All the passion my sister had not been able to give the King went to this tiny girl, with her unusually beautiful hands and the eyes which had turned dark, Howard eyes under Tudor hair of autumn red.

'She will catch cold,' Anne lamented after Elizabeth had been taken on her journey. 'To carry a babe so young through the cold December air, not even a roof on the litter! Why must she be apart from me?'

'It's the custom,' I said, 'A princess must learn to be her own mistress early.'

'*Mary* was not apart from Catherine when she was a baby – I found that out. Catherine was allowed to keep her child by her. Why?'

'That was different,' I said weakly. 'The Queen Dowager had lost so many babes . . . the King could not bear to part them.'

'He can bear to part *us*, it seems. Well, I shall make that young bitch pay for it. She shall stop her sulking at Hertford Castle and be taken to Hatfield to wait on my daughter. She – that proud-stomached thing – shall do the lowest nursery tasks, and think herself lucky to do them for a royal princess, as she is not one.'

There was a mutual loathing between Anne and the seventeen-year-old Princess Mary, now robbed of her title and known as the Lady Mary. Having decided to elevate Elizabeth, the King was not doing things by halves. Mary had suffered plenty of humiliation already, and this was to be yet another.

She took it badly. Word travelled rapidly back from Hatfield by means of our Uncle Norfolk (who enjoyed breaking bad news) that the Lady Mary had raved and stamped, insulting Anne and Elizabeth equally, referring to Anne as Madame de Pembroke and implying that her marriage was no marriage. As for Elizabeth, she said, she would call the child 'sister' exactly in the sense that she called young Fitzroy 'brother': bastards both.

Anne sent back an order that Mary should be slapped hard if she persisted in calling herself princess, and that she should be deprived of all her old servants and her confessor. It was vindictive, but she was dealing with a vindictive girl and I, who disliked Mary, secretly rather admired Anne for the line she was taking. Tudor offspring probably needed more slapping than they received.

Our Uncle Norfolk, ferrying to and fro between Hatfield and Whitehall with furious messages, thoroughly enjoyed setting one woman against the other. He smiled, for once, all over his hatchet face, and the cast in his left eye veered hideously.

But why do I talk about our hateful uncle, when I had begun to remember that Christmas masque? In one of the newest and most splendid chambers of Whitehall, two 'houses' had been built, of wood and plaster, one a Hell-mouth with great grinning teeth and a cavern of a throat, all covered with crimson dragon's scales. From this emerged the devils, male courtiers in scarlet tight-fitting doublet and hose, short golden goats' horns fastened to their heads and long tails attached to their rumps. They wore glittering eye-masks and false beards of wire, gold and silver and red, and imitation flames and smoke rolled out of the cavern behind them.

On the other side of the hall rose Heaven, a palace of milk-white feathers set with brilliants, and we, the Court ladies, were angels in snowy satin with little wings attached to our shoulders and gilt haloes (very difficult to keep straight) on our heads. We danced a formal measure of attack and defence, then partnered off, each devil wooing each angel into the ways of sin (but most decorously, the saints having their keen eyes on the proceedings).

My partner was a man I could not recognise from what I could see of his features, which were largely hidden behind a beard of scarlet wire which kept slipping off one ear, so that he constantly hooked it back.

He was not the most graceful of dancers, having considerable trouble with his tail, which kept getting between his feet. He murmured apologies as our steps faltered, and I found myself beginning to giggle. In despair of managing it, he hooked it over his arm.

It broke off, leaving him holding the tail like a tame snake. I laughed so much that I had to stop dancing. He began to join in, stared at by a few other dancers who were doing much better than we were. Young Weston danced like an angel rather than a devil, and George could never be other than graceful. But my unhandy partner and I were in a class of our own, for I had taken more wine than I should have done and my steps were unsteady.

I pulled him by the hand. 'Come,' I said, when I could speak for laughing, 'let's go out.' He followed me through the ranks of dancers towards the doors, down a corridor where guards, standing stiff and tall, regarded us calmly as though two wildly giggling people in costume were not a sight out of the ordinary.

The gardens where we found ourselves were beautiful and thoroughly unseasonable. Their carved stone pillars were twined round with ropes of artificial pearls, interwoven with bright flowers of silk and gauze; other false blooms clustered about where real ones no longer grew, the lights from coloured lanterns beaming over all.

I sank down on a bench, my hand to my side, where a painful stitch had developed. My partner sat down beside me and surveyed the scene.

'Extremely fine growth for the time of year,' he said, at which I began to laugh again.

He nodded sadly, 'You may well laugh, madam. I must be the worst dancer in the mortal world. I regret that I brought you into ridicule, but they would know it was not your fault. The trouble is, I am really a soldier.'

Wiping my eyes, I asked, 'Where did you serve? There have been no recent wars, to my knowledge.'

'In the army of the Archduchess – the late Archduchess – of the Netherlands, madam.'

'But I served her, too! Long ago, when I was a girl. She died three years or so ago, I remember. Where have you been since then, sir?'

He shuffled his feet awkwardly. 'The Emperor Charles was good enough to offer me a place . . . for a time. Then I joined the garrison at Calais . . .'

He needed to say no more. I knew without telling that he had been hanging about Europe for those three years, doing anything that came to hand, willing and amiable, but without any real ambition: my father would have had him kicked out.

'And now?' I asked.

'His Grace – His Majesty, I think I should say – was kind enough to take me as one of his Gentlemen-Ushers.'

What an honour, I thought cynically. Just one of the hundred and seventy or so gentlemen under the Lord Chamberlain's rule – ushers and grooms and pages and esquires and table-waiters. A little higher than the servants below stairs under the Lord Steward, but nothing very great. I asked him his name; it was William Stafford, but he did not add that there was a knighthood attached to it. He was, it seemed, of the family of the great Duke of

Buckingham who had lost his head for being too near the King in blood. He had been brought up at the dead Duke's home, Thornbury Castle in Gloucestershire; and indeed I noticed a faint pleasant West Country tang to his voice, which reminded me of the Devon in Will's.

Then, suddenly conscious of looking ridiculous, he pulled off the wire beard and the mask, with an exclamation of impatience at himself for wearing them so long. And I saw a face which also brought Will's to mind, a sweet indeterminate mouth and kind eyes – even hair that grew untidily, as Will's had done.

He was young, in his early twenties, I guessed. And instantly I thought of something that had not troubled me before – that in the coming year I would be thirty years old. An ageing, stoutening widow, already with grey threads in her hair, who should not aspire to courtship.

Yet that was what I wanted from William Stafford, even after so few minutes' acquaintanceship – that he should think me beautiful and desirable, and woo me.

We looked at each other, long and intently, in the flickering lantern light, the music for the dancing floating to us on the cold air, the sounds of the river beyond the garden, distant laughter, a girl's squeal of pretended dismay: there were others in the gardens.

He asked my name, in turn. Instead of remarking on my kinship with the Queen, and becoming deferential, as another might have done, he said, 'I knew George Boleyn – Viscount Rochford – at the Emperor's court.'

'Yes. My brother. And the Earl and Countess of Wiltshire are my parents, the Duke of Norfolk my uncle, Sir Edward Boleyn another uncle, and so on, down to the least Boleyn and Howard relation. And I am the least of all, I am nobody and I have nothing, only my pittance as Her Grace's lady.'

I had certainly drunk too much, for babbled all to this complete stranger. I talked as I had never talked to anyone before. Except Will, and I began to feel as if I were talking to him now, Will come back from the shades.

He interrupted me gently, touching my hand. 'Won't you take off your mask?'

'With pleasure. But don't expect beauty like the Queen's. I am only the ugly sister, *la laideronerette.*' I pulled off the pearl angel mask.

After a moment of studying my face, he said, 'Her Grace is beautiful, as you say. But her face is thinner than it should be and there are small lines on it: I would not have guessed she is younger than you. Also, when she smiles, two of her teeth at the top over-wrap a little. I would not say that was a fault, but yours are as straight as a row of pearls. You are not ugly at all – indeed I would call you very comely, though a little plump. I would guess you eat more than you should, to comfort yourself.'

I said, 'William Stafford, you seem to me to be a completely honest man. Too honest for a court. Be wary; take good care.'

'I will. And I would take good care of you, madam.'

He rose and offered me his arm. I took it, and we walked through those fantastic gardens, which now had a new enchantment which had nothing to do with imitation pearls and flowers of fabric.

Two nights later he came to my bed, in the cheap, obscure lodging I had taken. (I had told Anne that I missed Meg Lee's company since she had left Court to have her child, and that I would rather be alone than among the younger women. She seemed not to think it odd, and gave me a new gown as a Christmas present. Some of the ladies had received palfreys and saddles of Spanish leather, but what would I have done with a personal palfrey?)

I was very happy with William Stafford – happier than I had been with Will, for I had not the children to drag at me. I felt ten years younger, the extra flesh William had ungallantly mentioned dropping off me. People paid me compliments – me! I even caught the King's glance on me – he who usually avoided my eyes. But William and I were discreet, and nobody guessed.

But the day came – a beautiful, hopeful spring day – when I had to tell him, 'I am with child.'

There was joy in his face. 'I am heartily glad of it, sweet. We must be married – tomorrow, if you like.'

'No.'

'Ah, you're thinking of the banns that take three weeks. But you could speak to Archbishop Cranmer, who used to be your family chaplain – '

'I was not thinking of the banns. I was thinking that . . . the Queen will not like it.' She would look with no favour on a marriage of mine to yet another second son, landless, without money or prospects, related to Buckingham, who had been executed for no offence, and to his daughter, who had married Uncle Norfolk and caused a great deal of trouble to Anne. The Staffords were not a family greatly popular with the throne.

'Then what shall we do?' William asked helplessly.

I pondered. 'We could be married secretly, and then I could go away. Tell the Queen I'm unwell, or want to be near the children. At any rate, I must leave Court.'

'But then I shall not see you.'

'Alas.' I kissed him. 'We can hold out for a while yet – see, my waist is as slim as a bedpost.'

And so it remained, with a little help from my wearing of dresses to hide it. At all costs I must avoid inserting a panel of material into skirts, as Anne had done so proudly, flaunting her pregnancy. It seemed not worth the trouble of asking to be excused my Court duties until my condition became obvious. We had been married, rather furtively, by a priest who accepted that we were legally contracted.

It was George's wife, Jane Rochford, who caused my downfall: it would be. I was one of those whom Crazy Jane envied and hated. We were in a pleasant parlour at Greenwich, flooded by sunlight, as warm as they say the climate of Italy is. An Italian musician, Signor Bassano, who had recently come to Court with his family, was entertaining us, Anne and a few of us ladies. He was a handsome man, grey-haired with seductive dark eyes under thick brows, and he played the lute like an angel.

His son Baptista, an equally handsome boy with dark curls, sang to his father's accompaniment, a languorous song of his own country. Joining in with the occasional plangent chord was a young English musician, Marc Smeton, a groom of the King's chamber. He was only a carpenter's son but, as Anne said, so was another not unknown Personage. He was exceptionally beautiful, for a male and an Englishman, in a sensuous fashion, and he adored Anne quite openly.

The Italian song ended, to applause from us all. Then, at a nod from his father, Baptista began to sing. It was a setting of *Salve Regina*. After a few bars, Marc's voice joined Baptista's in lovely harmony. It was impossible not to notice that Marc's gaze never left Anne's face. The Hymn might celebrate the Queen of Heaven, but the worship was all for the Queen of England.

Anne relaxed visibly in that atmosphere of music and love. She was pale and looked unwell, since her last miscarriage, the second of the year, and she needed reassurance and consolation.

What I did not realise was that Jane was watching me, not the musicians. When the hymn was ended and servants were taking round wine, she stood up with a rustle of skirts and very deliberately went to Anne's side. She bent to whisper, and I saw her look hard at me, and Anne's look follow hers.

Anne beckoned to me. The musicians were talking animatedly to the ladies, the Italians flirting, Marc still more intent on Anne than any of the company. I stood before my sister, knowing too well what was coming.

'You are with child,' she said. It was a statement, not a question.

I whispered, 'Yes.'

Abruptly she dismissed her attendants and the musicians. Jane contrived to remain, hovering in malicious expectancy.

The storm broke. Anne threw at me all the things I had expected. I was a disgrace, a loose woman; single-handed I had done her more harm than anyone else about the Court. My very existence shamed the Boleyn name, and the names of Howard and Rochford. And so on, while I stood there hot-cheeked.

At last I managed to say that I was married, and to whom.

'William Stafford? Master Nobody. Could you do no better than that? Besides, I don't believe it. Who wed you, a drunken hedge-priest?'

'No, it was a Father Thomas of Clerkenwell . . .'

She laughed hysterically. 'Are you sure it wasn't the Blessed St Thomas of Canterbury? It would need a saint from Heaven to sanctify a marriage of yours. Tell me a better story than that.'

I could say nothing to calm her, and when she had raged herself hoarse she ordered me out. Jane, in the corner, laughed silently.

I knew we were defeated. I told William so, but he was more hopeful than I. I grieved, not only for us but for Anne. It was not like her to turn me away unheard, but she had suffered great disappointments in her own pregnancies; it must have been hard for her to see me thriving in mine. Besides, the King's fancy was swerving again: he had a new lady in mind, and not only in mind.

Anne told the King about me, which also was not like her. He might have taken my part, if only to anger her, but instead he sent William a contemptuous letter of dismissal, telling him to take his slut of a wife with him. Uncle Norfolk was delighted to inform us how much we had both disgraced his name and his wife's (his wife! He was living openly with a mistress). He threatened to have me beaten publicly and to order William to lose his right hand for stealing a woman of Howard blood. My father passed me in an antechamber without even a sideways look, and later sent a maid of my mother's with an icy note to say that he was discontinuing the poor allowance I had from him.

Even George cold-shouldered me. 'You're a fool,' he told me when I went to plead with him. 'You always were. God send you a better brain.'

Only, before we left the palace, Mistress Orchard came to us and spoke kindly, which astonished me, since I had always thought Anne her great favourite. She made me show her the wedding ring which I had been wearing on a chain between my breasts, and nodded. 'I knew you would not whore. Go to my sister at Lambeth and lodge with her, she'll charge you little more than the price of your food. Take this towards the babe's clothing.' She gave me a purse and left hurriedly before I could find that it was full of gold pieces.

Her sister treated us generously and we were well lodged. But the gold pieces were spent one by one, until we were truly poor and William talking of going back to serve in Calais.

Then I knew what I must do. I sat down and painstakingly wrote a letter to Thomas Cromwell, the King's Secretary of State, a very powerful man who had the King's ear in most things. Little did I think what an enemy we would have in him. I wrote (and I carefully copied my letter to keep):

Master Secretary: From a poor banished creature, this desires you to be good to my poor husband and me, for it is not unknown to you the high displeasure that both he and I have of the King's Highness and the Queen's Grace, by reason of our marriage without their knowledge. We know ourselves wrong in this, and grieve for it with all our hearts.

But, good Master Secretary, I beg you to sue for us to the King's Highness, and beseech him that it will please him of his goodness to speak to the Queen's Grace for us, for I perceive Her Grace is so highly displeased with us both that without the King be so good a lord to us as to sue for us, we are never like to recover Her Grace's favour, which is too heavy to bear. One thing, I pray you, consider – that my husband was young, and love overcame reason. And for my part I saw so much honesty in him that I loved him as well as he did me; and was in bondage, and glad I was to be at liberty; so that for my part I saw that all the world did set so little by me, and he so much, that I thought I could take no better way but to take him and forsake all other ways, and to live a poor honest life with him; and so I do not doubt but we should, if we might once be so happy to recover the King's gracious favour and the Queen's. For well I might 'a had a greater man of birth and a higher, but I assure you I could

246

never 'a had one that should 'a loved me so, nor a more honest man.

We have been now a quarter of a year married, I thank God, and too late now to call that back again. I had rather beg my bread with him than to be the greatest Queen christened.

It was not a good letter, I knew that – I had used 'poor' too much and shown my ignorance in other ways, I daresay.

Yet, within two weeks, a messenger came to us with a brief note to say that by royal grace and mercy I was to be granted a pension enough to keep us and the child. No more than that, nor anything to say whose was the royal favour.

And later, by the hand of Mistress Orchard, came another piece of paper, with my name, Lady Stafford, on one side of it and on the other some words from the English Bible: 'But one thing is needful; and Mary hath chosen that good part which shall not be taken away from her.'

I knew then that Anne was sorry: and that when she needed me most she would call me back to her.

Here ends Mary Stafford's narrative, written at Rochford Hall, in the County of Essex, in the year of Our Lord 1548.

SIX

TOM WYATT'S NARRATIVE

'But where is the sweet music on yonder green hill, O,
And where are all the dancers, the dancers in yellow?'
'Madam, they're here.'

I am perhaps confused in my mind, when I look back on that time. It seemed life lived in the darkness of a gathering storm.

There were rays of sunshine, if they had been true sunshine, not the false glitter of the lighting at a masque. The King smiled on me: I was made High Steward of West Malling near my family home, in Kent, which came very timely because I was so much in debt and was glad of the extra income. My father, with his brain for figures, could never understand why I was such a spendthrift – I owed money, too much, to the King himself. I had even had a short sharp sojourn in the Fleet prison for a silly fight with one of the City sergeants. Then I was given a lease on some rich land, in Yorkshire, and finally, on Easter Day of 1535, I was knighted. My father was pleased, and proud, and doubtful. I think he often looked keenly at my son Thomas, now in his fifteenth year, hoping that he would turn out to be anything but one who was a poet first and a courtier second.

Thomas Cromwell favoured me. He was Master of the Rolls now, and Vicar-General, and one of the King's great friends. I liked him and trusted him, though many did not. Why was I not easy in my mind, with the sun shining so warmly?

I was in love again. It had seemed impossible once. But Anne had been out of my reach for so long, and I was still young, separated from my wife for years, restless and romantic. When I first saw Elizabeth Darrell at Court I thought she was wearing a wig made from some other woman's hair, so fair it was, the light golden colour sometimes seen on the heads of children. She was very young, perhaps fifteen, of a Wiltshire family. Her complexion was country-fair and her look merry.

It was my sister Meg who presented me to her, for no other reason than to put two people in conversation who knew nothing of each other. I think she said I had a son of about Mistress Darrell's age. Certainly Meg had no intention that I should form a fancy for this young fresh nymph.

But I did, a fancy that would not leave my thoughts or dreams. I wrote sonnets to her, calling her Phillis, praising her bright looks and cheerful aspect. She could not have been more different from Anne, and I was not captivated as I once had been, yet my man's nature told me I needed a new lady in my heart.

I was not free of Anne's strange enchantment. Who could be, that had ever felt it? Only I no longer wrote sonnets to my 'Brunet', because I thought it not wise. Francis Bryan praised her fulsomely in his verse, as did her brother George (a better poet than either of us, to my mind). We sang these rhymes in her rooms, grouped about her like bearded Muses on Helicon; sometimes singing in twos and threes, with Marc Smeton and one of the Bassano family twangling on the spinet (Marc's particular instrument) or the lute.

I remember a morning when someone opened the ballet-book at a lyric of the King's, set by himself as a trio. It had been written for Anne in the days of their courtship, and ran:

> The daisy delectable, the violet wan and blue,
> Ye are not variable – I love you and no more.

I forget who stopped singing and began to laugh. Then we all joined in and the music turned to chaos.

'However dazzling my sister's charms,' spluttered George, 'it would be a skent pair of eyes that saw in her a daisy or a violet.'

Young Bassano looked puzzled. 'What is skent?'

'Squinting,' George explained. 'Crossed, like this.' He illustrated. 'Looking both ways for Sunday.'

'Hush!' Anne snapped. 'Have you no sense, any of you? George, for shame. And Tom, what would your father say?'

What, indeed? My father, a Wyatt loyal to the Crown, come what might, never criticised the King by even the whisper of a hint, much less made jokes. I remember that one of Anne's ladies rose and left the room during that silly dialogue. Who, I wonder?

Marc had not laughed. He murmured, as close to Anne's skirts as he dare be for the hound Urian, 'Her Grace is not a daisy nor a violet nor any common flower – she's a rose, a lovely damask rose, *rosa sine spina.*'

Anne threw him a glance half annoyed, half affectionate. She was glad of praise these days, anything to make her feel admired and safe.

Safe. There was another royal mistress, a girl Anne hated and tried to rid herself of, in vain. It was the old story – what had been good enough for Queen Catherine must be good enough for her. And something worse than a mistress. The King had met a cousin of Francis Bryan, Jane Seymour, a woman neither very pretty nor very young, and looked at her hard and long. She was modest, shy, virtuous. Hints were dropped: Brian persuaded her to come to Court as one of Anne's ladies. In her mousy way she was very clever; clever enough to catch and capture the King.

And there was menace in France: would François accept the baby Elizabeth as a bride for the Dauphin? Henry had refused to give them the Princess Mary, since she was now officially bastardised.

George came back from his mission to the French King with a refusal – such a marriage would offend the Pope too much, François said. Anne was distraught. She had hoped for so much from her old friend, the gallant tom-cat king who could have made her secure by the betrothal of her baby daughter. He had betrayed her, and Henry was angry. She no longer held a trump card in Elizabeth. She needed to conceive again, but God alone knew how, since the

King seldom even spoke to her, and then it was in a sharp tone, with that choleric look we all dreaded.

His choler was finding terrible expression. The wise and great Sir Thomas More died by the axe because he would not take the oath declaring the King to be Head of the Church in England. When the King heard that More's venerable head was off he was playing at dice with Anne. He threw them down on the table. 'This is all your doing – the honestest man of my kingdom is dead,' he bellowed, and stamped out.

And old John Fisher, Bishop of Rochester, went the same way. The Pope, Henry heard, had made Fisher a cardinal. Very well, said our King, he should have the head to put the hat on. In fact, the grey head went up on a spike at the end of London Bridge, with More's. Anne had been no friend to Fisher, but she protested, and again the King put the blame on her. She was rash enough to say that he should be grateful to her, for having brought him out of sin, made him rich with the spoil of the monasteries, and been the cause of his reforming the Church.

Only Anne would have dared. One did not say such things to Henry. She was as brave as a lion, but thought little before she spoke. As other beasts do when the lion is wounded, people began to turn against her. Her Uncle Norfolk, always her enemy, now publicly called her a whore. Even my friend Francis Bryan ceased to fawn on her and began to sneer. Old scandals were revived, new ones invented and the people listened, and chattered, and pointed.

She tried so hard to be a good queen. It was not for vain show; she was changing from the frivolous woman she had once seemed. She turned to the pursuits of any humble country housewife, working with her delicate skilful fingers not only at tapestries, but at shirts and garments for the poor – the common people who were chattering and pointing, not caring that their new garments came from her, or that the bounty provided for them in every parish came from her Privy Purse. She had reports made of boys who showed promise, and students her chaplains knew, and paid for their education. I think she now read and learned from the

Scriptures for the first time. Latin is all very well and a most noble tongue, but the young eye skips over it. Anne had rescued a bishop, Hugh Latimer, from prison, where he faced the awful fiery price of heresy, and made him one of her chaplains. He talked to her honestly, as though she had not been a queen, and she listened, and read for herself, and turned to good deeds.

I hoped for her, that winter, as she conceived again, carrying the child safely. 'It will be a son this time,' she said, serene and confident as she had not been before. 'My soul doth magnify the Lord, for He hath regarded the lowliness of His handmaiden.' Anne, to call herself lowly! I prayed for her, and so did Latimer, and good gentle Cranmer. I heard him rebuke a courtier who spoke scandal of her.

'Think shame,' he said, fiercely for him. 'Her Grace is no whore and never was. If your own wife is as good a woman, be thankful for it, and if she is not, send her to the Queen to learn wisdom.'

Alas for wisdom. On the day that followed Epiphany in this year of 1536 Queen Catherine died at last, in her lonely banishment. Anne rejoiced, openly, unable to conceal her joy and relief. The King too rejoiced. The next day, a Sunday, he had a special Mass celebrated, not to mourn his late wife but to celebrate the event with praise and the shrilling of trumpets.

That evening there was a feast and dancing in the Great Chamber at Greenwich Palace. Anne, though she danced only soberly because of the child, had herself and her ladies dressed all in yellow, and persuaded the King to wear it, and little Elizabeth. Some grave people pulled long faces, but Anne said, 'Yellow is the colour of mourning in France – I told my sister to wear it for the death of her first husband. What ails yellow? It becomes us all.'

The King picked up Elizabeth and carried her round the room, showing her off to all the company, making her laugh and chatter (she was the brightest of all children), then set her to the ground and danced with her, her tiny hand in his great one.

I thought: the Scriptures tell us it is better to go to the house of mourning than to go to the house of feasting. Will it be so this time?

We were still at Greenwich, three weeks later, snow a thick pall on the gardens and the decks of the winter-bound ships lying alongside. I saw Bess Darrell running towards me across a sludge-wet courtyard, and shouted to her to mind her footing. 'Tread more soberly, Phillis,' I called, in the jesting way I was used to speak, not wishing to risk serious courtship. 'Even a fairy's feet can go astray on slippery cobbles.'

There were tears running down her fair cheeks and she carried something in her arms. For one mad moment I thought it was an infant and that she came from another disastrous childbed. Then, as she reached me, I saw that it was a tiny dog, brown and white, and that it lolled with its head rolling away from her shoulder.

'Little Purkoy.' She showed me the small corpse. 'Poor little dog, oh poor little thing!'

I had no need to ask if it were dead. Its neck was obviously broken. 'He fell,' she gasped, between sobs, 'over a balcony, up there. A page was carrying him and slipped, letting go. And he fell, all that distance . . .'

Gently I took Purkoy from her, and gave her my handkerchief. I was strangely glad that she had so tender a heart and could be sad as well as merry.

'What will Her Grace say?' she cried. 'I dare not tell her. None of us us dare – as she is. Will you tell her, Sir Thomas? She is fond of you.'

'Go in,' I said, 'and keep warm. I'll do what I can.'

It so happened that on my way to the Queen's antechamber I met the King. He saw at once what I carried, and made a sort of tut-tutting sound of impatience, not regret. Turning on his heel as he strode away, I ventured to follow him at a distance, as far as the antechamber, having given the dog to a servant. There was the sound of his voice speaking loudly, and then Anne's in great distress. I wished I had told her myself.

*

I think myself a man of letters, yet I have no idea how to set down the next events. It was very soon after the death of Little Purkoy and, ironically, on the day of Queen Catherine's funeral, that Anne miscarried, at three and a half months, of a male child.

Some said it was because she had been told too suddenly by her Uncle Norfolk that the King had fallen from his horse while jousting and lay badly injured. My sister Meg, who was never far from her mistress's side, said it was because she had come upon her husband on his knees, toying with Seymour. 'She gave that cheese-faced slut plenty of hard words, and the King too.'

'How did he take it?'

'Badly. He . . .' Meg set her lips and said no more. She had been warned very often by our father not to speak against the King. A Wyatt does not utter treason.

One of those winter mornings my valet-de-chambre came to shave me; he was a garrulous man, as ready for gossip as any old woman. 'The Italians are going, post-haste,' he told me.

'What Italians?'

'The Bassanos, father and son. Giovanni and Baptista.'

'Where are they going – and why?'

He shrugged. 'To Whitechapel or Bishopsgate, where their sort live, I'd guess – even back to Italy, it may be. As to why, sir – the father said he was frightened, for his son.'

'Why, what sin has Baptista committed? He seems an amiable enough lad.'

The valet looked around nervously. 'There's some tale going round about Marc Smeton, their friend. That he's been too bold – too near the Queen.'

'With one of her ladies? Which one?'

'I can't say, sir.' Clearly he could but dare not.

I asked Meg, who answered roundly: 'What a rubbishy tale! That boy moons round under our feet until I long to kick him. Bold, he? I'd like to see him say boo to a goose. No, a mouse. He blushes if one speaks to him sharply.'

George Rochford was out of favour with the King. He had

quarrelled with Francis Bryan, and Bryan had complained of his manners.

Anne prayed, Meg told me, very often, spending hours in her oratory with Latimer or Cranmer. She read from the English Bible to little Princess Elizabeth (but secretly, for fear of being thought Lutheran). She tried to save an abbey which had not yet been despoiled, but the King would not listen.

I heard – again from my talkative valet – that young Marc Smeton had been invited to supper by – of all people – Thomas Cromwell, my powerful friend. My valet leered. 'Taking up with boys now, is he, the mighty gentleman?'

I said I thought it was highly unlikely, though Marc was a pretty lad, and great men have strange aberrations. I resolved to ask Cromwell, politely enough, why he favoured the boy.

But that meal was never eaten. Marc was seized and questioned as soon as he set foot in Master Secretary's house: about his relationship with the Queen. He stuttered and stammered, on which they rushed him off to the Tower and tortured him until he spoke. Poor Marc, with his nightingale voice and clever musician's fingers, would never play or sing again, because they had racked him.

May has always been an unlucky month for me. Now, this year, it could see my end. I am in the Tower, waiting.

My friend Cromwell had been instructed to hunt out treason: that form of treason which was conspiracy to cuckold the King or murder him. On May Day, Henry Norris was accused of adultery with the Queen, and imprisoned here. Francis Weston and William Brereton followed him. And George Rochford – George, accused of incest with his sister. They came for me last of all.

I asked of what I was accused. Of adultery with the Queen, they said. I protested that I was innocent, and demanded on whose testimony the charge had been brought. They said, on the Duke of Suffolk's.

Suffolk, Anne's enemy and the King's great friend, appointed one of the commissioners for treason. I had been pleasant with him long ago, before he turned so arrogant; and it came to my ears here in the Tower that one of his servants had lived with a woman of my household. He must have heard whispers at Allington. He was a spiteful, envious creature, a strange thing in so large a man. But in this case it was not merely his spite: he was being used as a cat's-paw . . .

I must not, dare not, say any more. A Wyatt does not speak treason or commit it.

I have told Cromwell that I am innocent, and that Anne is pure from any man's touch but her husband's. She is here, imprisoned in the apartments which were hers at her coronation, guarded by women who hate her. But they let her keep my sister Meg, and they allow her chaplain and Cranmer to see her.

Death is among us, young as we are, I and my friends and my poor dethroned goddess. We have been misjudged to our deaths, sacrifices to satisfy a Moloch. Our blood will stain the Tower's stones for ever.

I must not write any more. A Wyatt does not speak treason, even when the axe is poised to fall.

If they allow us the axe, in mercy. But for treason – which I have not committed, I swear – it might well be the rope, the knife and the fire.

My youth is gone.

20

The rat he ran up the wall,
And so the company parted all

Anne swept into the King's Hall which adjoined the royal apart-ments of the Tower of London. Notable trials usually took place in Westminster Hall, but the trial of a crowned queen was such a new, strange and weighty matter that for fear of public riots it had been decided to use the old battlemented hall of the Tower, so that the royal prisoner should not pass through the streets.

The people of London, not to be cheated out of a spectacle, had pushed and shoved their way in, hundreds of them. They shared the floor space with Court personages and anyone who could find the leisure. It was to be not only a royal trial, but a spicy one – adultery and incest, as well as treason. Better than a play.

To Anne they were no more than a blur of colours and moving heads. Ignoring them, and her judges, she sat down composedly in the chair provided for her at the improvised bar, and spread out her skirts to cover the maximum area, isolating her from everyone else. Nobody darted forward to help her. Behind her stood two of the waiting-gentlewomen appointed to her, Lady Boleyn, her Uncle Edward's wife, and Mistress Coffyn, wife to her Master of the Horse. Both were her enemies.

She straightened her back and looked about her as calmly as though about to watch a fairly uninteresting tournament. Chapuys, the Spanish ambassador, watched her with grudging admiration. A cool, fearless woman, Protestant though she might be.

Chapuys had not been a witness to her first days and nights in the Tower. She had wept and laughed and wept again, then laughed so wildly as to shock her jailer, Sir William Kingston, Lieutenant of the Tower. He was used to all sorts of behaviour from prisoners, but not the hysteria which followed extreme shock. She had talked, babbled, raved, her ravings all avidly listened to by the enemy women, the spies, so that they could carry incriminating evidence back to Cromwell.

But Cromwell, who had been the deviser of the plot to bring Anne down and ensure his own political safety, was disappointed: nothing but denials that she had ever been unfaithful to her husband. 'I can say no more but nay, unless I should open my body.' And she had pulled the panniers of her dress apart, tearing at the rich brocade so that the stitches ripped, showing the whole front of the under-kirtle. Kingston had looked away, embarrassed.

Now, none would have believed in the ravings, the turmoil of mind behind Anne's calm exterior. Certainly not the nobles gathered on the newly built platform, familiar faces ranged opposite her to judge her.

Her Uncle Norfolk, grimly smug under a Cloth of Estate which signified his temporary appointment as High Steward of England. His son, the poet Earl of Surrey, Tom Wyatt's friend, red-bearded, nervous. The overfed, bloated bull of a man who had been the handsome, dashing Duke of Suffolk. A young man, fiery-bearded like Surrey, but sickly, pale of face, huddled into himself by a mortal illness: Anne's old love, Harry Percy of Northumberland. Miserably he avoided her gaze, which swept impersonally over him.

Not a flicker of emotion, only sharp attentiveness, passed across her face as she listened to the monstrous indictment.

'Lady Anne has been Queen of England, wife of our Lord Henry VIII . . . for more than three years . . . she not only despising the most excellent and noble marriage solemnized between the said lord our King and the lady Queen herself, but also bearing malice in her heart towards the said lord our King, led astray by devilish instigation, not having God before her eyes and following daily her fickle and carnal appetite and wishing that several familiar and daily servants of our lord the King should become her adulterers and concubines . . . she most falsely and treacherously procured them by foul talk and kisses, touchings, gifts and various other unspeakable instigations and incitements . . . in accordance as her most damnable propensity to crime drove her on . . .'

They read out a list of dates and places. She had procured Henry Norris to violate and carnally know her on 6 October 1533, William Brereton on 8 December. Carnal knowledge of Sir Francis Weston on 20 May 1534. Marc Smeton on 26 April 1535 – at Westminster, the others had been at Deptford and Greenwich. The same charge, repeated, on various occasions.

And, on 2 November 1535, her own brother, George Rochford, with French kisses and gifts and jewels, until 'despising all the Almighty God's precepts . . . and every law of human nature, he violated and carnally knew his own natural sister'.

The faint shadow of an incredulous, mocking smile touched Anne's mouth. They had not even bothered to check their alleged dates with her pregnancies. Would she, in her high ambition, have risked losing the King's son for a moment's gratification? Not a man of them but must know what danger she would have been in at such a time. They had not considered, when they had settled on 6 October 1533 for her seduction of Norris, that only a month before that date she had borne her first child with great difficulty and agony. Still sore, unhealed, bleeding from the lochia, the least of her wishes would have been carnal intercourse. The King himself could bear witness to that.

One person with a memory for dates rose in protest. From her place in the audience at Mary Stafford's side, Mistress Orchard leaped to her feet and shouted.

'All lies! I was her close gentlewoman, I never left her side. After the Lady Elizabeth was born – '

Norfolk whipped round, scowling and squinting. 'Silence that woman!'

'But my lord, I must give evidence – '

'Not permitted.'

Mistress Orchard continued to shout as two men of the guard seized her and dragged her through the crowd to the nearest door. They flung her through it and bolted it again. Under the general noise the pummelling of her fists on the outside of the door was lost, and died away.

Mary Stafford put her head in her hands. Nobody knew better than she how her sister had been situated. But she was herself heavy with child, and dared not risk being manhandled as Mistress Orchard had been. Sick at heart, she heard the silly, flimsy accusations trail on, unsupported by witnesses or proof. It was even said that the King's great displeasure and sadness at his wife's adultery had caused him grave bodily injury. That would be the leg ulcer which had been worsening for years. Ever since he caught the pox.

Anne was standing, still as a statue, seeming hardly to breathe.

'Not guilty, my lord. That is my plea.'

Nobody could see her fists clenched within the wide sleeves, drooping over the whitened knuckles and the rudimentary extra finger. Mary prayed for her sister: then to the Virgin, to St Anne and St Barbara, whom Anne had represented in the masque. Only women saints seemed appropriate in this cause.

Anne spoke sensibly, briefly. She pointed out that there was no case to answer, since she had never committed adultery, as God was her witness. She had made gifts to some of the men named, but only in the way of friendship and generosity. She declared herself totally innocent and loyal to the King.

Among the onlookers there were loud murmurs of sympathy. Even the sensation-seekers boggled at the lies which had been paraded for their inspection.

She wouldn't, not the Queen, said some. Not so many times, with so many men. Once, with one, it might have been, if the

King's powers were failing, as the whisper ran that they were. That way she might have got an heir, and no finger pointed at her, if she'd been clever.

Besides, you could tell by looking at her that she wasn't a wanton. There were those who remembered Bessie Blount's opulent beauty, and the plump prettiness of the Queen's sister Mary, both ready and willing wenches, that was to be seen at a glance. But Queen Anne – so thin, like a saint who'd been starving herself for holiness, the skull under the skin pitifully visible, the eyes so shadowed with waking and weeping – she was no whore.

Many had called her so once, and they watched each other out of the corners of their eyes now, hoping it would not be remembered. For crowds are fickle. 'Good Queen Catherine' had been all their cry once, but she was dead, only a ghost in their memories. Nan Bullen, the Night Crow, had turned into their Queen Anne, being slandered to death by a pack of judges who appeared no better than they should be: Norfolk, in particular, as ugly as sin.

Norfolk cared nothing for what they thought of him. He interrogated the twenty-six nobles, silently demanding from them the verdict they were bound to give.

'Guilty.'

Some spoke loudly and confidently, conscious of being unshiftably on the right side. Surrey hesitated, on the edge of defiance, until his father's malignant eye forced the word out of him.

'Guilty.'

Northumberland stared at the ground between his feet, shaking his head frantically. The family stutter he had inherited chained his tongue, the cancer he nursed stabbed at him. At last, goaded by Norfolk, he muttered into his beard, weeping.

'Guilty.'

Norfolk pronounced sentence. He was a savage at heart, the more savage for concealing it under a quiet manner which might be mistaken for affability. When Wolsey had fallen, and Norfolk had engineered his removal from Whitehall to faraway York, he had been heard to remark that he would on the whole prefer the

Cardinal to stay, that he might 'tear him with my teeth'. It was rumoured that when his wife, being in childbed, had railed about his mistress, he had cut her head open and rolled in full armour on her naked body, until she spat blood.

Yet Anne was his niece, daughter of his sister Elizabeth (now lying ill at Hever), whom she very much resembled at this moment, and his voice shook as he told her what must be her fate.

'Because thou hast offended our sovereign, the King's Grace, in committing treason against his person, and here attainted of the same, the law of the realm is this, that thou hast deserved death. And thy judgment is that thou shalt be burnt here within the Tower of London on the Green, else to have thy head smitten off as the King's pleasure shall be further known.'

From the crowd came a sound, part moan, part hiss, of indrawn breath.

Anne stood without moving, only the hollows of her cheeks seeming to deepen. Then she put her hands together in prayer and bowed her head. Those near enough heard her say, 'Oh God, Thou knowest if I have merited this death.'

A gleam of sun through the long window above her showed up the grey French hood of silk and taffeta, and the soft gleam of the pearls framing her averted face. Then the sun went in.

She raised her head and turned to her silent judges. Her voice was quite steady and very clear, the French accent stronger than usual.

'I think you know well the reason why you have condemned me. My only sin against the King's great goodness has been my jealousy and lack of humility. But I have prepared myself to die. What I regret most deeply is that men who were innocent and loyal to the King must lose their lives because of me.' She paused, breathing deeply to keep her voice strong. 'I ask only a short time to dispose my conscience, before I must die. Pray for me, I implore you.' Almost under her breath she repeated, 'Pray for me.'

At the back of the hall women and men were openly sobbing. On the platform none of the twenty-six was looking directly at

Anne, but for Suffolk, who openly sneered. Then from one of them came a sudden, tearing noise of retching, as Harry Percy of Northumberland rolled from his stool and lay heaving at the feet of his neighbours.

Nobody went to his help, for Anne had turned and was following Sir William Kingston, Lieutenant of the Tower, out of the hall, the two impassive women behind her. She glanced aside only once, towards the man who was to be tried next, who stood between two guards.

George gave her a smile, which she returned faintly. They understood one another. He would be as brave as she had been, winning over doubters by his demeanour and obvious honesty.

But in George there was a streak of arrogance and levity which Anne did not share. He denied firmly enough the charges of adultery and incest. Yes, he had spent some time in the Queen's bedchamber on one occasion. She had been unwell, recovering from a miscarriage. He had brought her sweetmeats and had sat on the edge of her bed chatting, trying to cheer her up in her melancholy. He supposed that her women had gone in and out – some of them might have been there all the time, he had no recollection.

Nor did he recollect kissing his sister otherwise than as a sister should be kissed. And if he had done so, how, he asked reasonably, could anyone but themselves have known?

Even the judges exchanged glances. How, indeed? That hadn't occurred to them. And in any case the other sort of kiss would not constitute adultery, only depravity.

Prosecution brought another charge. Rochford had made remarks suggesting that he did not believe the Lady Elizabeth to be the King's true daughter, but the offspring of one of the Queen's lovers.

George stared back, silent. He would not demean himself to deny such a vile slander. But it would have been better if he had denied it, since his silence seemed like admission.

The next charge was a written one, on a folded paper. The

prisoner was not to read it aloud, he was told. His face changed as he took in the sense of it. Then he laughed, a short, loud laugh of defiance.

'By this paper it seems that my wife told me that His Majesty is – lacking in virility – that he has not the powers of a man – and that she learned this from the Queen.' He laughed again. 'Is it likely, my lords, that such a gross lie would be uttered by the Queen in the first place, or that Lady Rochford would have been disloyal enough, and rash enough, to pass it on? Judge for yourselves.'

They did judge for themselves. They had heard whispers, quickly suppressed, from those of the royal bedchamber who should not have whispered. They knew of Lady Rochford's spiteful nature. Of course she would have passed on the rumour, in the hope of just such a revelation in public to discredit her husband. And of course the rumour had some foundation, for how could a man be potent with a wife he hated enough to put her on trial for her life?

And so George laughed himself out of the reprieve he might otherwise have gained. This time Norfolk's voice did not falter as he pronounced sentence.

'You are to be drawn from the Tower of London through the city of London to the place of execution called Tyburn, and there to be hanged, being alive cut down . . . your members cut off, and your bowels taken out of your body and burnt before you, and then your head cut off and your body divided in quarter pieces, and your head and body to be set at such places as the King shall assign.'

The terrible sentence of a common traitor. George went white, but said nothing aloud. His lips moved as he prayed: 'Jesu have mercy.'

Mary Stafford stumbled to her feet and pushed her way through the press of people, who made way for her since she was big-bellied and might give birth among them – she was weeping and groaning enough already.

She was never to speak to George again, nor was Anne permitted to take a last farewell of him; by especial order of the King.

Of the other accused men, only the poor lad Marc Smeton admitted guilt with the Queen. He would have admitted anything, stretched screaming on the rack, or with an iron band round his head turned tighter and tighter until it threatened to burst his skull.

Anne commented dismissively that Marc would naturally crack under torture, since he was not a gentleman. She dared not show any feeling for any one of the accused men, even now. For she still assured her women that it was all a mistake, a test of her by the King. A joke. Her Aunt Boleyn observed dryly that he must have an unusual sense of humour.

'You shall see, then,' Anne flung at her. 'I shall be sent to a nunnery, that's all.'

Her aunt's eyebrows rose. 'At this time, with nuns being turned out on the streets to beg?'

Far from countermanding the sentence pronounced on his wife, Henry rejoiced. When news of the sentence came to him, he sent word of it at once to Jane Seymour. Worse, unbelievably to those of his gentlemen who waited on him as he dined that night, he remarked to his bishop companion that he had anticipated the sentence, and had accordingly composed a short verse-tragedy about the matter. He produced the manuscript and handed it across the table, smilingly awaiting the bishop's praise.

It was not forthcoming, even from a guest anxious to please. The bishop murmured thanks but let it lie unread by his plate.

Anne had wished that she had 'my bishops' with her, 'for they would all go to the King for me'. She had done so much for them. Yet only one spoke for her to the King: Thomas Cranmer.

He had known her as a young girl, had been her confessor as chaplain to the Boleyns. He thought more of her than of any woman living, he wrote to the King, he loved her particularly for her devotion to God and the new religion. But, of course, if she were guilty, he dithered, then it was all very dreadful . . . (He must save his own skin and the future of the Reformed Church. But he would have liked to save Anne as well.)

When she heard of the letter Anne uttered one of her wild laughs.

'They called Marguerite de Valois *le mère poule de la Réforme*. Will they call me the white falcon of the Reformation, since that is my crest? But the falcon would seem not to have feathered its nest very comfortably.'

The Lieutenant of the Tower looked censorious. Kingston was a keen supporter of the Catholic Princess Mary. 'Disobedience to the Church – ' he began.

'To what Church? Say rather to an old Italian fellow who knows less about the English people than I know about the habits of Indian savages. I was *glad* to be the means of freeing my country, *glad* to see the Holy Scriptures printed so that all can read them. I have done only good to England.'

Lutheran heresy, thought Kingston sourly, but he was still bound to be respectful to his royal captive. He could, in any case, deal her a crueller blow than by mere fencing with dialectics.

'Not much good to your brother, madam,' he said. 'He is condemned, with the rest of the prisoners, to hanging, drawing and quartering.'

Anne crossed herself and fell on her knees.

She talked no more of the King jesting with her. When Meg Lee, who had been Meg Wyatt, appeared in her apartments she knew the significance of it. The King was showing clemency, now that he was going to be free of her.

Meg told her gently that the sentences of butchery had been changed to beheading, the normal form of execution for nobles. Marc, the commoner, was to to be hanged, as befitted a mere musician.

Anne bowed her head in thankfulness, 'And I too. Not burning, but beheading. History will call me Queen Anne *Sans-Tête*.' Her hands went to her neck. She laughed, since one must laugh or scream.

'But Tom is spared, at least,' said Meg. 'They haven't even tried him.'

'God knows why.' Neither said what must not be said: that of the accused men none was guilty of anything beyond flirting with Anne, whereas against Tom Wyatt there could have been a true bill. But she had not been married then, so it would not have been adultery. Not that Justice, according to Henry, would have taken any account of that.

'Cranmer came to confess me yesterday,' said Anne. 'And he said that if I would admit myself pre-contracted to Harry Percy he would say something to the King, plead with him, for both me and George. God bless him. So I admitted it.' She shrugged. 'I would never deny my marriage before, since that would make me out to be no queen. But now what have I to lose? Only – Meg, will this make my little Elizabeth a bastard? Not that, surely!'

'Of course not. She was born in wedlock, as everybody knows, whatever you may have admitted or not admitted.' Meg held her tongue about what everybody also knew – that the King was desperate enough for an heir to face leaving behind him a progeny who were all bastards, Mary, Elizabeth, and young Fitzroy. And of these, of course, Fitzroy would be chosen as his heir, being male, and never mind the daughters he had professed at various times to adore.

Anne asked for news of George. Very brave, Meg said, for her husband had managed some words with him. Very happy that the dreadful first sentence had been commuted, both for him and his friends. Very devout, reading his English Testament and praying constantly. He sent his beloved sister all his love and besought her to lean on Christ, as he did.

'I do,' said Anne, 'I will, to my last hour. Meg, my father has not visited me. He must have tried, surely?'

'They say he's gone to Hever,' Meg replied shortly. 'Your mother has collapsed, and little wonder.' She omitted to add that Thomas Boleyn had volunteered to serve as one of Anne's judges; he had been refused the privilege and had left hastily for Kent before he could be drawn into the web of doom that had been woven round his family.

Anne sighed. 'Yes, he would hate to see me like this. He hoped for so much . . .'

Hoped? He had treated his three children as pawns to further his own ambitions, thought Meg bitterly. Even as a child she had never liked her friends' father. Let him swelter at Hever; if he was hauled back to the block, she for one would not be sorry. She forebore to tell Anne that her sister Mary had miscarried of her child after the shock of the trial, that labour pains had come on her within the precincts of the Tower, and that she now lay in childbed delirium in lodgings, nursed by her husband.

'Mall?' She made her tone convincingly airy. 'At home and safe, so far as I know.'

'*He* would never dare to touch her – would he? Innocent of everything as she is, except of being my sister and George's. Oh Blessed Virgin, protect Your daughter, and all of us. My poor mother – is she very ill, Meg? Yes, I can see it in your face. I knew this thing would kill her.'

She asked nothing about the King.

Henry made a habit of never again seeing his victims after he had ordered their destruction. Now he kept out of the public way too. Even he had an uneasy sense that his popularity was low. Female blood had never before been shed on the scaffold, much less the blood of a queen.

Besides, he had brought Jane Seymour to a house nearby, and was seeing all he could of her at private parties. She was the future mother of his heirs, it was quite right and proper that he should. The whole distasteful business of the traitorous Boleyn mob would be over in a few days.

Only two days from Anne's trial to her execution. George and their friends, Marc Smeton, Francis Weston, and Henry Norris, were gone sooner.

None of the five made any last confession. There was nothing to confess, and they were all gallants. George, the first to die, encouraged the others to be brave. He made the conventional pious speech, more sincere in his case than in most. 'Live according to the Gospel, not in preaching, but in practice.' He prayed for his enemies and particularly for the King. Then he knelt and bared his neck to the axe. Wit, mockery, charm, grace, royal favour and the love of women had availed him nothing.

As the axe thudded down there came a groan from the watching crowds. All the citizens of London who could get to Tower Hill were there.

In a house in Bishopsgate a very small girl was dancing, pointing her toes and flirting her skirts to the music of a lute played by the man she knew as father, Christopher Johnson.

'Well done, Margaret. Prettily stepped, my little pigsnie.'

The baby tossed her dark hair and smiled coquettishly over her shoulder, as she had already learned to do. Johnson played louder and quicker, to distract her from the boom of the Tower cannon, so close.

But her ears were sharp. ''Sat?' she asked.

'Only guns. Men shooting in the marshes. Never mind it. Now turn, bend the knees . . . so.'

Margaret dimpled at her father. But now, since a minute ago, she had no father.

They had kept Anne waiting for a day beyond her appointed time of execution, so that would-be spectators would get tired of waiting and go away. She had spent the long agony of suspense in constant prayer with her priest. All her fire and sharpness were gone now as she faced death. Again and again she vowed her innocence of the charges against her. All night she prayed, for her own soul, for her daughter, for those she had offended, Princess Mary among them.

On 19 May she stepped out from the door of her lodgings into the May morning sunshine. As she made her way to Tower Green, her four ladies were behind her, Meg closest, and all weeping. But Anne's eyes were dry, brilliant with a terrible excitement. Meg, dressing her, had felt the tremor which rippled through all her body, a continuous shiver of fright.

She wore a plain dress the colour of a black pearl, with a wide white collar which could be removed when the executioner was ready to strike. His weapon was a sword, and he was a Frenchman, specially imported for his skill. Anne was grateful, she had told Meg on hearing of it.

Now that she was only a few steps from her death she was unaware of Meg or the others, hardly conscious of the selected few who had been invited to watch. Thomas Cromwell was there, his double chins for once raised from his collar bands, a fat half-smile coming and going on his lips. It was the zenith of his hopes – almost. Anne's existence had threatened Master Secretary Cromwell and his plans for an alliance between his King and the Emperor Charles V. Her death left him free to press for the Seymour marriage, which would please the King and restore him to full favour.

Anne was at the steps of the low scaffold – purposely low so that not too many could see the block. As Kingston gave her his hand to mount them, she turned and put her little Book of Hours into Meg's hand. It would be a pity to let such a fine volume drown in blood.

Then she gestured to her attendants to stay where they were, and mounted the steps alone. On the platform she took off her headdress, the pretty velvet hat of black, with an embroidered coif beneath and, holding up the weight of her waist-length hair in one hand, covered it with a white linen cap. Against its whiteness her face glowed with the high flush of extreme fear.

But she stood still, controlling the shaking of her limbs. Afterwards, nobody would recall seeing her tremble, or hearing her voice falter, though the breeze carried it away from all but the nearest spectators.

'Good Christian people, I am come here to die, according to the law, for by the law I am judged to die, and therefore I will speak nothing against it.' The usual little speech, mild towards her murderers, in case they should revenge themselves on her family. She prayed for the King, adding that a gentler or more merciful prince there never was – 'to me he was ever a good and gentle

276

sovereign lord'. She spoke her last lie with her old sarcastic three-cornered smile which defied anyone to believe it.

She looked from one to another, steadily, speaking slowly and clearly.

'And if any person will meddle of my cause *I require them to judge the best*. And thus I take my leave of the world and of you all, and I heartily desire you all to pray for me.'

Then she knelt, in the sunlight, the soft wind from the river ruffling the frilled edge of her cap, and blowing about a strand of hair which had escaped from it. Her long white neck was curved like a swan's. But her head was still raised, her eyes darting frantically towards the black-clad men who stood around her.

'Jesu, receive my soul. Jesu, receive my soul . . .'

The headsman beckoned one of his assistants deliberately to rustle the straw, distracting her attention. As she glanced towards it the sword came down.

All the blood in her body was pouring over the block, the platform, splashing down against those who stood nearest. They were aghast, though it was what they had expected, had come to see. Many were weeping, all were horror-struck, her ladies, even the two who had hated her, sick with shock.

The executioner lifted her head by the long hair and displayed it. He had not enough English to say anything about its being the head of a traitor, nor was he inclined to, for he was gallant towards ladies, and her bravery and beauty had charmed him.

He laid the head down again, gently, as though he might hurt it, wiped the sword on straw and descended the scaffold steps. From an official he collected his fee of £23 6s 8d and vanished into the Tiger tavern, to be sluiced down at the pump in the inn yard, change his clothes and console himself with several strong drinks.

The limp body in the black-pearl dress, looking very small, lay half-slumped against the block, the head near it, the eyes open, their splendour glazing over.

Everybody was moving away, being directed off the Green by

men-at-arms. Soon the Green was almost deserted but for the huddled group of ladies. It was Meg who said, 'We must take care of her.'

It was Meg who organised the secret removal, during the night that followed, of the butchered corpse in its rough elm arrow-chest of a coffin, from its place on top of George's coffin. A cart was waiting outside the Tower to carry the arrow-chest by stages to Salle Church in Norfolk, where the Boleyns had been Lords of the Manor.

Among her ancestors, in a service conducted by a priest who could keep a secret, those who loved her laid Queen Anne 'in a place consecrate to innocency'.

EIGHT

ELIZABETH BOLEYN
AND MARY STAFFORD

I know how to curse . . .

Elizabeth Boleyn settled herself even more comfortably against the daisied bank and let the sun touch her face. With her complexion it would do no harm.

Smiling, she watched her children. George had escaped from Master Nicolas again and was fishing in the moat. There was Master Nicolas, wandering about on the other side of the pleached apple trees, full of red fruit like little suns. By the time he had located George, the boy would have got tired of fishing and bounded off to some other sport.

Mary was plaiting flowers into her gold-brown curls, as pretty as a flower herself – as well the little hussy knew, for her mother could see the glint of a mirror in her hand. How old was Mary now – eight, perhaps? Soon to be of marriageable age. Thomas would find her a good husband among the boys of their noble friends.

Thomas. The name brought her a twinge of unease. She shook her head irritably, as if a fly plagued her.

Something moved at the edge of the lake. Little Anne, in a kirtle as green as the grass, had put her arms round the neck of that great hunting hound she loved so much. The creature should not have been in the castle gardens at all, it belonged with the others, but Anne spoiled it. She would certainly catch fleas from its coat. She looked like a black-haired fairy, smaller than the dog itself.

Thomas – again that dart of unease – had scolded the child for associating with such work beasts as dogs, and had brought her back a monkey from London as a pet, but she had screamed and refused to touch it or have it near her. She said it was like an ugly little man.

'Oh fie, a maid shouldn't flout at men' reproved old Dame Joyce, 'or else how shall she get lusty sons and daughters?'

'Men are not kind,' said the child. 'Giles hung up a dog that was sick and I cried.'

But Anne was laughing now, her shrill sweet laugh, the hound licking her face.

Odd, she was getting nearer, yet Elizabeth had not moved from the warm grass. The child's pointed elfin face and the dog's rough one almost filled her vision. Then they suddenly receded to a pin-spot in the distance, and Elizabeth's whole being seemed to lurch.

The grass felt different under her fingers, more like linen. There was a cross in front of her eyes, many crosses, all together, a window, lead-lighted. Something bright-coloured, two creatures on their haunches, holding a shield that glinted blue and red and green . . .

'My lady.' It was a woman's voice, unknown. Elizabeth turned her head, raised on high pillows. It ached. She lifted a hand to her brow, and saw that the hand was wrinkled, blue-veined, brown-spotted. How could that be, and she the mother of three such young children? And why could she see the pulse fluttering on the inside of her wrist, beating the same rapid time as her heart?

Realisation came flooding back. 'Oh, sweet Christ,' she said. 'Blessed Virgin. No, no, no, it can't be.'

The waiting-woman's face was full of pity as she proffered a drink. Elizabeth drank it gratefully. Her mouth was dry and her throat ached. Then she lay back on her pillows, all too conscious now of reality.

She was in her own bed at Hever. The sunshine streaming through the window belonged to this summer of 1536. At some time, weeks or days ago, she had become violently ill with palpitations of the heart. Then a fever had set in, and the doctors bled her, so that she became faint and was frequently unconscious. She was glad of these black chasms of the mind, because they kept her from remembering that Anne was dead, brutally murdered in public, slandered and disgraced.

And George too. Both her beautiful, brilliant children rotting corpses buried in shallow graves without a prayer said over them or a candle lighted.

When she was well again she would go to London, to the church of St Peter ad Vincula in the Tower, and have masses said there for them, and let the King try to stop her. She would have Scriptures read in English, since that was what they both would want, little as she herself understood why they should.

For the moment she would rest and try to recover her health. They brought her aqua vitae and cordials and meat broth, and opened the windows, at her request, to let in the sweet air, though of course it was highly dangerous in a sickroom. The gardens were rich with the lushness of June, but no children played in them.

'Where is my lord?' she asked Dame Alice, who had taken over the post of head housekeeper when old Joyce died.

'Over at Penshurst, I think, my lady, with Sir William Sidney. Hawking,' she added.

'Ah, hawking.'

'Yes, my lady. He took Robin the falconer with him, two days since.'

'You are sure he is not at Allington Castle?'

'Quite sure, my lady.'

'Sir Henry Wyatt is alone at Allington?'

A slight hesitation. 'I think Sir Thomas has returned, my lady. Does your ladyship fancy a posset now?'

Elizabeth refused the posset. So Thomas had not gone to Allington, to his old friend, because Tom Wyatt had been released from the Tower, perhaps put into his father's custody. Why had he not suffered with the others? It might be hard to find out, since people would be nervous of discussing anything with her that touched on the tragedy.

Naturally, Thomas Boleyn would not be there, in a house tainted with treason. Instead he had gone to Sidney, a man conspicuously in royal favour. He was bound to have gone away somewhere, when she lay ill, for he hated sickrooms. If she had died in his absence, of course, he would have ridden back promptly.

When he returned from Penshurst next day she was dressed and seated in a chair by the window. He expressed joy to see her so much recovered.

'I am better, yes. God has seen fit to strengthen me.'

Thomas seemed to have shrunk in size. Perhaps it was because he no longer carried himself proudly. For a man who had been engaging in sport in the open air he was a bad colour, and his face had grown more lines, his eyes heavy bags of sleeplessness. His glance slid sideways away from hers, into corners, as though he expected an enemy to be lurking there. She, who had lived with him so long, knew that he was in great fear.

Elizabeth felt very calm. Today her heart was not beating its wild alarum, her head was cool: truly she had been given strength to deal at last with the draper's grandson who had been fortunate enough to wed her, a Howard, and through her to sire a Queen of England.

'So you escaped, my lord,' she said conversationally. He started.

'I – escaped?'

'My daughter and my son died, and their friends, but you escaped the King's anger. I wonder how? It may be because you volunteered to sit among those who judged their trial, as you had done at the trial of the others.'

'Only to plead Anne's cause, I swear it!'

'Yes? I think it was to placate the King. If her Uncle Norfolk presided, why not her father as one of the noble judges?'

'I . . . I was refused.'

'And so you ran back here, with your tail between your legs.'

'You were mortally ill, they told me.'

Elizabeth shook her head. 'If there was any mortality at question, it was your own. The King's wrath would have been loosed on you if you had stayed about the Court. You knew that those he does not see he puts out of mind, so you took care that he should not see you. Even now you fear that the next rider across the draw-bridge, the next knocking at the door, will be a summons back to London under escort. That's true, is it not, Thomas?'

Even for him, it was impossible to deny. He seemed to droop and collapse, a fool's bladder of lard pricked with a knife. He slumped into a chair, sitting like an old man under his wife's pitiless gaze. How like her Anne had looked in her last days, so gaunt and haggardly beautiful. His misery was the greater because he regretted so sorely that he had not stood beside his daughter and his son at the end, to give them comfort. In his way, he had loved them. He had seen many die, he would not have swooned.

'Have you heard any news from Court?' Elizabeth asked, as though they were discussing a game of tennis. 'How does the King bear up in his widowerhood?'

'Very merry, I hear. But not widowerhood. He was betrothed to – ' he gulped – 'Queen Jane the day after . . . the day after. They were married ten days later.'

'With great ceremony?'

'No, privately. I was not told where. But soon after, he showed her to the people in a progress by barge from Greenwich to Whitehall. And she was with him at the State Opening of Parliament.'

'And? Something else, I think.'

He had not been going to tell her. 'Anne's initials and heraldic badges have been taken down at Whitehall and Greenwich, and Queen Jane's put up instead.'

'So, he has wiped Anne off the slate, as though she had never been. Dead and finished and forgotten . . .'

Elizabeth's waiting-woman entered with robes over her arm.

'Will you be needing these with you, your ladyship?'

Elizabeth examined them. 'This, and this, I think. The river air is treacherous, even in summer. Not that. You should know better than to bring me any gowns of gay colours.'

When the woman had gone Thomas asked, 'You're going away? To Blickling? That will be a welcome change for you. Yes, I think you should go to Blickling. But it has no river, you know.' He spoke patiently, as to a mental defective.

'Lambeth has, however. I am going to my family's house at Lambeth. Nobody lives there except my stepmother when she visits London.'

Thomas looked shaken. 'How long will you stay?'

'As long as I live, and I think that will not be long. I can no longer stay under the same roof as the man who did nothing to save my son and daughter from death, then crawled on his belly to their murderer – and would do so again to save his skin, I've no doubt. I see their blood on your hands, your face is daubed with it. I sicken to look at you. I never loved you, Thomas, or you me, which is not uncommon in our state of life. But I think now that if Anne had seen some love between us she would have grown up to be a gentler woman, and married a man instead of a monster. And I hate you because your gross ambitions made her in part like you and brought her to destruction.'

'Unjust! Unjust! You came to Court, you wished to see her great! It was your blame too.' He was on his feet, red-faced, trembling.

Elizabeth put her hand to her heart, though it was not at its old fluttering. Nothing Thomas could do or say would agitate her now. But she said, 'Leave me, unless you wish to kill me too.'

The old Howard mansion was a quiet place. Few footsteps sounded in its rambling corridors and low-ceilinged rooms, whose windows looked out on the river and its scurrying boats like water-beetles and, on the further bank, a rambling collection of buildings, Chester's Inn, a bishop's house, tenements, the watergates of mansions Elizabeth had known in Anne's great days.

She stared steadfastly in the face of bitter memories, until they disintegrated and were swept away by the flowing river. In the old house she drew the mantle of the Howards round her and settled into a kind of serenity.

Never either completely well or completely ill, she kept herself reasonably exercised, continuing to be a part of the living world, when a different sort of woman might have become a religious recluse. Sometimes she crossed the river – once, as she had promised herself, to attend a mass in the church of St Peter Vincula for the souls of Anne and George. The priest was well paid, and the small band of choirboys who sang a requiem.

Elizabeth kept her eyes away from Tower Green, both going to the church and returning from it. She took a boat from Tower Stairs to Lambeth, so that she might not see the place where George had died.

One winter day she went to Whitehall Palace, to see the King and Queen dine in public. He was very obese now, the eyes and mouth almost invisible among the fat masses of the face. Constantly he pawed at Jane's arm and shoulder, once at her flat breast. She was as pale and pursy as ever, not flattered by her rich gown and jewels.

Some of these Elizabeth recognised as Anne's. She stood well to the back of the crowd of sightseers, just an ageing woman dressed in black, with a black veil over her face. Her lips moved behind the veil, silently, as she mouthed words that blasted Henry, his hopes and his health, and those who had helped him to bring about Anne's ruin. Then she turned those burning, sunken eyes on Queen Jane.

'May she . . .' But the words faded on her lips. Jane, and any others who in time might wed Henry, was doomed enough already.

In early spring 1537, she made her way by easy stages to Hunsdon House in Hertfordshire, some twenty miles north of London. In the village an opportunist kept a litter and four servants ready to carry Court visitors to the house, or ordinary citizens curious to see the little Lady Elizabeth or the Lady Mary, her half-sister.

They were not on public view: that was to be expected. But

Elizabeth Boleyn was used to ordering people about and had money for bribes. After an hour or so of waiting in a cottage, with a housewife thoroughly in awe of her, she was taken to a walled garden and positioned by one of its gates.

Her granddaughter was walking with Lady Bryan, who had chief care of her. Or not so much walking as prancing and skipping. She was three and a half years old, well grown for her age, slender and extremely lively.

As she cantered on, Lady Bryan puffing behind, she chattered continuously in a high clear voice, pointing and gesturing.

She was like, yet not like, Anne. Slim long neck, oval face, quick movements and, when she turned, Elizabeth saw with a shock two great dark eyes. But they were not, as Anne's had been, set at an alluring slant, they looked straight out at the world, and the hair above them was a fiery marigold colour. Tudor hair and Howard eyes.

From her dress she would seem to have had no new clothes for a year or so. Her skirts were too short, her bodice pinched her slight form, her sleeves stopped just below the elbows and her cloak and cap were shabby. Her nose could have done with wiping, but she drew her wrist across it, so that Lady Bryan had to proffer her own handkerchief.

Conflicting emotions tore at her grandmother. The child was pert, obviously unruly, stamping her foot at some reproof, talking too much for a small child in the presence of an adult. She was not beautiful or even pretty, and a faint look of her father at the widest part of her face caused Elizabeth a shudder of revulsion.

Yet she was blood of her own blood, Anne's daughter, all she had of Anne that was living. She had been born with great agony, and Anne had loved her as she had loved no other human thing.

And she had been disgracefully treated. From Princess of Wales to untitled nobody. Queen Jane would bear sons, doubtless, and then Lady Nobody might be considered a threat to the throne. One would not put it past Henry to have that small head severed from the thin shoulders in a few years.

A rush of painful love took Elizabeth by the throat. She stepped forward into the garden, swirling her cloak so that the movement should attract the child's attention. It succeeded. Attendant and charge stopped to see the stranger in black.

Lady Bryan recognised her at once, and stiffened. They were cousins by marriage, but had never been friends, and Francis Bryan, her rakish son, had turned against Anne in the last days.

The old woman at the gate called, softly but clearly. 'My lady Elizabeth.'

The child looked up sharply at her guardian, got no guidance, and was left to her own judgment. A person of consequence, and friendly to her. She dropped a perfect Court curtsey, no less graceful for that ridiculous brief skirt, and smiled a brilliant Court smile showing tiny front teeth. Her grandmother bent her head in response: for a moment their eyes locked. Then Lady Bryan caught at the child's hand and pulled her on, without looking back.

Thus was the last and only exchange of courtesies between the two Elizabeths conducted.

Neither beautiful nor pretty, yet intensely striking. Presence of mind, authority, self-will, pride, the power to charm. One day she would be a remarkable woman – if she lived to be a woman – would have made a remarkable queen, but that could never be, of course.

With horror, her grandmother remembered that she had wished barrenness on this little creature, when in the Banqueting Hall of Whitehall she had cursed Henry and his line.

On a warm spring day of 1538, when new heat brought out the marsh-gases at Lambeth, Elizabeth set out for a walk. Her waiting-woman Joan Hayling tried to dissuade her.

'It will tire you, madam. Better stay within the house or in the garden pavilion.'

In reply her mistress merely snapped her fingers for the fur-lined mantle which was her invariable outdoor wear. Joan sighed.

'At least let me come with you, madam. Or let John take you pillion.'

'You know I hate to be hauled onto a saddle like a sack of potatoes. I will walk.'

Joan watched the retreating figure, the back now bowed, the steps slower than the once-haughty gait, plodding steadily westwards. Soon it was almost out of sight round the great bend of the river, then it was gone, along the path which led to Lambeth Palace, the residence of the Archbishop.

Her imperious manner would have gained her admission, even if the guards had not recognised the Countess of Wiltshire. His Grace was in residence, and would receive her, said the messenger.

Thomas Cranmer, Archbishop of Canterbury, was on his feet to greet the lady whose family he had once served as chaplain. He bowed over her hand, guided her to a chair, noted with concern that she was short of breath and weary, and much aged and altered. They had not met since the execution.

'I expect you wonder why I have come to see you, my lord.'

His smile was singularly sweet, transforming the long plain face and lighting up the shortsighted brown eyes.

'I am too pleased to see you to ask questions, my lady.'

'It is I who must ask the questions. Will you confess a sinner? I have not been to confession these three years.'

Cranmer's heart sank. They were going to have yet another discussion of the changing, shifting theology of the times, dictated by the King's whims and policies. But at least confession was still a recognised sacrament.

'Gladly. Shall we remove to my private chapel?'

'Here, if you please. I remember your stairs, and my legs are old now.' She flicked at a knee contemptuously, then, before he could protest, slid down to a kneeling position before him, hands joined in prayer.

'*Mea culpa, mea maxima culpa.*' He was relieved to hear that she was not in mortal sin. Non-observance of the Church's rites, deliberate absence from her husband's bed, a general lack of charity towards others, wordly vanity in the continued use of paints and perfumes – so far, so good.

Then came the admission of her curse on the King and his lineage.

Cranmer shook his head, tut-tutting. 'Very wrong indeed, daughter. But such things are idle superstition, though dangerous.'

'Dangerous, indeed!' snapped the penitent. 'The thing works. In the year since I cursed him didn't Queen Jane die after giving birth to Edward?'

'But that is the common lot of women, and she left him a healthy son.'

'Healthy for how long? I've seen him – too fat, too pale. Sickly like his half-sister Mary, the bloodless cow.'

'Daughter!'

'Your pardon, father. But she is. And not married yet because no foreign prince will have her. And whatever bride the Monster chooses next will have no luck, and no child, and everyone knows why – because of the disease which has swollen his leg out like a bolster and keeps him away from killing deer in the same quantity as he killed the rebels in the north. What do you say to the burning of beautiful Margaret Cheyney at Smithfield, for no other offence than sharing her bed with a man accused of rebellion? What . . .'

Cranmer very gently but quite firmly raised her to her feet and put her back in a chair.

'You are overwrought, my lady. We have moved outside the bounds of the confessional, and we must not speak words that might be construed as treason.'

'Why? Are there spies behind the tapestry?'

'You know my mind. I am only a poor scholar, who never desired high office and all its burdens: I love justice and mercy above all things. There is much in today's happenings that I deplore, but we will not talk of that. You came here to ask if the curse you laid on . . . one who had injured you can be removed.'

'Only from my granddaughter, not the rest.'

Cranmer crossed himself. 'I love the little Lady Elizabeth. I am her godfather, I held her in my arms at her baptism. She is a noble child and deserves only blessings. Shall we pray for her together?'

His penitent, between Amens, reflected that he used her grand-daughter's proper title, the Princess Elizabeth, in his prayers. So he did not support the bastardy which had been imposed on her. Would he come out into the open and speak for her, persuade Henry to treat her as his only legitimate daughter?

No. For Thomas Cranmer, that good, gentle man, was weak, and afraid for himself, and an innocent in rapid double-dealing. He would change and change again, until the cruel times caught up with him. She pitied him with all the heart that was left in her.

When their prayer was ended she said, 'Thank you, my lord. I would ask you only one more thing. You were truly persuaded of Anne's innocence, when you confessed her before she died?'

He turned away, looking beyond her towards the river and the Tower.

'For you I will break the seal of the confessional,' he said at last. 'I absolved the Queen, but of no mortal sin, for she had committed none. She was in a state of grace.'

'I knew it. But I thank God.'

'I will tell you something else, my lady. On the morning she was to die, a man came here to see me, a Scotsman, a stranger. He found me walking in the gardens, and told me, in great terror, that he had been wakened at sunrise from a dreadful dream of . . . of an execution.' He would not tell Anne's mother that the dream was a vision of a severed head, in horrid detail.

'He had been ill in his lodgings and had heard none of the news. I asked him did he not know what was to happen that morning, and he answered that he did not. I told him, "She who has been the Queen of England upon earth will today become a queen in Heaven." And I wept.'

Elizabeth crossed herself, bent a knee, and kissed the long white hand which wore the Archepiscopal ring. Their farewell was grave and affectionate, the parting of two old friends.

She set off back towards her home, this time taking the short cut across the meadows, where lambs grazed under the apple trees. She felt peace of mind, for the first time in three years. But some hundred yards from the gate leading into her gardens she put her hand to her heart, and gasped and slid to the ground.

They found her there, among the long grass, her face turned up to the blue sky, petals of apple blossom lying pink and white on her brow, from which the deep wrinkles had faded.

They buried her in the Howard chapel of Lambeth church, under a simple stone bearing her name, her title, and the date of her death.

Thomas Boleyn died at Hever almost a year later, a lonely, bitterly disappointed man. His tomb in St Peter's church was the one he had designed and planned so long ago, a table tomb bearing a fine monumental brass of himself in the full robes and insignia of the Order of the Garter. None of his family lay by him except the infant son Henry, who had died before any of the other children had been born.

One of them lived still and had sat by his deathbed holding his hand between her own plump ones: his daughter Mary.

22

Kind sister, sweet Ophelia

The days passed, and the years. These increasingly fast, it seemed to Mary, so that a month ago seemed like yesterday. The 1530s were gone, leaving behind a trail of beauty destroyed, abbeys and monasteries pulled to pieces, the stones sold or pilfered for building. The shrines they had held were gone, too: the saints' relics burnt; the holy statues, which had smiled and breathed and bled, ridiculed out of existence. The only church now was the Church of England, Henry VIII's church, run on whatever lines he chose to dictate.

He had married three times within two years. Mary and William Stafford kept well away from Court now that William had organised himself a military appointment in Calais, but they heard plenty of rumours.

Thomas Cromwell, confident that he was the power behind the throne, had arranged a marriage for Henry with the Lady Anne of Cleves in Germany. It was a disaster from the moment he set eyes on her. Cromwell had lied to him about her beauty. The King was thinking of getting rid of Cromwell in any case, and was growing infatuated with little Catherine Howard, one of the Duke of Norfolk's nieces.

Anne of Cleves, still virgin, consented thankfully to a divorce. The marital merry-go-round continued with Henry's marriage to tiny, pretty, silly Catherine.

Wanton Catherine. Unlike her predecessor she was not still virgin. There had been licentious bed romps in the Sussex household of old Agnes Norfolk, during which Catherine had managed to get herself not only deflowered but betrothed to a young rakehell. All of which came as a severe shock to Henry.

'How could he not have known?' Mary asked William. 'I knew it. You knew it. It was common gossip at Court, and beyond. Such goings-on would never have been tolerated once.' She scarcely remembered the goings-on at the French Court, when she had been a girl no older than Catherine. Mary Stafford was a different person from Mary Boleyn.

Catherine, cousin to Mary and Anne, would go the same way as Anne, her tender neck severed by the executioner's axe.

'She was kind to Elizabeth,' Mary said wistfully. 'Poor child, with no mother.'

'Or too many mothers,' observed William.

The year after Catherine's execution, Henry had married yet again, a learned widow, Catherine Parr. So far as anybody knew it was going well, the new Queen keeping her head between her shoulders, dressing Henry's horrible leg ulcer, and bestowing something like a domestic existence on her stepchildren.

Cromwell was not present to interfere. He had died on Tower Hill, like the young men he had sent there four years previously. Men whispered that anyone could be judicially killed these days, for any reason.

It was one of Fate's ironies that after Jane Rochford, George's widow, died with Catherine Howard for complicity in her infidelities, Rochford Hall in Essex came into the ownership of Mary and William – a handsome house which would be their first real home. William resigned his commission at Calais: but, by another irony of Fate, he died before he could return to England.

Whether William took something of Mary with him at his death, or whether the transition from wifehood in France to widowhood in Essex was too much for her, it was noticed by those about her that Lady Stafford seemed to alter greatly when she moved to Rochford Hall. Always plump, she now grew heavy and lethargic, sleeping a great deal and not always returning a sensible answer to a sensible question.

Her son Henry Carey was a brisk, bluff young man with ambitions for a high place at Court. He, like everybody else, was well aware that he was the King's bastard and much resembled what his royal father had been in younger days. It would do him no good for those about the King to hear that his mother was losing her wits. Besides, he was mildly fond of her, though he had never known her well, having seen more of the ex-monks who had educated him than of his mother.

'She seems to remember nothing,' he complained to his sister Catherine. 'Even my name escapes her, sometimes – she confuses me with others called Henry.'

'Understandably,' snapped Catherine, who was preparing for her wedding. 'Seeing that everyone for the past generation or two has been christened Henry or Catherine, those that were not William or Thomas or Mary. *I* didn't choose to be named for a Romanist queen, I can tell you.'

'Oh, we all know you for one of our leading Puritans, long-nosed canting jackasses.'

She turned on him in fury. Her red hair, pale skin and tight-lipped mouth gave her a strong resemblance to her step-sister, the Lady Mary Tudor.

'Keep your jeers to yourself! You'll jeer on the other side of your face before long, when the New Religion takes a firm hold of England.'

Henry crossed himself, to annoy her. 'God forbid. What music are you and your high-minded Francis Knollys planning for your wedding? Lutheran psalms? And I suppose your children will be named Habbakuk, Obadiah, Keren-Happuch, that sort of thing?'

'You may laugh. They are godly names, all.'

Henry looked falsely pensive. 'How glad I am that my little Welsh wife is called merely Anne.'

Catherine bent her head over the sleeve she was working for her bridal dress, refusing for once to rise to the bait. She was bitterly ashamed of her Aunt Anne's scandalous death, even if her life had helped to banish Papistry. 'The Lord help your wife,' she said, mildly for her, 'married to a whoremaster.'

Mary was unaware of such sharp exchanges between her son and daughter. What other people said or did washed over her mind, like gentle ripples on a shore. She was aware of her youngest child, the only survivor of several, little Willikin, a delicate, fanciful child. They said he would not make old bones, but not in his mother's hearing.

She was aware of the beauty of Rochford Hall. It had long been a Boleyn house, coming into the family as the dower of her grandmother. There was peace for her in the little oratory, which had not been swept away when so many others were destroyed. For hours she would sit there, in a sort of pleasant dream, listening to the doves on the roof, the clip-clip of a gardener's shears in a flowerbed, the sweet faint tinkle of a virginals somewhere in the house: Willikin's music tutor.

The time came when she had to be gently reminded that it was time for a meal, time for bed. Her chaplain was worried because she was unable to remember the responses to the prayers he said with her every day, but only smiled at him and murmured to herself.

'My lady's wits are wandering,' he told her housekeeper. 'Is it that she lives in the past?'

'No,' said the housekeeper, a bowed old woman called Mistress Orchard. She had unobtrusively found her way into Mary's home, as she had into the old house of the Howards where Elizabeth Boleyn had spent her last days. 'No,' said Mistress Orchard, 'she lives in the present, where she's happy. She remembers nothing because she wants to remember nothing. Too much happened, too much sadness and badness.'

Mary Stafford died at Rochford Hall in her forty-fifth year, from no painful illness, simply because her life was over, the leaf was ready to turn to the next chapter. On her deathbed she smiled, turning round and round on her finger a heavy gold ring that she wore above her two wedding rings, now sunk deep into her flesh.

Only Margery Orchard knew the history of the ring. It had come from a tomb and she would make sure that it went back into one, still on her mistress's hand.

At the last, Mary knew none of those about her, only someone who stood at the foot of her bed.

'Nan!' she said, and held out her arms.

The young chaplain looked on her dead face with wonder, seeing for the first time that she was very beautiful.

NINE
HENRY AND EMILIA
1592

A whitely wanton with a velvet brow,
With two pitch balls stuck in her face for
eyes;
Ay, and by Heaven, one that will do the
deed
Though Argus were her eunuch and her
guard.

William Shakespeare

23

Ripeness is all

Henry Carey, Baron Hunsdon, Lord Chamberlain of the Household of Her Majesty Queen Elizabeth, sat with his feet up at a
window of his London residence, Somerset House, on the north
bank of the Thames. He was sixty-eight years old.

Somerset House was one of the grandest of the riverside houses,
all of them homes of the nobility. The Queen had graciously
awarded the keepership of it to her Lord Chamberlain, partly for
his long and distinguished services to her and to England, partly
because he was her first cousin officially and her half-brother
unofficially. This was never said aloud, though known to many at
Court. The name and dubious fame of his long-dead mother, Mary
Boleyn, was forgotten.

His gouty foot was plaguing him which was annoying, for this
beautiful late September of 1592, following a dank summer, had yet
no nip of cold in it. He sat comfortably in a broad cushioned
window seat, the latticed casement open to let in the air: a soldier
more than a courtier, he hated stuffy rooms.

The windows of the river side of Somerset House looked across
to Lambeth, and a scatter of neglected old buildings which had
been the mansion of the Howards. They had a fine new residence
now on the north bank, Arundel House.

Across the long gardens and the river's wide bend he could look
down towards Whitehall Palace, where his royal sister-cousin was
holding audience or eating her dinner in public for the edification
of her loving people, or dancing high and disposedly, or translating

Italian or Greek in her beautiful script, or any one of her famous accomplishments.

Elizabeth Tudor. So like himself, when they were both young, with fiery red-golden hair and dark eyes. He smiled. What a vain creature she was, at fifty-nine defying time and wrinkles with enamel face-paint and elaborate wigs and bodices cut as low as decency permitted, or lower. Her teeth were black, some of them missing, and her high nose was hooked with age, but you did not notice that (nor did she intend you to) because she carried herself so majestically and wore the air of a beauty, which she had never been.

She was always a-glitter and ablaze with jewels, great pearl drops swinging from her ears, gold and silver lace trimming the huge frames of her ruffs, her hundreds of gowns jewel-worked in Tudor roses or symbolical designs such as eyes and ears, to signify that she saw all and heard all that concerned her kingdom: 'my dear lover, England', as she called it. She was dazzling and brilliant and frightening, her smiles like sunshine and her rages like storms.

She had no other lover, though her courtiers and visiting ambassadors protested violent passion for her; had never known man – if what she told Carey privately was true. It had been a near thing with the late Earl of Leicester, her Sweet Robin, who had hoped and intended to marry her, but she had fended even him off. Had fended off all those foreign princes who had come courting, and so kept England in her own hands, by consummate statemanship.

She had also kept it Protestant. The brief reign of her half-sister Mary had swept England with fire and blood as hundreds of martyrs went to a dreadful death for the faith of the Reformed Church. The country had been left with a lasting fear of Catholicism, and Elizabeth was determined that it should never return. She had been very near losing her own head at one time. Only extreme cleverness got her out of that tight corner. Throughout her long reign she had lived under the threat of assassination from one source or another, chiefly the Catholic Queen of Scots' party. Carey thought she would escape that one, too.

It was not luck, but wit and a tremendous inner strength which had put Elizabeth on the throne and kept her there. When he came to think about it, the Tudors had not been a very lucky family.

His own father, King Henry, had died at fifty-six, a bloated, disease-ridden grotesque, hated alike by Catholics and Protestants for what he had done to their causes in his petulant rages. Only the man in the street mourned him as Good Old Harry, once their handsome giant.

His male heir, Edward VI, Jane Seymour's boy, had lived to only sixteen, poor sickly lad. His cousin Lady Jane Grey, the same age, had lost her young head on the block after a pathetic nine-day reign.

Mary Tudor, Bloody Mary, had married King Philip of Spain and had no children by him.

And Elizabeth? Well, glory had made up to Gloriana for the lack of domestic happiness – at least he hoped it had. But she had told him secretly that her barrenness was bitter to her. Women were made to bear, and she had not. 'I am accursed, Harry. I have always felt myself accursed in love.'

No, Venus had certainly not smiled on the House of Tudor. He felt himself fortunate, as an unacknowledged member of it, to have done pretty well in that line, with a fine sturdy Welsh wife who brought him a healthy dowry, seven sons and three daughters, and still warmed his bed. As did a succession of other ladies.

Whatever god presided over lands and possessions had also done well for him. Almost the first thing Elizabeth had done at the beginning of her reign was to give him the royal manor of Hunsdon in Hertfordshire, where she had been brought up in her early years. He had been knighted, created a baron, and enriched – though not as much as he would have liked, for Elizabeth was niggardly with money.

He had lost Hever, of course. After the death of his grandfather, the King had bought it (Carey's poor mother had actually been given a share of the money) and Hever had become the home of

Henry's fourth, divorced wife, Anne of Cleves. He had not seen it for many years. Pretty place, but small.

He bent to tickle the ears of his greyhound Jupiter, who was dealing with fleas on the costly carpet.

'Not done badly, your old master, Jupe. Even though they could never din learning into me, all their hic-hac-horums and quo-quid-quorums. Got along well enough without 'em. And now she's given me the Office of Revels, and my own company of jolly actors. Shall we write a part in for you, eh, Jupe? A cur in a comedy, to make the groundlings laugh? What, boy?'

The greyhound got to its feet and came to lay its long muzzle on his knee. Absently, he stroked its smooth neck, musing. His head began to droop in an old man's sudden sleep. The sounds of the great house, the cries of the watermen, somebody somewhere blowing a trumpet mingled in his mind, formed a dream. Somehow his old tutor at Syon got into the dream and began to admonish him.

The door burst open, startling him awake with a blasphemous oath. Doors in Somerset House were not supposed to do that – they were opened soundlessly by obsequious servants.

'What in t'other devil's name are you doing here?'

Emilia Bassano stood in the doorway, ripe and glowing like a plum tree in full bloom. Her dress was of many colours, as though she had dipped into a bag of rainbow scraps and flung them all over herself: reds, blues, greens in posies and bowknots thronging on her farthingale, great puffed sleeves of tawny yellow threaded with purple ribbon, and extravagant ruff framing her vivid face. He gave her plenty of money and she spent it in dressing like a gipsy. But it became her, the pretty wretch, she might dress as she pleased. A little mannish hat was perched on her nest of black curls, long amber earrings swung against her ruff, and there were six or seven good rings on her long fingers.

She swayed into a curtsey so deep that for a second she seemed to be sitting on the ground. It was an exaggeration, almost a mockery of the curtsey a Court lady would make: the Queen would have said something sharply witty about it. But then Emilia would not have the chance to curtsey to the Queen, and she was not a lady.

She advanced and kissed Hunsdon's hand with the same over-done respect, then turned over the hand and let her lips linger on the palm, which he enjoyed. She had a mouth that looked and tasted like a strawberry, he thought.

'Well, hussy?' He slapped her bottom affectionately – what he could reach of it through the stiff fabric of the bum-roll which held out her farthingale. 'You have been told to keep away from Somerset House. My lady would be mortally offended if she caught sight of such as you within doors.'

'My lady is at Hunsdon, my lord, as well you know. And Blackfriars is so tedious, no company but ruffianly players swarming up and down like ants.'

'They are *my* players, as you well know, Em. You think yourself above them, I suppose?'

She tossed her head. 'I hope I move in higher circles than jacks of that sort. My friend the Countess of Kent – '

'The Countess of Kent was your lady mistress, not your friend. You maided her not a bowshot from here, when Sir Henry was at Court, no more than that. But for her you'd never have come under my eye, so be thankful and stop your boasting and bragging.'

Emilia perched herself on his knees and changed the subject. 'How vexatious it is that so many men are called Henry. It's too old a fashion to please me, alas, with due respect to you, my lord.'

'There was no thought of pleasing you when I was christened, doxy. I was called so for the late King Henry, as were so many born at the time.'

The brown eyes, twinkling with mischievous malice, surveyed him thoughtfully.

'Ah, yes. Only there was a better reason in your case than in most, if I remember.'

'You'd better not remember.' His tone was sharp. Once, after a drinking bout, he had told her of his parentage, and had regretted it ever since. Emilia had a loose tongue, not made for secrets. She had sworn on the Bible not to tell, but Hunsdon would not have cared to put money on her silence. Heaven help her if it ever reached the ears of anyone who mattered.

'At least,' she stroked his beard to restore him to good humour, '*I* was not given a common name, like Mary or Margaret or Catherine or Anne or Elizabeth. Emilia is a very fine name, don't you think, my lord? They could have named me after my mother, Margaret, but they chose better, for my sister and myself. Emilia and Angela – how musical, how mellifluous! That comes of learning, you see, and living in foreign courts. My beloved father was a most learned man, speaking three languages.'

Hunsdon grunted. Her father had been an Italian musician, employed at the Court of King Henry in the service of Queen Anne Boleyn. They, the Bassanos, father and son, had fled to France about the time that their friend Marc Smeton was about to be arrested on suspicion of adultery with the Queen. The elder Bassano had seen trouble coming: they would be safer at the French Court. When the old King died they crept unobtrusively back to England and were welcomed as good Catholics by Queen Mary. That was how Baptista Bassano had come to speak three languages.

The merest touch of Italianate Cockney tinged the refined speech Emilia had learned to cultivate under the tuition of an impoverished scholar in Bishopsgate. Bassano had paid for her to be educated well, there was that to be said for him, and taught her well himself in music. Hunsdon pushed her off his lap.

'Less chatter. Play to me.'

She went to the instrument which stood in the corner. She had played it only once before, on a stolen visit to Somerset House, and had ever since longed to get at it again. It was not a common virginals, which had only one string to a note and were so called not in honour of the Virgin Queen Elizabeth, but because they were easy enough for young ladies to learn music upon. This noble thing was a harpsichord, with two or more strings to every note, made in Flanders by the Ruckers family, the lid painted with cupids and allegorical figures in a landscape of flowers. Emilia did not often get her clever fingers on such a fine thing.

She began to play. It was a set of variations on a simple tune, *Rosasolis*, moving from a plain statement of the melody to complex flights of the composer's fancy and ornaments of the player's skill, brilliant showers of notes cascading into one form after another, high trilling notes and soft purring low ones. She used the keyboard as a trained rider might use a mettlesome blood horse, showing off his own powers and the horse's. With a last triumphant flourish she turned and inclined her head in tribute to the listener.

He laughed, applauding. He had never ceased to admire her art. It was good to have a mistress accomplished otherwise than between the sheets – though she was that, no mistake, almost too much so for his years.

She went into a Spanish Pavane, a Galliard, a Morisco. Then, with a delicate clearing of the throat, played the prelude to a song. Her voice was good, trained, but not altogether pleasing because of a touch of professional harshness and a lack of feeling for the words, so that you heard and understood them without being melted or pierced to the heart. His own daughter Philadelphia's voice was sweeter. But still it was music.

The song was one made on the recent retirement of the Queen's Champion, Sir Henry Lee, presently Her Majesty's Master of the Ordnance. Now, thought Hunsdon, let me see, that would be the son of Lady Margaret, she that was a friend of my mother's and one of Aunt Anne's most devoted attendants: Meg Lee, he remembered her. She had been sister to that scribbler, Tom Wyatt, Knight of the Shire for Kent. Wyatt and Hunsdon's mother had been brought up as neighbours – and Aunt Anne, of course, for whom the poet was said to have entertained a great passion. But Tom Wyatt had not died on the block with her and the others; only, a very few years after, from a simple fever. Ah well, Cupid is a knavish boy.

Emilia sang.

His golden locks Time hath to silver turn'd.
O Time too swift, O swiftness never ceasing!
His youth 'gainst Time and Age hath ever spurn'd,
But spurn'd in vain; youth waneth by increasing.
Beauty, strength, youth, are flow'rs but fading seen:
Duty, faith, love are roots and ever green.

'Enough!' He clapped his hands. 'You make me feel old.'

'God forbid!' She rose and made her curtsey again, so deep, so – theatrical. Yes, she would have made a better Player Queen than any of the boys in his company of players.

She said solicitously that he must not feel old, he was not, only mature, ripe. He must need a cup of wine: would he graciously call for one? He hesitated a moment before letting his servants see that she was here, then tinkled the bell. Let them think what they liked, and devil take them.

The wine came, they drank, she as carelessly as though her stomach were lined with tin. He admired a free-drinking wench, especially when she held the cup in so excessively refined a manner. He tangled his own fingers in the wiry curls which had lost their little impudent hat, feeling the small sharp teeth biting his wrist in a way he found singularly provocative. She was being unusually kind to him – why?

'I have good tidings for my lord.'

'Good tidings? Then give them good words, good my mouse of dexterity.'

'I am fecund.'

'You're *what*?'

'I am with child to your lordship.'

His heart gave a fearful lurch before it began to beat faster. His brain swirled with conflicting emotions. With child, to one of his age: by Christ's blood, a miracle! Pride surged through him. Father of ten grown men and women, a grandfather several times over, in years almost the Prophet's three score and ten, and yet to have begotten a child on a young woman but a third part of his age.

The fool, the clot-poll. She was enough of a harlot to have known better. Now she would push her vaunting ambitions to the point of shaming him. Pride flew out of the window – he began to shout at her.

'How do I know you speak true?'

'I do, trust me.'

'Trust *you*! How do I know the child is mine, then?'

Her lovely eyes were limpid, her mouth drooping. 'Because I tell you, my lord. I have not meddled with another man since you took me out of my humble estate and raised me to your own heights.'

'Hardly that, madam! My lady is very hearty, you're no baroness yet. I gave you a handsome house, money and servants and a horse. Every rag on your back is mine – nay, leave them be, I'll not have you uncasing yourself here. You owe me all you have, and what do you give me in return?'

'A son,' she whispered, the eyes eclipsed under sweeping lashes, the heart-shaped face downbent. He was tender-hearted towards women, for all his flares of temper, and he hated to see one cry, as she was doing, very prettily, tears coursing down her cheeks, just as they did in madrigals (which never mentioned running noses).

Her news had certainly been a small shock to him. There had been one or two mis-throws, not long after he became her protector, but he had been younger then. He had thought her one of those who could not carry a child to term and here she was, 'fecund'.

He patted her thigh. 'Come, cheer up, I'll look after you. You're of ripe years for bearing . . .'

The tears stopped abruptly. 'Only nineteen!' She was twenty-three, and they both knew it.

'Yes, yes, nineteen. But we must take care.' He had been thinking rapidly. 'You shall be well married, have no fear.'

'Married!' Her voice shot up to a squeak.

'You heard me. Marriage is an honourable estate, especially in your happy condition – how many months gone are you?'

'Three,' she said reluctantly. So she had delayed telling him, for

309

fear she should lose her place. The sly slut. Well, she should not go about flaunting her belly to his discredit. The Queen was tolerant of masculine peccadilloes, so long as the men did not marry the women concerned – she hated marriage at Court – but he had no wish to be branded as a whoremaster. He said, 'Alfonso Lanier shall have you.'

For a moment she was speechless, then burst out, 'Lanier! That dull oaf! He has neither art nor wit nor a good favour nor anything worthy of *me*.'

'Her Majesty seems to have a better opinion of him, since she keeps him among her band of musicians – '

'Where he makes every tune sound as doleful as his own face. When he plays, one might mistake *The Carman's Whistle* for *Fortune my Foe*. He, indeed!' She snorted delicately. 'I'll have a better man, if I must marry.'

'You must, and you shall wed Master Lanier if I say so, make no doubt of that. I'll see him tomorrow. Bachelors are few and he is not promised yet – '

'Because nobody wanted him,' Emilia muttered.

'You and he shall be well-endowed and keep the Blackfriars house for the time being. God's wounds! Never pull that sullen face at me, wench, or I'll put you across my knee, *fecund* though you may be. Now get out of my sight, I'm weary. Send my man Gilbert to me and tell him I'll take my supper early. And remember, Em – make not your sail too large for your ship.'

She curtseyed at the door, this time with visible insolence. The greyhound left its master's side to follow her. With a flash of one small square-toed scarlet shoe she kicked it on her way out.

Hunsdon looked after her, stroking his beard. The besom. He wished Lanier joy of her. Yet she was a charming creature, a spell-binder if you kept a weather eye open for her faults; and she had just given him a startling, gratifying proof of his virility. He would make a hearty supper tonight.

*

On a blustery day in October, when the wind hurled fallen leaves and men's hats along Bishopsgate, Emilia Bassano, spinster, was married to Alfonso Lanier, bachelor. She had attired herself as a local version of the Queen, in all the glitter she could assemble, and looked magnificent. Her bridegroom, a man with the sort of looks that were difficult to remember, a neutral sort of visage, wore a worried expression: as well he might, thought Hunsdon, who gave the bride away. The bride insisted that the clerk put down her name as Aemilia – it looked more classical and showed that she had more learning than anyone present.

In April of the next year she bore a son, whom she pointedly called Henry so that there might be no mistake about his paternity. Among the family he was Enrico. He was promptly handed out to a wet nurse, who cared for him in the domestic quarters of the house, presenting him to his mother only when he was sweet-smelling and quiet. She was sorry to see that he was dark, like her, failing to carry on the Tudor red hair. Otherwise she took little interest in him. Another conception had followed quickly on the boy's birth (Alfonso proving himself a man, people said unkindly), which proved to be a girl. Emilia named her Odillia, after a minor saint, but the child was puny and lived only nine months. Without too much mourning she was laid in the churchyard of St Botolph's Bishopsgate, near her Bassano grandparents.

Now slender again and with a mature bloom which suited her greatly, Emilia began to entertain, on a lavish scale made possible by Hunsdon's generosity.

It was at this time that William Shakespeare saw her first.

She was Heaven, she was Hell, she was a fever which he had tried not to catch burning in his veins. He had seen her at first without taking much notice of her, his mind being on other things such as his new play for the Lord Chamberlain's Company.

Then his friend and co-actor Richard Burbage had taken him to a music party at the Laniers' house, which the Lord Chamberlain had given to the couple as a wedding present. Burbage, known as

Dick, was a highly popular player of leading parts and son of the great James Burbage, owner of The Theatre, Shoreditch.

Dick was twenty-eight, his friend thirty-one. Dick was a Londoner, Will a countryman. Will had appeared some years before from Stratford-upon-Avon in the English Midlands, a quiet, watchful young man of no small brain, normally reserved in manner but witty in flashes. He was known to be poor, with a wife and children to support at home.

Dick and Will got on famously, though so different. Dick was shortish, stocky, with thick dark curls and a pair of big come-hither eyes that thrilled the ladies. Will was slender and modest of mien, somewhat thin, as though he had never had quite enough to eat, balding early. His only charms were his beautiful voice with its slight rustic tone, and his eloquent hazel eyes, which seemed to change colour like jewels.

Mistress Lanier was not Will's ideal of beauty, more Dick's type. Will had never cared particularly for dark women. His wife was fair and had once been a nymph of loveliness, though she was now a shrew.

Emilia Lanier's mass of curled black hair was piled up under a slightly barbaric coronal made of coloured feathers and brilliants, and her cartwheel ruff twinkled with points of light. Her orange-tawny farthingale was the colour of a blackbird's bill, thought the countryman. Beneath the bright-beaded edge of the bodice an eyeful of creamy bosom showed.

Will was not fond of creamy skin, especially of such a dark tone. It brought to mind real cream, so often sour. Her curls had been stiffened with some glue-like preparation, which made them seem more like wire than hair. They looked as though they would crackle if one touched them – he almost put out a hand to try whether they did: he found it strangely hard to resist this impulse.

She was seated at a fine Flemish harpsichord, which not long ago had graced Somerset House, until Emilia cajoled it out of her protector. She was singing an Italian ballad, and playing the accompaniment with real professionalism. She liked to throw Italian phrases into her conversation, too, but Will noticed that it was markedly Cockneyfied: he knew this because he had been in Italy once, his quick ear soon picking up the genuine accent.

Dick Burbage, one arm round an obliging trollop brought by another actor, saw with interest that Will was leaning forward in his seat, so transfixed by the musician that the glass of wine in his hand was spilling over onto the floor. The expression on his long, mobile face was unmistakable.

Well, well. Will, bitten, caught, captured, besotted, enravished. He had not been noted for his amours – surprising, for a man whose wife lived elsewhere. A few, but nothing like the usual, nor any hint of a dose of the clap caught on Bankside.

And something else: Dick had more than once wondered whether his friend might not be a trifle this-way, that-way in such matters. His patron and friend, Henry Wriothesley, Earl of Southampton, was not above suspicion sexually, to a wordly mind. He was young, tall, willowy, almost girlishly pretty, delicate-skinned and long-haired. Had he been a player they would certainly have cast him for female parts. Will was devoted to the boy. He was still in a state of admiring awe about aristocrats, and charmed by youth and comeliness in either sex.

Dick decided to have a good-natured game with his friend. When the song was over and the singer receiving compliments and caresses, he tapped Will on the shoulder.

'A rare piece, isn't she?'

Will started, 'What? Oh, rare.' He sounded dubious.

'Showy, though. More hung with baubles than a tree with costards in gathering time. But be under no mistake, there's good blood in her.' He stroked his pointed beard. 'I might say, royal blood. In a manner of speaking.'

'How, royal?'

'Mark me. Queen Anne Boleyn, God rest her soul, had a brother, George, a merry young man and a favourite with the old King. He was raised to honours. Cinque Ports Warden, Viscount Rochford. You're not listening to me.'

'Indeed I am.' Will fixed his gaze on his friend and kept it there, with difficulty, as a high laugh rang out from the group by the fire.

'Well, George Rochford fell from power at the fall of his sister. They said he'd bedded her, so the charge was incest and treason. All a tale, lawyers' lies, but he lost his head with the others. Meanwhile, he'd fathered a little wench on a waiting-woman of the Queen's, who'd got rid of it after its birth to a dancing master and his wife in Bishopsgate. *That's* its daughter.' He nodded towards Mistress Lanier.

Will looked bemused. 'How do you know all this? You were not born.'

'No, but my grandmother was, and she had an ear for Court gossip.'

'Does *she* know – Mistress Lanier?'

'Of course she knows – peacocks about it, but only in hints, for two reasons: item, Margaret Johnson was of ill repute and was never married to Mistress Em's father, and Lord Hunsdon is also a Boleyn on his mother's side and doesn't care to have the family name bandied about.'

Will nodded but said nothing. Dick, somewhat disappointed by the failure of his scandalous story to astound or amuse, wandered away.

In fact, in his friend's eyes, it had encircled Emilia with a halo of borrowed light. To her odd personal attractions was now added the glamour of a dead, tragic Queen and a doomed handsome brother. He had written it somewhere: 'ladies dead, and lovely knights': Anne and George Boleyn, their blood running in the veins under that dark creamy skin.

And in the boy-child crawling round the floor under the feet of the company, the infant his mother called Enrico. In him ran that double stream of Boleyn blood, and that of Mary, Lord Hunsdon's mother. Will had heard that she had been both beautiful and wanton.

From that moment, the strange, alluring yet repellent young woman Mistress Emilia Lanier became his life, the best and worst part of him, his delight, his torment: his America, his new-discovered country of rich marvels, his restored youth, his shuddering realisation of age. He was hers, her Will, her poet.

She was vulgar, and he knew it. She was pretentious and false, and he cared nothing. She dabbled in spells and magic, and he smiled. She was a brilliantly accomplished musician, and he adored her.

He was violently, and, though he did not know it, immortally in love.

Will was working on a new play. Like most, it had had an old beginning, a tale from Boccaccio of intrigue and bawdry. His mind seemed to run upon such things. He was finding them less unsavoury than he had done once, and the Court enjoyed them. Trust the Queen to see the point of a blunt jest . . .

His landlady's daughter, a poor slut who smelt of onions, disturbed him to let him know that a young gentleman was below, desiring to see him. Wearily, Will laid down his pen. 'Bid him up.'

The young gentleman was not above medium height, but looked taller because of the high heels of his expensive riding boots. He was all in buff colours, fine leather, soft kidskin, velvet trimmings; his beaver hat bore a knot of bright feathers and a silver buckle. It was pulled down well over his face.

He whipped it off, with a sweeping theatrical gesture. But the visitor was not one of the Lord Chamberlain's players, nor from any other company.

'Emilia! What . . . is this a masque?'

'Not a masque. Call it a whim, a fancy of my own.' It was a guise which Southampton, who also had whims and fancies, greatly liked. Will found it part attractive, part repulsive. It amused her to find this out as she took off her gentlemanly finery, piece by piece. When it was over Will was faintly disgusted with himself, even more so to find himself madder than ever for her.

They drank wine, and Emilia tried to get a look at Will's writing. He covered it and put it on a shelf. 'I never allow anyone to see it before the last page. Except Dick, of course.'

'Not the Lord Chamberlain, if he asked?'

'He is too ill to ask.'

'Or my lord?'

'My lord?'

'Your gentle patron. And mine.'

His high brow was furrowed. 'Yours? I know you've attended and entertained him – but your patron . . .'

'Oh, I entertained him very well. And do so often.' She sat back on the bed, leaning against the wall, fastening the elegant horn buttons of her doublet. 'Phoo! How these tallow tapers stink. Can you not afford wax? Go without some other thing, but tell that slut downstairs to buy wax.'

Will was the colour of the tallow. 'What do you mean, you entertain him?'

She laughed, smoothing down her lacy cuffs. 'With singing and playing – what else? "Come away, Come Sweet Love". Or "My Lord Southampton's Jig", perhaps.' No one could have mistaken her meaning: he did not mistake it.

'What a face!' She pointed at it. 'Do you mean to cast up your good supper, or the bad wine?'

'I . . . knew nothing of this. I cannot believe it.'

'*Per Gesu!* I have a brother-in-law called Innocent, but you and he should change names. Do you not know me – and your friend – better than that? You cannot believe it, and you living in bawdy London these many years, country swain though you are? What else did you think we did, a young gentlewoman and a young lord, both of some attractions? Or, sometimes, two young gentlemen, as now. He gave me this gear.'

Will got to his feet, 'I should be pleased if you would go now. You see the door, the stairs are beyond it.' He turned his back on her.

Emilia had a moment of selfish compunction. Why had she told him, except for the fun of taunting him? She had smirched her reputation by telling him. What if he told, in his turn – Dick Burbage, anyone who would put it about?

But he would not tell. She shrugged, and ran down the staircase, whistling. He heard the door slam loud enough to fall off its hinges.

Many years later, the news that William Shakespeare was still remembered, thirty years after his death, came as a surprise to Mistress Lanier. She recalled him, of course. There had been some amorous nonsense between them, and she had read verses he had written to her – very poor stuff. But she was astonished that the King, Charles I, actually studied and admired the fellow's work.

Besides, she did not care to think of that time in her life. For many years now she had been an immensely upright character, quite changed from the Emilia of her wild youth. Poor she might be, a widow living and keeping her grandchildren on a pittance, but her virtue was beyond reproach.

For a time, after her husband's death, she had become a whore, to supplement her income. But it had not suited her, and had paid badly. She must find some other means: and here her good education, so long ago in Bishopsgate, came to her aid. She would become an author. If men like that poor thing Shakespeare could win fame by the pen, why not women?

Not filthy stage plays, of course – they were not serious literature. Since she had now become ardently religious, her first long poem was modestly dedicated to Jesus Christ Himself. Somewhat naturally, this produced no substantial benefits, the divine dedicatee being presumably happy to approve her work from a distance.

She therefore began to address in heroic verse some of the noble ladies of her acquaintance, such as her old patron the Countess of Kent. Oddly enough, they were politely uninterested, and very tight with the purse strings, and now there were so few of them left. In the hope of a wider audience, she gallantly set herself up as the champion and defender of womankind. As she pointed out in the Preface to her epic, 'It pleased our Lord and Saviour . . . to be begotten of a woman, born of a woman, nourished of a woman, obedient to a woman, and that He healed women, pardoned women, comforted women . . . yea, after His resurrection, appeared first to a women, sent a woman to declare His most glorious Resurrection to the rest of His disciples.'

How many men living could write like that? Yet nobody had taken much notice. Emilia's great work sank without trace.

Now, old and very poor, she must live on her wits, not her intellect, scrape what she could in the way of grants and pensions. She was writing to King Charles, not for the first time. He would be bored to get another letter from his humble petitioner, but never mind that.

Perhaps he had not noticed in her last letter that she had pointed out their relationship. Now she had worked out its exact degree: they were fourth cousins – or was it fifth? curse her memory. Boleyn, Carey, Tudor, Stuart . . . titles and lands, riches and honours and glory, as the Scriptures said. She was surely entitled to just a small share of the Ormonde estates.

She put down her pen and looked round the mean room in the mean cottage, and sniffed. To come down to the district of Clerkenwell, so far north of the City, of the Strand and the mansions and palaces, some of them the homes of her ancestors. Fine Arundel House, over the river . . .

Her mind began to stray in the past, in times she had known and places where she had moved in her vanished beauty.

She kept no mirrors about the cottage. Emilia's looks, ripened so early, had faded half a lifetime ago, leaving her sallow, almost yellow, shrivelled, deep-lined, the black hair turned white, the fine teeth fallen out. No different from any other old woman of Italian origin.

Even her splendid eyes had almost disappeared into folds of wrinkles. 'Thine eyes I love,' that over-praised scribbler Shakespeare had written, 'and they, as pitying me, Knowing thy heart torments me with disdain, Have put on black, and loving mourners be, Looking with pretty ruth upon my pain . . .'

She sighed deeply. Her great-aunt Anne's death on the block, so young, had been a great tragedy, but at least she had not lived to see her beauty fade.

The door creaked open to admit two small figures, her grandchildren, son and daughter of her own boy Enrico. Mary was eight and Henry six. They cost her dear to keep in food and clothing; they were the chief reason why she fought for her little bits of grant and pension.

Henry hung back shyly, being in awe of his grandmother. The only thing Henrican about him was his name, poor little scrawn, the Tudor and Carey stature seeming to have dwindled away down the line.

But Mary was going to be tall. Her glossy brown hair was swept back from a high brow to fall in long ringlets on her neck. Her figure was still childishly flat, but she carried herself like a queen, as Emilia had taught her with nips and blows. She wore a blue dress of cheap material trimmed with deep lace cuffs and collar, from some much-laundered stuff one of Emilia's noble patrons had given her.

It had been a toss of the coin, when the child was born, whether to have her christened Mary or Anne. But Mary Boleyn, Mary Carey, Mary Stafford, had been just a ha'porth or so luckier, a hundred years ago.

A hundred years. The twenty-seventh year of their ancestor King Henry's reign. Emilia suddenly felt very old and tired, as though she had lived through all those years herself.

But for the future, there was young Mary. She said to her granddaughter 'There is one verse of my great poem I urge you to remember, child.

> So shall you show from whence you are descended,
> And leave to all posterities your fame,
> So will your virtues always be commended,
> And everyone will reverence your name . . .

319

So much to remember, so much to remind the child of constantly. For the moment she had almost forgotten some of it. But she said again, 'Remember.'

Mary lifted her perfect heart-shaped face and met her grandmother's anxious look with her own great dark Boleyn eyes: Howard eyes.

'I shall remember,' she said.